I0777668

WHAT IF THE FUTURE IS ALREADY WRITTEN?

AFTER ALL THE Wreckage

WRITER'S DIGEST AWARD WINNING AUTHOR

LJ EVANS

AFTER ALL THE *Wreckage*

LJ EVANS

This book is a work of fiction. While reference might be made to actual historical events or existing people and locations, the events, names, characters, places, and incidents are either the product of the author's imagination or are used fictitiously, and any resemblance to actual persons, living or dead, business establishments, events, or locales is entirely coincidental.

AFTER ALL THE WRECKAGE © 2023 by LJ Evans

LJ EVANS BOOKS

www.ljevansbooks.com

Cover Design: © River Briar Designs

Cover Images: © iStock | fokkebok, Volodymyr Kazhanov

Chapter Title Images: iStock | Pavlo Stavnichuk, kotoffei, Userba9fe9ab_931

Developmental Editing: Evans Editing, Brayzen Bookwrym, and HEA Author Services

Line and Copy Editing: HEA Author Services

ISBN: 978-1-962499-10-1

Library of Congress Cataloging in process.

Playlist

https://spoti.fi/3qORevb

Author's Note

Dear Reader,

The heroine of this story and I have something in common—we both adore the *Veronica Mars* show! If you haven't watched the series yet and intend to, just be warned there are a few serious spoilers discussed in the book.

xx
LJ

Dedication

To all the women who have ever been underestimated,
may you kick ass and take names.

To Rob Thomas for creating a character who will
forever live in my heart and soul.

To all my readers, may your present be full of so much joy
that you don't need to look behind you or ahead of you for
more.

Chapter One

Rory

AM I ALRIGHT
Performed by Aly & AJ

If panic attacks could have babies, I'd be having *quintuplets*. The thought landed in my chest as I pulled my royal blue Honda Rebel into a tiny spot on the street outside my dad's office. It was the last place I wanted to be for more reasons than I could count. Some of those reasons were petty, full of old grudges and teenage hurts, and some were deadly serious.

The deadly part was why I'd swallowed my pride enough to come.

I slammed my foot on the kickstand and swung my leg over the seat before standing in my thick-soled Harley-Davidson boots and pulling off my helmet. I dragged the hair tie from my ponytail, slung it around my wrist, and ran a hand through the dark brown strands.

When I turned toward the small but expensive building that held Bishop Investigations & Security, my reflection caught in the two stories of glittering glass. I cringed, knowing neither my bike nor my appearance would help my cause today. My black jacket was naturally distressed with spiderweb cracks along the leather, and the hole in my black jeans was from a tussle with a cheater I'd been following rather than any designer styling. They'd be the first of many things my father would pick at today. A few more additions to the long list of my mistakes. But two could play at that game. After all, I had a list of his that I could recite too.

I shoved my shoulders back and strode through the doors. The inside of his office was professional and cold. Decked out in steel and gray leather, the lobby was elegantly arranged to impress Dad's clients. As if the surroundings screaming wealth proved he could get the job done rather than the fact he had a good interior designer. But the truth was, as much as it irked me to admit it, Dad always got the job done. Whether the client liked what he found was an entirely different story—one I knew firsthand.

My eyes drifted to my wrist and the black-and-blue fingerprints that had turned darker throughout the day. I tugged the cuff of my jacket down, clamping it against my palm with my fingers. If Dad saw the marks, any chance of asking him for the favor I'd come for would be lost. And I needed him to come through. For the first time in almost a decade, I actually needed my father.

I hated it.

At the desk, the latest receptionist in a long string of Georgetown grad students sat waiting. Each of them used their time with his company to launch a litany of justice and law enforcement careers. His name on their résumé was an exclusive D.C. insider's gold star that opened doors. Too bad I'd never been offered a chance to earn one. Maybe he'd known I would have rather been boiled in acid than sit at that clear glass desk answering his phones.

"Rory," Chanel greeted me with a snip to her tone. Her gym-toned legs below the hem of a gray pencil skirt crossed as she swiveled toward me, purple Prada pumps dangling from her feet. They were the only sign of color in the stark space. She fit into Dad's image perfectly whereas I looked like I'd been dragged in from the biker bar on the edge of Cherry Bay—the town I called home after leaving D.C. a few months ago.

"Dad in?" I asked her, trying to keep my voice light and

even.

Her gaze flitted over me briefly, barely withholding her judgment, but I could hear it anyway. The silent *How on earth is this Sutton Bishop's daughter?* Because the only thing I'd inherited from the blond-haired dynamo in a suit who was my father was the cleft in my chin. He was tall with a square face and wide shoulders, whereas I was almost all Mom with honey-toned Italian skin and a lithe, short frame. Dad's green eyes screamed their color even over a distance while the tiny bit of jade that flashed in my brown ones was only visible if you were close enough to kiss me.

Not that I'd been kissed lately. It had been so long, my lips and vagina thought I'd abandoned them.

"He has twenty minutes before he has to leave for lunch on the Hill," Chanel said primly.

It was exactly what I'd hoped for. Dad spent more time wining and dining D.C. bigwigs these days than he did investigating. Although, maybe that wasn't much different from when Mom had been his partner. Back then, he'd brought the business in and she'd executed it… or I did. Right up until the divorce split them down the middle and me along with it.

As I headed for the stairs, I tossed a jab over my shoulder. "Dad has dining with sleazy politicians down to a science. They should give him the oil prospector of the year award."

"First, not all politicians are sleazy. Second, you're one to judge. How's it going swimming with the cheaters?"

My foot stalled on the first step, and when I looked back, her eyes were narrowed. I almost laughed at her quick retort, but then I wondered if her defense of Dad came from a sense of loyalty that went much deeper than an employee-employer relationship. I wondered if Dad had tucked this receptionist into his bed a time or two… or more.

It made me want to heave up the cold mac and cheese I'd called breakfast.

I didn't respond, turning back around to take the stairs

at double time.

His office door was open, the low hum of his voice audible if not the actual words. He didn't have an assistant guarding the entrance. He didn't believe in having one. The fewer eyes and hands on sensitive information, the better in his opinion. And if for some reason the nearly perfect Sutton Bishop did need help, the highly paid receptionist downstairs would be tasked with it.

Dad had his chair turned toward the enormous windows looking out at the dome of the Capitol Building. I knocked, and he swung around to take me in. His eyes narrowed ever so slightly before a tight smile appeared on his lips.

"I'll have to call you back," he said into the phone, pausing to listen to the response. "I'm telling you, you're worrying over nothing, Roland. I'll see you tonight."

He hung up and watched as I moved to stand next to the pair of straight-backed chairs in front of his steel desk. The chairs weren't designed for comfort. Dad didn't want people to dally in his office any more than he wanted them lingering in his personal life.

Handsome and brimming with charisma, my father could have been a politician as easily as he'd become a private investigator. He could charm his way into just about anywhere… and anyone. It was a skill Mom said I'd inherited from him, and sometimes, I wasn't sure if it was a compliment or not.

"I'd love to say it's nice to finally see my daughter again, but I'm confident you didn't drive into D.C. on that asinine bike just to visit dear old Dad," he said dryly with a pointed look at the helmet under my arm.

I tossed it on the chair as he came around the desk to draw me into a one-armed hug. A catch and release he'd once shown me how to do while fishing. The nonchalance pricked at old wounds I couldn't afford to let show.

A wisp of pine from his cologne combined with a hint of smoke from his occasional cigar wafted over me. I was dismayed by the temptation to hold on to him longer, to use his strength to buoy me up. To once again be the little girl he'd beamed at when she'd handed him the proof of a certain congressman sleeping with a prostitute. Proof that had cost the man his reelection and his wife.

I gritted my teeth and stepped farther away. If I allowed myself to drop my shield even briefly, the weight I was carrying might slip off and I'd never be able to pick it up again. I wasn't even twenty-three yet, but I had both lives and a business resting solely on my shoulders.

As he leaned up against his desk, he scanned my outfit, his look lingering on the fresh cut and red skin visible through the hole in my jeans. I grabbed the cuff of my jacket extra tight, ensuring it stayed firmly in place.

"To what do I really owe the pleasure?" he asked.

I regretted the cold mac and cheese all over again.

Now that I was here, I didn't really want to make my request. I took a few seconds to run through the numbers in our bank accounts once more. Then, the image of Mom lying in the bed at the long-term care facility settled cruelly in my chest. Her skin was paler than ever before, and her eyes were always shut as a feeding tube, a host of cords, and beeping machines kept her alive. I forced back an unexpected rush of tears. I couldn't afford them any more than I could afford the damn hug to undo me. Tears never solved anything—the saying should have been monogrammed on our Bishop family crest.

"I need a loan," I told him.

I knew better than to ask for money straight up. Dad believed in earning what you got. Struggle built character. It was the one and only thing my parents had agreed upon after the divorce.

Dad crossed his arms over his chest. "How much and what's it for?"

If I said I needed it to cover the added expense of Mom's new facility in Cherry Bay, he'd object. He'd made it very clear he disagreed with keeping her on life support after the doctors had recommended shutting it off and the insurance had stopped paying because of it. But if I said I needed cash to cover Marlow & Co. bills, he definitely wouldn't give it to me. He'd be happy if the business Mom had created after divorcing him disappeared. One less competitor.

After my mistake in high school—getting suspended and almost expelled for stunning a drug dealer in the boys' bathroom—he and Mom had pretty much switched sides. Once he'd seen me as an integral part of their business, now all he saw were my errors.

Because neither of the real reasons I needed the money would sway him, I gave him the fake one I'd come up with on the commute into D.C. "I want to get my master's."

I tried to keep my face impassive through the partial lie. I'd once planned on going to grad school before applying to the FBI, but these days those ideas seemed like Neverland dreams, and I was out of pixie dust. After missing the spring semester because of Mom's accident, I'd transferred from Georgetown to Bonnin University in Cherry Bay where I was weeks away from squeaking out a bachelor's degree. Even though it was less expensive, I'd still had to take out a loan as every penny from the sale of Mom's D.C. condo had gone toward keeping her breathing.

Dad's eyes narrowed as if he was attempting to read me. My face remained stony, but I made the mistake of shifting ever so slightly on one foot, and he caught the small movement.

"You've applied and been accepted to grad school? Where?"

He wasn't buying it. Why had I humiliated myself like this when I'd already known it was a futile effort? Mom's face flashed in my head again, and those fricking tears I never let out threatened once more. I grabbed my helmet and headed for the door before I further humiliated myself.

"Never mind. Forget I was even here," I said.

"I didn't say I wouldn't give you the money. I just want to know the truth."

Gripping the chin guard of my helmet with one hand, I waved at him with the other. "Why does it matter? Your daughter needs a loan. I'm not asking for a handout. I'm not asking for anything I won't pay back. You set the terms, and I'll meet them."

The second he strode toward me with anger flashing in his eyes, I realized my mistake.

He grabbed my arm, demanding, "Who hurt you?"

"It isn't important." It was embarrassing was what it was. A stupid wardrobe malfunction that had let the cheating bastard lay a hand on me.

"Damn it, Rory-girl! How many times do I have to repeat myself? You aren't cut out for this business. You're going to end up dead just like your mother."

"Mom isn't dead!" I growled back, pushing him away from me and taking a step into the hall.

He sighed, the sound full of frustration and sadness. "She is, Rory. Even if, by some miracle, she comes out of it, she'll be a shell of a person. She won't ever be Hallie again."

"Just because you've given up hope doesn't mean Nan or I have," I hissed. "And Mom didn't die because some asshole cheater came after her. She crashed into the Potomac."

I stomped toward the stairs.

"Because someone messed with her car's computer."

As his words sank in, my feet stalled. My heartbeat sped up, doing triple time, as I whirled around to face him. "What?"

He rubbed his forehead. The regret and exasperation on his face were a clear message he'd let something slip he'd never intended for me to hear. I'd repeatedly asked the detective in charge of Mom's accident for the cause, and Muloney had told me they'd never know for sure. There hadn't been another vehicle involved. She'd just gone over the edge and into the river. A submerged tree had pierced the right side of her head, and she'd drowned before the rescue people got to her. They'd resuscitated her, but she'd never woken up. She'd gripped my hand a few times, her lids had fluttered open and closed, but she'd never really been cognizant.

And now it had been eleven months… Eleven months I'd survived without her. But it felt like twenty years. An eternity in which I'd lived in some alternate version of what had once been my life.

"Who told you that?" My words were garbled as pain and fury roared through me. He didn't respond, and it only goaded me further. "I can't believe you! You told Muloney to cut me out? You're not her next of kin. You don't get to make any decisions about her. You lost that right when you divorced her. Like it or not, I'm the one who's responsible for her now."

"Except you want my money to keep her alive."

"That's not what it's for."

"Isn't it?" he demanded, brow rising again. "I know you've gone through the tiny profit you got out of the condo, Rory. I know you've had to change facilities more than once. This bullshit idea about a master's degree? You and I both know it isn't what the money is for."

God, there were times I hated how good he was at his job. He really knew everything. He always had. It was why clients flocked from all over the Northeast to his doors.

"Keep your damn money. I'll do this alone, just like Mom and I have done everything else for the past ten years, and I'll figure out why someone wanted her dead while I'm at it."

"I don't want to lose my daughter *and* my wife."

"Ex-wife. Your latest girlfriend would hate to hear you call her that."

He blew out an exasperated breath. "You're not cut out for this, Rory," he repeated. "It's my fault you started down this path. I can admit I was wrong. I never should have asked you to do any of the things I did, and Hallie should never have let you coerce her into picking up where I left off.

"Jesus, look at you." He gestured toward me. "You're battered and bruised, racing around town on that deathtrap, for what? An idea that you can be some real-life Veronica Mars? Real detective work isn't anything like that goddamn show."

Each syllable was a hit to my already bruised psyche. Scars and scabs hidden deep in my soul started to bleed. Veronica had saved me. And ever since Mom's accident, my life had taken on an even more decidedly Veronica-like vibe. She'd stayed to help her dad after he'd gotten sick just like I was helping Mom. She'd gone back to running the family PI business, and I'd done the same. The clients and money I brought in weren't nearly enough, though. I was doling out more each month than I was bringing in, and Nan didn't have any extra cash to offer. She was barely getting by on Pop's widow's pension.

I swallowed hard, striking back the only way I could with words I wasn't sure were true but would hit home anyway. "At least Keith Mars loved his daughter. Fake show. Real love. The complete opposite of this." I waved a finger between us and then turned on my heel and headed down the stairs.

He followed me to the railing, calling after me. "Rory, don't leave like this."

I didn't respond.

"You know there are a lot of companies who would give someone with your computer skills a hiring bonus. If you're looking for money and don't want it on my terms, at least consider it. You need to leave this business behind and concentrate on what you *are* good at."

Chanel was pretending not to watch the show as I stormed past her desk, but I saw the smirk, and it only fueled the rage inside me. I wished I could slam the door to the building, but all it did was swing back and forth.

As I stalked over to my bike, the realization that Dad might be right caused bile to hit my throat. Maybe I did need to get some eight-to-five desk job in some corporate office peddling my computer skills. Not because a buckle had gotten caught in a trellis and the cheater had pulled me from it by my wrist, but because a job in a corporate office would pay a helluva lot more than my handful of clients.

But then Dad's slipped admission came back. Someone had messed with Mom's car! Someone had done this to her on purpose. There was no way in hell I'd let that go. I'd borrow money from Tall Paul, the biggest loan shark I knew, before I'd just walk away.

Just like Veronica Mars had once said, this was where I belonged. In the fight. It was who I was. And I could guarantee whoever had done this would regret it.

As I pulled on my helmet and merged into the heavy traffic of D.C. at lunchtime, I wondered how much Dad had paid Baloney-Muloney to keep the truth from me. Was Dad investigating it on his own or was he leaving it to the tiny force that made up Cherry Bay's police department?

If Dad had any information, I'd find out. I had a backdoor into his network that he was clueless to. I'd find out what he knew, and if it was nothing, there were other doors I'd start banging on—or hacking into.

Dad was right about one thing. I'd die before I let anyone get away with this.

Chapter Two

Gage

Performed by The Guess Who

I tapped my fingers along the edge of the Pathfinder's steering wheel, trying to push down the impatience I felt sitting at the back of the car line in front of Cherry Bay's only middle school. I had a long list of things to get done at the bar, which meant I barely had time to manage picking Monte up and getting back to the apartment before opening.

The car in front of me inched forward, and I did the same thing as I scanned the sea of tweens sidling down the sidewalk past the car. No copper-topped waves in sight. Had Monte worn a baseball cap today? I couldn't remember. My younger brother did more often than not. He hated his red hair. Hated the curls more. Hated that kids teased him about being Orphan Annie's twin brother. How the hell they even knew who she was beat me. I'd had to look it up.

"Bubba, I have to pee," a tiny voice from the back seat whispered.

Shit. I glanced in the rearview mirror, meeting Ivy's gaze. My sister's pale blue eyes were just like our mother's, but at the moment, they were wide and desperate. A look I wasn't sure I'd ever seen in Demi's. I'd seen fanciful, whimsical, and even clouded, but never desperate. More often than not, Demi's were strangely serene, even in the face of my anger.

Ivy wiggled in her seat, and panic filled my veins. I definitely didn't have time for a bathroom accident. Didn't have time to clean the car seat, the car, or tame the shamed tears that would flow. It wasn't her fault. What three-and-a-half-year-old hadn't had an accident or two?

"Hold tight, Ives," I ground out.

I flipped on my blinker, zipped out in front of a car in a way that earned me a loud honk, then cut off another car before it could block the driveway of the school's parking lot. After sideswiping the orange cone set up to keep people out, I pulled up along the sidewalk near the flagpole in front of the nondescript square building.

I was in the red zone, but I didn't care as I jumped from the driver's seat and jogged around to help Ivy unbuckle even as she protested. Holding her tightly to my chest, I ran toward the bathrooms outside the gym—smelly spaces I knew well from when I'd attended the school a lifetime ago.

I skidded to a halt outside the boys' and girls' restrooms, debating which to use.

"I don't know if I can hold it," Ivy's small voice squeaked out.

Her alarm raced through me. I rushed into the boys' room. When I didn't see anyone standing at the urinals, I sent a silent thanks to the universe. Two stalls were empty. I'd barely set her on her feet before Ivy was jumping up onto the seat. I winced, trying not to think about what was on the toilet. It wasn't like middle school boys were known for their hygiene. But the look of pure gratitude on her face eased the chokehold that had taken over my chest.

Her ponytail was askew. Little wisps of curls had escaped, surrounding her elf-like face dusted with a light sheen of freckles. If there was anything in my life that could make me feel like a failure, it was her damn hair. How did other parents do it? Every time I picked Ivy up from preschool, all the other girls seemed to have their hair still perfectly assembled—neat and tidy—while Ivy's seemed to come loose the moment I put it up.

How was I, at twenty-seven, even in a position to be thinking of a little girl's hair and where the nearest bathroom was? My life was so far from where I'd imagined it would be that there were days the simple weight of it was like an anvil sitting on my shoulders. I was living the wrong life. With that thought came the spike of anger and frustration that usually followed it. Fucking life. Fucking Demi.

Once Ivy was done, she leaped off the seat, and her face burst into a smile so bright it felt like heaven was shining a beam right down on us. It took every thought I'd just had about living the wrong life and all the rage, and zapped it away. She was worth it. She and Monte both.

"All better?" I asked.

She nodded, slipping her tiny fingers into mine, and we made our way out to the sinks where we both washed our hands. With our damp palms joined, we made our way back to the SUV as Ivy tried to skip. She looked like some malfunctioning robot, but it made my lips twitch upward for the first time all afternoon.

I was definitely going to be late now. But I had help at the bar. River would be there, and he'd pick up the slack by unloading the delivery. Audrey would handle the setup inside, and between the two of them, they'd shoulder the tasks I hadn't been able to get to. It would be fine. It always was.

When I got back to our gray Pathfinder, I lifted Ivy into the back seat and watched as she struggled to buckle up. She was extremely proud of being able to do it herself and would get frustrated if I tried to help. It took her five times as long as it would have if I'd done it, but it all came down to that old saying about teaching someone to fish… No one ever mentioned how much patience and energy it took the teacher to do so.

I hopped into the driver's seat and moved to a spot that had opened up near the school's front office. I left the car idling, pulled my phone from my pocket, and shot Monte a text.

ME: Ivy had to use the bathroom. We're parked in the lot.

A couple minutes went by, and the number of kids wandering past dwindled. The vehicles in the car line beyond the sidewalk started to fade. Still no sign of my brother. He knew the timing was tight from pickup to the bar opening, so he usually did his best to get out quickly. I flipped my phone over to see there was no response.

ME: Hey? Did you have practice today?

I had his basketball schedule taped to the refrigerator, logged into the calendar on my phone, and burned into my brain. But that was the other thing I'd found out the hard way—nothing was predictable with kids.

The principal meandered down from the head of the car line, picked up the cones in the driveway, and set them aside. Three kids tagged along behind him, backpacks weighing them down, phones in hand, and walking while texting in the way teens did despite the warnings that it could be dangerous.

An inkling of something that wasn't quite fear but close hit me in the chest.

Nothing is wrong. Everything is okay.

It was a mantra I lived by these days.

Except last night Monte hadn't slept, and neither had I because of it. His eyes had been shadowed this morning, a sense of despair clinging to him as he'd shoveled in the eggs and toast that his growing body demanded.

"What's the point of even having the visions, Gage?" he'd asked. "I'm useless to stop whatever they show me. Nothing I can do. Nothing you can do. We've both tried."

What if he'd gone on his own to D.C.? That singular thought caused more alarm than any kind of pee accident could.

While waiting for his response, I shoved my hand through the pitch-black of my thick waves. I looked nothing like my brother and sister. They were all Demi—strawberry-blond strands with pale eyes and soft white skin that showed off their freckles. I was Dad from my dark hair, gray eyes, and square chin down to my skin that always carried a hint of tan year-round.

As the minutes ticked away, my anxiety grew. I stabbed out another desperate message.

ME: Please tell me you didn't go to D.C. I'm at the school. Ivy is about two seconds from melting down.

It wasn't Ivy who was having the meltdown. It was me. But Monte would do just about anything for our little sister. When she'd first been born, he used to crawl into bed with me for comfort whenever she was crying, even when it was just a normal *I'm hungry* type of cry.

My phone buzzed with a reply from Monte, and relief washed through me.

MONTE: I went home with India, remember? I'm spending the weekend with her to work on our science project.

My relief was quickly replaced with guilt. Had he told me and I hadn't paid attention? I'd been so focused on his vision, sleeplessness, and growing restlessness that I might have missed him telling me.

ME: Are you sure that's a good idea with everything happening?

MONTE: It'll keep my mind off it for a while.

In my gut, I knew the truth. He was doing this for me as much as himself. He didn't want me hovering over him, worrying. But it was my job to protect him, not the other way around.

I put the SUV in gear and backed out of the spot, heading toward the bar.

The asphalt roads at the edge of town quickly turned into cobblestone streets in the town center. The first village in Cherry Bay had been founded in the late 1700s, but the college that had been built on the bluff overlooking the

Potomac in the 1940s was what had put us on the map. It drew students and academics from around the globe.

I hooked a right at the alley between two stone buildings that would have been perfectly at home in a medieval English village and headed into the small parking lot at the back. The Prince Darian Tavern had been in my family for over two hundred years. It had first been a post inn, and now it was a bar and restaurant with a two-bedroom apartment and extra storage space above.

While Dad had leased out the restaurant several decades ago, the tavern had been run by a Palmer since its inception. Between the renovation loans I hadn't known he'd taken out and the pandemic closing us down, we'd been almost wiped out financially. After Dad had died, I'd had to sell the house, and we'd moved into the apartment that he used to rent to college students. We were squished together in a space crowded with furniture that didn't fit, but I refused to get rid of those last pieces of our family history. Selling the Victorian we'd grown up in had been painful enough.

I parked the Pathfinder and waited with gritted teeth while Ivy fumbled with her buckle. My gaze journeyed to the next parking lot over, and my heart skipped a beat at the sight of a dark-haired woman. I could practically feel the energy vibrating from Rory Bishop as she headed toward the doors of the Cherry Bay Police Department. The aura of brave confidence was the same as it had been when she'd been fifteen. A self-assurance that mimicked the fictional heroine she'd worshipped back in the day.

Lithe and edgy in all black, I was hypnotized by the way she moved. Unable to draw my eyes away from her.

How long had it been since I'd seen her? How many miles, years, and traumas had filled the space between us?

I was just about to call her name when Ivy jumped out of the car and landed on my foot. It turned any sound that would have emerged from me into a deep grunt, and I had to catch my sister as she wobbled and balance myself at the same time. When I looked back over to the station, Rory was gone, and something a bit like sadness filled me.

Which was ridiculous. I didn't even know Rory anymore. I'd barely known her as a teen.

I pushed aside any thoughts of her, stepped around the wrought iron staircase leading to our apartment, and headed for the rear entrance of the bar with Ivy's hand in mine. A delivery truck had its door rolled up, and as I'd expected, River was already unloading it on his own.

His wide shoulders flexed as he hefted a case of vodka onto his shoulder. His height and build along with his shaved head, pierced nose, and plethora of tattoos intimidated most people. They had no clue his aura radiated nothing but kindness when all they saw was a scary giant.

River had been working for my dad since he'd been in college himself, and decades later, he was still here. Although I was pretty sure that had more to do with not abandoning me and my siblings than because he needed the job. Not when his art was in high demand around the country.

"Sorry we're late," I offered before looking down at my sister. "Go into the office and get a snack from the snack drawer and your coloring books from the shelf. I'll be in after I help River."

"Can I have a chocolate cwinkle?" she asked, eyes wide, knowing I normally didn't let her have sweets this close to dinner. But with my nerves feeling frayed after the scare I'd just had at the school, I didn't feel like arguing with her.

"Yes, but only one," I said, narrowing my eyes at her.

She grinned and then took off down the hall, her messed-up hairdo bouncing around her.

"Hey, Squirt! Don't I even get a hello?" River grunted after her.

She waved her stuffed otter without ever looking back as she hollered, "Hi, Uncle Wivuh!" her R's lisping into W's.

"I expect a hug later."

I grabbed another case off the back of the truck, hauling it to the storage room above the bar. The dark interior stairs were small and groaned with age, but they were smooth and stained to perfection. Everything in the building might be old, but it wasn't shabby. Dad had made sure of it, and I'd picked up where he'd left off.

While River and I unloaded in silence, my thoughts kept drifting back to the brown-haired dynamo I'd seen next door. A piece of me longed to go back in time to when I'd known her. When I'd had nothing to worry about but internships and college tuition. To a time when I'd been adored by a girl who I'd known would take the world by storm and set some guy's heart on fire.

Last I'd heard, she was at Georgetown, but I vaguely recalled some mumblings late last year about her mom being in a car accident. I hadn't paid much attention to the talk because Rory and her mom hadn't lived in Cherry Bay for almost a decade. Plus, I'd been hip-deep in another of Monte's visions and finalizing the paperwork on Ivy's and Monte's adoptions. I'd barely been able to breathe at the time, let alone think of a young girl from my past.

But now I couldn't shake the image of her.

Why was she in town? Was she visiting her friend Shay, whose family owned the Tea Spot across the street? Or was she visiting her grandmother? Regardless of why she was there, I didn't have any more time now to let my thoughts dwell on her than I had a year ago.

I signed the receipt from the delivery and walked toward the tavern's office. I pushed open the antique wooden door with its beveled glass to find Ivy at a claw-foot table that had been there probably since the tavern had first opened. She was on her knees in a burgundy brocade armchair, draped in a mosaic of color from the stained-glass window that made her seem like one of the paintings of our ancestors hanging on the walls in their gilded frames.

When I got up close to her, the mirage broke, and a

chuckle rumbled through my chest. She was covered in chocolate from forehead to chin. It never failed to surprise me how quickly and absolutely she could become a mess when eating. She'd need a full body scrub before dinner.

Which reminded me, I needed to call our babysitter and beg her to come over. I'd expected Monte to be home to watch Ivy, which only reconfirmed I hadn't known my brother would be at India's. Unease settled in my chest once again—a worry I couldn't shake. I was an Olympic champion at worrying these days.

I pulled my laptop from the old captain's desk on the other side of the room and brought it over to the table. I kissed the top of Ivy's head as I set it down in front of her. "Give me a few minutes, Ives, then I'll take you upstairs for dinner. Do you want to watch something while you wait?"

She nodded. "Scooby-Doo?"

Her addiction to the cartoon made me smile. "Sure."

I loaded the streaming service, started an episode, and then looked at her chocolate-covered face and hands. "Don't touch the computer. And wash your hands when you're done with the cookie."

She nodded absently, already watching Scooby and the gang as they scurried over the screen in the opening song. I stepped away, watching her with regret curling through me. She was loved and cared for, but she didn't have a normal childhood. Then again, none of us had been allowed one. Not with Demi in and out. Not with the abilities she'd branded us with.

But we had each other, and that was all that really mattered.

Chapter Three

Rory

NO ONE

Performed by Aly & AJ

My first stop on returning to Cherry Bay was the police department. The building was several hundred years old, sitting at the edge of Main Street and butting up against the acres of green that made up the Bonnin University campus. Even after it had been retrofitted multiple times, the station still had a moody, Gothic vibe with its original stone, brick, and iron mixing in with high-tech cameras, computers, and bulletproof glass.

Harriet sat at the front desk where she'd been for as long as I could remember. Her dark hair was cropped short. She had a lean, toned frame and dark eyes in a narrow face. One of Mom's best friends and the department's dispatcher, Harriet was the first to know everything that happened in town. It tugged hard on my heart that she might have been hiding the truth from me.

"Look at what the cat dragged in," she said with a smile that faded once she saw my glower. "Is it Hallie?"

"Not in the way you're thinking," I said, and relief coasted over her face. I felt a twinge of guilt before I demanded, "What the hell, Harriet? Her wreck wasn't an accident, and you kept it from me?"

Her eyes widened in surprise. "What? No!"

Her reaction seemed genuine which meant she hadn't

known either. My teeth gritted as I headed for the swinging half door that led to the desks in the back. "Where is Baloney-Muloney?"

She shook her head, reaching out to stop me. "Muloney isn't here, Rory. He drove to New York to bring his daughter home for Thanksgiving."

My emotions swung back and forth. A part of me wanted to storm into the bullpen, tear up the detective's desk and his computer, and get what I'd come for. Except that wouldn't win me any favors with anyone in the department. It would likely ban me from the precinct forever. The smart course of action was to pull out the Bishop family charm and win him over when he returned. With the way my anger was bubbling and growing, I wasn't sure I'd be able to channel it when he returned.

"When will he be back?"

"Sunday," she said.

Another two days wasted. I was already too far behind on Mom's case. Almost a year too late. Why hadn't I demanded more from him sooner?

"He lied, Harriet. He lied and kept the truth from me. He's lucky I haven't put out a hit on him yet."

"I haven't heard even a whisper of it being anything but an accident. I would have told you." She squeezed my arm again, and we shared a tormented stare before she patted my cheek. "Come to the house on Thanksgiving. Please. I told Kora I wanted you both there. Hallie wouldn't want the two of you sitting alone in a room at the recovery center."

That was the thing no one seemed to understand. My grandmother and I weren't alone. We were with Mom. And I wasn't much for holidays these days. It felt wrong to celebrate while Mom was lying there, but the hope in Harriet's eyes had me swallowing back my automatic no. Instead, I told her I'd talk to Nan about it and said goodbye.

It was a short drive from the station to Shady Lane Rehabilitation and Recovery Center across from the hospital. Both were square buildings built in the fifties, but they'd kept the charm of the town in their stone and plaster facades. Shady Lane was the second facility Mom had been in since the D.C. hospital she'd been airlifted to had kicked her out. Nan and I had moved her here, not only because the staff knew us, but because it didn't require Nan and me to commute in the horrendous beltway traffic. The downside was it cost even more than the last place.

I signed in at the front desk and made my way along the sterile hall to Mom's room. The quiet hum of the machines and the antiseptic smell were almost unnoticeable to me after eleven months of practically living in similar facilities. My grandmother was there, sitting in the same chair she always was, knitting a creation that wouldn't be straight and wouldn't fit right. It was a hobby she'd picked up to fill the long stretches at the side of a hospital bed.

"I was surprised when you weren't here," Nan commented as I strolled in and tossed my helmet onto the loveseat under the room's single window.

Nan's hair used to be as dark as mine but was now mostly white. It was cut close to her head for ease, but it suited her. She was only in her midseventies, but the loss of her parents, her sister, her husband, and now her daughter had aged her in an irreversible way, adding wrinkles that shouldn't have been there.

"Where's the Jeep?" Nan asked, head tilting toward the helmet I'd tossed aside. Technically, the Jeep I'd been borrowing ever since Mom's SUV had been totaled was my grandfather's. Nan had kept it running right along with her green Volkswagen Beetle from the sixties even though she definitely didn't need both vehicles. After twelve years, she still couldn't part with a single piece of him. It was why their closet still held his clothes, and the shed out back of their house held his woodworking tools.

"I had some business to take care of in D.C., and the bike needed to be driven."

I hadn't told Nan I was asking Dad for a loan because she would threaten to sell the cottage again. A home she and

Pop had bought in their twenties and was mortgage free, but that she could still barely afford because the property taxes and insurance stretched her meager income.

"You got a new case?"

I nodded. It wasn't a lie. I had Mom's case now.

"How is she today?"

Nan's knitting needles slowed ever so slightly, and she didn't respond right away. When she finally looked up, I saw hopelessness in her eyes. It had been a bad day, and I'd been off on a useless errand.

I went to her, crouching down and surrounding her hands with mine. "What happened?"

"Doctor Huan showed up. She basically said we were wasting time, money, and love holding on to a physical body when Hallie is already gone." Nan choked on the last words, and my anger flared back to life.

How could everyone just give up? I knew the odds. I knew the miracle we were looking for was rare. Mom's lack of eye movement, the lack of any response, and the stupid Glasgow Coma Scale they administered all told us the numbers were not in our favor. But every time I looked at my mother, I felt like she was still there, and I'd read enough stories about people who'd recovered even a year later that I couldn't just remove the life support and let her body die. Not yet. Not when we were still within those miraculous months.

"Screw her, Nan," I said gently. "She doesn't know Mom. She doesn't know us. She has no clue what kind of fighters we Marlowes are."

Nan sniffed, grabbed a tissue from the side table, and dabbed her eyes with it. "You didn't get that fight from the Bishops, that's for sure."

After giving her a weak smile, I winked. "I got my charm from them."

I stood and Nan smiled. "The Marlowe women have been known to make a few siren calls ourselves. You got the best of both families. Which makes me wonder why you haven't been luring any hot bodies to your bed lately."

I laughed and went over to Mom's side, grabbing her cold hand and rubbing it between mine. I didn't answer because I didn't have to. Nan and I had been consumed with Mom's recovery. But even before that, my sex life had been pretty hit or miss. Especially when most of the guys I'd tangled with in high school and college had been overwhelmingly immature. Or maybe it had nothing to do with them but a flash of stormy gray eyes I couldn't forget. Memories of a boy who'd burned himself onto my soul without even knowing it. Without even a single kiss.

A man I'd purposefully ignored since moving back to Cherry Bay.

I wasn't exactly sure why.

Liar, my soul screamed. The harsher truth was that I didn't want him to see me this way. I didn't want him to look at the girl he'd thought could be Veronica-Mars-strong and see her struggling to hold herself together.

I didn't want to be pitied by him. Not him.

I sat on the edge of the bed, moving Mom's legs, massaging them, and doing all the things the physical therapists and nurses had taught us to do. She'd be weak when she eventually came back to us, but she was going to recover. She had to. The Marlowe strength was part of our doggedness. We didn't give up once we set our minds on something.

And it would be a hot day in space before I gave up on the most important person in my life.

♫ ♫ ♫

I spent Friday night and most of Saturday on my laptop in Mom's room, doing what I always did—working on my cases and my classwork.

Normally, whenever Nan wasn't in the room, I talked aloud to Mom because the first doctors we'd seen had said it was important for a coma patient to hear their loved ones' voices. I'd ramble on about the Department of Defense background checks I was running, the cheating partner I was following, or the deadbeat parent I was tracking down for child support. I'd talk about my classes or brag about Nan's latest gardening achievement.

This weekend, my silence hung oppressively in the air.

As I was researching her accident, I didn't want her to relive the trauma if she could hear. The most recent reports insisted she didn't have any brain activity and that nothing I said mattered anymore, but I couldn't believe that because if I did…

I shook my head, concentrating on the final string of code I needed to create a backdoor into the Cherry Bay Police Department's server. I smiled when I got in, covering my tracks as I went, like brushing away footprints in the snow.

There was nothing like the thrill of a good hack in the morning.

If I wanted to, I could tell the department how I'd done it so they'd be protected in the future, and maybe I would. But not until Mom's case was solved.

I rooted around their system, learning the ins and outs, and finally found Mom's file. It was suspiciously thin. I didn't know if it was because Muloney had done a shit job or because Dad had told him to be careful what he put online in case I came looking. Whatever the reason, there was nothing about her car's computer being compromised like Dad had insinuated. The handful of notes were about where the Pathfinder had been towed, the stops she'd made before her trip to Cherry Bay, and people they'd interviewed at those locations. There weren't even photos from the actual accident scene, which raised the hair on the back of my neck. The lack of information made me all the more determined to see Baloney-Muloney when he returned. I wanted photocopies of his handwritten notes and the pictures someone had to have taken.

Turning away from the disappointing search, I pulled up Mom's calendar in our Marlowe & Co. system. There was nothing out of the ordinary for the day of the wreck. She had time blocked for yoga in the morning, a meeting with the DoD about our contract for background checks, and then a client meeting in the afternoon. The only thing that made me raise a brow was that she hadn't referenced a case file for the client meeting. I'd check her physical planner later at home.

Still not prepared to give up, I turned my attention to scouring security footage from the day of the accident. I didn't have video saved from our D.C. condo because I'd wiped the server clear when I'd sold the place, but I did have recordings from our office cams. I was still running security for the wannabe game development company who'd subleased the space from me.

Swiping through the stored files, I found the day of the accident. Mom had worn a black-and-white-checked blazer, a black turtleneck, and dress pants. Formal for her. Likely due to the meeting with the DoD. Her steps were hurried as she headed for the door, but nothing to make me think she was upset. I froze the screen, fingers lingering on her face.

Regret was like a computer virus. It ate away at your insides until nothing was left but spoiled zeros and ones. I wished I'd said something more important that morning. More poignant. More lasting. At least I'd shouted *I love you* as I'd left. But had she felt the full impact of it? Had she heard how much she truly meant to me?

"I miss you," I whispered, and then instantly felt guilty as my eyes landed on my breathing mother lying in the bed next to me.

I swallowed hard. Were the doctors right? Was she gone already? Were the thousands of dollars Nan and I had spent to get her into Shady Lane and keep her body breathing doing anything? Would she ever open her eyes, register me, and talk to me… say anything so I would have something besides *See you at dinner* as my last words from her?

Unexpected tears filled my eyes like they had at Dad's office the day before. *Nothing gets solved by crying, Rory-girl.*

I rubbed my eyes and returned to my hunt for video evidence. Most businesses only kept security cam footage for thirty days unless it was subpoenaed by the authorities. Had the police done that for the places Mom had visited? I'd found none of it on the department's server, so I doubted it. I searched each of the businesses only to be handed more disappointment.

If I'd done this last December, we'd be ahead of the game instead of miles behind.

As the sun sank behind the spirals of the buildings on the Bonnin campus, I kissed Mom's cheek and said, "I love you. Maybe think about waking up, okay? You can hand Dad a healthy dose of fuck-you that would make both of our days."

Then, with a heavy heart, I headed back to the cottage and Nan.

The porch light was shining on two pots of multicolored chrysanthemums that would bloom for a few more days. Nan and Pop's place had always been full of color, almost year-round due to Nan's love of gardening.

The half-timbered style of many of the homes on this side of Cherry Bay reflected the Englishmen who'd built them from plaster, stone, and maple wood that had been on the land before the cherry trees had taken over. Once thatched, Nan's roof was now a bright blue tile, giving it a fairy-tale quality. The cottage had been remodeled several times over the centuries until it now accommodated three bedrooms, a single bathroom, a spacious kitchen, and a living room.

I parked my bike behind Pop's yellow and rust-colored Jeep inside the detached two-car garage. Nan's Beetle wasn't there. She'd gone to bunco with friends for the first time in months. It was good she was doing something normal, but it also seemed like life was moving on without

Mom. Like we were leaving her behind. Giving up.

I gritted my teeth, unlocked the front door, and punched in the alarm code that would have made the CIA happy. I made my way directly to Mom's bedroom which I'd temporarily converted into an office. Once she was better, we'd figure out a new place to do business.

I tossed my things on a chair and went straight to the boxes sitting in the corner. They were Mom's things I hadn't had the heart to unpack yet. It took me two boxes before I came up with her scratched leather day planner. I opened it, and her tight but slightly slanted print caused my heart and throat to squeeze closed. I forced myself to flip the pages until I found the day of her accident. In the two-o'clock slot for the client meeting, she'd written *Space Force, Lincoln Memorial* in a shorthand code that only she and I knew.

I sat back, drumming my fingers on the pages. I'd closed all the outstanding cases, and we definitely hadn't been working with anyone from the Space Force. Why hadn't she logged it into our case files? She'd been nervous enough to use our shorthand code instead of writing it out. Unease filled me. Was this what had caused someone to mess with her car's computer? Had the person she'd met done it, or had someone hacked their way in? There were only a couple of ways to get into a car's systems—the easiest through the online navigation or by attaching a device to the car's computer directly. If it had been the latter, the evidence was probably gone. Crushed with the totaled car at the junkyard.

Irritation and impotence whirled through me. Had Dad checked it out before the car had been picked clean and then destroyed?

I turned toward the window and the quiet street outside, searching for peace or answers or a wormhole into the past. The lantern-shaped streetlights barely shimmered through the fog that had rolled in from the Potomac River.

What the hell did Dad and Detective Muloney have that proved it hadn't been an accident? And why hadn't they been able to find out more in the eleven months since? For all his faults, Dad was damn good at his job, so if he didn't have more, it was either because he wasn't inclined to go looking, or it was hidden deep. Neither was an answer I liked.

I looked down at the day planner again, absentmindedly flipping pages until it fell open to a month before her accident. More coded notes, but this wasn't our normal one. A stab of pain slid through me as I realized she hadn't wanted me to be able to read it either. That stung more than anything Dad had said to me yesterday.

On the other side of the page, she'd drawn an icon of some sort. It almost looked like the Avenger symbol, except instead of an A and an arrow, there was an A and an S with a zig-zagged line inside the circle. I snapped a picture, loaded it into a search engine, and went down a rabbit hole trying to find anything that looked like it.

My phone rang, and I glanced down, tempted to ignore it, but then guilt ran through me. My best friend had left me several messages over the last two days, and I hadn't returned them. Instead, as often happened when I was on a case, I'd lost sight of anything but the trail I was following.

"Hey! I was going to call you."

Shay snorted. "Liar." But there was no malice to it. Not anger or frustration either. She was exactly the forgiving angel she'd always been. "I need my wingwoman tonight."

I groaned internally. "Shay—"

"Please. You know I have a good feeling about this one. But…"

She didn't trust herself. Not after the last cheating bastard who'd stomped all over her heart and then had the audacity to say it was her fault.

"Where am I meeting you?"

She hesitated, and I knew what she was going to say before it even escaped her lips. "I know you've been avoiding it…him… But I didn't want to make it feel like a date, so I agreed to meet up with Devlin and his friend at The Prince Darian."

I didn't know which part of her statement elicited more twists and turns in my chest—where she wanted to go or the fact that it would be a foursome.

"He's bringing a friend?"

"I promise I'm not trying to set you up."

"Two couples in a bar on a Saturday night… definitely not at all date-like."

She chuckled. "This is just Devlin and me trying to get a feel for each other without Dad hovering around us at the café."

Devlin was new to town and the campus, carrying his newly appointed associate professor's title like a badge. His visits to the Tea Spot where Shay worked for her dad while going to college had increased until the guy was practically eating every meal there. She'd begged me not to go all "Rory" on him, but I'd still done the basic search. Enough to know he didn't have any priors and no complaints had been filed against him at his last college.

"What time are we doing this?" I asked, and my friend literally squealed. It simultaneously made me feel worse for neglecting her and made me smile.

"If you'd answered my texts, you would've had more time. They're meeting us in thirty minutes."

I put a hand to my messy ponytail, flattened from wearing a helmet, and then rubbed my makeup-free cheeks. I didn't need to look in a mirror to know they were pale and lifeless and that my eyes were shadowed after months of tossing and turning instead of sleeping. This was certainly not the way I wanted to stroll into the tavern for the first time in years. Definitely not how I wanted *him* to see me for the first time in years.

"I look like I've been on a stakeout."

"Come over. I'll have you fixed up in ten minutes."

The debate within me was strong. But I couldn't

abandon Shay. Not again. So, I hung up, grabbed the keys to Pop's Jeep, and left a note for Nan before walking out the door. The Jeep smelled like oil and ancient vinyl. Like salt and sea and rust. The scent was one more reminder of things I'd lost. A grandfather who'd been one of the only people in my life to truly spoil me. He'd been gone two years before Mom and I had moved in with Nan the first time. We had stayed barely a year, but those months had branded themselves on my soul just like a certain gray-eyed boy once had.

A gray-eyed boy I wasn't prepared to see again.

I wasn't ready to walk into The Prince Darian.

But I'd do it because Veronica Mars's words were true. The people who really deserved your time, faith, and love were the ones who came through even when you hadn't loved them enough. And that was Shay for me. I'd always been more caught up in my tragedies than hers. So, if she needed me, I'd be there.

If that meant seeing Gage Palmer for the first time in seven years, I'd just have to take the hit and hope I could get up and walk away when it was over.

Chapter Four

Rory

FOREVER YOUNG
Performed by Rod Stewart

TEN YEARS AGO

The first time I met Gage Palmer, I was twelve and he was a stunning seventeen-year-old. A heroic male figure coming into my world just as the number one man in my life had become the villain.

And I'd become his vile sidekick…

With my parents' marriage having disintegrated because of my mistake, Mom had moved us to Cherry Bay with Nan. There she'd joined a single parents group the members laughingly called the 5-H club because all the members' names started with an H. They were meeting that night in Holland Palmer's closed bar, and I was being forced to mingle with the other 5-H children in the empty rental apartment above it. Mom thought it would be good for me to meet a few of the kids I'd be starting school with in the fall, but I didn't see the point. Not when we'd be moving back to D.C. once the divorce was final. We'd only be in this tiny town for a few months. Weeks maybe.

I needed us back in D.C. so I could fix what I'd broken.

As I stomped my way up the steps behind the bar, the sound of little kid giggles and soft girly laughter poured from the apartment's windows along with the lyrics to a song I knew well. My feet came to a stop as "Could This Be Love" by The Guess Who drifted down to me. Most kids my age didn't even know who the band was, but I'd listened to them on vinyl with Dad for years.

Curiosity filled me as I approached the open doorway. There was a girl about my age with long blond hair and green eyes holding the hands of two toddlers as they danced to the music. Both boys stared up at her as if she was an angel. One of the toddlers had dark hair and dark eyes while the other had a riot of red curls bouncing around a chubby little face. He was barely able to stumble through the moves on his tiny legs. I was just about to ask how they knew about The Guess Who when another boy emerged from the hallway off to the side.

No… not a boy… a guy… a man. Or maybe not a man yet either, but somewhere close. He was tall. Taller than my dad. And he had ebony-colored hair that shimmered in the fading light. His face was the kind movie superheroes had, square and strong, but it was his eyes as they found mine that made my heart forget to beat. They were the gray of storm clouds. A summer storm full of electricity and thunder that might pelt you with hail. That's what it felt like. As if my entire body was being pricked with falling ice.

"Hey, you must be Rory," he said.

His voice was deep, even gruff, with a rasp to it that sent a shiver down my spine and made my legs shake. He took a step toward me, sticking his hand out. "I'm Gage."

And all I could think was that it was the best name I'd ever heard in my life. It fit him. Dark and stormy. Like the bad boy on a motorcycle your parents wouldn't want you to date.

When I took his hand, the lightning I'd felt in the air seemed to shoot through me, and I let go, jumping back almost as soon as I'd grabbed it.

"You okay?" he asked, but he rubbed his palm on his jean-clad thigh as if he'd felt it too. When I simply nodded, he turned to the others, saying, "Hey everyone, this is Rory.

Rory, that's Shay." He pointed to the blond-haired-angel girl. "Harriet's son, Maverick." He aimed a hand at the dark-haired toddler. "And my brother, Monte."

My eyes widened in surprise. Monte and Gage looked nothing alike. Gage looked like the tavern owner, Holland. They both had the same black hair, square features, and big build, but Monte looked like a little cherub.

I raised a hand in greeting. The song ended and "Broken" came on. My heart flip-flopped like a fish out of water.

I turned to Gage. "Did my mom tell you I like The Guess Who?"

One brow rose, and I wondered how he could do that. It made me want to practice it in a mirror until I could do it as well.

"Wait, you know The Guess Who?" he asked with surprise.

"Only the best band of any decade."

He put a palm to his chest, a grin taking over his face that made those gray eyes light up like the sun had come out from behind the clouds.

"A girl after my own heart."

And I fell hard and fast with no chance of stopping myself.

♫ ♫ ♫

NINE YEARS AGO

The second time I fell for Gage, it was because of a fictional character.

"I can't believe you didn't watch any of the episodes. You won't even understand what's going on!" I shoved Gage's shoulder with my fist. I couldn't help it. I seemed to be drawn to touching him whenever we were together. It felt wrong and right and sort of decadent.

"I've been a bit busy, Pipsqueak. College applications, basketball, and now finals."

"Plus, Lori Martinez," Shay said dryly from the other side of me.

Lori was his girlfriend. Whenever I saw them together, it made me feel like I'd eaten a live eel.

Gage approached the ticket booth and said, "Three for *Veronica Mars* at eight."

My heart scrabbled out this weird pattern because he was buying tickets for us even though I knew it wasn't a date. I was with Gage *and* Shay. He was taking two thirteen-year-olds he basically considered little sisters to a movie because neither of their parents were able to take them. While Gage didn't understand my obsession with *Veronica Mars*, he did understand single parents who worked way too hard and had succumbed to my beg with hardly a blink.

Gage bought our popcorn, drinks, and Reese's Pieces before leading us into the darkened theater. We'd come early enough that we had our pick of seats and ended up right in the middle. I had my best friend on my left and the guy I adored on the right. What could be better? Almost a year ago, I'd thought moving to Cherry Bay was the worst thing to happen to me. Now, I was terrified it was all coming to an end.

With my parents' divorce final, Mom and I were moving back to D.C. this summer. Mom had gotten the money from her share of the house and business, and it had been enough to start over with a condo and an office of her own downtown. If it weren't for the hours she spent each week commuting because of me, I might have pleaded with her to stay in Cherry Bay.

"You okay?" Gage asked, leaning in to nudge my shoulder with his.

The warm sparks that always covered me when he was near hit me like a shock wave. I looked up into his eyes that were almost black in the dark of the movie theater. He was the most beautiful person I'd ever met, and I craved every single moment I got with him. Which, in nine months, had been almost as rare as the times I'd spent with my father. But I would have traded every moment with Dad for a single extra minute with Gage.

"Yep," I finally responded, determined to not let anything ruin this day. I ripped open the Reese's Pieces bag and poured some into my popcorn container, carefully mixing it up.

"What the hell are you doing?" he asked with a frown.

"Do *not* dis this snack perfection until you've tried it, Gage Palmer," I said in my very best adult-sounding voice. I shook the container at him, and he made a face.

I grabbed a handful of popcorn with some of the candies mixed in, and shoved it at his mouth. Half of it fell to the seat and beyond, but as he started to laugh, some of it made it inside. His lips were surprisingly soft, and my fingers tingled at the touch. A now-familiar heaviness grew in my chest and stomach as I watched him chew around his laughter.

"So?" I asked. "What's the verdict?"

"It's not entirely despicable." The saying was his little brother's. Whenever anyone got Monte to try something he thought he'd hate and ended up liking, he would say the same thing but in his cute toddler voice that couldn't quite get all the syllables right.

Sometimes, I wondered if my parents would have stayed together if they'd had another child besides the one who'd driven a spike down the middle of them. But then, I thought about Gage's parents and how having Monte hadn't healed their broken parts. According to the gossip I'd heard, Gage's mom had stuck around for longer than normal after Monte had been born, but she'd still left. Like she always did.

I wasn't sure what was worse, knowing you'd never see your parent again because they'd died like Shay's mom or knowing your parent *chose* not to see you because they prioritized everything in their life over you. My hero,

Veronica Mars, would know. She'd been abandoned by her mom the way Gage and I had been abandoned by one of our parents.

The theater lights lowered, and I almost squealed. The previews lasted way too long, and then, there she was—Veronica! With her snark and attitude, coming back to the town she'd sworn never to get stuck in, doing everything to solve the case for Logan. The antihero. The morally gray kid who grew up to become a Navy Intelligence officer. The guy no one thought she should end up with… except the fans. They were perfect in their own imperfect way. I didn't see them *ever* getting married, which was fine by me. I didn't want to get married either.

I didn't want a husband. A cheater. A man who left.

I wanted someone who chose to stay because they couldn't imagine doing anything else.

When the lights came up at the end, I was filled with loss because I didn't want it to be over. I needed more of Veronica. I needed to know how her life turned out because, in some strange way, I felt like it meant something in the scheme of mine.

As we left the theater, Shay darted inside the bathroom, leaving me alone with Gage. He put his arm around my shoulders, drew me close, and my entire body lit up like a sparkler.

"Pipsqueak, you don't seem all that happy for someone who just watched her hero on the big screen."

I looked up at him, and it was as if he could read my mind. As if the turmoil in me over my dad and leaving and my future was all laid out for him. Gage tugged a strand of my hair.

"She seems pretty badass for a marshmallow," he teased. "Maybe a bit like someone else I know."

How could I not fall for someone who saw me in that light? Who saw through the broken parts to the person I most wanted to be? There was no way I could stop my heart from giving itself to him even knowing I was moving back to D.C.

in a few months. Even knowing he'd be off to Kansas, chasing his dreams about tornadoes and weather.

No matter how our lives pulled us apart, there'd always be a part of me that belonged to him.

♬ ♬ ♬

SEVEN YEARS AGO

The third time I fell for Gage, it was for his motorcycle.

I hadn't been to the enormous Victorian Gage lived in with his dad, his brother, and their housekeeper for over two years. But Mom and I were in Cherry Bay, visiting Nan for a few days, and Holland had invited us to an end-of-the-summer party. It wasn't an official gathering of the 5-H club, because Gage's mom was back. She was upstairs, laughing and chatting with the other adults while the kids congregated in the finished basement. I wondered how long she'd stay this time. I wondered what Gage thought of her being there.

When I went in search of him, I found him leaning with his elbows on the patio railing, staring out at the darkening sky. A storm was coming. Would it be anything like the ones he'd spent his summer chasing with a storm company in the Midwest? This one promised to be full of lightning and thunder, bolts of electricity shifting through the air just like they shifted through me whenever Gage was near.

Standing at the base of the garden stairs, I took a moment to catalog the differences in him since I'd seen him last. If possible, he was even more beautiful, with wider shoulders and a narrower face. He hadn't shaved, so there was scruff along his jaw that made him much more man than the teen I'd first met. As I watched, he dropped his head, shoulders sagging as if a heavy burden had suddenly hit him, and my entire being cried out.

I was just about to call his name when the French doors behind him opened and a woman stepped out. She looked like Monte. All strawberry-blond hair and blue eyes. Thin.

Willowy even. From inside the house, I heard Monte call her, "Mommy!" and come running after her. She bent and said something to him that made him smile before he skipped back inside.

The woman crossed over to Gage on feet so light it was as if she was floating.

When she reached him, the look on his face made me inhale sharply—dark fury. I'd never seen Gage angry. He'd always been calm. Easygoing. Even laughing.

"You can almost feel the electricity buzzing through the air, can't you?" she asked.

"Why are you here?" Gage growled. I instantly wanted to go to him. To reassure him, but I also knew, from years of listening at doors and windows and hallways, that this wasn't a conversation to interrupt. "How can you do this to Dad and Monte? He's calling you *Mommy*."

The word was scathing. As if it was the worst word in the world. She stared at the sky for several seconds before she finally responded. "I want to be here, Gage. It's the only place where the darkness doesn't drown me. Where I can stand in the light for a few moments."

"It's selfish," Gage grunted out. "Because when you leave, as we both know you will, you'll take the light with you, and we'll be left in the dark. Monte's going to cry himself to sleep for days. Dad's going to retreat into his quiet shell. But you won't give a shit because you'll be out there flitting around like a queen bee going from flower to flower, sprinkling the light you took from us onto others."

"Gage—"

"No. I don't want to hear whatever ridiculous excuse you have about wandering feet and an inability to stay in one place, Demi." The way he refused to call his mother by anything but her name was telling. As much as I was hurt by my father's cold indifference, I still called him Dad.

Demi reached out and covered Gage's hand with hers. A strange look ran over her face. As if she'd plugged herself into a computer and was getting a download. Her eyelids fluttered, and when they opened again, they were hazy.

"Sometimes," she said with a faraway voice, "sometimes, in order for something to grow into what it's supposed to be, it has to be left alone. The roots need to struggle through the clay and soil to the water below without help. They're more powerful that way. Stronger. Harder to rip out. I want you to have the joy I see ahead of you, even if it's a long way off, but you're going to have to fight to keep it. You'll need to grow roots that are deep and strong and sturdy to make sure you can, and you'll have to do that on your own."

"Fuck that. You aren't doing this for me. Or for them." He waved toward the house and his family. "And you won't leave us again as some noble act of self-sacrifice. You're doing this because you get bored. Because you don't love him—any of us—as much as you love yourself."

My heart broke apart in my fifteen-year-old chest.

I knew what it felt like to not be enough for a parent. Even when you were loved completely and wholly by one, the missing parent left marks you could never heal.

Demi pulled back a little and said, "I know it seems that way."

"Not *seems*, Demi. It *is* that way."

I couldn't take it anymore. I couldn't take his anguish. His anger. I bounded up the steps, my boots pounding on the wood and causing both of them to glance my way.

Demi's eyes widened on seeing me, and then, she smiled. She had Gage's smile. Except it made her look like a fairy—mischievous and spirited and good all at the same time. I wanted to hate her. I wanted to hate her with every fiber of my being for what she was doing to him, and yet, it was impossible when she looked like goodness personified. Our gazes locked for several seconds. My pulse picked up as she seemed to read my soul and all the mixed-up feelings I had for Gage.

She winked at me, taking my confused emotions and notching them up another level. Then she turned back to

Gage, patted his arm, and drifted into the house without another word.

The silence she left behind felt as loaded as the sky.

Finally, I forced out an, "Are you okay?"

Gage pushed a hand through his black hair that had grown longer and wavier since I'd seen him last. He shrugged in response and then asked, "How are you, Rory?"

I'd almost forgotten the rasp of his voice. How it seemed to coast over me, electrifying my nerve endings. Just like I'd almost forgotten how those stormy eyes were the only ones to ever see the truth of me.

When I didn't respond right away, he raised a brow. He took me in slowly, a curious look on his face. As if he was surprised to no longer see the thirteen-year-old who'd bit her lip trying not to cry while saying goodbye after his high school graduation party. Now, I had curves in places I'd never had, I wore makeup, and my hair was down and styled. I'd worn my impress-Dad's-latest-girlfriend outfit today— tight jeans and a purple tank with half booties.

"Look at you..." A grin played at the corners of his mouth.

"Yeah, yeah. All grown up, yada yada."

He chuckled, and I was thrilled to be the reason for it after all the grief I'd witnessed.

"I'd hardly call fifteen all grown up."

I rolled my eyes. I felt older than fifteen, and working the front office of my mom's PI business meant I'd heard and seen things many adults, let alone teens, probably never would.

Monte's laugh drew our eyes toward the kitchen.

"He's calling her Mommy," Gage said, swearing under his breath. "Do you know what it's going to do to him when she leaves again?"

We both knew I did. I threaded my arm through his, leaning my head on his shoulder, trying to give comfort by my presence like he'd done for me in the past.

"Maybe this will be the time she stays," I said softly.

I realized it had been the wrong thing to say when his entire body tightened. He pulled away, heading for the back stairs.

"I gotta get out of here for a while," he said.

For two heartbeats, I debated before following. I had to almost run to catch up with his long legs. As I trailed him inside the detached garage, he mounted the back of a cherry-red Indian motorcycle. My heart stopped and started. He looked perfect there. Not the bad boy I'd once imagined him based on his name, not a misunderstood rebel, but a god on his flaming steed.

"You got a motorcycle!" I said and then felt stupid. "I mean, duh, but you know I've always wanted one. Can I come with you?"

"Don't think it's a good idea, Pipsqueak." The long-ago nickname hit me like a brick to my chest. It sounded too good coming from his lips. Growly and grown-up and addictive.

"Come on. Knowing this is my dream, you'd really refuse me?" I half teased, half begged.

"I'm not good company at the moment, and I doubt Hallie would like you riding my bike."

"I told her I'm getting my own as soon as I get my license," I said, putting my hands on my hips. His eyes followed the motion, slowing on the skin exposed by my cropped sweater.

He looked away, throat bobbing, and I wondered… wondered if he saw me as something more than a little girl. It didn't matter. He'd go back to college, I'd go back to high school, and we'd go years without seeing each other again. But we had this moment. This moment right here, and I wasn't letting him leave without me.

"Please, Gage," I said, trying hard to keep the whine out of my tone.

"Fine. Grab the extra helmet," he responded with a chin

nod to the shelf behind me.

I smiled, scurrying to grab the helmet before he changed his mind. I stood at his side while I tried to hook the strap, and when I struggled to tighten it, he leaned in to help. His fingers brushed along my jaw, and electricity zapped through me—sudden and fast like the lightning that was threatening to course through the sky.

He drew back, wiping his hands on his jeans before pulling on his helmet.

I climbed on the back and slid my arms around his waist. When he started the engine, it vibrated through my body. The tingle joined with the energy I felt drifting between me and Gage, settling low in my stomach. He revved the engine and a laugh escaped me. When he turned his head sideways, the grin I saw through the visor took my breath away.

Then, we were out on the road, leaving the cobblestone streets of Cherry Bay and the trees hinting at fall behind us. We cruised along the winding roads at the edge of the Potomac. The air was full and thick, the breeze carrying the humidity along with it. The waves crashed on the shore as if the ocean was trying to dig itself into the land. The smell of the silver maple and sycamore trees mixed in with the dankness of the water. In front of us, lightning zapped, crashing to the ground in a magnificent display. It was near enough that the thunder chasing it boomed around us, shaking the earth.

I loved it. Just like I loved Gage when I shouldn't.

I tightened my thighs around him, flung my arms into the air, and let out a scream of exhilaration and joy and freedom.

His deep laugh joined my cry, the wind whipping it away, leaving the remnants to mix with the intense emotions of this moment. The memory we were making felt huge. Monumental. Irreplaceable.

But fleeting.

Somehow, I knew enough to savor every second. As if

I knew the truth. As if I knew it would be the last time I saw Gage Palmer for seven years.

And by that time, my entire world would have changed.

And his too.

Chapter Five

Gage

DEAR HEART
Performed by Nate Smith

PRESENT DAY

The Prince Darian was packed to capacity. The cherrywood bar top allowed me to easily slide the drink over its lacquered surface to the woman sitting across from me. She didn't fit in with the college students elbowing their way through the space behind her, looking more like one of the professors who'd made the mistake of coming in on the wrong night. She glanced my way with a flutter of lashes and a raised brow. Her aura all but screamed lonely and available. Once upon a time, I would have spent the night flirting with her, and it would have ensured a huge tip, if nothing else. But these days, nothing seemed to appeal to me.

River joined me, toting a rack of clean glasses still steaming. I didn't have the money to hire an official barback, so Audrey, River, and I split the role, keeping the bar stocked as well as serving drinks. As we unloaded glasses, my phone buzzed, and I looked down, hoping it was Monte. Instead, it was some damn social media alert. I hadn't heard from my brother since this afternoon, and my insides were crawling.

"Still no word?" River asked.

I shook my head. I'd promised myself not to be a helicopter parent, but it was damn hard. There was a heaviness in my gut that spoke of a thunderstorm brewing. The feeling clung to me in a way I couldn't shake.

"If it wasn't for the dreams, I wouldn't be worried," I replied.

River and Audrey both knew about Monte's visions. I'd had to tell them the truth back when the FBI had knocked on my door, and I'd needed them to take care of my siblings while agents had questioned me. But we rarely talked about it. It was a darkness we all pretended wasn't there.

"He tell India the truth?" River asked.

"He said no. But what the hell is she going to think if he wakes up screaming?" Not only screaming but trembling as images of blood and death chased him.

"She'll think he had a nightmare," River said with a shrug.

I didn't respond.

"Go. Call him."

River grabbed the glass from me, and I made my way toward the back, weaving my way through the crowd. The Prince Darian was dark and moody. Full of worn wood, copper, and old leather. Enormous roughhewn beams traveled from front to back, lowering the ceiling but adding a rustic coziness to the space. Booths ran along one wall, ending with a corner unit pushed up against the mullioned, stained-glass windows depicting a scene from a local fairytale about the prince the bar was named after.

We didn't have a stage or room for a live band, but there was a tiny dance floor and enough space for a DJ who played Tuesdays, Fridays, and Saturdays. The music the college kids liked was nothing I listened to. But then again, the little-known classic rock bands I preferred weren't liked by many people. Except once upon a time by a teen girl who'd flirted around the edges of my life. Whose presence seemed to have haunted me since yesterday when I'd caught a glimpse of her all grown up.

As soon as I closed the office door behind me, I dialed Monte's number. It went straight to voicemail. I texted again, but he didn't reply. I was debating calling India or her parents when shouting in the corridor drew me into the hall.

A college-aged guy and a girl were arguing furiously.

"Everything okay here?" I demanded.

They both jumped.

"Fine," the girl said. "Just a dumbass being jealous for no reason."

She stomped back down the hall, and he followed her into the bar, nearly knocking Audrey and her tray over. Audrey's white-blond hair streaked with blue and pink was up on top of her head in a messy bun, and her lean body was cased in leather from head to toe. She had almost as many tattoos as River, and when they stood next to each other, you could tell they fit. As if they were two pieces of the same whole. Hell, some of their tattoos even bled from one to the other.

"Watch it, jackass," she exclaimed with no real heat. She and River were two of the calmest people I'd ever met. It was their serene energy that had stabilized me after Dad had died and Demi had taken off once again.

The Cherry Bay residents had come out in force after Dad had died, grieving his loss alongside us and wanting to help, but I'd only been able to stomach River's and Audrey's assistance. Maybe it was because they'd already been working at the bar for almost two decades, and I could pretend it wasn't pity or charity I was accepting, even when my subconscious knew it wasn't true. With Audrey's mammoth art sculptures in high demand and River's miniatures thriving online, they hardly needed the paltry money they made at the bar.

"You get a hold of him?" Audrey asked as I joined her.

I shook my head.

"He's just a teen lost in the moment. I'm sure you remember being that way," Audrey said with a wink.

It made my stomach churn for all sorts of new reasons. He was only thirteen. Too young for him or India to be even thinking about kissing, let alone more. I'd had the sex talk with him. It had come out when I'd insisted we move Ivy into the room Monte and I'd been sharing and give him his own.

Monte had protested the room change at first, saying if anyone needed space, it was me. I'd just stared at him, trying to figure out what that meant. When his cheeks had turned fiery, I realized he was talking about me bringing a woman home. I'd barely held in a scoff. There was no way I was bringing anyone back to our apartment.

I could barely remember the last time I'd had sex, kissed someone, or even thought about kissing someone. Even if I'd had the time for a hookup, it wouldn't have been anything more. I wouldn't have introduced someone into my siblings' lives who wouldn't stay, and I couldn't think of adding anything permanent to the pile of responsibilities I already carried.

As if the gods were laughing at me, the crowd parted to reveal the spitfire I'd seen across the parking lot the day before. This close, I could feel the energy crackling around Rory, bright and furious, singeing the air and leaving the scent of lightning in its wake—burned ozone and danger.

Her hair was long and straight, falling well past her shoulder blades even in a ponytail. It left her high cheekbones exposed and accentuated her large, amber-colored eyes with the trail of green fire blazing around her pupils. She was dressed in a black tank with a neckline low enough to show the swell of her breasts and tight black jeans that clung to slim hips and the perfect curve of an ass she shouldn't be allowed to have. On her feet, she wore a pair of biker boots with chunky heels and rows of metal buckles and studs.

She looked like both hell on wheels and the sweetest of delights.

My body reacted violently to the image of her, making

me feel like an asshole even though I knew she was no longer fifteen. She had to be twenty-two going on twenty-three, but it still didn't feel right for my dick to be responding to her. Not after years of training myself to bury any thoughts except the platonic kind.

She was with Shay, and they were talking to two men who had an academic look about them in button-down shirts, sleeves rolled to their elbows. They weren't who I'd ever expect my edgy, quick-witted Pipsqueak to end up with.

Except she sure as hell wasn't mine.

I couldn't afford to have anyone be mine at the moment. Especially not a feisty fireball who didn't even live in Cherry Bay and was just visiting.

As I stood there staring, the noise of the bar all but disappeared around me, and I was overwhelmed again with the sense of an approaching storm. A premonition that Demi's damn psychic abilities had forged into me. Abilities that were never wrong.

All I could hope was that the storm would be a real one with rain and winds and lightning rather than another traumatic event my family couldn't sustain.

Chapter Six

Rory

USED TO BE YOUNG
Performed by Miley Cyrus

While I was doing my best to concentrate on Shay's conversation with Devlin and his friend Luis, I was on high alert waiting for Gage to show up. Since I'd been in town, I'd listened to the gossip, and I might have even done a little digging on my own. The only nights he wasn't behind the bar at the tavern were Sundays and Wednesdays.

I wished it were Wednesday.

Liar, my brain said as my heart picked up its pace.

The music had kicked in, making it almost impossible to talk. My friend leaned into Devlin, and he tucked a curl of her shimmering blond hair behind her ear. Her pale skin was flushed with more than blush. Her green eyes sparkled and her heart-shaped lips turned upward, the bright pink lipstick a perfect accent to the magenta sweater she was wearing. She looked like the cherry blossoms that bloomed in spring. Sweet. Kind. Iridescent. We were complete opposites. She was the light, elfin fairy who'd grant your wish. I was the warrior you feared showing up at your door.

The truth hit me out of the blue like malware… For the first time since everything that had gone down with her ex Rico, Shay was happy. Unlike a computer virus, this thought brought a bit of joy to my heavy heart. She deserved to be happy.

I shifted my gaze away from them to scan the room as an old sensation bled into me. My stomach flipped like I was on a roller coaster. Like it used to do when I was in the room with only one man. After going years without ever feeling again the spark of electricity I used to feel when Gage was nearby, I'd thought I'd imagined it. But tonight, as my eyes found Gage behind the bar, the spark returned, just as strong, if not stronger. As if it actually might burst into a full-on flame. As if something was in the air more than the normal push and pull of particles. As if a banked fire had finally received the oxygen it needed to come fully to life.

He seemed at ease behind the bar, but then that had always been Gage—calm and sure. He was smiling, maybe even flirting a bit with the woman across from him as he twirled a bottle. His biceps flexed as he caught the neck before it crashed to the ground. And while I'd never seen him behind the taps, mixing and pouring, it seemed like he belonged there—as if he and the building were one. Maybe the tavern had been in his family for so long that it had become a sentient part of his DNA.

Maybe I needed to stop drinking my Jack and Coke before my brain melted. I didn't believe in that kind of paranormal bullshit any more than I believed in sappy fairy tales spouting magical wishes and true love.

Shay elbowed me, drawing my attention away from Gage and back to the men we were with.

A group shuffled out of the large booth up front, and I said, "Grab the table before it's gone."

We hustled toward the soft burgundy leather, and Audrey showed up to take our order. She knew Shay on sight, asking about her dad and how things were at the Tea Spot. Shay asked if Audrey had sold any new sculptures in return. As Audrey walked away with our order, I realized she hadn't recognized me. It had been a long time since my mom and I had hung around Holland, the 5-H club, and the bar. Too long. And now Mom might never be there again.

I forced back that thought, turning to give Luis a smile,

and asked, "What do you teach at Bonnin?"

He shook his head, leaning in a bit, his blond hair glowing in the dim lights. "I'm just here visiting Devlin. I'm actually an associate professor at Wilson Jacobs in New York. Are you a grad student like Shay?"

Before I could respond, my friend jumped in. "Rory's finishing a double major in criminology and computer science while working as a badass private investigator. Someday you're going to turn on the news and see her in an FBI windbreaker with a man in cuffs on the ground at her feet."

Luis's eyes turned wide, and I couldn't help but tease, "Putting a man in cuffs is one of my favorite things."

Shay snorted, Devlin cleared his throat, and Luis flushed bright red.

I turned away so I wouldn't be rude and laugh in the poor guy's face, and for the first time in seven years, my gaze met Gage's. Across the dimly lit space, you wouldn't know his eyes were the color of gray storm clouds flecked with lightning that could scorch you, leaving a crater behind, but his dynamic chemistry seemed to pull the air from the room. His aura screamed power and control. A man who would get things done. A man who was used to being the center of attention.

A man who could handle handcuffs.

The sleeves of his Henley were pushed up to the elbows, exposing a tattoo on his left forearm he hadn't had the last time I'd seen him. I wanted to run over and examine it. To find all the differences in him, both externally and internally, from when he'd been the teenage boy I'd repeatedly fallen for.

The intensity of that look—of him—on top of everything else going on in my life seemed to land on me all at once. A damn screw that had been wrenched too tight. I couldn't catch my breath, and a sudden, desperate urge to escape rose within me when I'd never been the running type.

I scooted out of the booth, and Shay shot me a pleading

look. "You're not leaving, right?"

"Just using the restroom." But I think we both knew I might bolt.

I made my way through the crowd, feeling Gage's eyes follow me. I wasn't sure whether I was surprised or not that he'd seen me. That he'd not only seen me but was now trailing me with a penetrating look I could feel across the room.

In the bathroom, I stared at the woman in the mirror. I felt like a shadowy reflection of myself—of the girl Gage had first met. It was as if I was losing pieces of myself day by day. As if Mom's coma was somehow reaching out to haul me into the abyss with her.

I shook my head, trying to clear the dark thoughts and calm my racing heart.

It didn't work. I needed to get out of there. I wasn't good for Shay or her joyful not-date date. I was covered in a sluggish haze that had followed me here like the fog creeping in from the Potomac. The only thing that might clear it was a few hundred rounds to my punching bag or maybe losing myself in a tricky computer hack.

Straightening my shoulders, I strode to the door with determination, pushing it open and colliding with a thick body. Hard, muscled, and tall. My instincts flared to life— not the usual, put-up-my-fists reaction, but the slow-burning fire that had always swirled through me when one and only one man was nearby.

Gage's large hands steadied me, and the warmth of his touch only intensified the storm brewing inside me. By the time my eyes finally reached his, one of his brows was raised slightly. An alluring, teasing lift I'd once adored and longed to mimic.

"Where's the fire, Pipsqueak?" he asked, lips quirking upward.

The nickname flew through me like a match to gasoline. I loved it and hated it. It made me feel seen and special while at the same time it forced me back into the role of a teen girl who idolized him.

I stepped away, and he did the same, and I instantly missed the heat of him. That warmth—that low pull deep inside my stomach—was what had been absent in the touches of other men I'd let briefly into my life. Those interactions had been all perfunctory motion and momentary satisfaction. This was a fire that would brand me, that had already branded me.

Could a person spontaneously combust from years of untended flames?

"Hey, Gage," I managed to get out, glad when I sounded almost nonchalant instead of like a drooling idiot or the adoring teen he'd last seen.

"Are you here visiting Shay and your grandmother?" he asked.

Surprise filtered through me at the question. With the way the locals talked, I'd been sure he'd heard I'd moved back. Did this mean he hadn't heard about Mom either?

"I moved in with Nan while I'm finishing my degree at Bonnin." It was a struggle to keep the bitterness and sadness out of my voice. I didn't want him to see me as the girl who needed to be pitied—the one struggling to keep her shit together—when that was exactly why I'd stayed away from the bar to begin with.

"What happened to Georgetown?" he asked, brows drawing together.

His question confirmed he'd heard enough to know I'd ended up at the college of my choice, but that he hadn't heard the worst.

I made a pointed glance around the tavern and said, "You should know better than anyone that life throws you curveballs."

He glanced away as if I'd struck him, and I instantly wanted to take it back. I reached out, my hand settling on his bicep. "I'm sorry. Not just for my words but about your—"

"What the hell, Rory?" He yanked my wrist up to his

face where he examined the bruises that were now turning an ugly shade of green. "Who hurt you? Was it that guy out front?"

He dropped my hand and strode toward the end of the hall, forcing me to jog after him. I didn't know if it pissed me off or thrilled me that even now, all these years later, he instantly wanted to protect me. It was wrong, wasn't it? To have those feelings? Those screwed-up threads that had somehow tied us together?

I grabbed his arm, yanking him to a halt. "No. Geez, Gage. Don't go all he-man. I just met Luis tonight. He's Shay's boyfriend's friend."

Gage turned his stormy eyes on me. Eyes that had always seen through me.

"So, some other guy did that to you?"

I crossed my arms over my chest. To my surprise and delight, his gaze fell to the swell of my breasts peeking over the neckline of my tank before it jerked back to my face.

"Just an altercation with a sleazebag cheater," I told him. "Don't worry—he ended up looking worse." And he had. The guy had ended up with a stun gun mark and my boot imprint on his back. He'd be remembering me for longer than my paltry bruises would last.

"A cheater?" Gage's face was a furrow of confusion before the realization dawned. "You're working with your mom?"

I opened my mouth to respond just as two bodies came flying out of the men's room. Two college kids—one guy with another in a headlock. They rammed into the wall, making the old paintings rattle and shake.

"You fucking asshole." The one in the headlock grunted, reaching up to try and free himself.

"Stay the fuck away from her," the other man barked.

"Hey, break it up!" Gage growled, his deep voice booming around the darkened space.

In one smooth move, he pulled the two of them apart

and shoved the first one toward the exit leading to the parking lot out back. The guy who'd just been released from the headlock went after them and would have started slinging fists at Gage if I hadn't stepped forward, grabbed his arms, and twisted them behind his back.

"What the hell?" he said, trying to turn around to get a look at me, but I'd been trained to handle exactly these kinds of situations. I pulled up, putting pressure on his shoulders and propelling him in the same direction.

"Both of you cool your jets and take off before I call the cops," Gage thundered, giving the kid he'd hauled out of the bar a shove that sent him sprawling onto the pavement.

I let go of my guy, but instead of stepping away, he rounded on me, swinging. The surprise of it hurt more than the fist barely grazing my face.

"Did you just fucking hit her?!" Gage roared. He shoved the guy in the chest so hard his back hit the ancient stone of the building's exterior. Before I blinked, Gage had his forearm shoved into the man's windpipe.

"She assaulted me first," the man choked out.

The kid Gage had tossed to the street got to his feet. "This is fucked up. I'm out of here. Just stay the hell away from Suzie." And he scrambled away in the dark.

"Call the cops, Rory," Gage said.

The guy struggled against Gage's hold, scratching into his skin and the tattoo I'd ached to see just minutes before.

"It's fine. Let him go," I said.

"No. He hit you. He was fighting in my damn bar. Call the cops."

"Do you really want to spend half your night filling out paperwork for something that isn't going to get prosecuted? Just let him go."

Gage glared at the kid, pressing into him more and causing him to gurgle, before releasing him and taking two giant steps backward. "Get the hell out of here. And if you ever step foot in my bar again, you'll regret it."

"Fuck you and this shitty place anyway," the guy said. As he went to move away, I stuck out my boot. He went sprawling onto the pavement face-first.

"You bitch!" he said, standing up, face contorted in rage, blood dripping from his chin.

Gage stepped up between us, and a standoff as old as time beat through the air as they stared each other down. Finally, the kid sprinted away.

Gage flipped around, scouring my cheek for marks. He lifted his hands, caressing the skin with a gentleness that brought tears to my eyes. The touch was intimate and familiar even after all our years apart.

I swallowed hard, every single synapse coming awake as the rough pads of his fingers stroked along my jaw. When I dared to meet his eyes, my body froze, snagged in Gage's vampire-like lure. The chemical reaction zipping between us was so strong I expected to see flashes of light dancing in the tiny space between us, threatening to consume us.

As if he felt it too, he dropped his hands and moved back.

But it was too late. I'd already been scorched.

There wasn't a moment where I'd come in contact with Gage Palmer and not been burned.

Except now, it was the last thing I could afford.

The last thing I wanted.

A maniacal voice inside me laughed. *Liar*.

Chapter Seven

Gage

BROKEN DOWN ANGEL
Performed by Nazareth

She'd been hurt. She'd been hurt before tonight by some unseen guy in a way that made me want to rip his head off, and now by some ridiculous college kid while I'd stood by.

I wasn't a violent person by nature. My coaches in school and Nick at my internship with Storm Dominators had all commented on my cool head. But at the moment, I didn't feel anywhere near calm and collected. All the frustration and anger and heaviness that had been building in me for the last two days—hell, the last four years—attempted to pour out of me.

I might actually have done something I would've regretted if Rory hadn't stopped me.

What was even worse than wanting to beat the crap out of some stupid kid was the feeling I had when I touched her. The feeling I had simply when looking at her. She'd always been beautiful, but now, she was so much more.

When my fingers landed on her cheek, the feel of her bled into me in a way I wasn't prepared for—into my skin, my chest… my groin. It could consume me if I let it. I might actually be able to lose myself in her. Lose myself and forget, for a few minutes, every burden and responsibility that had been drowning me.

Monte. Ivy. The Prince Darian.

I stepped back.

Startled by those thoughts. No. Not startled. Panicked.

Losing myself in anyone, let alone Rory, was not in the cards for me. Not in my present.

"That was a stupid move," I told her. "I had it handled. You didn't need to step in and risk getting hurt."

Her chin went up. The stubborn fierceness I'd once admired in a teenager suddenly looked extremely sexy and utterly enticing in a grown woman.

"Believe it or not, Gage, I probably know how to handle myself in a fight better than you do. If I hadn't had your back, that guy would have taken a cheap shot at you from behind."

I found so many things wrong with those statements. Her knowing how to fight. Her protecting me. Damn. Did her parents really know she was doing all of this? Chasing cheaters and breaking up bar fights? Had she taken her hero worship of a television character and turned it into reality?

None of that sat well with me. My worries increased, adding to the pile of concerns I already had boiling inside me. But she wasn't my responsibility. There was no way I could add Rory to the list of things I needed to take care of. She had family and friends. They'd have to look out for her.

"In my bar, the only people who break up fights are me, River, and Crank."

She snorted. "I never took you for a misogynist."

I just stared at her for a moment. The statement and her attitude were so typical of the tween I'd once known that my lips twitched. It loosened the tightness inside me, allowing a chuckle to find its way out. A strangely weird and unused sound.

"Misogynist," I repeated, shaking my head, and her lips quirked in response.

We stood there with the dim light of the EXIT sign coating us in neon as if we'd entered an alternate universe.

As if we were actually on an episode of *Veronica Mars*. That thought made me grin, and I uttered the surprising truth, "It's really good to see you, Pipsqueak."

She returned my smile with her own. As a young girl, she'd had a vibrance that almost made her glow. But now, as I took in those full pink lips pushed upward, I realized some of her light had dimmed. Her smile didn't have the full strength it'd once had.

She had dark shadows under her eyes, reminding me of Monte's, and her aura flickered with pain and loss instead of sass and attitude. Grief clung to her, and it made me almost as furious as the bruises on her wrist and the hit she'd taken to her cheek. I didn't want her sad or grieving. I wanted the flirty badass who'd stuck her arms into the air on the back of my motorcycle and dared the lightning to strike her.

I closed the distance between us again, desperate to know the truth of what had really happened to her, when just two seconds before I'd been equally desperate to walk away. "What's wrong?" I demanded.

Her eyes widened, her look darting away and then back. And at first, I wasn't sure she'd respond.

A quiet "Everything" escaped her lips. She immediately stiffened as if regretting her words. She spun around, adding over her shoulder, "Coming here tonight was a bad idea."

Worry spread through me all over again as she headed into the crowded bar with me right on her heels. "Rory," I called, willing her to stop, and she did for half a second, pushing at her eyes. When her fingers came away, her makeup was slightly smudged, and it made her look like a watercolor version of the brilliant oil painting that she'd always been.

"I'm sure I'll see you around," she said before fleeing.

Her boots were sure and steady as she weaved through the crowd. I was so stunned by all of it, by the difference in her, by the fierceness that had turned almost tortured, that I hesitated too long. By the time my feet followed, she was already back at the booth with Shay and the academics. As I strode toward them, she grabbed her bag and flew out the door.

All that remained was the taste of ozone and regrets.

♫ ♫ ♫

For the rest of the night, my body and brain were stuck in overdrive, thinking about a brown-eyed firecracker who'd lit a fuse inside me I'd thought had been burned out. I couldn't seem to escape the scent of Rory, the softness of her cheek, or the energy vibrating off her.

She was still on my mind when I stumbled into the apartment after closing the bar, exhausted and revved up all at the same time. I ached to touch her again. My thoughts seemed wrong and right and badly timed. Because even if I got over the fact that it was Rory—a girl I'd once basically babysat—I still couldn't have her. It would be wrong to bring anyone into my life when I had so little time to give. I barely had time to shower, let alone date, and I certainly wouldn't just sleep with her and leave her. Not her. Because even though I hadn't seen her in years, there was too much between us already for a casual hookup.

So there would be nothing. And my body would just have to get on board with it.

I took an ice-cold shower, determined to wash away the lingering heat of my thoughts. After stepping out, I pulled on a pair of pajama bottoms I'd forced myself to get accustomed to once Ivy had moved in with me. Then, I made my way into our shared room. Her little feet were outside her blankets, her arms and legs sprawling in all directions on the toddler bed, and her stuffed otter covering her face. My heart lurched at the sweet sight of her, and my mind finally landed where it should have been all night. On Ivy and Monte.

I tucked Ivy back under the covers, moved the otter to the side, and then took the five steps to my full-sized bed shoved against the opposite wall of the bedroom.

I'd get a few hours of sleep before she woke, demanding the Sunday morning breakfast and cartoons that had become our new tradition. Monte would come home. Life would return to normal.

But even as my eyes drifted shut, I wasn't sure I believed it.

♫ ♫ ♫

Ivy's tiny hand prodded me awake, and I'd barely registered it from the depths of my sleep-filled haze when she said, "Monte's scared."

I sat straight up, noting the fear in her eyes before I pushed aside the covers and went in search of my brother. Had he come home and I hadn't known? The alarm would have beeped. I would have heard something. I scrambled into the hall, looking inside his room before darting into the living room. Ivy followed me, dragging her stuffed animal behind her.

I'd searched the entire apartment before the reality set in.

He wasn't there.

I squatted down in front of her. "Where is he?"

Ivy frowned, and that's when I saw it—the blank look she got after she'd had her own vision. She was tied to us somehow through Demi's abilities. When Monte or I were really upset or hurt, Ivy sensed it. She'd go into an almost trance-like state, telling everyone how we were feeling, and when she came out of it, she hardly ever remembered it.

"Go turn on the television," I told her. "I'll be right there."

I jogged back into our room, grabbed my phone from the charger, and hit Monte's number. It rang and rang and rang. When I got no response, I jotted out a text.

ME: Call me. Ivy had a little episode. She's worried about you.

I hit the restroom, splashed water on my face, and then went into the kitchen to start the coffee. The place was small, too small for the furniture we had shoved into it. But I'd been determined to bring as much of Dad and the feel of home with us as I could. The old walls and wooden floors were now covered with antique furniture and knickknacks gathered by generations of Palmer families that had once been in the Victorian. The only modern pieces were a cushy couch you sank into and a television so big it barely fit on the claw-footed buffet table that did double time as a television stand and linen cupboard.

I dialed Monte's number again, and he still didn't pick up.

Panic washed over me worse than when he hadn't shown up at the school on Friday. This was an entire weekend's worth of feeling like something was wrong, topped off by the cherry of Ivy's vision. So, I did the thing I promised I'd only do in an emergency or if he fucked up and lost my trust. I called India.

She answered groggily. "Hello?"

"India, it's Gage. I'm sorry to call so early, but I need to talk to Monte. Did his phone die or something?"

India was quiet for a moment, and when she spoke, her confusion made every kernel of anxiety that had been residing inside me pop and bloom. "Isn't he with you?"

Fuck. Fuck. Fuck.

"He told me he was with you, working on your science project."

Where the hell was he? Where had he been all weekend while lying to me, sending me texts, pretending everything was okay? Anger and frustration blended with my fear.

"We finished our project at school on Friday because I was going out of town with my parents for Thanksgiving."

God damn it.

India was the one to speak again, and this time, concern bled into her voice as well. "He's not with me, Gage… If he's not with you either, where is he?"

With a sinking feeling, I knew exactly where he was. Exactly where I'd thought he'd gone on Friday when he hadn't turned up in the car line. He'd gone to D.C.

As if sensing my emotions, Ivy came into the kitchen and wrapped her tiny arms around my leg, pushing her face into my thigh. My hand went to the top of her head, trying to reassure her, while pure adrenaline laced with terror slid through me.

"I'm sure it's just a misunderstanding. I'll let you know when he shows up," I told her before hanging up and jabbing out another text.

> *ME: India says you're not with her. Shit Monte, please tell me you didn't go to D.C. Where the hell are you?*

No response. My chest felt like it was going to break apart.

I picked Ivy up and pulled cereal and milk out. Normally, I made my siblings a big breakfast on the weekends because we weren't scrambling out the door to get to school, but today, I could barely think about feeding her.

Monte had felt useless and desperate all last week. He always felt that way with the visions. It had only gotten worse after our few futile attempts to do something about them. When we'd first gone to the authorities, no one had ever taken us seriously, and the one time they had, it had backfired on us. I'd taken Monte's visions to the police, making it seem like they were mine so I could protect him from the backlash. But instead of them thinking I was actually giving them a warning, they'd thought I was some wackadoodle sharing my threats ahead of time. I'd almost ended up in prison.

Now, every time he had the visions, we did nothing. He'd be a fucking mess until they were over. Until whatever god-awful event played out, this was his life—our lives. He'd get very little sleep with the images growing more intense the closer it got to the tragedy happening. It wasn't like his dreams gave us a specific location, time, and place. No. That would be too easy. Instead, he just had vague descriptions and a horrific glance at blood and guts and bones.

My phone buzzed and relief started to coast through me before I saw it was India.

> *INDIA: I just texted him, and he didn't respond to me either.*

Trails of sweat slid down my back, and my hands shook as I messaged her back.

> *ME: I'm checking with the guys on the basketball team.*

Which was a joke. India knew as well as I did that Monte wouldn't be with them. He was barely friends with them. The guys tolerated him because he was tall for his age and had good ball skills.

After I set Ivy in her seat at the counter, I placed the cereal bowl in front of her. I was trying desperately to rein in my emotions because she'd go off if I let them out. I stepped away from her, farther down the small hallway leading to the bedroom we shared.

When I called River, he answered in a husky, fuck-you-it's-too-early tone. "Better be an emergency."

"Monte's missing."

Silence for a beat.

"What do you mean? I thought he was with India."

"She's out of town and hasn't seen him since Friday."

"He never called last night?"

"No. And now he won't respond. He…" I choked on the lump that had formed inside my throat.

"We're on our way," River said.

The phone went dead, and I looked down at my naked chest and flannel pajamas. *Fuck*. I jogged into the bedroom, pulled on jeans, a long-sleeved T-shirt, and my work boots. I grabbed a baseball cap to hide the wild tufts of hair sticking up after my restless sleep.

As I made my way back into the main room, my gut turned violently. Something was horribly wrong. It had been all fucking weekend, and I hadn't listened to it. But I knew better. My inner voice had saved me more than once. In high school, they'd had me ducking a fist, and when I was chasing storms in the Midwest, it had earned me the nickname the Storm Whisperer.

And yet, I'd fucking ignored that instinct for days now.

"I want Monte," Ivy said. Her tiny, fairy-like voice cracked with emotions as she finally sensed what was going on.

I swallowed hard, kissed her on the top of her head, and talked around the lump. "Soon, Ives. Soon."

But if he'd gone to D.C., how the hell was I going to find him?

And why had he stopped responding? Where had he been all weekend? On the streets? That thought curdled my insides further, thinking of my tall but innocent-looking brother wandering the streets of the city at night… in the dark… where bad shit went down all the damn time.

With another inward curse, I finally remembered the app on my phone showing our locations. When I pulled it up, I expected to see the Capitol Building because he'd been desperate to talk to Representative Dunn and warn him. Even if there was no way he would have gotten in to see the man, that's where he would have gone first. But if he had gotten to talk to the congressman, after two seconds of listening to Monte's wild talk, they would have tossed him out. He'd be home by now.

It took longer than I wanted for the app to ping his last location. It was some random street in D.C., but now the phone showed as offline.

Crap.

Had he been mugged? Was he bleeding out somewhere?

Had something worse happened?

Some fucking guardian I was. I hadn't helped him, and he'd decided he had to go by himself. I debated what to do. Call the cops? Go to D.C. myself and search the streets? I felt paralyzed. Then, a different fear curled through me. If the cops thought I wasn't doing my job, if they thought I hadn't been watching over Monte as I should have been, would they call Child Protective Services? Would they take Monte and Ivy away from me?

There was no way I was letting them take my family from me.

No. Fucking. Way.

They were mine. I couldn't lose them. Not like this. Not after everything I'd done, everything I'd given up, to keep us together.

A key in the lock drew my gaze to the door as Audrey and River rushed in. She was in a pair of sweats covered in paint and clay, which meant I'd dragged her out of the studio. River was in jeans and a flannel shirt, looking as wild-eyed as I felt.

They glanced from me, to Ivy, and back.

I motioned my head down the hall, and we ended up in my bedroom with the door shut and voices hushed.

"He went to D.C. That's his last pinged location," I said, waving the phone at them.

"I was going to ask if you'd tried to find him that way," Audrey said, worry creasing her brows.

"His phone is offline." My voice was thick with emotion.

"Try not to think the worst," River said. "His battery might just be out of juice."

"But where the hell has he been staying? If he's been on the street…" God, I couldn't think about it. Demi had lived on the street multiple times. Or in her car. Anywhere the mood took her, flitting around as if the norms of society didn't matter. She'd sleep in people's backyards, sometimes even people's she didn't know. She went to wild parties and stayed with strangers. She said life was too short to stay in one place for too long.

Jesus, was Monte going to end up like her?

No. He wouldn't. He absolutely wouldn't. He hated what Demi had done to us. To Ivy. There was no way he'd do the same thing.

"I'll stay here with Ivy," Audrey said. "You two go. See if you can find him."

It didn't escape me that she hadn't suggested calling the cops. Maybe it was because she and River had a bad history with law enforcement. They'd been roughed up a time or two simply because of the way they looked. As if they were part of the biker gang mixed up with drugs and chop shops who frequented Tall Mike's. Or maybe she'd simply had the same thought I'd had—that if we called the cops, they'd see me as unfit and take my family from me.

Hell, maybe I was unfit.

But I wouldn't give my siblings up. I'd die first. I'd run for the border before I'd let anyone take them from me. I'd promised myself Monte and Ivy would always have one person who'd be there for them, no matter what. A constant in their lives.

Except I hadn't been.

I'd let Monte down, and he'd gone to take care of things on his own.

If something happened to him, I'd never be able to forgive myself.

Chapter Eight

Rory

GOING WHERE THE WIND BLOWS
Performed by Mr. Big

I woke on Sunday morning with the spiral of Mom's notebook embedded in my cheek. What time had I fallen asleep? I rubbed a hand over my face, my gaze landing on the time in the bottom corner of the computer screen. It was after eleven. Shit. I'd actually slept. In a horrible position that made me groan as I moved, but I'd slept.

When I'd first gotten home from the bar, I'd been wired. Thoughts of Gage, the feel of his touch, and the way he'd stepped up to defend me had all whirled in my brain. No one had ever done anything like that for me. Not Dad. Not Mom. I'd always been solo on the job. So, Gage shoving the guy up against the wall for touching me had tugged at an unspeakable longing deep inside me.

With my brain refusing to turn off, I'd picked up where I'd left off before Shay's call, searching websites for the emblem in Mom's planner. I'd found three company logos that looked like the drawing. One was for a literary agency in Los Angeles, another was for a Montana ranch, and the last was for a weather-related company in Colorado. None of them were anywhere near D.C., and none of them had any military contracts tying them to the Space Force.

I stretched, easing my stiff muscles and rubbing the mark on my face. My stomach growled. I needed to get to the station to grill Muloney. But first, I had to get some food in me, visit Mom, and apologize to Shay for leaving her.

When I got out of the shower and entered the kitchen, Nan was placing plates with cheese omelets on the table. It was quiet as we ate, but instead of the sense of comfort I normally had around Nan, the air was tense and heavy. I was just about to ask what was wrong, when she pushed her half-eaten food away and said, "I think we need to consider the doctors' advice."

My fork dropped, staring at her in torn silence.

She looked at me and then down, before glancing back up. "Your mother wouldn't want you living this way. She'd be upset you sold the condo and furious you're giving up on your dreams to run the agency. She wouldn't want us going bankrupt to keep her body breathing when her soul is already gone."

"She's there!" I growled, frustrated that I was fighting tears once again.

"Is she? I look at that body lying in a bed, withering away, shrinking, becoming smaller and smaller." Her voice cracked. "And that isn't my daughter. That isn't my vivacious, energetic, full-of-life girl. That's a shell that no longer holds everything I loved about her."

"There are studies, Nan. They show people recovering after a year." My voice was thick with emotions just like hers.

"We're almost at the year mark, Rory," she said sadly. God… part of me couldn't believe it had been that long. "I didn't tell you, but they're raising their rates."

"Who?" My brow furrowed. "Shady Lane?"

She nodded. "It's going to be another five hundred a month."

Fuck. There was no way I could swing that. I instantly thought of Dad, wishing I hadn't fought with him. Wishing I'd done anything to convince him to loan me the money. Then, I thought of what he'd said, about getting a job using my computer skills. I was damn good at finding—or creating—security issues. Someone would hire me as a white hat hacker protecting their systems. Maybe they'd even give me a bonus like Dad had suggested. I could continue to work cases on the side. Most importantly, Mom's. I could even handle the background checks we did for the DoD.

I got up, tossed the rest of my uneaten meal, and washed the dishes while Nan watched.

"Say something," Nan finally begged.

I dried my hands and looked at her. Nan had been the only one on my side, and now I didn't know how to feel—what to think. "I'm the one in charge of her advanced health care directive. So ultimately, it's my decision, and I'm not giving up on her."

I grabbed my messenger bag loaded with my gear and walked out the door.

I hated myself a bit for leaving that way. But then again, I hated everything about this situation.

I drove my motorcycle to Shady Lane, and when I got to Mom's room, I was struck by what Nan had said. Somehow, I hadn't seen it before, but Mom did look withered. She looked like some tiny version of herself. Nothing like the person I'd idolized almost as much as a fictional character.

I greeted her with a kiss, but for the third day in a row, I didn't talk to her about what I was doing as my fingers flew over the keyboard. This time it was because I didn't want her to hear I was looking for work. I found a couple of local IT jobs and even a government job that might suffice. As I hit submit on the applications, it all felt wrong, but I wasn't giving up on her.

I couldn't.

A tiny piece of me, the logical part that was good at assembling pieces of a puzzle to solve a case, whispered that I was being irrational. Murmuring that maybe the doctors and Dad and Nan were right. But I couldn't listen to it yet.

It hurt too damn much to think of giving up hope. Giving up when she'd never given up on me, even after the mistakes I'd made.

I turned on one of the *Real Housewives* shows Harriet had gotten Mom hooked on and lay down on the bed with her, careful of the cords and wires. My entire body shook as I realized how frail she felt. I held her hand and talked to her about the show as if she were there. And when the sun started to set, I kissed her goodbye with a heavy heart and more weight added to my shoulders.

On the way to the police station, I forced my thoughts away from Mom in the hospital and back to why she was there in the first place. The accident that wasn't an accident. Harriet wasn't at the front desk. It was some new person I hadn't buttered up yet. I waved to her, acting like I had every right to be there, and strode past the swinging gate into the bullpen, only to find it eerily empty.

Voices drew my attention to the conference room. Detective Muloney was in the doorway, talking to a group of people strewn around the long table I could only partially see. Something was afoot because the energy vibrating through the space was tense. Maybe there'd been a break-in or an assault on campus. Crimes like those occurred near most universities, and this department prided itself on handling them fast and efficiently. Which only spiked my irritation because they hadn't handled Mom's case the same way.

Muloney turned his head toward me as I wound my way through the desks. He was in his fifties, but still fit, without the bulging gut that sometimes found its way onto older officers. Mostly bald, he made up for the lack of hair on his head with an abundance of it on his face.

He leaned over to one of the rookies at the table and said something that caused the younger man to look my way before Muloney came out of the room to head me off. One look at my angry face, and he seemed to realize why I was there. He let out an exasperated sigh, tugged his scraggly beard, and then sat on the corner of the nearest desk.

"You lied to me, Dexter. You've really earned the nickname I gave you."

"I don't have the time or energy for this today, Rory. We've got a missing kid that takes priority over everything."

Surprise, sympathy, and sadness instantly filled me, and I shot a look toward the conference room. No wonder the desks were empty. For two heartbeats, I felt bad that I was pulling him away from it. Missing kids were the worst. Kid cases of any kind were a strain. But my regrets flew out the window with his next words.

"I did what your dad asked and what I thought was best. I don't need you going half-cocked all over the damn place, chasing imaginary leads because you think you're some big shot PI. Leave the real investigative work to the men who've got the experience to do it."

My teeth ground together as his words stabbed at me. Men. Experienced. Half-cocked. I might have been only twenty-two, but I'd been working for Marlowe & Co. for nearly ten years and I'd double majored in criminal law and computer science. I'd been on the streets since getting my PI license at eighteen, and that had given me more experience than the rookie cop coming out of the propped-open conference room door fumbling paperwork. Instead of responding with my résumé and demanding the respect I'd earned, I gave him my best saccharine smile and acted like he hadn't said anything.

"Exactly what have you uncovered in my mother's case, Baloney-Muloney? How did you determine her car's computer had been messed with? What have you done to follow up on it? How did you trace her movements that day? Because you damn well haven't asked me what cases she was working on or where she'd been. You haven't asked for the security footage from our home or office. You haven't even asked me who I think might have had it out for her."

"The list is long," he said with a grunt. "Your mom made more enemies than friends."

That pushed me into full pissed-off mode. "Because she

didn't let cheating bastards, sneaky thieves, or deadbeat parents get away with anything. And she had plenty of friends. Just ask Harriet," I said, waving toward the front desk even though my mom's friend wasn't there.

"Your dad gave us most of what we needed. I've had James combing through it when he's had time."

I stepped closer to him, shoving a finger into his chest. "You've got James working it? For God's sake, the kid barely has a badge. And whatever Sutton Bishop told you, it isn't nearly enough. He didn't have access to our cameras, notes, or our case files, so whatever he gave you, you knew I could've given you more. The more you needed to do this investigation right."

For a moment, Muloney looked completely chagrined, and my stomach fell as realization hit me. I'd tapped into Dad's computers, and he'd followed it back. He must have. I'd made a stupid rookie mistake. I'd let the fox into the henhouse. Not only let him in, I'd opened the door and practically laid out the welcome mat. All my anger turned inward.

I hadn't been myself since I'd gotten the call from Muloney letting me know Mom had been pulled from the Potomac. I was exhausted, living on mere hours of shut-eye while juggling the bills, our cases, and school, and trying to spend as many minutes as possible with Mom and Nan. And I'd slipped up because of it.

Dad wasn't right and neither was Muloney. I was good at what I did. But I'd been desperate to keep all the balls rolling, and my desperation had blinded me.

I stepped back. "I want everything you have. And I mean everything. Have Harriet send it over to me. If I don't have it by first thing tomorrow, I'm going to Edith at the *Mercury* and telling her how you violated every code in the book to get information you had no right to."

I was almost to the lobby when he responded. "You need to stay out of this. I'm serious. You're too close, and you're going to get burned. Your dad and I don't want to see you hurt."

I shot him a scathing look.

"What would you do if it was your mom, Baloney? Or your wife? Or one of your daughters? I'm certainly not going to sit on the bench while you send Tweedledee over there chasing his tail. I have double his experience even if I don't have a dick swinging between my legs."

"Jesus, Rory. Don't make this into something it isn't."

"It's exactly what I think it is. You and Dad made a decision based on what you believed I should or shouldn't be doing because of my age and gender. You kept the truth of what happened from me, her next of kin, for almost a year! You stole information from my office and are now blackballing me out of the case. We both know you wouldn't have done that to Tweedledee if it was his mom who'd landed in the river."

I didn't wait for his response, slamming my way out of the department, fury swelling along with hurt pride. What did I expect? I would encounter this same attitude if I entered the FBI. I'd be underestimated, patted on the head, and treated like I needed to be sheltered. I had to lose this chip on my shoulder or it would likely keep me out of the bureau altogether.

But who was I kidding? That dream had likely set sail last December with a hacked car computer and icy waters. Instead, I was going to end up at a desk in some stuffy office, keeping spam and identity thieves out of corporate servers.

I was going to be everything I'd scorned.

The antithesis of Veronica Mars.

A washed-up has-been at twenty-two.

Chapter Nine

Gage

MAN AGAINST THE WORLD
Performed by Survivor

My entire being radiated with frustration as I watched Muloney excuse himself and walk out of the conference room. The other officers shifted uncomfortably as I sat at the table, filling out paperwork.

Goddamn paperwork, while my brother was missing.

River and I had scoured D.C. the best we could. We'd flashed Monte's picture around to anyone remotely near the location his phone had last pinged. The only shred of comfort I'd had was that the alley near the Capitol wasn't the worst part of D.C., and yet it still wasn't anywhere I would have wanted him to wind up alone for an entire weekend.

Guilt and regret mixed in heavily with my fury and disappointment.

This was my fault.

And Demi's. If she hadn't passed down these abilities to him in the first place and then left us alone while he tried to navigate them, maybe things would have been different. Instead, she'd done what she'd told me years ago was for the best—she'd left us to grow our roots into the hard clay of life by ourselves.

"Any other friends you can check with? Other places he likes to hang out?" the younger of the two officers asked as he came back into the room with a stack of copies he'd made of my brother's picture. The officer looked like he was barely out of high school. How the hell was he going to find my brother?

My fingernails bit into the palms of my hands.

"None that I haven't told you," I said. "Isn't there an AMBER Alert you can issue or something? Anything?"

A hush fell in the room, allowing Muloney's voice and a woman's to echo through the open conference room door. My body instantly recognized the woman's, going on alert just as it had last night. What was Rory doing here? Had she heard about Monte?

I got out of my chair in time to see her put a detective nearly three times her age and size in his place with a simple finger to his chest. Her voice drifted over to me. Something about investigating a case.

Her words shot through me like a shock.

Rory found things for a living. Found people and information. Damn, I should have gone to her right away. I started to make my way to the conference room door just as she stormed from the building with anger blazing behind her. Feelings I could absolutely relate to even though I didn't know why she had them.

Muloney headed my direction, rubbing his hand over the top of his bald head, his aura flickering remorse and annoyance.

"What was that about?" I asked, brows drawing together.

He glanced toward the door and back. "Nothing but trouble. Girl thinks her little PI license makes her a cop or some modern-day Nancy Drew. Let's get back to your brother. Are you sure he hasn't just taken off? Kids do that sometimes."

"He didn't run away."

But I heard what he wasn't saying. They thought he was like Demi. Everyone in town knew she was notorious for running off. But there was no way in hell Monte would have done that to us. Not to me or Ivy, just like he wouldn't turn off his phone.

Except he'd done both.

It ate at me for all of two seconds before I trusted the instincts I'd ignored all weekend. I had to get out of there. I had to talk to Rory. Something had happened to Monte in D.C., otherwise, he'd be home by now. Otherwise, he'd have found a way to contact me because he knew I'd be sick with worry. My chest was squeezed so tight I was afraid I might have a heart attack at twenty-seven instead of fifty like my dad.

"His phone is off or disabled. He wouldn't do that to me exactly because of what you're thinking. He hated what Demi did to us as much as I did. He's missing, damn it!"

All four police officers looked at me, and I sensed the pity I despised wafting from them.

I pushed past Muloney. If I didn't get out of there, I was going to put my hands on someone like I had the stupid college kid the night before. I'd shake them. Rattle them. Throw them against the wall and demand they search for my brother.

"We'll put his information in the national database, and we'll talk with the students and staff from the school, but I bet he shows up before long with his tail between his legs," Muloney said, as if Monte had just gone to some off-limit weekend-long party at the beach. Kids being kids. Boys being boys.

My anger grew, but I didn't respond—I couldn't. I just kept my feet headed for the door and the dark-haired spitfire who'd walked out.

I hurried around the back of the building to where I'd left the Pathfinder just as Rory zipped out of the parking lot on the back of a Honda Rebel. It shouldn't have been unexpected as she'd told me as a teen she planned on getting one, and yet the vision she made caught my breath. She was sexy and enticing in all the right ways—or wrong ways.

By the time I got into the SUV and caught up with her, she was stopped at the only light in Cherry Bay, two blocks from the bar. The other night, the idea of her chasing down some guy who'd left his fingerprints on her wrist had pissed me off. Made me angry at her parents and a fictional character for leading her into this business. But now, all I felt was relief, because I knew Rory. I knew her determination. She wouldn't give up. She sure as hell would do more than just put Monte's name in some goddamn national database.

I just had to convince her Monte hadn't run away. That he wasn't like Demi. And that thought made my chest tighten all over again because it might mean telling her a truth I wasn't sure she'd believe. Hell, even having been surrounded by it my entire life, there were moments I didn't think any of it was real.

I barely caught sight of the motorcycle as Rory turned down the darkened road in the older section of town that led to her nan's place. The street was lined with cottages dating back two or three centuries mixed in with Victorians. It was only two streets over from our old home. Another ache stabbed at my gut thinking about the house. Yet another loss we'd weathered. But it had been worth selling it to keep my family together.

To keep my brother… who was now gone.

Tears filled my eyes, but I refused to let them loose. I ground my teeth together and turned my attention to what I needed to do at the moment. I knew better than anyone not to dwell on the past or the future. The only way I'd survived the last few years was by concentrating on the right now.

And right now, I needed Rory to help me find Monte.

She pulled into the driveway of a cottage halfway down the lane and headed straight for the detached garage. The door slowly closed behind her, shielding the bike from view as I parked across the street and cut the engine. I flexed my hands on the steering wheel. What was I going to say to her? How much of the truth could I afford?

Was I even doing this? Asking Rory to help? God… it felt like she should still be the twelve-year-old kid I'd first met with a love of The Guess Who and Veronica Mars. The kid who'd looked at me with adoring eyes as if I was a hero to worship. But if there was the slimmest chance she could help us, I couldn't drive away. In my heart, I knew minutes mattered. Those same kind of minutes that had once meant getting in and out of a storm in one piece or becoming part of the wreckage.

Just as I reached for the handle, a knock on the glass with something metallic made me jump. It was Rory, holding what looked like a flashlight that flickered with electricity as she pushed a button. It took me a minute to realize it was a stun gun. The same minute it took her to realize it was me in the soccer-mom-type SUV.

"Gage? What are you doing here? Why were you following me?" Her voice sounded muffled through the window.

I didn't know whether to be impressed or worried that she was fast enough and sneaky enough to have gotten the drop on me.

She dropped her stun gun back into the bag she had flung across her chest as I pushed open the door. Her stance was exactly the Rory I'd known at fifteen but with an extra confidence to it. A bravado she'd shown off by pushing around a detective three times her age, but below the bold daring, I felt the loss and heartache I'd sensed last night. It was newly scored. Not healed. Barely even scabbed over.

I couldn't afford to worry about any of that now. Not with my brother's life on the line.

"Monte's missing. I need your help." My voice cracked, emotions pouring out.

It was dark, but the moon was full, so it was easy to read the surprise that bloomed on her face.

"It was you at the station just now? With Muloney? What happened? What are they doing? Where are they looking?" The real concern in her tone made tears hit my eyes all over again. The relief of having someone actually care that he was gone. River, Audrey, and I had been on our own all day. I needed all the help I could get, and I hadn't gotten any from the people who should have given it.

"They think he took off. Like Demi… or just to attend some damn party. That he'll show up when it's over with his tail between his legs." It hurt, the flicker of similar doubts I saw in her eyes. It caused me to growl when I should be begging. "Monte didn't fucking run off. He wouldn't do that to me."

She turned and headed for the cottage, and I followed. Even though she was a good eight inches shorter than me, I had to almost jog to keep up with her fast stride.

"I realize you haven't seen Monte since he was little and you don't know him. But I do. And you know me well enough to believe me when I say he wouldn't do this to me or Ivy."

Her footsteps stuttered at the mention of Ivy, and she came to a stop, turning to really take me in for the first time since I'd gotten out of the car. Her gaze eased down over every inch of me, from my mussed black hair to my work boots and back up to the day-old stubble on my chin. It was as if she was taking me apart and then putting me back together. I wished it would be that easy for me to do the same—take all the broken pieces and assemble them into something greater than the bits that remained.

"Come inside," she said softly. "Tell me what you know, and we'll try to figure it out."

She unlocked the door, turned off an alarm, and threw her bag into a wicker basket by a side table before heading for the back of the house.

I'd never been inside her nan's place, but I'd been in some of the other cottages along the lane growing up. They all had low ceilings with exposed beams and small rooms shaped from years of use. She strode past the living room archway to the kitchen at the rear. Reaching into one of the modern gray-and-white cabinets mixed in with teal fifties-styled appliances, she brought out two old-fashioned glasses. She poured a hefty dose of bourbon into them and pushed one across the counter toward me.

I didn't pick it up. I couldn't. Not when I needed my brain clear while I figured out what the hell had happened to Monte.

"How long has he been missing?" she asked.

I tucked my hands into my pockets, rocking slightly back on my heels. "I thought he was with a friend for the weekend. He texted me a couple of times, even called me, so I didn't think anything of it, even when he didn't respond to me last night. I thought they were just goofing off or his phone had run out of battery. But this morning, when I still couldn't get a hold of him, I called his friend, and they said they hadn't seen him since Friday…" I swallowed hard, trying desperately not to lose my shit as I had earlier.

Her eyes widened ever so slightly, and I could see the doubts reemerging.

"I know what you're thinking," I said, shaking my head.

"He was texting you—"

"He didn't fucking run away!" It was loud and pained. A roar. A wounded animal. Cut and bleeding and waiting for the hyenas to pick at its bones.

"Okay," she said in a gentle tone, attempting to soothe the wild animal. She set her phone on the counter, turning on a voice recording app. "This is for me. So I can listen again if I need a specific detail I might not remember. Just tell me what you know."

Frustrated from repeating the story several times, I knew I sounded snippy as I shared what he'd been wearing on Friday, and how I'd gone to D.C. looking for him after finding his last pinged location on the app. I told her how River and I had scoured the streets near the Capitol, but I bit my tongue when I started to mention the congressman and the vision. Instead, I focused on Muloney's halfhearted offer to talk to his teachers and friends.

When I trailed off, she was still watching me with an intensity that had always been Rory's. With eyes you thought were the softest of browns until you were up close enough to kiss her and could see the tiny flash of green. Except I'd never kissed Rory. Never even been tempted to kiss her when she was twelve or thirteen or even fifteen. But ever since I'd seen her last night, I'd wanted to with a ferocity I couldn't shake, even when it made me feel like a creep.

Finally, after the silence had remained between us for a beat too long, she asked, "What aren't you telling me? What didn't you tell the police?"

My eyes skittered to the voice recording and then back. "Nothing."

She reached over and turned the recording off. "Don't lie to me! Not me! You want to coast around the truth with Baloney-Muloney, fine, but not me, Gage!"

That she saw through me wasn't a surprise. Her frustration and the hurt layered under it made me ache to tell her the truth about Monte's abilities. To unburden myself of all of it. I bit back the words, doubting the truth could help me tonight. When I didn't say anything else, she tossed back the rest of her drink, set it on the counter, and headed out of the kitchen toward the front door.

Pure panic welled through me. "Don't kick me out. Fuck. I need someone to do something. God. It's Monte… my little brother." My voice cracked again pitifully. I was a pitiful human being.

Her eyes were wide and sad. "If you can't be honest with me—if you can't tell me why I should believe he didn't just run away like Demi—then I can't help you. One of the most important things Mom has taught me is to not get involved with someone lying about their case."

"I'm not lying! My thirteen-year-old brother is out there somewhere. Maybe alone. Maybe with someone targeting his innocence…" I pushed the heel of my palm against my eyes and the rush of tears. When I lowered my hands, she was watching me. Analyzing. Cataloging. "He wouldn't run away. He wouldn't do this to me. Something is wrong."

"We like to believe our loved ones won't hurt us, but you and I both know they're the ones who leave the biggest cuts. The wounds that never completely heal and easily bleed with the slightest of bumps."

Pain echoed through her words. Bitter and raw. This was more than what had happened with her dad. New wounds I didn't have the time to uncover. Had no right to uncover. Monte and Ivy were all that mattered.

"Monte wouldn't just leave."

"Tell me what you think really happened." It was a plea, begging me to trust her just as I was begging her for help. But she didn't understand the enormity of what she was asking. The truth only our family knew. Dad was dead. Demi didn't give two shits. That left me holding the bag and protecting my brother and sister the best I could. Shielding their powers from the world.

Sadness filled her face, and she finished walking down the hall, but I didn't follow.

"Please," I whispered. A tortured cry.

I didn't really know Rory beyond a handful of conversations with a teen girl. I certainly didn't know the grown-up, stunning person she'd become. But it felt like I'd never see my brother again if I walked out without securing her help. Maybe it was Demi's abilities flowing through me. Maybe it was just my fear, but it seemed real. As if this woman was the only hope I had of seeing Monte again.

Chapter Ten

Rory

SUNCHOKE
Performed by Aly & AJ

Layers of emotions were captured in that singular plea Gage sent drifting down the hallway. I was exhausted. Mentally. Emotionally. Physically. What I needed was another stiff drink and a full night in a real bed. But it was the last thing I was going to get tonight.

I had no intention of letting Gage walk out the door without helping him find Monte—the little cherub boy I remembered with his bright red curls and freckles. There was no way I'd let Gage lose his brother after everything else he'd already lost. He'd given up everything to take care of his family. When Shay had told me how he'd adopted his half sister after Demi had left town, I'd admired the way he'd stepped up to the plate for her. He'd been a twenty-four-year-old kid raising other kids.

In my life, I'd rarely seen anyone act with such selfless nobility. I wasn't going to let one more thing damage this man who already had more than his fair share of permanent scars. Wounds that remained after the wreckage that not one, but two parents had left behind. They sliced at me as much as him. All of those losses and aches belonged to me too. I understood them in a way not many people could.

But I also had to get the truth from him, and he was holding back. It stung. Not only because my twelve-year-old self had wanted Gage to be able to tell her everything, but because twenty-two-year-old me still felt the barbs from her father and Muloney. It was as if Gage's silence was threaded with the doubts of those other men.

"Please," he begged again, and I barely stopped myself from running to wrap him in my arms.

Instead, I crossed them over my chest and met his gaze with one I hoped showed only strength and determination as I said, "Tell me the truth."

He pushed his palms up against his eyes for the second time, and my heart twisted, falling to the pit of my stomach as I realized he was trying not to cry. I broke. I couldn't resist. I moved on silent feet until I was standing in front of him, reaching out to barely graze his arm.

When he dropped his hands, the pain swirling in his stormy eyes stole my breath.

"I only left out the pieces you wouldn't believe," he said quietly.

It tore at me all over. "When have I ever not believed you?"

He scoured my face as if searching for the truth. Looking for an answer I couldn't fully give because I didn't know what he was going to say. And yet the moment felt enormous. As if everything in my world might change with whatever came out of his mouth, and it caused the first spark of panic to rear somewhere at the back of my brain. A neon sign warning me to back the truck up before it was too late.

His jaw flexed and his lips tightened as he fought some internal debate that raised the tension in me. Finally, he exhaled, saying, "Monte gets… visions."

Surprise had me taking a step back as I tried to process his words. "Visions?"

He rolled his eyes up to the ceiling as if he thought I was already doubting him, when really, I was trying to make sure I'd heard him right.

"He sees bad things before they're going to happen.

The train derailment outside Philly two years ago? For six weeks before it happened, that's all he could see. When he slept. While he was awake. He lost ten pounds he couldn't afford to lose. He knew enough to know the car was going to derail in Pennsylvania. Knew it was a passenger car, but we didn't know a date or a time or what route. The closer it got to the event, the harder it was for him to think of anything else. I tried to tell Amtrak, but they laughed me out of their offices. When I got angry, they called security. When I sent a follow-up email, they filed a restraining order. But that wasn't even the worst of it. After the derailment happened, the FBI showed up at our door. They searched the bar and the house as if I'd planted the bomb myself."

My eyes narrowed as I finally caught on to what he was saying. He was trying to tell me his brother saw the future. The shock of it hit me in waves.

My doubts must have shown because he brushed past me toward the door, anger and frustration radiating from him. "I knew you wouldn't believe me! This is why I don't mention it to anyone. Never mind. Forget I said anything. I'll find Monte on my own."

"I didn't say I didn't believe you."

"It's written all over your face." He waved a hand at me.

I swallowed because I *was* struggling to believe even though I *knew* Gage wasn't lying.

"You wanted the truth, Rory, and here it is. Monte is missing because he saw a vision of Congressman Dunn being shot and felt compelled to warn the man. The nightmare was driving him crazy, and it will only get worse the closer it gets to the actual event. So he went because he had to do something even though no one ever listens to us. And now he's disappeared, and that scares the hell out of me. Somewhere between texting me yesterday afternoon and this morning, he vanished. Unlike my brother, I don't have the *gift* of vision to help me find him."

He whirled around, ripping open the door so hard it

slammed against the doorstop before bouncing halfway shut again.

"Gage!" I called after him.

But he didn't stop. By the time I got to the edge of the sidewalk, he was already in the Pathfinder, flipping a U-turn, and heading back toward town. The taillights blinked as he disappeared around the corner—an ominous omen.

But I didn't believe in omens any more than I did ESP or hocus-pocus or visions. Just like I didn't believe in fairy tales and happily ever afters.

Crap!

I set the house alarm, pulled my laptop from my bag, and took it with me to the kitchen table. Gage's untouched drink sat there. I tossed it back. I hadn't had anything to eat since… the half-eaten omelet Nan had made this morning. Where was Nan? I scrambled to the refrigerator and the notepad where we scrawled our schedules for each other.

Gardening club. It was late for the gardening club to still be meeting, but at least she hadn't witnessed the showdown between Gage and me.

I returned to the table and my computer. My eyes felt blurry and tired, but I pushed on, logging into the Marlowe & Co. system with the password I'd thought was foolproof but had done nothing to keep Dad out of our system. That was my fault.

I took a moment I wasn't sure I could afford to bring up the backdoor I'd set up into Dad's computers and shut it down. Technically, we were both at fault for spying on each other. What kind of family did that? What kind of family had to resort to spying in order to get what they needed? I hesitated as I typed in the code, and decided to leave a little present he'd recognize as coming from me. A little Keith Mars epithet. Veronica's dad had requested one time that they try to do something that normal dads and daughters did. Maybe this was the only thing my dad and I would ever have in common. A distrust of each other that had us digging in the dark for the truth.

After I'd left my gift, I clicked on the backdoor I'd placed in the Cherry Bay PD and brought up Monte's file. Tweedledee had entered a report into the National Crime Information Center database, but that was it. No follow-up had been conducted yet with the school, his teachers, or his friends. Worse, no one seemed to have asked why a thirteen-year-old boy was "itching" to go to D.C. and meet a representative who wasn't even from Virginia. Or if they had, they hadn't written down the answer. No one had called the Capitol Police or Metro PD to make sure they were on the lookout.

I slammed the keys. The lack of follow through wasn't necessarily incompetence given the family's history. It wasn't too far of a stretch to think that whatever caused Demi to drift in and out would have been inherited by one of her sons. I didn't know Monte, and maybe he had inherited her wandering ways, but something told me that Gage was right. That Monte wouldn't do this to the brother who'd given up everything to take care of him. At least, I hoped that was the person Monte had grown into.

I thought about what Gage had said. How Monte was tormented by the image of the congressman being shot. What kind of person could see that on repeat in their brain and *not* try to warn the person? Real or not…I'd be tempted to do the same thing, wouldn't I?

While I was in the station's system, I pulled up Demi's files. Holland Palmer had made his first report over twenty-three years ago. Gage must have been a toddler. Demi had shown up three months later. There were no other reports filed by Holland from all the times she'd gone missing when Gage was a kid, and I didn't know what that said about Holland and Demi's relationship. It was Gage who'd filed the next report, and that had been less than three years ago when she'd left Gage and Monte with their one-year-old sister and not come back. He'd had to file in order to gain custody of his siblings.

There was nothing in any of those files that would help me find Monte.

Had Gage been as scared the first time Demi had gone missing as he was now? He'd been so little that first time, maybe he didn't even remember it. But he'd certainly remembered every time afterward. I'd heard the anger in his voice when he talked about it.

It had left wounds.

Wounds that would have spiraled and grown when he'd gotten the call about his dad.

Pain I understood all too well.

I'd been in a department store, splurging on Nan's perfume for Christmas when Muloney had called. Seeing the Cherry Bay PD name scroll across the notification banner had made me instantly worry about my grandmother. I'd accepted the call as I'd stepped away from the counter. Muloney's words had seemed like a nightmare. I'd stood there, frozen. Unable to move. Barely registering what he'd been telling me.

They'd airlifted Mom to a D.C. hospital, and when I'd gotten there, when I'd finally seen her, she'd been hooked to machines that were breathing for her. Much of her face had been covered in bandages. She'd already become some alternate version of my mother.

I'd had Nan and Shay at my side then, just like I had them now. Even Dad had shown up. He'd be there again if something horrible happened. His help might come with strings I'd hate, but he'd be there. Who did Gage have? River and Audrey were a pair of artists and part-time bartenders. They wouldn't be able to help him navigate the system to find a missing kid.

I turned back to my computer. I'd be able to find out exactly when Monte had left the school on their cameras. I could figure out how he'd gotten to D.C. and follow the trail of video footage he'd left behind. Over an entire day had already gone by since Gage had last heard from Monte. That was a lifetime in missing kid cases.

I straightened, and my fingers found the comfort of the keys. Veronica Mars had taught me a truth. When tragedy tore through your life like a catastrophic storm, leaving nothing but destruction, you could deny the wreckage existed or you could stand up and find a way to rebuild.

I was trying to do just that. Gage had rebuilt repeatedly. But if he never saw his brother again… Somehow, I thought that might bury him beneath the rubble forever. I couldn't let that happen. I *wouldn't* let it happen.

I was going to find Monte.

Chapter Eleven

Gage

BORDERLINE

Performed by Ed Sheeran

I stared at the coffeepot, willing it to brew faster. I was going to need it to get me through the next few hours. Hell, the day.

I'd thought time and exhaustion might dull the agony I felt the longer I went without a word from Monte, but it hadn't. Instead, the pain grew, eating away at my insides until I was sure there'd be a cavernous hole appearing before long.

After I'd left Rory's, Audrey had stayed at the apartment while River and I had gone back to D.C. and retraced our steps. We'd driven around the back roads and alleys, getting side-eyes from shadowy figures as drug deals went down. Panic had shoved itself through me as I'd thought of Monte out on the streets with people who'd make mincemeat of him. Monte wasn't small. He'd had a recent growth spurt that had brought him close to six feet already, but he was young. Naive. Maybe a bit too trusting.

We'd driven around aimlessly for too long before we'd ended up at the Metropolitan PD and repeated the entire process I'd gone through with Muloney in Cherry Bay. They'd given me contact information for the National Center for Missing and Exploited Children that Muloney hadn't. I'd called the center on our way back to Cherry Bay, surprised to find it was available twenty-four hours. They'd assigned me a caseworker who told me they'd follow up with both police stations and keep me informed as well.

All night, I'd called Monte's phone, hoping it had come back online.

This morning, after a couple of hours of tossing and turning but never sleeping, I'd showered and put on clean clothes. When I'd looked in the mirror, I'd seen the same ghost of a man who'd been there yesterday. Shadowed eyes with lines between my brows and around my lips that felt permanently etched there. I'd looked worse than I had after Dad had died. Even after I'd driven all night to get home to Monte… and Demi.

When I'd arrived in Cherry Bay from Kansas, our mother had told me, crying and sobbing, that Dad's heart attack had been her fault. I hadn't believed her. But then she'd told me about their fight, her pregnancy, how she'd tried to run, and how he'd tried to stop her. And I'd known the truth. She'd cracked Dad's heart open one last time. If I hadn't already half hated my mother, the fact she'd brought another chasm of suffering into our lives was enough to push me over the edge.

I'd wanted to send her away. I'd wanted to tell her to go wherever the hell she'd been heading before Dad had tried to stop her. But she was still legally married to him, and even though Dad had listed me as the executor of his estate, Demi still had rights… to the house…the tavern… to Monte. It ate at me, but it was easier to let her stay than to try to fight her for any of it. Because I knew the truth. She'd take off again, and then I could work my way through the mountains of paperwork it would take to keep my family safe. I just had to bide my time.

I'd never expected her to stay as long as she had. Through the funeral and her pregnancy. Through the first part of the pandemic, adding her uninsured hospital bills to the pile of debt we already had hanging on us. With no income coming in because everything was shut down and our renter moving home while the college was closed, what little money there'd been had dried up.

And just as we'd started to come out of it, just as Monte had started to adjust to living in an apartment instead of a huge house with a large yard, Demi had left once more. But not before cleaning out the cash in our parents' joint bank account.

I'd never understand why Dad hadn't divorced her. Never understand why he hadn't taken her off everything. Not even love could be that twisted, could it? To have you repeatedly turning the other cheek while blow after blow after blow slowly destroyed you?

Until his heart had actually fucking given out.

A hand on my thigh had me jumping out of my dark thoughts.

I looked down to find Ivy, curly hair sticking up in all directions, pale blue eyes sad, her normally smiling lips turned down, and my heart spasmed another notch tighter. She wore her favorite otter pajamas that matched the stuffed animal in her hand. I sent a silent thanks to Audrey for knowing they would comfort her.

"Monte?" she asked.

I picked Ivy up and squeezed her tight, that sweet baby shampoo scent that followed her everywhere surrounding me. Raising her was the hardest and most rewarding thing I'd ever done. A million times harder than driving the storm tank into a tornado. But whenever she smiled at me, face full of adoration, as if I were a real-life superhero, nothing else mattered.

Today, I felt nothing like a superhero. I'd let my family down.

A rapid one-two-three knock on the apartment door had me frowning.

River and Audrey had keys. They might knock, but they'd just let themselves in, and neither of them knocked like that. As if they were impatient. Or angry.

I headed for the door with Ivy in my arms, flipped the

deadbolt, and opened it.

Rory stood on the landing, the early sunrise haloing her, making her look like an angel for all of two seconds before I noticed the scowl on her beautiful face. She had two to-go cups from the Tea Spot in her hands, and the shadows under her eyes had grown, just like mine.

Her gaze bounced from me to Ivy and back before she looked over my shoulder and demanded, "You going to let me in?"

I tried not to get my hopes up. Hope that somehow I wouldn't be alone in this. The NCMEC coordinator last night had tried to reassure me I wasn't alone, but it had felt empty coming from a disembodied voice over the phone. I had River and Audrey, but they seemed as lost as I was on how to navigate this situation. Worse, they actively hated the cops. Just going to the station with me in D.C. had made River antsy as hell. He'd walked out about halfway through the interview, his normally calm self all but dissolving. He'd whispered that if he didn't leave, he might punch someone.

Standing in front of me now was a fierce woman who I'd never seen back down from anything in her life, even at thirteen. I needed that. I needed someone who was going to battle for Monte just as much as I would. Someone who knew the rules of engagement. Someone who knew *how* to fight the battle because I damn sure didn't.

I stepped back, and as she brushed past me, my body spasmed. Relief. Desire. Hope.

I shut the door and turned to see her taking in the apartment. What did she see? The last time she'd been here, it had been full of inexpensive furniture Dad kept for the college renters. Now it was packed with generations of our family's belongings. It was cluttered, but it wasn't dirty.

Rory looked at Ivy as she handed me one of the cups. "It's coffee. Black. Wasn't sure how you took it, but was pretty sure you'd need it."

It was the second time she'd handed me a drink in less than twelve hours. "Thanks."

She walked over to the counter separating the living area from the kitchen, put her cup down, and yanked a laptop out of a messenger bag flung over her shoulder. She was in a tight purple sweater instead of the black I'd seen her in since Friday. The cotton knit clung to her curves, putting them on display in a way that was both modest and sexy at the same time.

Ivy's little hand slid along my cheek, and I turned to my sister. Her eyes were wide, darting back and forth between Rory and me. "Who she?"

I made my way over to the counter. "Ivy, this is Rory. Rory, Ivy."

Rory looked up, fingers pausing on the keyboard. She stuck out her hand. "Nice to meet you, Ivy."

Ivy smiled, and it landed in my heart. When I looked into Rory's face, I saw a wealth of emotions cross it as Ivy accepted her hand. They did a sweet little shake that made my sister giggle.

I put Ivy down, squatted in front of her, and said, "Go brush your teeth and get dressed. I'll do your hair once you're done."

She nodded and headed down the short hallway to the bedroom she and I shared, dragging her otter behind her. When I turned back to Rory, she was watching me with eyes full of sadness. I suddenly hated that look more than I'd ever hated the pity directed our way by the other Cherry Bay citizens. I'd prefer hate over sadness. I'd even prefer fury and frustration. But what I really wanted was the adoration she'd always sent my way. And maybe pleasure and satisfaction after having had the best orgasm of her life.

That last image had me shutting down any and all thoughts of her emotions.

She shoved a piece of paper in my direction and then handed me a pen. "Contract."

I picked up the paper. The logo read Marlowe & Co., and the hourly rate made my insides scrunch up. But I'd do anything I needed. Anything. Even if it meant we had to sell the building the bar and our home was in.

"I'm not really charging you," she said as if reading my mind. "That's just so I can legally do things on your behalf."

My stomach rolled. Charity. Had she and her mom discussed it and decided to do this for her old friend Holland's kids? Was her mom going to help? Or was she doing this on her own?

Muloney's words from last night hit me. *Girl thinks her little PI license makes her a cop or some modern-day Nancy Drew.* Both her parents were in the business. She'd picked up the mantle by working with her mom. If anyone could find Monte, I had to believe it was Rory and her family.

"You'll find him, right?" My voice was thick and scratchy.

"I already did," she said, and joy flew through me for half a second before she squashed it again, "and then I lost him. Let me show you. Sign the contract first."

I signed where she'd told me, handed it back to her, and she brought up a video. It was a view outside Cherry Bay's middle school. She hit Play and said, "Watch."

A black sedan showed up with a CarShare app sticker in the front window. Monte appeared from the gates of the school. He had on a green baseball hat, a gray windbreaker with the name of the bar written on the back, and faded jeans. His favorite kicks were on his feet. White and lime-green neon. His black backpack hung from one shoulder until he threw it into the back seat and followed it inside.

My heart sped up. He'd hired a car. That should be easy enough for anyone to trace.

"He booked it using your credit card," she said.

I started to ask how she knew and cut myself off. This was her job, and I could only imagine that despite Muloney's derision, she was good at it because Rory had wanted to do this her entire life.

"I had him put the app on his phone a while ago. I wanted to make sure he wasn't stuck without a ride if there was an emergency with Ivy or just… I should have checked my card. I didn't even think about it."

Frustration brewed in me again. I'd wasted so much time yesterday. I could have found out exactly where he'd gone and traced his steps from there to the location his phone had last pinged.

"It's hard to think clearly when someone you love is missing." She minimized one computer tab and brought up another. "I followed the sedan through as many traffic and bridge cams as I could. But based on what you'd said about Congressman Dunn and the time he left Cherry Bay, I was able to pick him up at the Capitol on Friday."

This time, the video showed the same car dropping Monte off on a corner near the domed building. God, it was good to see his face. But then I realized this was Friday, when he'd still been texting me. Grief washed over me so strongly I had to grasp the back of the barstool to steady myself. I would have taken him. If he'd insisted, I would have gone with him.

My stomach sank as the truth hit me for the first time. He hadn't wanted me to be involved. The last time we'd made a fuss, the FBI had shown up at our door and put me in cuffs while they searched the house. Thankfully, Ivy had no recollection of it, but Monte's eyes had been terrified. He hadn't relaxed until the FBI had let me go. Then he'd hugged me so tight I thought he'd break a rib.

He'd blamed himself.

Damn it, Demi. How could you leave him to deal with this on his own? I don't know how to help him through it. And yet, would I really want her back even if she showed up? Could I ever forgive her? I didn't want her screwing up our lives and taking our money. Not again. We couldn't handle any more cracks to the barely put together bones of our family.

"I'd hack the cameras inside the Capitol, but even as good as I am, someone will eventually notice, and the last thing we need is for me to get arrested. Instead, we'll use a friend I have who works there. We might be able to see who Monte talked to and trace his steps from there. Even if he lost his phone or it went dead, he might go back today if he's determined to talk to Dunn. We'll head into D.C. as soon as you're ready."

I should have thought of that too. If he hadn't seen the congressman this weekend, he'd definitely try to get to him today. Everything I'd been doing had been all screwed up. Rory was right. I'd been lost in panic. Lost in kicking myself over my failures instead of really putting my head on straight. But her ideas gave me hope in a way I hadn't had a few minutes ago. Hope I tried to tame in case we didn't find him.

Ivy's little voice, singing in the bathroom, drew our eyes in that direction. I wanted to rush out the door and head to D.C., but I needed to get her to preschool first. River and Audrey would take her, but they were going to search for Monte in the coves and beaches along the Potomac where the college kids held their weekend parties. Plus, taking Ivy to preschool meant keeping her schedule as normal as possible. Wasn't that what you were supposed to do with little kids? Keep their worlds normal?

"I need to drop her off at day care and make sure I'm back to get her."

Ivy came running down the hall, her hair flying all over the place. She had on a pink dress and sparkly pink tennis shoes, and she'd put a pink cape on her otter.

I'd never understood until I was chartered with looking after her just how drawn some little girls were to pink. It certainly wasn't because I'd forced the color on her, but if she chose anything for herself, it was in some shade of pink, including ice cream, milkshakes, and cookies. If we bought frosted animal cookies, she only ate the pink ones.

She handed me a brush, comb, hairbands, and two enormous pink and white polka-dot bows. Inwardly, I groaned but took the items and plopped her on the stool at the counter. I felt Rory watching me as I tried to divide Ivy's hair neatly down the middle and pull it back into two high ponytails.

Reaching over the counter, I flicked the sink on, wetted the comb, and did what I did every day—my best with a mess of curls. Just as I went to put a band around the first one, Ivy turned her head to ask Rory a question and the movement caused her hair to slip from my grip. I bit my cheek, trying not to swear.

When I risked looking at Rory, her lips were twitching. The last twenty-four hours had been hell. The worst hours of my entire godforsaken existence. And now, in less than an hour, Rory had added a light to it. Hope and light. It did something funny to my chest. It did something that made me wonder for the first time since Dad had died what it would look like if I didn't have to do any of this alone. What if I had a partner… What if I had Rory? Ridiculous thoughts that weren't going to happen, but that snuck in and wouldn't let go.

Chapter Twelve

Rory

BABY LAY YOUR HEAD DOWN
Performed by Aly & AJ

As a girl, I'd never been into Barbies or playing house. I'd never wanted to babysit. Even before the divorce and working in Mom's office, I'd been much more interested in Matchbox cars, racetracks, and skateboards. I'd wanted to beat everyone at whatever game we played at school. Not because I wanted them to lose, but because I wanted to win. I wanted to be the fastest, the smartest, the toughest. I certainly didn't want to spend time with babies, toddlers, or any human of that variety.

But when Gage had opened the apartment door this morning with Ivy tucked up in his arms, it had done something funny to my stomach. And for the first time ever, I understood the phrase *my ovaries nearly exploded*. I'd felt an ache deep inside that had only grown the more he'd interacted with his sister, every moment loaded with a sweet tenderness.

My body's reaction to him and to Ivy, but especially them together, was surprising and unexpected. Unwelcome, even. It added a layer of admiration to my teenage memories of him. But the bitter truth was, even if there'd been a chance for Gage and me to be something, seeing him with his family and understanding what he'd done to keep them together would keep me from taking a chance with him. I had my own family's responsibilities to handle. I couldn't add his to my list.

And yet, here I was.

Doing this job for free. Because it was fucking Monte. How could I not be here?

Ivy waggled a stuffed animal in my direction. The fur was matted and the neck was a bit wobbly, causing the head to tumble forward. "Aw you a fwend of Monte's?"

Gage looked from me to Ivy and then said softly, "Rory's helping us look for him."

Her eyes grew wide. "You aw?"

"Yes. I'm going to do my best to bring him home to you." My eyes met Gage's over the top of her head, and I saw tears fill his eyes that he fought back by closing them.

He looked harrowed and exhausted. I knew those feelings well. I'd been living them for almost a year. He pushed the long sleeves of his T-shirt up, revealing the tattoo on his arm. The one I'd wondered about on Saturday. The cursive font wound like vines around a sword, and the words caused my heart to skip several beats.

In a world that loves its villains, be the hero.

They weren't a Veronica quote I knew, but they felt decidedly Veronica Mars-like. And maybe… maybe that was the moment I fell all over again for Gage. Not for the bright and shiny teenage boy he'd once been, but for a man who'd chosen to be the hero.

I swallowed hard, looking away as waves of emotions flooded me.

After he finished struggling with Ivy's hair and the two bows that somehow looked askew even though he'd just put them on, he handed her a banana. "Don't make a mess." I wondered briefly what kind of mess a banana could make as he turned toward me and said, "Let me just go grab a few things and call River."

He disappeared down the hall, leaving me with his sister, and that made my gut twist way more than if he'd left me sitting next to Tall Paul and his beefy henchman who got his money back at any price. Paul's muscle I could handle. A tiny human? Not so much.

I could feel her watching me as I scrolled through the live cam footage along the street outside the Capitol Building.

"What show is that, Wowy?" she asked. The way she said my name with the R's mixed up snagged at my heart all over again. I glanced up to see the banana was looking decidedly goopy and there was some of it smeared along her cheeks and fingers. How had that happened in mere seconds?

"It's not a show. It's video footage from a camera. I'm hoping I'll see Monte."

She leaned over so she could see my screen better, and her cheek brushed my sweater, transferring some of the smudged banana guts. "Monte's on TV?!"

"It's not TV. It's like, watching… Never mind. He's not on there yet, but if I see him, I'll let you know."

She sighed and leaned back. I brushed the banana off my sleeve, watching with a sense of dread as she waved it dangerously close to my computer.

"I like *Scooby-Doo*. Can they find Monte?"

Scooby and the gang had been one of my favorite shows as a kid, and it made my heart soften a bit more, my ovaries clenching in that strange way all over. "I don't think they'll be able to come. They have a pretty tight schedule."

Her little fingers almost touched the screen, and I grabbed her wrist just in time to save it from being streaked with the slime that had now taken over her entire hand. That was… fast… and disgusting.

Gage reappeared behind us, and I caught a hint of soap and clove—a heady scent that had always been his. "Go wash your hands and grab your backpack," he told his sister.

After she'd slipped off the stool and run off toward the bedroom, he turned back to me. "She didn't get you all slobbery, did she?"

I shook my head. "I prevented the worst of it."

"I've never met anyone who can go from perfectly clean to utter disaster faster than Ivy."

My lips twitched as I glanced around the clean apartment and wondered how much work it took to keep it that way with a little terror like her on the loose.

"I drove around most of the night, looking for him on the streets," he said with a chin nod toward my screen where the steps of the Capitol buzzed with people coming and going. "I know his phone's last location, but the phone company might be able to send me his history if I asked, right?"

"After you left last night, I tracked him via a GPS cell tracker website and got nothing more than his last location." When I saw panic return to his eyes, I added, "It could just mean his battery died and nothing more. Did you turn on the Notify When Found option?" He looked at me funny. "Give me your phone."

He pulled it out of his back pocket, swiped to unlock it, and handed it to me.

I flipped through the screens until I found the right app, located Monte's number, and toggled through the options before handing it back to him. I didn't tell him I'd already found the IMEI number and searched it the way the police would if they tapped the carrier. I'd found nothing beyond the Capitol Building and the side street where his phone had last pinged. Which in and of itself was weird. But I kept my concerns to myself.

Ivy came out of the bathroom, a tiny pink backpack in her hands with so many sparkles they shed as she walked. She looked like Monte had when he was her age. Shiny and bright and cherub-like.

I will bring him home to them, I swore to myself.

Gage led Ivy to the door, grabbing his keys from a bowl on the table nearby. I stuffed my laptop inside my bag and joined them.

We followed Ivy down the stairs at a snail's pace that had me itching to pick her up and carry her. When we got to the ground, the two of them headed for the Pathfinder he'd been in the night before. I hadn't known it was him at first when I'd spotted the car following me. It was the last vehicle I'd ever expected to see Gage in.

He lifted Ivy into the back where she crawled into the car seat and buckled up at the same slow pace as she'd taken the steps. Then, he opened the passenger door and waved at me.

I shook my head. "I'll follow you."

He looked at my bike parked one spot over. "Seems pointless to take two vehicles into D.C."

I hesitated for multiple reasons. I needed an escape from the emotions that pummeled me when I was with him, but I also liked to control the vehicle I was in. Ever since I'd learned to drive and had taken the evasive driving course Mom had recommended, I'd preferred being the driver than the passenger. Those feelings had only intensified since Mom's accident. But Gage was right—it was silly to take two cars into D.C. I instantly regretted not bringing Pop's Jeep with me.

Our arms brushed as I got in, and it felt like I'd been hit with a low-level zap from my stun gun. The electricity spiraling up over my shoulders and into my chest was amplified a thousand times from the feelings I'd had around him as a kid. Our eyes locked for one beat… two… three. Then, he stepped back, shutting the door behind me and striding around to the driver's side. My brain felt like it had short-circuited.

I'd had good sex before. Fulfilling. Satisfying. Maybe a bit mundane, but still good. And yet, never once had someone simply brushing against me set my body off like a fireworks display the way Gage did.

As we drove toward the day care center near the college campus, I pulled my phone from my pocket with a shaky hand. I swiped through the screens until I found the cameras

I'd been watching on my laptop and continued my search through the sea of people arriving at the Capitol.

After parking in front of the preschool, Gage waited for Ivy to fight with her seat belt. How many times a day did he physically hold himself back from helping? I wasn't sure I'd be able to do the same. I could sit in a car staking out a place all day, but what Gage did required a different kind of patience.

"I'll be right back," Gage said, and they started to walk away, but Ivy pulled her hand out of his and ran back to the Pathfinder. She looked up at me with wide eyes full of a fear that hadn't been there all morning. I opened the door.

"Monte's side hurts. His fingers too," she said. "He's scared. Really scared."

A weird sensation crawled over the back of my neck. My gaze flew to Gage's. His jaw was locked tight, his lips a straight line of anger or disapproval or... reluctant acceptance.

"Wh-what?" I forced out, my breath seeming to have left my body, as I looked down at the little girl. Her expression had turned blank as if she hadn't just dropped a huge bomb in my lap. As if she hadn't said anything. She seemed confused at being back at the SUV as she turned to her brother.

Gage scooped her up, held her close to his chest, and murmured something in her ear. She nodded, resting her head with its two enormous bows on his shoulder as they strode toward the building once again.

My heart was pounding furiously.

I hadn't ever believed in any kind of extrasensory perception. Clairvoyance, channeling, and telepathy were all scams people ran on the weak-minded. At least, that had been the opinion of both my parents. One I easily subscribed to.

And yet... The look on Ivy's face... It hadn't been normal. It had been spooky as hell. And that voice... She'd said all her R's perfectly.

Another shiver ran up my spine.

I was ready to climb out of the Pathfinder and run back to my Rebel to escape all the emotions that had buffeted me since walking into The Prince Darian Saturday night.

He's really scared, she'd said.

I thought about the tattoo on Gage's arm. I thought about Veronica's words about the hero being the one who remains in your life while the villain is the one who takes off. I didn't want to be the villain. I didn't want to be my dad, walking out when things didn't go the way he'd planned.

A little bit of spookiness wouldn't send me running. I needed to do this for Gage's family—to ensure the pain and heartache radiating from Gage disappeared. So Ivy's smile was all joy and not sadness. So the little cherub boy I hadn't seen in years could come home to his family.

But maybe, just maybe, I needed to do it for myself as well.

Chapter Thirteen

Gage

HURRICANE

Performed by The Fray

Everything was going halfway decently with Rory until Ivy had one of her visions. I wasn't even sure she'd be in the car when I got back or if she'd have run for the hills.

I signed Ivy in, held her tight, and whispered, "I love you," before watching her wander farther into the day care center with her stuffed animal clutched to her chest. She didn't look terrified anymore as she sat next to two kids on a carpet woven with brightly colored letters and animals, and yet my heart remained heavy. I had an overwhelming desire to keep her close, even though it didn't make sense to take her to D.C.

Reluctantly, I turned away from my sister and headed back to the car.

Rory wouldn't let what had happened slide. She'd want to talk about it. Analyze it. Understand it. But the truth was, what happened with us—what Demi had given us—wasn't something you could understand unless you experienced it personally.

A piece of me sighed with relief when Rory was still in the SUV, but her narrowed eyes told me she'd considered bolting. It wasn't just Ivy's words that were freaky, it was the way she said them in a voice that wasn't quite hers. With wild eyes. And then, when it left her, and she looked at you with vague forgetfulness, it was even creepier. As if, for two seconds, she became someone else. Someone much older and wiser and weirdly connected to the people she loved most.

I sat behind the wheel, and the tension radiating between Rory and me was no longer of the sexual variety.

"I'm still heading to D.C.," I told her, without glancing over. "You coming or not?"

"You really think I'd abandon you over that?" Her words were sharp. Angry. And they jerked my gaze to hers.

She'd been freaked out—it was still there in her eyes—but her shoulders were back, and she was full of the same stubborn defiance I'd seen the very first time I'd met her. At twelve, she'd had more assurance than many grownups.

I swallowed. Admiration and longing welled through me in equal measures.

How had I never seen exactly how special she was?

You did, a little voice whispered.

The memory of her sitting behind me on my motorcycle hit me. We'd ridden toward a storm with lightning flashing, thunder booming, and Rory screaming her head off as if she was standing on a hilltop daring the gods to come and get her. We'd laughed. A sense of joy and freedom had surrounded me that day, spurred on by Rory's pleasure, taking the place of the ugly words I'd just had with Demi.

Rory had *always* been special. I'd just purposefully put blinders up. I'd had to. She'd been fucking fifteen that day to my twenty. Was it any better now simply because the numbers on our driver's licenses were different?

I started the car, backed out, and headed down the cobblestone streets until they bled into the paved roads and eventually the highway leading to our nation's capital.

The air around us grew increasingly strained. The tension wasn't just about Ivy, but it was the one thing I could address at the moment. The only thing I could handle discussing. So, I finally said, "Just ask."

"What's there to ask? She's a little girl who's worried about her missing brother. I'm sure she believes he's scared. He probably is. Even if he's holed up somewhere that he chose to go, being alone in the city at night by yourself can be terrifying."

I heard in her voice what she wasn't saying. *I don't believe in any paranormal bullshit.*

I didn't respond right away, wondering how much of my family's truth to expose.

"She doesn't have visions in the way Monte does," I admitted. "But she's tied to us somehow. One time, I sliced my hand on a broken bottle at the bar. I ended up at the ER getting stitches, and the day care called while I was there. Ivy was crying and complaining about her hand hurting, but they couldn't see anything wrong with it. She was inconsolable and didn't calm down until I arrived. She was holding her hand right where I'd cut mine."

I risked a look at Rory. Her eyes were still skittish, and she tugged on the sleeve of her sweater, pulling it over her palms. "What's your supposed superpower? Do you see visions too?"

"No." The retort came quickly and naturally. I wasn't sure why I was willing to tell her the truth about my siblings but not me. Maybe it was an intimate line I couldn't yet cross with her. Maybe I never would.

It didn't matter, because the abilities I had—the sense of a person's innate character and the ability to feel a storm brewing—were nothing compared to what Monte and Ivy had. Nothing that kept me up sleepless. Nothing that would allow me to save someone's life if we could ever get the authorities to listen to us.

As if she had picked up on my lie, she huffed out a little sound of disbelief. "I should have added *no lying* to the contract you signed."

My gut twisted, but I still didn't come clean. "So. You're working with your mom now. Were you supposed to be on a different case today? Something with her?"

She scooted sideways in the passenger seat, leaning against the door so she could look at me while I drove.

"You really haven't heard?" Pain filled her voice. The anguish I'd seen clinging to her from the moment she'd walked into the bar on Friday. "She crashed into the Potomac a few days before Christmas last year."

My gut clenched. "I'd heard there'd been an accident… I didn't think… I didn't know…" My entire being revolted at the idea of Rory getting that call. I knew excruciatingly well what it was like. The fucking agony.

I almost said I was sorry but stopped myself. Because it wouldn't matter. It wouldn't ease any of the goddamn pain. It wouldn't even be the comfort people thought it was.

"She's in a coma," she said quietly.

"She's still alive." I breathed out a sigh of relief.

"The doctors don't think so…" She shook her head, lips turning grim. "They want us to turn off her life support."

Every molecule of heartache I felt for her tripled. Quadrupled. Zoomed out of control. How could they expect her to make that call? How could they expect anyone to make it? To essentially kill the person you loved most?

I'd thought my life was hard. I thought finding out Dad was dead had been the worst thing to happen to me, but God… What if I'd had to be the one to stop him from breathing?

I wouldn't have been able to do it.

As if she sensed the enormity of my own emotions, she looked away again. Tugging her sweater again before flipping her phone over in her lap half a dozen times.

"I should have brought my motorcycle. We could have gone in two directions after the Capitol and covered more ground."

I knew her suggestion wasn't just because of Monte and our search. It was because she didn't like being in the car with me, sharing her life… her feelings… the overwhelming emotions.

I completely understood. I didn't want to think about Monte alone and scared, and she didn't want to think about her mom on a ventilator. So, I did what I could for both of us and tossed out a tease I knew would rile her up.

"The Rebel is cute, but I'm not sure it qualifies as an actual motorcycle."

In a flash, I saw the defiance I adored. She pointed a finger at me and then waved her hand around the abused Pathfinder with its airbags and safety features I'd been prompted to buy after Ivy had been born.

"What the hell would you know about motorcycles anymore? You're driving a dadmobile," she said with scorn.

My lips curled upward ever so slightly. "The Rebel is a little shit-spitter. Mine… Mine's a real motorcycle."

She hesitated for a beat. "You still have it? The red Indian?"

I shook my head. "Traded the Sport in for an Indian Chief."

She snorted. "That totally makes sense."

"What's that supposed to mean?"

"Safe. Sturdy. Road cruiser." She said it as if she was saying it about me instead of the bike. As if I was safe and sturdy… As if I'd take sex slow and easy.

And hell, sometimes I would. Lazy Sunday mornings were perfect for taking your time. But there were also moments for fast and furious up against a wall or on the back of my bike parked on the shore. Still, the hint of condescension and teasing picked at my ego.

"I think you mean burly, highly responsive, and can beat your little 471cc four-stroke off a starting line in any race on this earth," I tossed back.

"Burly? Isn't it against the law for a man to use that word?" Her face burst into a smile, and it almost made me drive off the road.

It had been so long since I'd seen that kind of smile on her face. Full of joy and recklessness. Lightning. It was a smile that turned her from an avenging angel into a teasing sprite. Mischievous. Promising things I shouldn't want.

Her phone pinged, and when she looked down, her smile disappeared and my heart faltered.

"Monte?" I asked, not even bothering to hide the fear in my voice.

She shook her head. "No. Sorry. This is my dad."

She hit the side button, ignoring it, and the phone buzzed a couple more times, which she also ignored. Finally, it started making music with an incoming call.

She lifted it to her ear, annoyance in every syllable as she said, "I can't talk right now. I'm in the middle of something."

I couldn't hear the voice on the other end, but I could tell by her posture that whoever it was, they were royally pissing her off. If it was still her dad, it didn't surprise me. They'd always had a rocky relationship. Not quite as rocky as mine with Demi, but close.

Rory's back went straighter, tighter, and her chin rose. "I barely got the file Baloney-Muloney sent me this morning, I haven't even had a chance to go through it. I'm in the middle of a case, Dad. A missing kid. You know how time sensitive it is, so I'm going to have to put your bullshit on the back counter and deal with it later."

Monte. For a few brief seconds, I'd let myself think of something other than my brother. But her words rammed his absence back into me, and guilt swarmed with it. I shouldn't be thinking of anything but my brother at the moment. And definitely not her smile or her eyes or having fucking sex with her on my Indian.

Her dad obviously hadn't liked her response because I heard the growl of a deep voice as we pulled up to a light after getting off the highway. Instead of showing the least bit of remorse, she only got fiercer.

"Well, it's a good thing I'm an adult and don't have to follow your orders. I'm not your employee. I'm barely your daughter, so let's just leave it at that. It was a mistake going to you the other day. Forget the lapse of judgment ever happened."

She hung up without waiting for a reply.

The word *adult* hung in the air around us. She was an adult. She'd always been an old soul, but now, she was running a business, dealing with the enormity of her mom's situation, and helping me with my brother. She wasn't a kid anymore. Far from it.

That should ease my guilt about the way I'd been looking at her.

And it did, but it also brought up a whole new round of regrets. I didn't know the ins and outs of her life, and yet, it felt like I knew all the important things. One parent basically dead and the other driving her batty. Why was fate so cruel to take the one parent you could actually depend on and leave you with the one who didn't know how to stick?

I wanted to shake her dad until he saw the light. Until he saw what he had in front of him so he'd keep her close instead of pushing her away. But those were more likely my feelings about my mother manifesting than the truth of her relationship with her dad.

All I knew was that after today, I'd never look at Rory the same again.

And I realized I didn't want to.

She wasn't a kid. She was a stunning woman.

Which was shit timing to realize it. Shit timing added to a messed-up life because just seeing her in a different light didn't mean I could ever add the burden of my responsibilities to hers. She'd let me. She'd try to shoulder mine with her own.

And hadn't I already been tempted by that idea back at the apartment? The idea of Rory being the person at my side. The person who saw me as more than a makeshift father and a bar owner. But after hearing how her life was already burdened, understanding how much she was holding up, I'd never do that to her.

I was pretty sure neither of us would remain standing if we attempted to carry the weight of one more life on our shoulders.

Chapter Fourteen

Gage

NOTHING ELSE MATTERS
Performed by Metallica

The only conversation we had after Rory hung up with her dad was her directing me to a parking garage down from the Capitol Building. We were both lost in our silent, complicated reflections. Mine turned from Rory to my missing brother and where the hell he'd been spending his nights in D.C. and why Ivy had said he was scared, not once, but twice. I wished again I could feel and see the things they did because maybe it would help me find him.

"My friend works in the security control room. I'm hoping she can access the camera footage from Friday. She's agreed to meet with us on her break." Rory glanced around my Pathfinder. "I can't bring my weapons or my computer inside. You have a cargo cover back there we can pull?"

I was just about to ask what kind of weapons when she leaned forward and pulled a gun from the waistband at her back. She placed it in her messenger bag where it joined the flashlight-like stun gun she'd pulled the night before and some kind of aerosol spray. Mace? Pepper spray? Jesus. My pulse picked up. Did she know how to use all of those? To shoot a gun? I'd never even held one.

"There's a cover," I said, doing my best to keep my voice steady.

We walked to the back of the vehicle, she tossed the

bag in, and I pulled the cover over it, latching it in place. Once I'd locked up, I noticed her eyes darting around the parking garage as if she expected someone to jump us and steal everything. I'd always known she was serious about her future job with the FBI. But now, seeing her hacking computers, carrying weapons, and scoping out the joint, it hit home how close she was to making her dreams come true.

As we exited the garage, I expected us to make our way toward the entrance to the Capitol Building, but she headed in the opposite direction. "Where are we going?"

"Rayburn Building. It's where my friend works and where Congressman Dunn's offices are at. He's moved up the food chain fairly fast and has a coveted spot on one of the best floors. Makes me wonder what he traded to get it."

"You know a lot about D.C."

"I should. I've been working it since I was a kid."

I glanced down at her, surprise filtering through me. "What do you mean, working it since you were a kid?"

She flinched as if regretting she'd let the words slip.

Images of a tiny Rory twisting through ventilation shafts and planting bugs flashed in my mind. My lips twitched upward but my stomach rolled with additional worry. When she didn't say anything, I pushed. "What the hell does that mean, Pipsqueak?"

"I really don't want to talk about it, Gage. It was a mistake. Let's leave it at that."

"Rory." I pulled her to a stop, looking down into eyes that glimmered. Rory hated to cry. Her jaw worked while she appeared to debate telling me whatever dark secret she was keeping.

Finally, she blew out a breath and said, "I'm the reason they got divorced. I fucked up and got caught. Mom found out Dad had been sending me in to collect evidence without her knowledge, and she freaked out. She moved us to Cherry Bay until the divorce paperwork dried."

I wanted to strangle her dad all over again. She'd been twelve when she moved to Cherry Bay. Twelve! I could understand her mother's anger. "What were you doing when you got caught?"

"Planting a bug in a senator's home office during a sleepover with his daughter."

I stared at her, stunned. Her love for *Veronica Mars* took on a whole new meaning. She'd been living it long before she'd ever watched the show.

"Jesus…"

"Don't even. I knew what I was doing. It was just a fluke that he came into the office." She turned and started walking, and I followed. "I know this city. I know how it works. And I know the people in it. Mom wouldn't let me take the same risks as Dad, but after I convinced her I wasn't giving up the life, she put me behind the computer instead. I ran her office and did most of her research. When I started driving, she'd let me do the occasional stakeout for some low-risk cases. When I turned eighteen, I got my investigator's licenses in Virginia and D.C. and went to work for her as a partner. This job paid my way through college."

I grew quiet. I'd worked at the tavern a few hours a week as a teen. Stocking and cleaning, nothing too hard, just basic barback activities as I couldn't legally bartend until I was twenty-one. Overall, my life had been fairly easy. Even once I'd gone away to college, Dad had footed the bill as much as he could so I didn't have to work too many hours while studying. Then, I'd gotten my paid internship with Storm Dominators, and it had covered the majority of my school expenses. But I'd still had a lot of free time I'd filled between classes and studying with the normal parties and dates.

Rory had basically been working like a mini adult for most of her life, which made me suddenly ashamed of the irritation I'd felt at becoming the head of our family at twenty-three. Everyone had to grow up at some point. But she shouldn't have been thrust into it so early.

As if she'd read every thought that had crossed my mind, she said, "Don't feel sorry for me. I loved it. I loved every moment. The only regret I have is the mistake I made that cost my parents their marriage."

"I very seriously doubt you were the reason they got divorced."

"You don't know. You didn't live with them."

"I know it takes a lot more than one screw-up by a parent, or a kid, to make a marriage fail. It takes two people and years of disagreements. Look at my dad. He was still married to Demi when he died. Even after…"

Rory and I drifted back into silence, lost in our thoughts—mine of my parents, our childhoods, and the wounds they'd left behind—as we made our way around to the front of the Rayburn Building.

The classic white-and-gray building had the same stately, reverent feel of the Capitol Building, with a series of steps flanked by two ten-foot marble statues staring at each other. Above the doors, six Ionic columns supported a portico carved with an eagle.

We stepped inside and got in line at the security booth where Rory took over with a smooth smile. She navigated us through, all the while laughing and joking with the security guards, calling them by name, and asking about their families. She seemed to know more people here than I did at the bar when the locals came out in force for Tango Tuesday.

After one last tease she directed at a large officer who dwarfed even my six-foot-three frame, we headed for the enormous staircase drifting up from polished marble floors.

"We have time before we meet up with Lucidia to flash Monte's picture around Dunn's staff and see if anyone recognizes him," she said.

When we walked into the congressman's suite, the guy at the desk didn't even look up from his laptop. Instead, he waved toward a clipboard on a sideboard.

"The congressman has a full schedule this morning. If you sign in, we'll see what we can do to give you a call later in the week."

Rory wasn't put off by the guy's no-time-for-you-peasants attitude. Instead, she hung a photo of Monte over his laptop screen. His eyes flickered over the image and then up to her face.

"This is Monte. He came here Friday. We'd like to know what happened when he did."

"We see hundreds of people every day," he said in a dismissive tone.

"But this is a red-haired thirteen-year-old. I doubt you get many of them in here. I'm betting he would have stood out."

The guy squinted, irritation blooming. "I don't know what to tell you. I don't remember him."

A weird silence settled in the room. In the middle of it, the inner door opened, and Representative Dunn emerged. He was a large man with a clean-shaven face, dark blond hair graying at the temples, and blue eyes sparkling as if he was a jovial uncle. Next to him was a lean, muscled man with black hair, black eyes, and a goatee. They reminded me of that old nursery rhyme about Jack Sprat and his wife.

"Good morning," Dunn said, turning his camera-ready smile at us.

"Morning," Rory replied as she stepped toward him.

The skinny man moved to intercept. "The congressman has a busy schedule today, as I'm sure Pat here told you, but if you put your name on the list, someone from our office will be in touch."

Absolutely nothing about the situation or any of the words that had been spoken since we walked in were cause for alarm. Irritation, sure, but nothing to cause the hairs on the back of my neck to rise like the time Tall Paul and his lackey had come into the bar offering to buy me out. And yet, that's exactly what happened.

Maybe it was just their jobs, the way they were taught to lie through their smiles as they bartered deals and told the folks back home exactly what they wanted to hear to be re-elected. Maybe it was the fact that Monte was missing, and he'd come here to try and save this man's life with an absurd story. Either way, my senses were going off like a shotgun blast. Something was wrong. Something didn't fit.

There was nothing good or jovial or even congenial about the men in front of me.

Instead, I got the same sense I'd gotten from Tall Paul and his thug. As if they were biding their time, waiting for me to crash and burn. Worse, they were ready to help tip me over the edge if needed.

All the inner tumult I'd been dealing with since realizing Monte was actually missing came bubbling to the surface. I stepped around Rory, going toe-to-toe with the black-haired man in a gray pinstriped suit.

"My teenage brother is missing after he came here to see Dunn, so pardon me if I don't give two cents about the representative's time, schedule, or next dirty deal." I ripped the photo from Rory's hand and shoved it toward the man.

"Just tell me what happened when he got here."

Chapter Fifteen

Rory

ATTACK OF PANIC
Performed by Aly & AJ

Shit. Gage was two seconds from slamming someone against a wall. Fury radiated through every ounce of him, muscles rippling with the effort of holding back.

The last thing we needed was to get tossed out of the building. He'd ruin my chances of ever getting information from anyone in the Capitol again. All my work schmoozing, bartering, and trading over the years would be lost.

I planted my feet and pushed against Gage's ginormous biceps to shove him aside. Caught off guard by the force I'd used, he actually took two steps back before turning an almost deadly frown my way.

"You'll have to excuse my client here," I said, ignoring Gage's look and using my sweet-as-frosting tone. "I'm sure you can understand how stressful it is to have someone you love go missing. We're just chasing down any leads we have. Can we walk with you to your next meeting so we don't keep you?"

The skinny man, who I'd identified in my search last night as Connolly West, Representative Dunn's chief of staff, stiffened. His eyes narrowed, darting from Gage back to me, determining that I was the lesser threat.

"We're sorry to hear his brother is missing. We're heading down to the subway. Feel free to walk with us."

Dunn made a noise that wasn't quite a huff of disapproval but close, and yet his face never broke from his suave, charming smile. For some reason, it raised my hackles. I suddenly wanted to wipe his grin right off, and if I was feeling that way, I could only imagine how Gage felt, knowing this man might have been the last one to see his brother before he disappeared.

Praying Gage wouldn't do anything stupid, we followed as the two men stepped out of the office heading for the elevators. I shot Gage a glance that said *Let me handle this.*

This was why you didn't take clients with you. They lost their shit when faced with things they didn't like because they couldn't be objective. They couldn't keep their emotions out of it. Hadn't Dad burned that into me enough over the years? Emotions lost cases.

But I'd somehow forgotten that important detail with Gage as my client. Years of thinking of him in a very different light were clouding my judgment. I needed to get my head on straight before I made another mistake. One that could be much worse than costing my parents their marriage. This could impact us finding Monte before something bad happened to him.

In the elevator, I took Monte's picture back from Gage and showed it to the two men. "This is Monte Palmer. He left school Friday afternoon to come and talk to you."

There was a beat where the air went frigid, and I knew the next words weren't going to be the whole truth even before the congressman spoke.

"Isn't that the kid who talked to us in the plaza? Red hair is hard to forget," Dunn said, sliding a look toward West. The two men were talking with their eyes the way I'd been attempting to do with Gage. They'd had years more practice at it.

West gave a curt nod. "Yes. He was talking about guns and shootings, wasn't he? We told him he should make his petition in person at our office."

Dunn's gaze barely slid past me. I was uninteresting to him, but they took in Gage with something akin to curiosity. "You're not from Colorado. What made your brother decide I was the one he needed to talk to?"

Gage hesitated, and my stomach tightened. If he spilled his guts right now about visions and future threats, there was no way we were going to keep their attention.

"You're on the Education and Workforce Committee, so maybe he thought you'd be more apt to listen than Congressman Addison."

It was quick thinking on Gage's part. I was surprised he'd known that much about either Dunn or Cherry Bay's representative.

Dunn smiled widely. "Plus, Harry loves his NRA money."

It was a slam against his fellow statesman, but I didn't expect anything else from the politicians who filled the halls and tunnels of the Capitol. There were good ones. I'd seen them in person, and my friends on the Capitol Police could tell you instantly who they were, but it was, unfortunately, rarer than it should be.

"Did you see where he went after you talked?" I asked.

The two men did that eye exchange again, and my gut sank.

"Sorry, we were late for a meeting and didn't stay to talk," West said.

We approached the entrance to the subway station in the basement that joined the Rayburn Building with the Capitol itself, and I slowed my steps, pulling Gage to a halt beside me.

"Thank you for your time," I said, and let the men continue on without us.

Gage simmered next to me. Once they were out of ear range, I turned on him and put a finger to his hard-as-a-rock chest. "Don't ever do that again."

His eyes widened, glancing down to where my finger

rested. Heat and awareness zapped through me. I pulled back with a jerk.

"If you can't control your emotions, I need you to walk back to the car."

His eyes narrowed. "They know more than they're telling."

To most people, Dunn and West would have appeared friendly and helpful, but the conversations they'd had with their eyes said otherwise. Something more had happened than just a conversation about school shootings. It was a nice cover story. If Monte had been ranting about what he thought was going to happen to the representative, they could pull it off as having thought he was talking about shootings in general and not Dunn getting shot.

"There are a thousand and one reasons for them to be holding back, including something as simple as Monte saw them talking to another congressman they don't want anyone to know they're dealing with. Everything here is shadowed in secrecy, and sometimes the most powerful information you can have is who is talking to whom."

"I don't give a rat's ass about any of that. I care about finding my brother."

"Pissing them off and getting tossed out won't help us find him."

I turned on my heel, heading back the way we'd come.

Gage was quiet next to me, but I could practically feel the frustration vibrating from him.

As we made our way back up to the main floor where more politicians and staffers poured in for their workday, the energy in the building increased, the pace similar to standing on the Metro platform. By the time we made it to the cafeteria, a swirl of bodies hurried in various directions.

I scanned the tables and found Lucidia at the back. Her thick black braids were pulled into a knot atop her head, and she had a large smoothie in front of her. She spotted me when we were halfway through the sea of tables, and her eyes widened slightly at the massive, broody man behind me.

When we sat down, she shifted nervously, and once again, I realized I should have left Gage outside. Nothing Lucidia and I were doing was illegal. None of it should technically get her in trouble, but people in the Capitol were persnickety about their privacy.

"Lucidia, this is Gage. Gage, Lucidia."

He reached his hand across the table, and she shook it firmly before withdrawing.

"Like I told you on the phone, we're looking for his brother. Representative Dunn just told me they had a conversation with him in the plaza."

Her brows went up. "He was out front? There had to be reporters there. You should be able to pick something up from one of them, but we can head over to the control room and see if we can spot anything on the video feeds."

I kicked myself for not thinking about the news vans camped out regularly at the foot of the building sooner. I turned to Gage. "Did the police put you in touch with any of the news outlets to run his photo?"

Gage shook his head. "But the NCMEC coordinator said they'd have someone contact me."

"How old is he?" Lucidia asked.

"Thirteen," Gage responded, voice deep and scratchy with emotion.

"Tough age. My sister left home when she was fourteen."

Gage's entire body stiffened, and his face turned dark. "Monte didn't run away."

Lucidia eyed him and then me. She lifted an eyebrow again, but didn't say anything. She grabbed her smoothie and made her way through the tables with us following her, and led us through an Employee Only entrance into the warren of corridors in the subbasement of the building. She stopped at a door that looked like a storage closet.

Disguised to look like it wasn't anything important, the control room was the heartbeat of the building's security. It was similar to several other rooms placed carefully throughout the buildings and tunnels making up the Capitol's grounds.

Lucidia turned to us and said, "He can't come in."

Gage's jaw ticked.

"Why don't you touch base with Detective Muloney and whoever you spoke to at Metro PD while Lucidia and I see what we can find?"

Gage didn't respond. He just turned away, pulling his phone out of his pocket and walking down the hall to lean against the concrete wall.

Inside the room, Lucidia was on me in a flash, dropping into the Spanish of her Puerto Rican homeland. She kept her voice hushed so the other officers in the room wouldn't hear. "What the hell, Rory? You know I don't talk to anyone but you."

"It's a kid, Lucidia," I responded in Spanish, grateful to have kept it up in college. "Thirteen-year-old kid who's gone missing after talking to Congressman Dunn. You think anyone is going to try to find him if something bad went down? No way Dunn and his cohorts want it to get out that he was the last person to see Monte."

She blanched, swirled around, and pulled out a chair from the desk in the corner. She pounded away at the keyboard, asking, "What time frame are we looking at on Friday?"

I gave her the range, and she pulled up video footage from the enormous steps most of the world associated with the entrance to the Capitol. She zipped through the time range, and I searched the people speeding past for bright red hair.

I'd almost given up hope when Dunn and his chief of staff appeared. Suddenly, there was Monte. He was tall for his age, so from the back he looked like a full-grown man. With his baseball cap lowered and his backpack hanging from one shoulder, I was surprised someone hadn't stopped him long before he'd gotten close to the congressman.

In the video, Monte was waving his hands, talking animatedly. What had me narrowing my eyes was the way both Dunn and West stopped completely, heads turned, looking very interested in what Monte was saying. West responded to Monte and then started to direct Dunn away, but Dunn stopped and turned back. He asked Monte something. Monte hesitated, a look of shock radiating from his face, but then he nodded. Dunn said something else, and then he and West walked away, traveling down the steps to where a group of reporters was waiting.

When I'd gone online last night, I hadn't found any recent press statements or interviews with Dunn. Certainly nothing from the Capitol steps on Friday. There actually hadn't been much about him in the news in quite a while. The most recent footage had been from this summer when he'd been at a women's shelter.

"Can you rewind it to the part where Dunn is talking?" I asked.

I wasn't an expert at reading lips, but years of stakeouts and following people had given me some skill. We watched the footage again. "Can you play it one more time and slow it down?"

Lucidia did her thing, and I watched the screen carefully.

"Did he ask about his mother?" My brows creased, my heartbeat jumping.

Lucidia played it again. Working in her job, she had a lot more experience watching silent footage. "I think so. He said a name. Like is your mom so and so."

My pulse sped up. *Crap.* How did Dunn know Gage and Monte's flighty mom?

Lucidia let the video play out, and this time I watched not Dunn but Monte. He watched the congressman as he went down to the gathered media. Monte's face was a war of emotions, but desperation was the most prevalent. He pulled his cap down further, hunched his shoulders, and headed toward New Jersey Avenue and Longworth House. His feet moved slowly. My heart sank as he disappeared from the camera's view.

I needed to dig out other cameras along the street. Ones that weren't locked down by the government and the different law enforcement agencies all staking a claim in and around the Capitol.

I returned my scrutiny to West. While I'd been watching Monte, he'd stepped away from Dunn and the reporters. He had his phone pressed to his ear, and his head was turned in the direction Monte had gone.

"Back that up a bit again, please," I said, reaching over Lucidia's hand as if I were going to do it myself, and she swatted me away.

Right before they got to the reporters, Dunn and West stopped, faces covered by hands as they exchanged a few words. Dunn's face was absent of his jovial smile for less than a minute, but then it returned as he walked down toward the media.

West was immediately on the phone, watching as Monte walked away.

The hair on my arms curled, goose bumps emerging.

Double fuck.

Upstairs, they'd acted like they'd only half heard what Monte had said, and yet, they had to have known this footage existed.

Just as I had the thought, Lucidia's screen went black.

"What in the blazes?" she said. She scowled, trying to bring it back up.

I knew in my heart what had happened before she said the words. I was astonished it had been left in the system this long, rather than disappearing on Friday after they'd talked to Monte.

"It's gone," she said. Her wide eyes met mine.

"Can you find out who deleted it?" I asked quietly,

darting a look at the other two people in the room who I didn't know.

"Not them." Her voice was even more hushed than mine. Barely a whisper. "Someone with higher clearance. I can dig a bit, but if I do too much, it'll attract unwanted attention. I could get in trouble for showing it to you."

Our eyes locked, and it was clear we were thinking the same thing. Monte hadn't run away. Fear curled through me, goose bumps reappearing over and over. What was I going to tell Gage? What if the worst had already happened? And what the hell did it have to do with their mother?

I swallowed hard, determination swimming in over the fear and sadness. We'd find him, damn it. We'd find him, and he'd still be alive. The split that threatened to rip through my heart at just the *thought* of the opposite being true was nothing compared to what Gage must already be feeling.

"Whatever you can, Lucidia. I'd appreciate it."

I headed for the door, and she followed. Turning back to her, I added, "You still hoping the Capitols will make it to the Stanley Cup this year?"

Lucidia snorted. "No hope involved. It's a sure thing."

"Give me a date, and I'll have a pair of tickets waiting for you at the stadium."

"My grandson will love it."

I wasn't sure I could afford it, but I'd make it happen somehow. Maybe I could barter tickets for services to someone at the stadium.

When I walked out the door, Gage looked up at me with a hopefulness that sliced through me. He traveled the couple of feet it took to reach me in two long strides. "Did you see him?"

I looked up at the cameras I knew were watching us.

"I need my computer. Let's get back to your car."

Knowing I would have said something instantly if the news was good, his face fell, my words wiping away any optimistic thoughts he might have had. I hated it. I didn't want to be the one bringing more anguish to his life.

But I didn't have another option. I'd do the job, whether it was ugly or not, because Gage needed someone in his corner, putting on the gloves and fighting for him and his brother until we had the truth. Like my television hero had taught me, there was no way to be declared the winner if you walked out in the middle of the fight. So I'd do what I always did. I'd buckle down and do the job and hope it didn't end up tearing us apart a bit more.

Chapter Sixteen

Gage

Whatever Rory had found out, it wasn't good. The sliver of hope that had started to lift my heart disintegrated, melting away. I tried twice to start a conversation about what she'd found as we left the building, and both times, she ignored it, shooting me annoyed looks.

I was the one who should be annoyed. Annoyed and furious.

Monte had been there. A thirteen-year-old kid by himself, and no one had thought anything about it. Not the CarShare operator who'd dropped him off. Not the congressman and his flunky. How was that possible?

We were out of the building and halfway to the Pathfinder when I finally reached out and hauled her to a stop. People swirled around us, most heading the way we'd just come from.

"Just fucking tell me," I demanded.

"How does Dunn know your mom?"

My jaw dropped and my heart slammed against my rib cage as her question rebounded through my brain. What the hell did Demi have to do with any of this? My tongue refused to work, and I couldn't respond for several long seconds. Finally, I choked out, "He doesn't."

But how would I really know if he did? I knew nothing

about Demi's life outside of Cherry Bay. Not where she'd been or who she'd spent her time with.

Rory shook off my hand and kept walking, telling me what she'd seen on the video in the control room. My emotions flew all over the place as we retraced our steps to the Pathfinder. Dunn and West had lied, no surprise there, but the look Dunn had given me in his office made a hell of a lot more sense. It was like… he knew me somehow.

What the fuck had Demi done now?

The hair on the back of my neck rose as I realized Monte's vision hit closer to home than ever before if somehow Dunn and Demi knew each other.

"It's worse, Gage," Rory said quietly as we climbed back into the SUV and sat in the darkened garage.

How the hell could it be worse? Monte was gone. Demi was involved. Dunn had lied. Jesus.

"The video feed…" She took a deep breath and then continued, "It disappeared while we were watching it. Someone erased it."

I stared at her for several seconds before letting out the words on a stuttered breath, "We scared them."

Shit… My fear for Monte's life grew impossibly larger, wiping out any hope Rory had brought me this morning. I should have been there when Monte had talked to Dunn. I should have fucking got into the car with him last week when he'd had the first vision and had been determined to warn the congressman. I should have done anything to protect him. Instead, I'd let him go to school every day haunted and tortured by what he'd seen in his dreams.

If something had happened to him…I swallowed. The pain dragged through my middle. I'd vacillated between fury, frustration, guilt, and fear for days now. Ivy's tormented voice saying Monte was hurt and scared ran through me again like a bell going off. An alarm.

But then it hit me. She'd said, *Monte is scared.*

She'd said it like it was happening right at that moment.

She'd been practically inconsolable when I'd simply cut my hand. If anything worse had happened to Monte, Ivy would have known.

A measure of relief wafted through the ache.

"He's not dead," I said. The strength of my conviction made my words come out as a growl.

Something crossed Rory's face. Worry…doubt…who the hell knew? But I could tell she didn't entirely believe it.

"He's not dead," I repeated. "If he was, Ivy would know. She said Monte *is* scared, not *was*. She isn't desolate with grief. She'd know, Rory." Doubt crossed her face, and I sighed. "I know you don't believe me. I get it. No one ever does, but I'm telling you, my brother is alive. He's scared but alive."

She swiped through a few screens on her phone, thumbs going a mile a minute as she typed messages. When she looked up, there was a steely resolve in her eyes. The grit I'd seen over and over again since I'd first met her at twelve.

"Take me to where his phone last pinged. I want to see it in person and make sure we aren't missing anything."

I turned the engine over, backed out of the spot, and headed out of the garage into the snarling traffic that surrounded the Capitol Building corridor. A few blocks past the Metro station, I pulled into the alley where his phone had last pinged. River and I had come by the spot four times yesterday, scouring the doorways and the dumpsters, while fear sped through us.

Two buildings towered on either side, both going up four floors. One was apartments and the other an office building. I barely had time to put the Pathfinder in Park before Rory was climbing out.

Instead of looking at the ground, searching for his phone as River and I had, Rory had her head turned upward. She jogged along the apartment building to where a fire escape wound down, the bottom rung hanging several feet off the ground.

"Give me a boost," she said. I simply raised a brow. "Monte's tall, right? Taller than me by at least a couple of inches. I bet he could have reached that bottom rung no problem."

I understood where she was going and gripped her waist, lifting her. She was such a force of nature that I expected her to be heavier than she was. Instead, even with her lean muscles, she was light and easy to maneuver. My skin burned every place we touched, the heat of her soaking into me, speeding through me like aftershocks.

Our gazes locked for a long beat, then she grabbed hold of the rung on the bottom of the escape and hauled herself up. I waited until she'd reached the first landing, and then followed her. As we wound upward, she checked each of the windows, but they were locked. At the top, we pulled ourselves onto the roof. The wind whipped against us, colder than it had felt down between the buildings.

Above us, the puffy white clouds that had led us into D.C. had been replaced with dark gray ones. The air seemed to crackle with the strength of the oncoming storm. I almost expected a tornado to be forming off to the right.

Chasing them back in the Midwest had always come with a wild risk. There'd been a thrill to it, standing on the edge of something large and untamable, and that wildness seemed to surround us now. A promise of violence hovered about us that threatened lives and limbs.

Damn if I'd let it take my brother's.

Rory moved away from me, ducking into the dark spaces between the equipment boxes and ventilation shafts. She came around the corner with a blanket and a bag of Mother's Circus Animal cookies in her hand.

I jogged over to her, touching the blanket. We had one just like it. Green and red plaid. A Christmas blanket that had been in our family for almost as long as I could remember but that was rarely used. I wouldn't have missed it for weeks or months.

I grabbed the bag of cookies, but even before I opened

it, I knew what I'd see—all the pink cookies had been left behind. My heart spasmed. A rush of tears hit my eyes, and I had to swallow hard to keep it all inside.

"He was coming home," I told her over a lump in my throat. She raised her brows in question. "He left all the pink ones for Ivy."

I handed the bag back to her, and she looked inside. Emotions ran over her face.

I rounded the corner where she'd come from. "Where was all of this?"

She pointed to a nook between one of the air ventilation shafts and the backside of the rooftop entrance to the building. He'd been camped out there, maybe planning to go back to the Capitol today, just like she'd said.

Had he woken up screaming? Had he had vision after vision and been huddled there alone? My heart couldn't take it. I thought I might throw up. I leaned my palm against the brick wall with my eyes closed, trying to get control over my trembling body.

Two arms surrounded me from behind. Soft and strong. Muscled and gentle. The heat of her mixed with a well of sorrow, bleeding into me.

"He was smart enough to get out of sight, Gage. Maybe we just missed him, and he's gone back to Dunn's office. The pain and fear Ivy felt could be for a hundred different reasons. Maybe when he tried to jump down from the fire escape to the ground, he fell wrong. Or he was sore from huddling all night on the cold cement."

I turned my head toward her voice, looking over my shoulder and finding her eyes watching me. "You believe us. About the visions. About Ivy's abilities."

She swallowed hard, and I read the doubts that still lingered there. "I believe you believe it."

My chest took another nosedive off a cliff.

I desperately wanted this woman—because that's all I could see her as now—to believe the truth of us. For some inexplicable reason, it felt like Rory believing us was the difference between finding Monte and not… of having my family whole again or not. What would it be like if we forever had someone like Rory on our side? Not just for Monte's sake… but for mine.

I swallowed hard again, twisting in her arms, so our fronts were touching. The swell of her breasts in that damn purple sweater brushed against my chest in nothing but a T-shirt. The fierce chemical reaction drifting between us was as strong as the electricity in the thunderclouds above us.

If we'd been there for any reason other than searching for my brother, I would have let the view of D.C. and the tempestuous energy of the storm pull us into a heated embrace. I would have kissed her until she had no other choice but to believe me. Until there was nothing but desire and passion in the air.

Her dark lashes lifted, and those amber eyes hit me. The tiny green rays around her pupils were a shimmering eclipse, as if hiding the truth of her just like her dark and edgy outfits obscured the softness underneath. The little girl who'd thought she'd broken her family was trying to be tough and emotionless when really she was swimming in them.

"I've never lied to you," I said, my voice low and rough. "Not when we were teens and not now. Why would I make any of this up? Why would Monte?"

My heart pounded as those all-seeing eyes stared into me. Reading me. Uncovering my truths just like I was uncovering hers.

"You're right. You wouldn't," she said softly.

My cracked and bleeding heart felt like it was wrapped momentarily in cotton gauze. As if she had the power to heal it. But it was there for only a mere second before she pulled herself away from me.

I cursed myself silently for multiple reasons.

For thinking, even for half a second, of spreading my burden onto hers. For getting lost in Rory for a heartbeat. My brother was missing, and I was thinking of the heaviness of my burdens and the way my body felt aligned with hers, proving I was more fucked up than I'd ever thought.

She held her phone up, waving it around as if trying to get a signal.

"What are you doing?" I asked.

"Trying to pick up RF signals."

I raised a brow.

"Some cameras put out a radio signal. If anyone is using one nearby, I might be able to tap into them."

She stopped, pointing at the office building next door.

"I need my computer."

She all but vaulted over the wall, booted feet banging on the metal of the fire escape. Once again, she left me jogging to catch up. Rory moved as if she were in a race. Like I should have been moving all along. Time was everything with my brother missing.

She was at the back of the Pathfinder with her hand out, waiting for the key fob in my pocket by the time I caught up.

"No lock picking?" I said as I handed the keys over.

"I could, but I didn't bring the right equipment with me today."

I'd been joking, but she hadn't even noticed.

She pulled her bag from the back, stuffed her gun into her waistband, and dragged her sweater over the top of it with an ease that proved once again that this was her reality. I wasn't sure I'd ever stop being surprised by it.

She climbed into the passenger seat and pulled her laptop out.

"Do you have a concealed weapons permit?" I asked, joining her inside the vehicle.

She barely glanced my way, fingers flying over the keys.

"Yes."

"So you know how to use that gun?"

She huffed as if I'd insulted her. "Yes. I've been shooting almost since I could walk. Both my parents trained me."

"It doesn't seem like your dad wants you doing this even though he was the one to bring you into it. Why?"

She didn't look up as she talked to me, just kept hammering away at her keys. "I think the black eye and broken rib I got my junior year in high school finally pushed him over the edge."

"What?" My voice was a low growl, thinking of teen Rory beaten up.

"There was a kid selling drugs in school. Steroids to jocks. ADHD meds to the A students. Recreational stuff to anyone who wanted to party. He was a meat hook of a guy. Beefy. On roids himself. I was taping a deal going down in the guy's bathroom, and my stupid uniform shoes slipped on the toilet seat. When the guy tried to stop me from getting out the door, I took a couple of hits before I incapacitated him with my stun gun."

She said it like it was nothing. Like every teenager in high school filmed drug deals and took down the ringleaders by zapping them. I stared for a moment. Not sure what I felt. Awe. Fear. Pride. What had her parents felt? The same? Worse?

She looked up, caught the mix of emotions on my face, and hers turned stoic before she turned back to her computer. "I was fine. Really. If you're going to be in this game, you're going to take a couple of hits. Dad just forgets that because he has employees who do all the street work for him. The school wanted to expel me, but Mom used some inside information she had on the principal to reduce my sentence to a week of suspension. Dad and Mom fought about it. The ugliest argument I'd heard since the divorce. She blamed him for starting me on this path, and he blamed her for letting me work for her while watching too much *Veronica Mars*. Sometimes, I think she trained me just to spite him. To prove she could do a better job than he had."

Rory shrugged as if it was nothing, never looking up from whatever she was doing on her computer. But I knew the truth. After all these years, I could still see the real Rory. She was paying penance for a sin she perceived was hers—the divorce—and demanding perfection of herself to try and earn her parents' respect and her father's love. To try and fix what she thought she'd broken.

Rory shut her laptop and looked over. "I need inside the office building."

She opened the door and looked back at me as I opened mine. She shook her head. "No. Find a place to park. We don't want to draw unwanted attention from a patrol car by sitting in the alley. Text me your location, and I'll meet you when I'm done tapping into the building's cameras."

My jaw flexed. So many things about what she'd just said were wrong. The idea of leaving her on her own while she snuck in to tap video feeds. The legality of it. The danger of it. Seeing this side of her made me feel both protective and proud. Made me want to stand up and give her an ovation while also pulling her close and using my body as a shield.

She must have felt my hesitation because she lifted a brow, lips quirking. "Honestly, Gage, it'll go much faster without you. No one will even know I've been there. You, on the other hand"—she waved her hand up and down my body—"no one is going to miss you. And then they'll be chatting about you tonight over drinks with their friends. The hot guy who popped by the office."

My eyes narrowed. "And you think you're what? Invisible? I hate to break it to you, Pipsqueak, but no one on Earth would be able to forget you."

My words legitimately seemed to surprise her, and I couldn't understand why. Guys had to have been jumping over each other to earn a spot at her side in high school. And college guys? Her sexy, edgy attitude had to have called to them. She was the opposite of invisible. Power and confidence radiated from her.

"Believe it or not, being invisible is one of my specialties. I know how to blend in and go unnoticed when called for, what to say to charm information out of people, and how to get what I need from just about any electronic device there is."

Someone other than me might have taken her words as a brag, but I knew she hadn't intended them that way. To her, she was just stating the facts. She did this job, and she was damn good at it. Not only good, but proud of it. She loved it.

It felt like a lifetime had passed since I'd done something I loved.

The first drop of rain hit the windshield as if taunting me.

She swirled on her foot, slamming the door behind her, and took off around the corner of the building. I put the car in gear and punched the gas, heading back toward the street, looking for an indoor garage not far from our location, and hoping Monte wasn't stuck outside in what was going to become a deluge.

Hoping Rory would get in and get out safely with information we could use to find my brother.

Chapter Seventeen

Rory

EYES OPEN

Performed by Taylor Swift

The first drops of rain splashed against my face as I ducked into the lobby of the office building. A handful of people were inside. Some waited on the couches placed in a square in front of the reception desk while others headed toward the elevator banks farther back.

The building was a combination of neoclassical columns and modern steel and glass as if it didn't know which era it belonged to. I'd pulled up the blueprint while sitting in Gage's SUV. There was a limited security office in the basement. The owner of the building obviously expected his renters to pay for their own if they needed additional protection. The lobby didn't even have a guard, just a receptionist.

I found the door to the emergency stairwell and traveled down the concrete steps until I hit the bricked hallway in the building's service area. I pulled a lanyard with a badge hanging off it from my bag, slid it over my neck so that the badge faced toward my chest, white back outward, and opened the door to the security office.

One man sat inside at a desk with a half dozen monitors. He wasn't much older than me and wore the uniform of a company I'd encountered before. They were hardly considered top of the line.

"Hi. Here to remove the malware Tommy found yesterday," I told him, stepping with confidence over to the computers running below the video feeds. I'd set my laptop down, pulled out my cables, and hooked them up before he even responded.

"I didn't hear anything about malware."

I didn't look up at him but knew there'd be a small frown on his face.

"No? Messed things up over at Wyatt and Schueller so bad they couldn't get the cameras working for two days," I said, dropping the name of the law office I knew his company protected.

I could feel the guy watching me, but he never once stopped me from doing my thing.

Five minutes was all it took for me to get inside, plant the backdoor I needed, and get back out. I unhooked the cable, stowed everything in my messenger bag, and stood. "All set."

"That's it?" the guy said, and for the first time, I met his look straight on.

"Simple extraction. But I have six more stops to go."

For a beat, I thought he'd say something, but his eyes drifted to the inverted badge and then back to me. I stepped past him, saying, "Have a good day."

Then, I was out in the hall, letting the door shut with a slight slam behind me as if I was in a hurry. It was amazing how trusting people could be of a young woman who looked and acted like she belonged.

I jogged up the steps, let myself onto the main floor, and slid past the elevator bank heading toward the front. When I glanced up at the shiny, reflective board listing the companies in the building, my feet skidded to a stop.

The logo for one of the three companies I'd researched after finding Mom's drawing in her appointment book stared at me. Confusion ran through my brain as I looked at the Argento Skies, Inc. name next to the logo. This company was supposed to be in Colorado and hadn't listed a D.C. location on its website. Its primary business was cloud seeding and hydrological research, which was especially high in demand out west. The government of Utah was its largest customer, but other states were clamoring for its services as well.

Every instinct shouted at me to run to the fourth floor and demand to know if anyone there had hired my mother. Instead, I took out my phone and was about to snap a photo of the logo when my gaze caught on something behind me in the mirrorlike sign.

A man who'd been walking toward the elevators had stopped to watch me. He was maybe six feet tall but seemed larger due to the breadth of his chest and shoulders. Military-grade boots, black combat pants, and a black jacket clung to his thick wall of muscles. His head was shaved, so there was hardly anything left of his brown hair. He had to be military. Maybe even special forces. He wore aviator glasses inside, and that tickled my alarms as much as the way he'd hesitated on seeing me.

I stepped back pretending to adjust my camera's zoom until I ran straight into him. Phone in hand, finger on the camera button, I whirled around, quickly apologizing while the camera whizzed silently. "Sorry. My fault."

His lips were set in a straight line, and he didn't so much respond as let out an irritated huff. Behind the glasses, I felt him taking in my face, my clothes, the phone in my hand. I lowered it, apologized again, and sidestepped him.

He stared at me for a few more beats before heading toward the elevators. I leaned up against the wall, pretending to text. When he strode inside the car and the doors had whooshed shut, I hustled over, watching until the elevator stopped at the same floor as Argento Skies.

My intuition told me this was important, my gut urging me to press the Up arrow. But I hesitated as turmoil set in. While I was desperate to find out what this man and the company had to do with my mom, I didn't have the time right now. Not if I intended to find Monte before the worst happened. Before the black screen in the Rayburn security room became more significant—if it hadn't already.

Nothing was going to change for Mom right that second whereas minutes mattered for Monte. The best I could do was run this guy's photo through the facial recognition software I'd "inherited" and see what came up.

I strode back to the sign and took a photo just as Gage walked in the front entrance, a black umbrella dripping onto the marble floor. His eyes met mine across the distance, and as I hurried over to him, he lifted his chin in the direction I'd come, asking, "What was that about?"

"A different case," I told him. I patted my messenger bag. "But I'm locked and loaded here. I told you I'd meet you in the car."

"You left without a jacket or an umbrella, and it's raining pretty hard."

He opened the door of the building for me, raising the umbrella and holding it over my head. My feet stalled again, stomach and heart flipping over once more, but this time it was at the sweetness of the gesture.

When was the last time anyone had held an umbrella for me? Maybe not since I'd been a little girl. Nan and Pops had driven into D.C. to pick me up from school so I could stay with them for the weekend while my parents worked some big event. Pops had opened the umbrella as I'd walked out the doors of the posh private school Dad had insisted I attend. It wasn't until later I'd realized it had nothing to do with making sure I had the best education and everything to do with *who* attended the school alongside me.

"Rory?" Gage's concerned voice dragged me from the memory to my feet lodged to the sidewalk as if I'd stepped into wet cement rather than the past.

"Thanks," I said, and we headed down the street toward a parking garage.

I tried to shake off the tender, gentlemanly move, but the way our arms kept brushing as we huddled under the umbrella only sent my body into overdrive. Just like it had when I'd held him in my arms on the rooftop when the need to comfort him had taken over any other thought. My heartbeat banged wildly, louder and harder than it had while sneaking into the control room or taking pictures of a suspicious man.

What I felt for Gage was stronger than anything I'd ever experienced. That all-consuming flame I'd felt burning as a teen was threatening to spiral out of control. But neither of us could afford for me to let it because the cost of a mistake now would be too great, and I refused to be the reason Gage lost his brother.

Inside the garage, he pulled the umbrella down, shaking it off, and I put more space between us. If he noticed, he didn't say anything. But then again, I was sure all he was really focused on was his missing brother. I was the one who needed to pull her shit together and stay focused.

The car smelled of rain and damp and Gage. It reminded me of autumn days. Of spice and falling leaves… Home.

I swallowed hard, propped my laptop on my knees, and opened the backdoor I'd just put in place on the server. I swiped through different cameras, finally finding the one on the side of the building overlooking the alley. It was an older system and the camera was somewhere in the scrollwork on the roof, which meant it was neither a great angle nor very clear.

I rewound the footage until I could start it close to the time Monte had left the Capitol on Friday, and then hit Play at four times speed. Nothing out of the ordinary appeared at first. A garbage truck emptying the dumpster, a few vehicles, and several people in suits using the alley as a shortcut. The sun went down, making the footage even more difficult to decipher. Then, a shadowy figure appeared that could possibly have been Monte.

Gage inhaled sharply as I slowed the speed back down.

We watched as Monte did exactly what I'd thought,

jumping up to grab the last rung on the fire escape. He moved upward, checking the windows on each landing just as we had. The camera lost him before he pulled himself up on the roof, but it was obvious that was what had happened.

I repeated the process, speeding up the video and slowing down whenever Monte came into view. We watched him come and go a couple of times during the day on Saturday.

A twisted hope rose in my chest that his phone had just run out of battery. That we'd see him climbing down from the rooftop again this morning and we'd be able to pick him up on other street cams I could tap.

But then, late on Saturday, the worst happened.

It was dark again as Monte walked back into the alley with a fast-food bag in hand. Two men in ski masks jumped him from behind, throwing a hood over his face.

Fear and anger rolled through me as Gage growled out an anguished "Fuck."

We watched Monte struggle with his assailants. He nailed them with his elbow and fists, but they were two large, muscular men and he was just a teen boy. They had him subdued with his arms zip-tied behind his back in under a minute. A dark sedan skidded into the alley, and they tossed him into the trunk. The men glanced around to make sure no one had witnessed the kidnapping, picked up Monte's fallen backpack and food bag, and took both with them into the car before speeding off.

"Fuck! Fuck! Fuck!" Gage hit the steering wheel over and over again.

My heart tore apart at the pure torture in his voice. His body was tightly coiled. His jaw clenched. He pushed the heels of his hands into his eyes, fighting tears that flooded mine.

I shouldn't have felt this much for him or Monte. They weren't my family. They were people I'd known for a handful of days once upon a time. But I did. I felt every ounce of fear and horror and anger that Gage did. The connection I'd always felt for Gage drew me to his emotions, an invisible noose contracting around my heart and lungs.

I swallowed hard, turned back to the video, and squinted at the impossible-to-see driver before attempting to make out the license plate. The footage was so grainy and so dark, the plate was nearly impossible to read. The streetlights barely bled into the alley, turning everything into a hazy, gold-like nightmare. I thought the sedan was gray rather than black, but I couldn't even be sure of that.

"I'll run the video through software to try and clean it up. See if we can get a better view of the plate, but we should take this to Metro PD right away," I said softly.

"I would have brought him, Rory. I would have brought him. He didn't need to do this on his own." Every syllable was a tormented cry.

I set the computer on the floorboard, pulled his hand from his face, and twined my fingers with his. When he turned to me, the agony in his eyes sliced through me like a knife.

"I know this is the worst scenario you wanted to see, Gage. I know it's hard to think of what we saw as being good in any possible way, but it means the police will finally take you seriously. They'll put out an AMBER Alert. They'll be all over it."

"Two days late!" he growled. "Why would those men take him? What could they possibly want?"

A list of things popped into my head. Human trafficking was at the top. But I wouldn't say that to him. Couldn't. And there was still the weird interaction with Dunn and West at the Capitol. The way they'd asked about Gage's mom. The way the screen had gone black when I'd watched the video with Lucidia. Maybe it was nothing more than Dunn not wanting to be tied in any way, shape, or form to a missing kid, especially if he knew the family in some way. But my instincts said somehow this was all tangled together.

"Do you want me to drive?" I asked, squeezing his hand.

Confusion bled through him for a moment, as if he was trying to figure out where he was and what to do next. His grief was so great, it washed out of him in a wave that threatened to pull me under with it.

"Gage, do you want me to drive to the police station?"

His face contorted, and he pulled away from me to slam a fist into the steering wheel a few more times before he turned the ignition over, jammed the gear shift into Reverse, and squealed out of the parking spot.

I wanted to comfort him.

Instead, I did the only thing that would really help. I picked up my computer and tried to find street cameras or store footage from the same time as the kidnapping. I needed a better look at the vehicle, its driver, and the two thugs. Maybe they would have removed their masks and we'd get an I.D. It was the only hope I had left.

Chapter Eighteen

Gage

SAFE & SOUND

Performed by Taylor Swift, with Joy Williams and John Paul White

My chest felt like it was cracked open and bleeding out. I was trying, and failing, to get my emotions in check. I was fearful Ivy would sense them as she usually did. It was never the good stuff she felt. Never the joy or love. She always latched on to the dark emotions. And right now, I was feeling so many it was hard to keep up. Anger at myself. Frustration with Monte for coming by himself. Hatred for the men who'd taken him. I wanted to destroy them. I wanted to pull them apart limb by limb for taking a sweet kid off the street just because they saw an opening.

It had been over forty hours since they'd taken him. Forty. Fucking. Hours. The trail had gone cold already. No one had believed me, and now my brother was gone.

My lungs compressed so tightly it was hard to inhale. I forced myself to take a ragged gasp of air. The last thing I needed to do was pass out and crash the car. Then, no one would ever know what Rory had found.

Rory. We never would have gotten this without her.

Gratitude wormed through the agony.

"Thank you," I said. It didn't sound like I was grateful. It sounded like I felt—angry and raw and broken.

"We're going to find him, Gage."

Her voice was full of confidence, but I wasn't sure I could believe it.

All I felt was pure panic and fury.

I parked along the curb outside the Metropolitan Police headquarters and stormed through the doors. As I stalked toward the elevator, Rory tugged my arm as if to slow me down, and I looked at her, confused.

"Gage. Listen to me. You're pissed off and scared and I get it. But you've got to calm down or you'll alienate them. Or worse, they'll put you in cuffs because you're tossing one of them around."

My jaw clenched tightly as her words settled in my chest. She was right. The way I felt… I wanted to slam every cop I'd talked to against a wall for not believing me. I wanted to take my anger—and yes, fear—out on someone. Anyone.

My nails bit into my hands as waves of emotions moved through my body. The only way to help Monte now was by getting my shit together. I took another deep breath, and then opened my eyes to find her watching me. It was a strange comfort. Her being there. Helping.

Unable to respond over the lump in my throat, I simply nodded.

When the elevator opened, there was a different officer at the front desk than the one who'd taken River and me to the Youth and Preventive Services Division last night. As I approached, I struggled to get the words out, "My brother has been kidnapped. I filed a report with Detective Bradshaw last night. I need to talk to him."

"Monte Palmer?" the officer asked, her eyes going wide, gaze drifting between me and Rory and then toward the back.

"Yes."

"Wait right here," she said, and then headed back into the warren of desks.

I gripped the edge of the counter so tightly I thought I

might break it or my fingers in the process. Rory's soft palm settled over my hand, slowly pulling it away from the desk and squeezing.

"Breathe," she said.

I kept forgetting to do that. The simple action of inhaling and exhaling.

Every nerve. Every muscle. Every organ was wound tight.

Full of terror.

What were they doing to him? Was he hurting? Right now?

God. Please let him be okay.

The glass door opened, and the detective from the night before walked out. He was a large man with dark brown skin, buzzed hair, and a neck the size of a defensive linebacker. His brows were drawn together in a frown.

"I was just about to call you. How did—"

"We have video of him being kidnapped," I barked. "Is that fucking good enough for an AMBER Alert?"

The detective's eyes widened. "Monte—"

"Two guys in masks stuffed him in a goddamn trunk." Every ounce of disgust I had for myself and for their lack of interest in my brother was twisted with the fury that raged through me.

"Mr. Palmer. Your brother is here."

It took way too long for me to register his words. It was Rory's surprised voice that finally clicked them into place.

"What? He's here?"

The detective raised his brows and nodded. "Walked in about twenty minutes ago."

Goose bumps littered my skin as a wave of shock washed over me. Every thread of tension in my being let go at the same time. My legs wobbled, and I would have hit the floor if I hadn't grabbed the counter just as Rory slid an arm around my waist. How could someone so small have so much strength?

"Jesus…" The word slipped out. Tortured relief.

"Let's get the two of you reunited, and then we can get everyone caught up. If you have a tape of the kidnapping, it will help considerably," the detective said.

He held the glass door open. I stared at it for a moment, took an unstable step and then another, all the while being buoyed up by Rory.

Bradshaw led us down a bland, white hallway. He paused outside a door, looking down at Rory. "I think it's better if it's just Mr. Palmer at the moment."

I felt Rory nod against me and then she stepped away, causing my unsteady legs to waver. I willed my body to behave, forcing myself through the door the detective held open.

Nothing about the room registered except my brother.

His freckled face was dirty and tear-streaked, and his hair was a wild mess of short curls sticking up in all directions. His clothes were filthy, but it was the sadness in his eyes that really held me.

We both moved at the same time until I finally had him in my arms.

I squeezed him as tears rushed down my face. He held on to me with a death grip. His face shoved into my shoulder blades, sobs racking his body. My tough brother, dissolving. But I was right there along with him.

"Thank God, Monte. Thank God!" I said into his hair. He smelled like sweat and fear as we clung to each other.

"I'm so s-s-sorry," Monte mumbled. "I—"

"Shh. It's okay. You're safe now. I got you. I got you."

We stood like that for an eternity. After seeing that video, I'd lived the worst handful of minutes of my life. Worse than realizing he was missing the first time because even then there had been hope… hope that he was doing all of this on his own and would show back up. And then the video had ripped that possibility away. On the drive to the station, I'd been tormented by images of him dead… pale… and cold. The same wax mannequin our father had appeared in his casket. I'd been plagued with thoughts of all the awful things that could be done to a human body and the even worse things that could be done to a human soul. What had they done to him in those forty hours? God… I needed to know and yet I didn't want to. I just wanted him to be okay. To be alive and okay. To be able to recover from this.

What if he never did?

I was jumping too far ahead. Too far. All that mattered at the moment was him being here. I was holding him, and I wasn't ever going to fucking let him go.

The detective cleared his throat. "I'll give the two of you a moment. Then we'll try to put together the pieces and see what we can do to find these bastards."

He closed the door, and I squeezed Monte even tighter. He hugged me back, equally fierce. Like he had when he was little, and he'd had the first horrible vision after Dad died. He'd crawled into bed with me and held on just like this. As if his world had ended all over again.

"It's going to be okay. You're alive. You're here. Everything else can be fixed."

It was a lie. We both knew it, but he sobbed again and sagged into me.

These days the world tried to make teenagers into mini adults while at the same time holding them back from true responsibility. It was a strange dichotomy, and my brother, seeing me pick up the pieces Dad and Demi had left behind, had tried to shoulder some of those responsibilities. Tried to become a man before he should. But now, with him struggling to control his tears, it was just like holding Ivy when she'd gotten hurt or had a nightmare. He was still a kid. Still needed protection and consolation and love.

Monte took a step away and wiped his face on a dirty sleeve. But he wouldn't look at me, and that twisted my insides right back up. Was it shame? What the fuck had they done to him?

My hand went to his chin, pushing it up until he was forced to meet my gaze. I scoured his face for the truth. His eyes were enormous, fear still lingering there, but also guilt. His cheek was bruised and his hands were wrapped in gauze, but what really caused terror to grow inside me was the parts of him I couldn't see. How bad was the damage?

"Monte…" I took a breath. Not wanting to ask, knowing that once the truth was spoken, I'd never be able to go back. But fuck, he'd lived it. I could at least hear it. I could at least be there to listen. "Did they…" My voice died away.

He shook his head. "No. I mean… they roughed me up a bit, but mostly because I wouldn't stop fighting them. They told me if I stopped, no one would hurt me."

Goose bumps littered my skin again. Thank God for small favors.

"Why are your hands wrapped? Where else are you hurt?"

"I think I might have a broken rib or two." He lifted his shirt, and anger raged through me at the black-and-blue marks along his side. "My hands are fucked up because I was digging at the concrete of the basement trying to find a way out."

Shit. He'd been alone. Afraid. Trying to find a way out.

I pulled him to me again. "You're safe now. But we need to get you to the hospital."

He pushed back. "I just want to get this over with." He waved a hand at the room, and I realized for the first time we were in an interrogation room. Metal table screwed to the floor, heavy metal chairs, a two-way mirror, and a video camera rolling in the corner. What the fuck? They were interrogating him?

I stalked over and yanked at the half-propped open door. Detective Bradshaw was leaning up against the opposite wall. He stepped forward once he saw me.

"You're interrogating him?" I demanded.

His eyes widened, and he shook his head. "No. Not at all. We were just keeping him somewhere safe until we could get you here."

I realized Rory wasn't there with him, and my heart lurched. Ever since she'd shown up this morning, I'd felt like I wasn't alone. Like somehow, I was stronger than I'd been before. The thought of her leaving now that we'd found Monte caused my gut to twist all over again.

Seeing me search for her, Bradshaw said, "Rory went down to the lab with one of my guys. She's working on the video with them, seeing if we can enhance the license plate on the vehicle."

I let go of another held breath.

The detective motioned to the room behind me, and I stepped back inside. He followed me in. Monte was sitting at the table, drinking from a supersized water bottle. Sandwich wrappers lay on the table, and for the first time, I was grateful for the detective. He'd at least fed him.

"My brother needs a hospital," I said.

"We were taking him there, but he refused to go until you showed up."

"I just want to get all this over with. Go home," Monte said, wiping his face again. His sweatshirt was so filthy, it didn't do anything but smear the dirt around.

The detective dropped into a seat on the opposite side of my brother, and I took the chair next to him.

"You came to D.C. to talk to someone on the Hill?"

Monte twisted one of the wrappers in his hand. "I wanted to talk to—"

"Someone about the mass shootings and gun violence," I cut in. I didn't look at my brother. I kept my eyes on the detective. I couldn't have Monte telling this man about his visions. If he did—even with the proof that he'd been kidnapped—they might just think it was all a big hoax.

The detective was a smart guy, so he knew I'd stopped my brother from saying something important. His eyes narrowed a bit, but he let it go as he asked, "Who'd you speak to?"

"Congressman Dunn," Monte said. "And that guy who helps him. West?" He shrugged. "They didn't really want to hear what I had to say."

"But you stayed in town anyway?" Detective Bradshaw probed.

Monte shook his head, finger running along the table. "It was stupid…"

Guilt and shame seemed to bleed from him. I dragged his chair closer to me and wrapped an arm around his shoulder. "It wasn't stupid, Monte. You wanted to make a difference. That's okay. But you should have trusted me to help you."

Monte's eyes turned wide. "I didn't want you involved. Not after…" he trailed off, looking at the detective.

"After your brother was investigated for being behind the Philly train bombing?" Bradshaw offered up.

It pissed me off all over again. The fact the FBI had suspected me just because we'd tried to warn them. The fact that this detective might have used the train derailment against me when I'd reported Monte missing last night. As if it was a reason my brother might have run away.

But losing my temper wouldn't help our cause. Like Rory had said, I had to keep it together so I didn't alienate them. So they didn't just let the men who'd taken my brother get away with it.

Chapter Nineteen

Gage

WHEN THE CHILDREN CRY
Performed by White Lion

Monte pulled away from me, indignant at the detective's insinuation about the bombing. "My brother is the best human being on this planet. They had no right!"

"What happened to Monte this weekend has nothing to do with the past," I grunted out.

The detective glanced at me and then turned back to Monte. "Where'd you stay Friday night?"

"I holed up on a rooftop. I thought I might be able to see Dunn again over the weekend, but he never showed up. I had to stay. I had to get his attention," Monte said, shoulders slouching.

"So you went back to the Capitol on Saturday?"

Monte nodded. "A couple of times. And to that building on Independence. You know, where his office is at."

"When did the men take you?"

"I'd gone to the fast-food joint around the corner to use the restroom and grab some food around eight or so on Saturday night. It was dark, but I'd never really been scared before, you know. There weren't many people in the alley and the rooftop had been quiet..."

He trailed off, and my heart lunged.

"They must have been waiting for me because they

came out of the shadows as soon as I rounded the corner. I fought…" Monte looked up at me, eyes full of anger and indignation. "I fought, Gage. I swear…"

Another sob choked him.

"Listen to me," I said, squeezing his shoulder. "You did nothing wrong. You have nothing to be ashamed about, Monte. Nothing."

He wiped his face again.

"What can you tell us about the assailants?" Bradshaw asked.

"They were big. Like as big as Gage. Black masks. They both had dark eyes, or I couldn't see any other color in the dark. Black clothes. One of them had a gun, but he never pulled it until we were going down the stairs into a basement and I wouldn't stop fighting."

"How long were you in the car until you reached the location where you were held?"

Monte shrugged. "I don't know. Not long. It felt like maybe fifteen minutes. I couldn't see, but I kept searching until I found the child safety handle in the trunk, but they'd disabled it or something because it wouldn't pop open."

I was so proud of my brother for thinking of those things. Fighting. Trying to get away. But I was also furious that he'd had to do any of it.

"When they pulled me out of the trunk, I could hear water splashing and smelled the river, you know. Like it was close? The ground was blacktop, or at least it wasn't dirt. It was hard. The door they opened sounded metallic, like a roll-up door. We went down steep stairs, and it was cold and damp, so I assumed it was a basement. I struggled with them on the steps… I didn't want to go down. I thought… I thought they were going to kill me. And when they yanked the hood off and shoved a gun in my face, I r-r-really thought it was o-o-over."

God damn it. I could feel his fear wafting off him, and it made me want to strangle the men who'd taken him all over again. It also meant Ivy was probably frantic. But I couldn't call the day care center. Not yet.

"Were they still wearing masks?" the detective asked.

Monte nodded. "Every time I saw them, they wore them. Once they got me down into the basement, they zip-tied me to some old pipes. One of them came down later and brought some water. But I was afraid to drink it. I didn't know if it was drugged… I didn't want to sleep in case…"

His cheeks turned a furious shade of red, and it magnified the discoloration there. My fingertips bit into my arms so hard I thought I'd leave marks.

"They ever say what they wanted?"

Monte's eyes shifted to look at me, and he adjusted himself in his seat. He shook his head.

Being the smart guy he was, the detective read the hesitancy.

"Look. If we're going to catch these guys, we need to know what they wanted. Where they were at. How you got away. If you aren't honest with us, it limits our chances."

"They asked what I'd talked to the congressman about," Monte said.

Detective Bradshaw's eyes flickered. "They asked about school shootings and gun violence?" he asked, disbelief filling his voice.

Monte nodded.

"And you don't know Dunn otherwise?"

Monte shook his head. The detective looked at me.

I raised a brow, adding my voice to my brother's. "We don't know the congressman."

That settled for a beat between us before Bradshaw asked, "That's all they wanted to know? What you'd wanted with the congressman? They held you for a day and a half, and that's it?"

"Th-they recorded me."

My stomach flipped, and even Bradshaw's jaded eyes

turned worried. "Recorded you how?"

Monte shook his head, disgust in his voice. "Not like that. Maybe an hour or two after they brought me down, they came back with a video camera. They had me repeat what I'd told Dunn. That was it. I didn't see any of them after that. I tried to dig my way out, tried to break the zip ties…"

He rubbed his wrists, and for the first time, I saw the torn skin there. More fury roared through me. I was going to kill these men. I was going to end them.

"So, after they recorded you, you saw no one? They just left you alone? But you told me earlier they dropped you off."

Monte swallowed hard and nodded. "Yeah. An hour or so before I got here. They came down. I could tell they were upset. Pissed about something. They were arguing and whispering in both Spanish and English. I heard them say they didn't like the idea of letting me go. One of them had a knife, and I thought I was going to die all over again, but then he cut the zip ties. The other one aimed a gun at me and told me to go up the stairs. Before I stepped through the door, they put a hood over my head again and had me climb into the trunk. When they stopped the car, they told me to count to fifty before I took the hood off or they'd shoot me. When I finally did, I was in the alley across from the police station. I ran as fast as I could here."

"We pulled the street cams," the detective said. "We got a shot of a sedan that matches the description of the one on the video your friend brought in. No license plate, and we weren't able to get a clear view of their faces. The alley where they let you out doesn't have any cameras."

Silence settled, and I could feel my brother shaking next to me as he relived the experience. I hated it. I hated everything about this moment.

"They took a big risk letting you go," Bradshaw said. "I don't get it. Why take you, ask you about school shootings and Dunn, and then just let you go?"

His question sank into me, and a realization hit. They'd

let Monte go after Rory and I had shown up asking about my brother. After she'd already seen the video of him talking with Dunn and they'd erased it. Our poking around had likely freed my brother.

But my relief was quickly followed by fear because they had to know we would put the pieces together. Which was why it didn't make sense that they'd let him go. It would have been cleaner for them to kill him.

That thought tore through me like a knife.

None of it mattered. They'd let him go. He was here. I'd keep him safe.

"I don't know why they let me go. I thought… I thought they were going to kill me, you know? I thought…" Monte's breath was uneven, and he put his face in his hands, another giant sob racking him.

"I think we're done here," I said, standing. "I want to take my brother to the hospital and get him home. He's been through enough."

Detective Bradshaw stood. "I'd like to talk to Gage outside for a second before we send you both on your way."

I rubbed Monte's back gently. "I'll be right back. We're leaving. I promise."

Monte put his arms on the table, resting his face on top, eyes closed. My heart bled out just looking at him. He was exhausted and frightened and drained. I wanted to wrap him in a hug and get him the hell out of there.

Outside the door, I crossed my arms over my chest, wondering which part of the story the detective was going to pick apart the most. There was no way we could tell him the truth, and I knew, just like he said, it would hurt their chances of catching these bastards. Then, Rory's face popped into my head. Maybe we could still figure out what happened, with or without the police. I was pretty sure she'd continue to help us.

"What aren't you telling me?" Bradshaw demanded.

I just stared at him. Lying wouldn't help. He already

knew we were holding back.

He let out a frustrated exhale. "Whatever you're mixed up in, whatever brought trouble to your brother's door, it isn't going to go away. I can't help unless I know the truth."

"I don't know why they wanted my brother, Detective. Isn't it your job to figure it out?"

"You know what I find the most confusing about all of this?"

"I'm sure you're going to tell me."

"Why Congressman Dunn? I mean, he's not from Virginia. He doesn't have an anti-gun platform, but he also doesn't take money from the NRA. His stance on gun bills has been decidedly neutral. So… why him?"

My teeth slid against each other as my jaw flexed. I turned away from him, grabbing the handle on the door, ready to get my brother and get the hell out of there. But his next question hit me like an ice storm, freezing me to my bones.

"Where's your mom these days?"

I shot him a look over my shoulder. "Don't know. Don't care."

"I read the missing person reports you and your dad filed. Talked to a Detective Muloney out in Cherry Bay. He says your mom runs away a lot. Makes me wonder, did she run here? To someone? Does she know Dunn?"

My insides flipped over as, for the second time that day, I was faced with the same question. "I have no idea, Detective. Demi never shared what she did while she was gone, and we haven't seen her in nearly three years. My dad isn't around for her to wheedle her way in anymore, so I don't think she'll be back. I won't have the same empathy for her that he did. Not after she stole money from us when we needed it for food and electricity. If I never see her again, it will still be too soon."

I didn't wait for him to respond. I opened the door and motioned for Monte to come on out. The chair scraped back against the concrete floor, and he walked over to me, shoulders slumped, one arm cradling his bruised side.

"Do you have your backpack?"

Monte shook his head. "They never gave it back."

I put my arm around him and led him toward the exit.

Bradshaw followed us, his words hitting me as the glass door opened. "We'll keep you posted, but I'm not hopeful we'll find anything with the limited information you've provided us."

It pissed me off. I left Monte standing by the counter, swung the glass door shut so my brother wouldn't hear me, and stepped close to the officer. He didn't back away. I wouldn't expect him to. After all, I was the one who would be fucked if anything went down between us.

"Trust me, Detective, I know how little you'll do. We've lived it our entire lives. So just go ahead and wash your hands of the Palmer family. That's what every officer before you has done."

He had the grace to look the teeniest bit chagrined. Good. The Palmers may not have had a reason to hate the authorities like River and Audrey did, but we had enough reason to distrust them. To have no faith in them doing anything for us.

I left Bradshaw standing there to go back to Monte, guiding him into the elevator and out of the station toward the SUV. Monte went to get in the passenger seat, but I motioned for the back. "Lie down. It'll be easier on your ribs. We'll leave as soon as Rory gets here."

"Rory? Like… Rory from when I was little, Rory?" he asked, climbing in the back and slouching along the seat.

"You might not remember, but her mom was a private investigator. Rory works with her now, so I asked her to help find you."

Monte's eyes widened, but he didn't say anything.

I brushed a hand over my face, exhaustion filling me. I couldn't even imagine how Monte felt… and Ivy through him. "What didn't you tell the detective in there, Monte? Was it about Dunn? Rory saw some footage of you on the steps of the Capitol Building with him. He asked you something about Demi, didn't he?"

Monte's eyes closed. "It was so weird, Gage. I told him the truth. Told him it was going to sound crazy, but that I knew someone was going to shoot him. I'd seen it. Knew it was going to happen in a warehouse near the river. Knew it was going to happen soon. He and that West guy… they didn't freak out or scoff. They just shook their heads and moved away, but then he looked back at me, he looked at my hair and my freckles, and he asked if Demi was my mom."

"He knows her." The words slipped out.

Monte nodded but kept his eyes closed. Pain was crawling over his face, and he shifted with a groan, grabbing his side.

"When they came down and recorded me, they wanted me to repeat everything I'd said to Dunn."

"So, whoever took you at least knows him. Or at least overheard what you said." Fuck. What did that mean? Would they just leave it at that… a recording and letting him walk? Or would they be back, looking for more answers?

My eyes went to the doors of the station. No Rory. I pulled my phone out and texted her.

> *ME: We need to go. I have Monte in the car.*
> *Where are you?*

"I think that's why they didn't freak out," Monte said, his voice drained and tired. "They must've heard Demi spout the same kind of bullshit before."

"It's not bullshit. Just because people don't believe it, doesn't make it not true," I growled. Monte was never wrong. The events always went down the way he saw them.

The door of the station finally opened to reveal Rory with her face twisted in irritation. Someone had pissed her off.

"There's Rory."

She started toward the car, pausing to turn back toward the building, shielding her eyes and searching the sidewalks before twirling around and jogging toward the SUV.

Monte inhaled sharply, and I turned in my seat to look at him. His eyes were glued on Rory as he let out a shocked, "Holy shit!"

"What's wrong?" I demanded, pulse ratcheting right back up.

But none of that, nothing that had happened over the last two days would have ever prepared me for the words that came out of my brother's mouth.

"It's been so long since I saw her… And in the vision, I just see her from the back, but Gage, Rory's the one who shoots Dunn."

Chapter Twenty

Rory

CHEMICALS REACT
Performed by Aly & AJ

I stormed from the station, pissed that Bradshaw had basically kicked me out of the tech lab. The video I'd given them was still processing, but he was annoyed that Gage and Monte had held back and now he was taking it out on me. He'd basically threatened to blackball me with the entire PD if I didn't tell him what was going on.

When I'd told him I was just hired today and had nothing more to tell him than whatever Gage and Monte already had, he'd snipped back with, "That's interesting since you don't even know what they told me."

And he'd been right. I could have kicked myself for giving him even that. My worry for Gage and Monte had me speaking before thinking. I wasn't sure if it was exhaustion or emotions or just a pile of mistakes, but I needed to pull myself together before I did something really stupid like tell a truth that wasn't mine to share.

My heart skipped a beat… The truth. Somewhere along the way, I'd gone from disbelieving Gage to believing. Maybe it had been when Ivy had sent me her spooky look and said Monte was scared, or seeing Dunn *not* freaking out while Monte told him about a future where he got shot. Or maybe it was simply the connection I'd felt to Gage from the very first time I'd met him. Whatever the reason was, I knew they weren't lying.

My dad would have a field day with this. Forget letting my emotions rule. If he ever found out I believed in visions and psychic connections, it would be all the proof he needed that I wasn't cut out for this work.

As I stomped down the steps, the hair on the back of my neck rose as if I was being watched. I looked back, trying to get a glimpse of whoever it was, expecting Bradshaw or one of his minions. I saw nothing at first, but then from my peripheral I caught sight of a large man in a leather jacket and aviator glasses disappearing around the corner. My pulse sped up. Was it the man from the Argento Skies building?

My instinct was to chase him down, but I couldn't now anymore than I'd been able to follow him into the elevator earlier. Gage's text had practically been vibrating with the urgency to get Monte to the hospital. So, instead of running after the guy like I longed to do, I turned back to Gage's SUV.

As I opened the door, two pairs of eyes met mine. It took me a heartbeat too long to realize the look Gage sent me was one of distrust.

As if I was suddenly the enemy.

My gaze swung from Gage's stormy eyes to Monte. I hadn't seen Monte in person since he was a little kid, but the shape he was in now still tore me up inside. His lids were swollen, a bruise bloomed on his cheek, and dirt covered most of his visible skin. His short, cropped curls were a tangled mess pushed into his head in places and sticking up in others, and his hands were wrapped in gauze.

But none of that shocked me as much as the alarm on his face as he looked at me.

Monte was afraid.

Of me.

What the hell had happened?

I slid into the passenger's seat.

"What's wrong?" I asked.

Silence.

Gage leaned in, frustration emanating from him. "You told me you didn't know Dunn."

My eyes narrowed in confusion. "I don't."

"You know lots of people on the Hill, Rory. I saw it clearly today. You got in and out of there with ease, calling people by their first names and asking about their families. You told me not to lie to you, so don't lie to me either."

"I'm. Not. Lying." I shoved a finger into his chest. "I don't know Dunn. If he'd known me when we showed up today, he would have said something. I know lots of security, so I can get in and out when I need to, but that doesn't mean I know all four hundred and thirty-five representatives personally."

"Then why are you going to—"

A moan from Monte drew our attention to the back seat. The two brothers exchanged another look, and it twisted something in my heart. Whatever had happened—whatever had been said while I'd been gone—Gage had suddenly lost faith in me.

It broke open the scabs covering the wounds from my dad's disappointment that would never fully heal. The look my father had sent me the day my parents had picked me up from the sleepover—this felt the same. Actually worse, because it was Gage and he'd looked at me with hope in his eyes all morning. And now, his bitter disillusionment tore through me.

Why would they think I knew Dunn? Had Bradshaw dropped something along those lines?

Gage leaned back, slammed his seat belt into the latch, and started the car. "I don't have time for this. I need to get Monte to the hospital."

He flipped a U-turn and headed toward East Street.

"Can you make it to the hospital in Cherry Bay?" Gage asked his brother. "I'd prefer to have you close in case they need to keep you."

Monte nodded with his eyes closed and then said softly, "I really just want to go home."

"Soon, bud. Hospital first."

Gage's fingers tightened on the steering wheel, and sadness filled me. Sorrow for whatever had happened to make Gage distrust me but also for Monte. I didn't know what the kidnappers had done to him, but at a minimum, he'd been roughed up pretty good.

The tension in the air was as thick and heavy as the storm outside while we drove. Every time I started to talk, Gage shook his head. But I couldn't stop my mind whirling with questions that needed answers. So, when it looked like Monte had fallen asleep, I leaned in and asked as quietly as possible, "What happened to him? How badly is he hurt?"

Gage knew what I was asking. Just thinking about what might have happened was enough to make me want to throw up. I didn't want to imagine the worst. Couldn't stomach the idea of Monte having lived through hours of abuse. And I didn't want Gage to have had to listen to his brother telling him about what had happened all the while feeling helpless and angry and somehow responsible.

Gage glanced over, and maybe my worry was clear on my face because the tightness on his face eased ever so slightly.

"Nothing like you're thinking. They mostly left him alone, but he fought back pretty hard when they took him, so they beat him up… A fucking kid…" He shook his head, swallowed hard, and continued, "We'll see if he has any broken ribs. Overall, I'd say he was lucky."

"Did anything that happened explain why they'd taken him? What they wanted?"

He shook his head, but he was holding back. His distrust burned deep inside my chest.

"Tell me why you suddenly don't trust me," I demanded.

Barely an hour ago, he'd been sweetly holding an umbrella over me and muttering thanks for helping him find his brother. Now, it was like I was the person who'd kidnapped him.

"Monte's here. You did your job. We can say our goodbyes and leave it at that."

My mouth fell open as the coldness of his words washed over me in brand-new waves of pain. I admired the hell out of Gage. Not just some superhero worship of a teen girl, but a deep respect for how he'd taken responsibility for his family even though it meant crushing his own dreams. Gage losing respect for me, for reasons I didn't even know, was a new nightmare I'd be reliving for months.

I tugged viciously on my sleeves before burying my nails into my palms. I fought to find my voice, bitterness coating the words as I said, "So we say goodbye. Just like that."

His jaw flexed, but I couldn't read his emotions. "Just like that."

Three emotionless words had never stabbed so deep. The careless rejection. The easy toss of me from his life burned like a wildfire.

I'd done nothing to earn this. I should at least have had a chance to defend myself before he decided I was now the villain, and yet it was clear he wouldn't give me the chance.

So, screw him. Screw all the men like my dad, Bradshaw, and Muloney who looked at my five-foot-five frame and thought I was just some little girl playing *Charlie's Angels*.

All my life, my parents had pounded into me that emotions were an investigator's downfall. And yet I'd let myself get caught up in Gage's fear and grief. I'd been sucked right in, putting my heart into it, clinging to memories of a boy I'd once thought I'd loved in that fierce and devoted way of a teenager. Or maybe I'd done it because of the wild attraction simmering between us now. Attraction that still pulsated through the air even with him pulling away from me.

Regardless, I'd broken another cardinal rule of investigators and gotten too involved.

Gage was right. We needed to say goodbye. I was truly happy Monte had been released and seemed to be somewhat okay. But now I needed to focus on *my* family. I needed to figure out how to pay for Mom's facility. I needed to find out the truth about her accident. Those were my priorities. I'd put the Palmers behind me, just like Gage wanted me to.

So why did the idea of walking away from them feel so wrong?

The quiet remained loaded as we made our way to the Cherry Bay hospital. Gage parked outside the emergency room doors, and when I looked across the street to the rehabilitation center, I easily spotted Nan's green Beetle in the lot.

For a few moments today, in the thick of it with Gage, even though everything we'd been doing had been for dark and terrifying reasons, I'd been able to forget about my burdens. I'd been able to concentrate on something besides what waited for me at the end of the day. But now, the heavy weight of my life slammed down on top of me.

Tears pricked my eyes, but I wouldn't cry.

Gage helped Monte out of the back of the Pathfinder, and his brother leaned heavily against him. Gage's strong arms held him up easily. A piece of me yearned for the same thing. Even though I had Nan and Shay who I could count on to always be there, my body craved Gage. Ached for it to be his arms keeping me from falling, shoring me up as the worst came at me.

I pushed aside those ridiculous thoughts. They were just leftover dreams of a disillusioned teen who'd tried to replace a father figure with a new hero.

As they stepped toward the hospital, I called out softly, "I'm sorry this happened to you, Monte. I'm truly glad they let you go, and I hope you'll be okay."

Then I looked at Gage whose eyes still held all those new doubts about me. "I'm going to see my mom. Nan is there"—I pointed across the street—"so I'll catch a ride with her. I wish you both good luck."

I turned and strode away, hating the tiny piece of my heart that waited for him to call me back. To apologize. To say thank you again. Anything that meant there was still something between us besides suspicion.

Chapter Twenty-one

Rory

HAUNTED

Performed by The Guess Who

As I pushed through the doors of the rehabilitation center without Gage's deep voice ever stopping me, my heart sank further into the pit of despair that was now my gut. Tears filled my eyes, but I forced them back.

I raised my chin and stiffened my shoulders. I'd spent a lifetime trying to shake my father's lack of faith in me. I wouldn't spend one more minute on another man who didn't believe in me.

Nan was knitting in Mom's room when I walked in. She did a double take when she saw my face.

"What's wrong?"

I swallowed hard, tucking away my feelings in the way I'd gotten good at, and shook my head. "Nothing. Just working a case."

"You work too hard." Her voice sounded sad.

I squeezed her shoulder before going around to the other side of Mom's bed. I kissed her cheek and picked up her hand, massaging the palm and the fingers. Wishing with all my heart that she'd feel my touch—my love—and wake up. My throat clogged, and those tears that had threatened moments ago swarmed again like a sledgehammer to an already cracking wall I fought to shore up.

"Miss you, Mom," I finally said. "Worked a missing

kid case today. Those are the worst. And the best if it ends up good, right? This one ended well. The family got him back."

"Oh, Rory. No wonder you look like hell," Nan said quietly.

She didn't tell me she hated me working dangerous cases, even though I knew she wasn't overjoyed with the work Mom and I did. I couldn't imagine any parent really wanted to see their kid put themselves in harm's way on purpose. But Nan had never told us we weren't strong enough to do it. Never told me I was too impulsive, too emotional, or made too many mistakes.

She trusted me.

More proof that walking away from the man across the street who'd wheedled back into my heart had been the right thing to do.

Normally, I didn't like to have anger and frustration in me when I visited Mom, and yet I had a hard time shaking both of those emotions. So, when Nan said she was ready to leave after I'd only been there a couple of hours, I walked out with her. Unfortunately, the tension that had begun my day and never really let go stayed with us as Nan drove in silence to The Prince Darian, where I'd left my bike.

"I really think we need to consider the doctors' recommendation." She broke the silence, exhaustion and loss in her voice, but also a resolve that scared me.

"I can't talk about this now!"

"Do you think your mother would want this for you? Buried in work. Spending all your free time with a body that doesn't speak? I want you to have a life, Rory. She would too. She'd hate that you haven't laughed in months. She'd hate that you've practically given up on the FBI and spend your time darting between jobs in order to take care of her. It has to stop. I can't support this decision anymore. She wouldn't want me to. She'd tell me it was selfish to keep her here at the cost of you living the full life she saw for you."

The sledgehammer finally broke through the wall I

hadn't had the time or strength to fix completely. Silent tears hit my cheeks, and I brushed at them furiously. Hating them. Hating the emotions and doubts that swelled with them.

"The decision isn't yours," I finally said, my voice wavering.

"We promised we'd make it together."

"We promised we were on her side!"

"I know she'd want this, Rory. I know it in the way only a mother knows her child."

The strength of the conviction in her voice sent goose bumps over my skin. Doubts pricked inside me. Dark whispers about a truth I couldn't handle and that I had to shut down fast.

Nan pulled up behind my bike. Gage had parked his Pathfinder next to it. Despite everything that had gone down this afternoon, I still longed to know what the doctors had said about Monte's condition. Worse, I wanted to know how Gage was holding up. Was he keeping it together now that he had his brother back, or were the doubts about Dunn and Demi that plagued me tormenting him as well?

"Parents don't always know what's best for their kids," I said.

"Don't start comparing me or your mother to Sutton Bishop."

"Then don't give up on Mom and me like he did."

I could see the hurt in her eyes as if I'd slapped her.

I hated myself a bit.

Hated all of this.

I opened the door, pushed out, and turned to look at her. "I'll see you back at the house."

She didn't say anything, and I just shut the door. She put the Bug into gear and headed out of the lot as I made my way to my bike. I looked up, eyeing the apartment above the bar. The warmth of the lights shimmered against the dark storm clouds. It called to the raw, unprotected slivers of my heart that had been revealed by the wall inside me that had broken.

I craved the coziness of the apartment. The sweetness of the little girl tucked inside. The heat of Gage when our bodies brushed. A part of me wanted to stomp up the stairs, pound on the door, and demand answers to why he'd pushed me away. A part of me wanted to kiss him just to see what he'd do.

But if he didn't trust me, nothing would ever work between us.

I'd known it when I was twelve, and it wasn't any different a decade later. Our lives weren't meant to collide in that way. We were simply ships, stopping for a few minutes in each other's ports. We'd never be the permanent shelter either of us needed.

♫ ♫ ♫

When I got home, Nan was in the kitchen, banging around. I didn't say anything, and I didn't join her. Not because I was throwing some teenager-like tantrum, but because I couldn't risk facing her with my emotions so unprotected.

Instead, I headed to the office and the manila envelope Detective Muloney had sent over this morning before I'd left for Gage's. Inside was a note explaining that he was only giving me the information so I'd see there wasn't much of a trail to follow and to back off and let them do their job. I snorted. I'd stop just like a runaway truck. I was going to tear through every lie and every barricade that got thrown up.

My hands stilled on the photos of the accident scene. Black skid marks led off the pavement and into the brush where she'd gone off the road. Some of the images showed her car partially submerged in the Potomac, the tree ripping through the driver's side. Others showed it after it had been towed back onto the road, the front end decimated.

Bile rose in my throat and my skin crawled.

It was a miracle she'd been pulled out at all.

I pushed my fingers against my eyes, fighting another wave of tears. Trying desperately to stack the bricks up against these raging emotions and failing. A few drops squeezed past, dotting the copies Maloney had sent as if they were the rain pelting the cottage windows.

I inhaled and exhaled slowly, wiping my face and forcing myself to concentrate again on the images. What had Dad seen that had made him think it wasn't an accident?

I shuffled through the stack, assembling the photos in a line as if they were movie stills. Reels frozen in time. The tire marks started pretty far back along the road. Black smudge lines on the dark pavement. I tried to visualize her car in motion. Tried to visualize being at the steering wheel and turning the vehicle in order to make those lines on the road.

And that's when it hit me. The lines were all wrong. Based on the trajectory of the curves, the skid marks should be on the opposite side of the vehicle. The brakes should have applied on the passenger side and not the driver's side. If the wrong set of brakes had engaged, they would have caused her to spin out instead of helping her through the corners. They'd sent her over the cliff instead of toward safety.

Dad was right. Something had gone wrong with her brake system. It would have been nearly impossible to control the car with it acting this way. In the movies, you always saw the bad guys cutting a brake line, but the truth was that modern cars made it almost impossible for a cut line to cause an accident like this. No, the only way to really achieve this kind of accident was to get into the car's computer system. It also meant it would be nearly impossible to track. Had someone put a physical device on the car to hack in? Or had it been done remotely using the manufacturer or the navigation systems?

My simmering anger spiked all over again. Finding answers now would be that much harder. The culprit would have had plenty of time to erase the computer trail he'd left behind. If I'd known the truth, if I'd done *my* job and asked to see the scene, I might have had a better chance.

But my emotions had blocked me. I'd been focused on Mom in the hospital and not how she'd gotten there. I couldn't afford to be blinded anymore. I took another deep breath, closed my eyes, and then turned back to the rest of Muloney's file.

It didn't take long to go through it. The physical file was almost as thin as the online one had been. It included a handwritten note from his talk with the mechanic at the tow yard confirming his suspicions about the brakes failing, and a list of places Mom had been that day.

Muloney had sent the rookie out to interview the attendant at the garage where she'd parked near the Lincoln Memorial and a clerk at the gas station outside D.C. where she'd filled her tank. I hadn't even known she was coming to Cherry Bay that day, just like I hadn't known anything about her meeting with the Space Force guy. Why hadn't she told me? What other secrets had she been keeping?

Sometimes, in order to see what I was missing, I needed a visual image of all the data we'd collected—like putting together a real-life puzzle. I went out to the garage, dug through some of the things from our condo that we hadn't had room for at Nan's, and found an old corkboard I'd had in my bedroom.

Taking it back into the office, I spotted a plate with a grilled cheese sandwich sitting at the edge of the desk. My throat bobbed. Even after our argument, Nan was looking out for me. She wanted what was best for me. I believed that, but there was no way I could choose my life over Mom's. It wasn't going to happen.

I unwrapped the corkboard from its brown paper and stared at the pictures pinned to it—my life on display. There were plenty of photos of Shay and me, and one of a teenaged Gage holding a tiny Monte with me grinning up at him instead of looking at the camera. Other photos showed

Mom, Nan, and me on a trip to the Bahamas after my high school graduation.

My eyes stalled on a lone picture of Dad and me from before the divorce. We were fishing. Except, looking back, I was pretty sure he'd been on a stakeout and had used fishing as an excuse to keep me quiet. There were a lot of good memories reflected here, but they felt shadowed by all the bad that had come later. The divorce. Losing Mom.

My jaw clenched as tears pricked my eyes again. She wasn't lost. Not yet.

I carefully took the photographs down, replacing them with an enlarged map of D.C. that I'd printed over several pages of copy paper. I stuck red push pins into the locations where Mom had been on the day of her accident before adding blue tacks for locations she'd been throughout the week leading up to it.

Cutting out names of people she'd met with, I taped them next to the pins along with a one-sentence summary of her business with them. I also included one-sentence summaries of the interviews the police had done. The biggest question mark was at the Lincoln Memorial.

I had no idea what she'd discussed with the unknown Space Force person, but I included a pin for the Argento Skies building near the Capitol, adding the company's logo to it. Finally, I printed a picture of the man in the building's lobby, noting that there'd been a possible sighting of him at the police station.

After I was done, I stepped back, hoping I'd see a pattern or a glaring hole. Nothing jumped out, but I wasn't discouraged yet. Sometimes it took a day or two for me to see the overlaps. Sometimes it took digging more before it came together.

Tomorrow, I'd head back to D.C. to the Argento Skies office, and see if they'd hired Mom. If they hadn't, then she had to have been researching them for another case. Maybe the Space Force case. I'd pick at that a little bit and see if I could find out who she'd met with.

I also needed to find a way into the companies responsible for the computers in Mom's car. That would take quite a bit of effort as those systems were guarded with serious firewalls. I wasn't in the right frame of mind to do it tonight because if I made a mistake, I'd get caught—possibly arrested—and I certainly couldn't afford that.

I turned back to the computer and the bills waiting for me. The money from the cheater's wife had come in. It would allow me to pay the invoice for Shady Lane this month. But I still had other expenses to pay.

A year ago, I'd planned on being almost two semesters into my master's by the time I applied for the FBI in February. But now I was barely going to have finished my bachelor's, and continuing my education felt like choosing between my future and Mom. I hated the voice at the back of my head whispering Nan was right. That my mother would despise me choosing her over myself.

I straightened my shoulders. I could do both. I could and I would.

What I needed was more money. None of the jobs I'd applied for had responded yet. Not that I'd expected them to with Thanksgiving looming in two days, but waiting added another unknown to the pile of uncertainty sitting on me.

I shut off the light in the office and headed into the bathroom, needing to get rid of the stench of the day. The grief. The sadness. But as the heat pounded on my back and my shoulders relaxed, I was surprised to find tears pouring from my eyes once again. For Mom and Nan. For me. For Monte and what he'd been through. For the guilt I knew Gage was still feeling even though his brother was safely home. I even cried for the loss of my childish attraction to Gage and whatever it was that had started to bloom between us since I'd first seen him on Friday night.

It wasn't until the water turned cold that I stopped crying, but once I did, I felt surprisingly better. As if I'd purged enough dark and ugly from my soul to actually move forward again. Maybe my parents were wrong after all.

Maybe, like Shay was fond of saying, you just needed a good cry once in a while.

I changed into sweats and a T-shirt and climbed into bed, hoping for sleep and knowing it would elude me. It wasn't just Mom's case that hung on me as I stared at the ceiling. My mind whirled with questions about Dunn's and West's strange reactions, the disappearing footage, the men who'd kidnapped Monte, and why they'd let him go.

What haunted me even more was Monte's expression as I got into Gage's car. Why would he be afraid of me when I hadn't seen him since he was a toddler?

My eyes had just started to close when the realization hit me.

I was in his vision! Holy shit. That had to be it.

He'd seen me in the vision of Dunn getting shot.

What had Gage told me about it? Not much. But his words in the Pathfinder were the key. *You told me you didn't know Dunn.*

There was no way I could sleep after that thought registered, so I went back to the computer. This time, I searched Dunn's and West's backgrounds even more thoroughly than I had the day before.

As I picked around the internet, searching for them, I realized someone had done a more than decent job of cleaning up their digital footprints. Some of the sites I normally used to find out about people had been scrubbed clean. An ugly feeling rose in the back of my throat. I recognized this code. I knew it like the back of my hand because my mother had taught it to me… just like she'd taught my dad.

One of them had done this. One of my parents knew Dunn. Worked for him, even.

Dunn wasn't an on-the-book client of Mom's. If she'd worked for him, it had been like she'd been working for the Space Force—without my knowledge. But it was Dad who was better known for cozying up to politicians.

When I'd closed the backdoor into Bishop Investigations, I'd had every intention of never logging in again, but now I had to risk it. It took me a bit longer to break Dad's firewall this time. He'd added extra encryption and a wildly complicated trip wire. But eventually, I got in. And sure enough, there was a file on Representative Roland Dunn. I didn't know him, but Dad did.

A bitter taste filled my mouth as Dad's voice from Friday morning came back to me. He'd been talking to a Roland when I'd walked into his office, hadn't he? What had he said? Something about taking care of it? Having it handled? I hadn't registered it. I'd been too worried about asking for a loan.

Too goddamn emotional.

Dad had placed the files on Roland under extra encryption, and that was even more surprising than the ones at his backdoor. It was going to take me hours of running code to try to break it. Even then, it might be impossible without knowing the key.

My phone buzzed with a call. I glanced over at it with every intention of ignoring whoever it was until I saw Dad's name. Shit. Had I tripped a secondary alarm? Whoever was doing Dad's IT work now was damn good if I hadn't seen it.

> *DAD: If you keep breaking into my system, I'm going to have to start charging you for the information.*

Fuck! I'd back out, but it was pointless now.

> *ME: If I had a dad who was honest with his daughter, I wouldn't have to break in.*

> *DAD: What do you want with Dunn?*

Double fuck. He'd watched every keystroke I'd made.

> *ME: Who's running your coding now?*

> *DAD: The person you misjudged sitting at my front desk.*

Chanel? Chanel in her designer stilettoes and perfect hair was his computer security analyst? My fingers slowed on the keys. I'd thought maybe she was sleeping with my father, not locking down his computers. I *had* misjudged her. I hated that almost as much as I hated that I'd tripped her silent alarm.

> *DAD: I answered you. Only fair you answer me. What do you want with Dunn?*

No way was I answering him. Instead, I left his system and went to the dark web. I hid my research behind several VPNs and layers of encryption. I pulled everything I could about both West and Dunn from their births on. Elementary schools, high schools, colleges, club memberships, and early political careers were all dug up and sifted into my own secure file.

It wasn't until I opened a list of Dunn's campaign donors that my heart took a gigantic leap. Right there, halfway down the page, was Argento Skies, Inc.

My palms turned sweaty.

There were several things my mom had pounded into me while teaching me her craft. One was to trust your instincts, which I hadn't always done lately, and the second was that there were no such things as coincidences. If you were in the thick of an investigation and threads started to overlap, there was a reason for it.

And now those threads were knotting around not only my parents but Gage's family and Dunn all at the same time.

Acid curled through my gut.

My dad was clearly involved with Dunn. Had my mom been too? Had my dad known about what happened to Monte? Had he even orchestrated the kidnapping?

I shook my head. No. Dad was an asshole. He didn't

know how to maintain a relationship with anyone but his clients, but he wouldn't stoop that low. He'd never be okay with kidnapping a thirteen-year-old.

I had to believe there were hard limits to what he'd do.

One thing was certain, I wouldn't be able to rest until all these threads had been pulled. Until all the pieces were revealed. I just had to hope that when the truth came tumbling out, it wouldn't give Gage and his family a real reason to hate me.

Chapter Twenty-two

Gage

HEY JUDE

Performed by The Beatles

I leaned up against the wall, legs sprawled along the edge of the mattress, as I watched my brother sleep with Ivy tucked up against him. The curls he'd kept shorn close to his head over the last year had dried while trying to spring to life. His face was free of dirt, but it made the purple-and-black marks on his pale skin stand out even more. My throat nearly closed thinking about how much worse it could have been than a few bruises and scraped-up hands.

The anger I'd kept buried all evening returned. My fingers clenched. I wanted to repay the favor, giving the grown-ass man who'd hit my kid brother a permanent mark that wouldn't fade the way Monte's bruises would.

One look at River's face as he and Audrey had rushed into the apartment tonight had told me he felt the same. They'd hugged us—held us tight—and then gone down to cover the bar for me yet again. I owed them more than I could ever repay, but whenever I brought it up, they got upset.

"We're family, Gage. And family takes care of family," River had said. And the truth was, if the roles were reversed, I'd do the same for them. But I'd never been good with pity. Or feeling like I owed someone something.

My eyes closed briefly, exhaustion pulling at me, but

every time they shut, the entire day played on repeat. I wanted desperately to feel nothing but relief at having Monte home. Instead, the storm felt like it was lingering over us. A momentary pause before we'd be battered all over again.

Dunn was still alive, which meant Monte would continue to see Rory shooting him.

For a few seconds in the car outside the police station, I'd panicked. I'd felt Monte's fear, and it had become mine. And then I'd been frustrated, thinking Rory had hidden something from me. But those feelings had passed in a flash with the look of hurt and incredulity on her face.

That's when I'd realized the worse truth. If Rory shot the congressman, it was because of us. Because she was protecting us, and I couldn't allow that. In that panicked moment, I'd thought if I could keep her away from us, it would keep her away from Dunn.

But the truth was, Monte's visions were never wrong.

Which meant Rory was going to shoot the congressman.

I closed my eyes, and all the versions of her I'd seen today scrolled across my mind. Determined and sure while handing me a contract. Smiling and teasing with the officers at the Rayburn Building. Fierce and confident climbing a fire escape. Sad and lonely, thinking of her mom in a coma. Devastated because her father had left her behind after she'd given him what he'd wanted and he'd deemed it a failure.

Rory and I had never shared more than a platonic hug in the decade I'd known her. And yet, an inexplicable bond seemed to be knotting us together. One that I'd never acknowledged until she'd sauntered into the bar this weekend. Part of my overreaction in the car had everything to do with those threads tightening around me because I doubted our abilities to take on the added burden of each other's complicated lives without collapsing.

But hadn't I learned in my physics courses that it wasn't the strength of a singular pillar that kept a bridge standing?

If a bridge only had to sustain its own weight, and if it was perfectly rigid, then a solo column might be able to bear it. But instead, a bridge fought the external forces of vehicles crossing it and the natural inclination of materials to bend under pressure. This was why engineers used multiple columns to help transfer the mass from one to the other, redundancies in case one failed.

Sharing the weight helped each perform the job of holding up the whole.

Family taking care of family.

Monte whimpered, and my hand immediately went to his leg, hoping the simple touch would soothe him. Instead, he thrashed his feet and sat up straight with eyes wide in fear.

My hand on him tightened. "You're safe, Monte. You're at home. You're safe. I've got you."

He drew in a ragged breath, glanced down at Ivy, and scooted away from her to join me with his back to the wall.

"I saw the warehouse again," he said quietly. He looked frightened but also worried. "Gage… I saw… I saw Demi there too."

My blood ran cold, a shiver running up my spine. "What?"

Usually, Monte's visions slowly came into focus, giving him more pieces each time, but this felt like an entirely new vision.

"She's at his side," he said, voice shaking. "She looks like shit… like a skeleton. Eyes hollowed, clothes hanging from her."

I swallowed hard. "And Rory is the one to shoot him? With Demi standing right there?"

Monte's brows creased, and he nodded. "She's got a gun. She's aiming it at him, but by the time the gun goes off, I'm looking at Dunn in the dream. He's moving, and I can't tell if it's because he's trying to protect Demi or if he's trying to run or what. But then there's blood pouring from his forehead, and he gets the same stunned look I've been seeing all week. But now, instead of just seeing him on the ground, I see Demi… She sort of catches him as he falls, and they both end up tangled there on the ground… There's so much blood… I don't know… I don't know…"

He banged his head against the wall, and acid eroded another layer of my stomach lining. Fuck. Was Demi killed too? Would Dunn and our mother die at the same time?

With Rory pulling the trigger?

"I don't know why Rory is there," I said. "But I'm the one who brought her into this. Tomorrow," I said as I glanced at the alarm clock on the side of the bed and saw it was two in the morning, "or later today, I'll call her and make sure she stays out of it. That she drops anything to do with us or Dunn."

Monte's eyes closed. "It won't help. It never does."

The despair in his voice slayed me.

"This is different than us trying to get the police to listen, Monte. This is someone we know. I can get her to stay away."

But could I really? Would Rory even take my call after how I'd reacted?

I had to believe Monte had these visions for a reason. Something—some force in this universe—wanted us to do something about them. Maybe this was the time we could actually make a difference. Maybe this was the time we could save someone. And maybe this time it would be Demi.

More chills ran up my spine.

I put my arm around my brother, tugging him closer. His head landed on my shoulder. We didn't say anything else. He was lost in his nightmare, and I was stuck in my churning sea of emotions.

I shouldn't care what happened to Demi. She hadn't cared about us when she'd taken everything in the bank account and run once again. But as much as there were days I hated her, as much as there were days I wished Dad had survived and she'd been the one who'd lost her life, I didn't really wish her dead.

I was here, and Monte and Ivy were here because of her. We were a family because she'd created us. She wasn't my responsibility any more than we were hers, but I also knew I couldn't just let her be killed without attempting to do something about it.

I couldn't let Rory be the one to do it. God… It made me sick to even consider it.

Monte's breathing evened out, and his body sagged into mine. My eyes closed, the weight of exhaustion and duty dragging me down until I landed in a dark abyss.

♫ ♫ ♫

Rap-rap-rap. The sharp, annoyed knock on the front door woke me.

Monte had moved while I'd slept. He was back next to Ivy, and they were conked out, dead to the world. I wondered what it would be like to sleep through anything the way they could. Especially Monte. After weeks of tormenting nightmares, he'd sometimes sleep for twenty-four hours straight. The first time it had happened, I'd been so worried, I'd almost called 9-1-1.

The knock sounded again, and I stumbled to my feet. I ran a hand over my face, the thick coat of stubble that I hadn't shaved in days prickling my palm. On bare feet, I lurched out of the room and toward the front door. Whoever the hell it was needed to go away because even as hard and fast as my siblings slept, they would wake up with the repeated hammering.

"What?!" I growled, tearing open the door.

Rory stood in front of me with a scowl on her face that matched mine.

She was wearing blue jeans and a vivid green sweater. It made that hint of color around her pupils stand out. Her hair was down, the long dark strands spilling over her shoulders and landing on the curve of her chest exposed by the low scoop of the sweater's neckline. She looked sexy and fierce. Sinfully beautiful.

My body instantly reacted to her, and wearing nothing but gray sweats, it was impossible to hide. I knew the moment she saw it because her eyes widened and then darted away. I crossed my arms over my chest, refusing to be embarrassed.

Instead of stating her business or walking away, she brushed past me into the apartment. I shut the door and turned to stare at her, hoping my glower would send her running. I couldn't afford for her to be here. She couldn't afford to be next to us.

I'd intended to call her this morning. Calling would have been safer. That way I wouldn't feel the electricity zigzagging between us, tempting me to chase after it just as I'd once chased after tornadoes.

She held out a piece of paper.

"What's that?" I demanded, keeping my voice low, but not bothering to reach for it.

"Your invoice. Like you said. I did my job." Her tone was perfectly neutral. Cold, even, and as much as I'd seen Rory in control, I'd never seen her cold, and something deep inside me objected to it.

Yesterday she'd said she wasn't billing us, and I'd disliked the idea of being a charity case. But now I wanted to rip the invoice to shreds because it meant I'd wounded her enough to have her standing in front of me as if I was just some random client. I didn't respond, just took the paper from her hand and slid past her to dig in the desk drawer where I kept the checkbook I rarely used.

As I wrote out the payment, I could feel her eyes boring into my back, stirring emotions I'd tried to tame over the last few days. Desire and lust. An almost raw and uncontrollable need to have her. During our search for Monte, the need had been dulled, but now that my brother was home, it flared to life in her presence until it felt almost uncontrollable.

I ripped the check out, took two long strides, and held it out.

Her fingers brushed mine as she took it, and the mere touch rushed through me like a wildfire in dry brush. Hot. Fast. Dangerous.

She glanced down at the paper, and her throat bobbed before she looked back up. "What's this?"

"Your money."

Her eyes narrowed. "That's double what my invoice said."

"You did your job. I got my brother back. Now I need you to stay away from us, Dunn, and anything related to him." I tried to keep my voice steady, but my emotions broke through on the last few syllables.

Her brows raised in shock and then a scowl returned to her beautiful face. I hated it. I doubly hated that it was sent in my direction.

But this was for the best. For all of us. I needed her far away from this mess. I needed the future Monte had seen ending with Demi's life being taken to disappear. And if keeping Rory away did that, I had to try. Even if she ended up despising me for it. Even if it meant walking away from the strings binding us. Even if it meant each of us having to be a singular column holding the weights of our individual bridges alone.

Chapter Twenty-three

Rory

RENEGADE

Performed by Big Red Machine and Taylor Swift

Gage's words stung as much as his distrust had the day before. After a sleepless night, I'd driven here, determined to get him to come clean. But when he'd opened the door in nothing but a battered T-shirt and a pair of sweats, every thought went out of my head.

Instead, my body instantly flamed at the sight of his sleep-mussed self. The stubble coating his jaw had grown another layer, making him even sexier than he was on a normal day. I was overwhelmed with the desire to comfort him… and kiss him. To give us both some sort of relief from tortured days and nights through arms and lips joined.

I'd given him the invoice only as a ploy to get inside. I'd never intended to actually take his money. Now, staring at the check he'd written for twice the amount due, every investigative instinct in me flared. He was paying me off. He was trying to push me out of his life.

Fine. If he wasn't going to say it, I would. "Monte saw me in the vision, didn't he?"

Gage didn't respond. He simply crossed his arms over his chest, fingers biting into his arms as if he was holding himself back.

"I'm the one who shoots Dunn." The way Gage's jaw tightened and his eyes darted to the hallway gave me the answer. "Holy shit. I'm right. I mean. I knew it, but wow. He really thinks I'm going to murder a U.S. congressman."

While I had to believe I'd never shoot someone in cold blood, I would in self-defense, and I definitely would to save an innocent person. I would also use a gun as a tool—as a negotiating tactic or to get someone to comply.

But even if Dunn had been the one to send my mom into the Potomac, I'd get my revenge by delivering him to the authorities. I'd stand in a courtroom while he was declared guilty rather than pull the trigger.

"What else does he see? Why am I there? What's happening at that moment?" I demanded.

"It doesn't matter. What does matter is you staying away from us and Dunn."

Instead of being rough and brutal as his words had been before, these were softer, accompanied by a plea in his stormy eyes. My heart sped up, pattering out a ridiculous beat.

This wasn't just about Monte's fear of what he saw in his head. This wasn't about Gage not believing me or trusting me. This was him trying to protect me, and he thought by sending me off with a tidy little check he could.

"If his visions are never wrong, why go through all the trouble of warning people?" I asked. "If nothing can be done, then why tell them?" He didn't respond, and I continued. "Because you hope that at least one time you can make a difference. Let me be the difference, Gage. I won't let you down. I promise."

He lifted an arm, rubbing the back of his head, and it raised his T-shirt, showing a tantalizing strip of skin and dark hair that had my body reacting all over again. But neither the instant flare of desire nor the bittersweet way he was trying to keep me safe would stop me from working on this case. Not with both our families involved somehow.

I stepped closer, and he didn't move away. I pressed the check to his chest, resting my palm there and feeling the rapid rhythm of his heartbeat beneath it. Our gazes locked as I said, "You can't buy me off, Gage."

"It was just a job, Rory. Monte is safe. You don't need to worry about us anymore." His voice was deep, guttural, and I could feel the concern vibrating through it.

"This isn't just about you and Monte anymore."

"What?" His brows furrowed in confusion.

I shrugged and told him the truth. "My dad works for the congressman. My mom was working on something related to one of Dunn's donors. Like it or not, I'm tied up in this."

His eyes narrowed, a flicker of hurt crossing his face. "You said you didn't know him."

"I didn't. Don't. I found out last night while digging for more information. And what I found requires me to keep going." I stopped to take a breath before continuing. "My mom's wreck wasn't an accident. Someone messed with her car's computer."

His eyes widened in surprise. "And you think it's all related?"

I nodded.

His eyes closed and then opened again. "Demi... She's in the vision with the congressman. She's at his side. They fall to the ground together in a mess of blood."

"What?" It was my turn to be hurt by things he'd held back. I didn't want our relationship to be like the one I had with my dad. Half-truths that had to be hacked to find the real answer. "You never said, not even when Dunn asked if Monte knew your mom."

"Because I didn't know. The closer Monte's vision gets to actually happening, the more he sees. Like a camera lens placed too close to an object and slowly coming into focus. It's never enough to give a time or location, but more details pile on."

I let out a breath. We'd both uncovered more in the dark of the night. "Please let me help, Gage. Let's help each other. This is exactly what I'm good at—putting the puzzle together piece by piece until the whole comes into view."

He raised his hand, pushing a strand of my hair back and tucking it behind my ear. My entire being convulsed at the gentle movement.

I couldn't tear my eyes from his if I tried. We were locked in a heated debate without words. A debate I wouldn't be the one to turn away from because it was about much more than me working this case or shooting Dunn. It was about us. Who we were at our core. It was about the burning flame flickering between us.

His gaze fell to my lips, and the energy between us grew, particles of electricity building. If they didn't release soon, they'd turn us to ash. His head lowered, my fingers fisted in his T-shirt, and the check fluttered to the ground as our lips met.

My soul sighed, my teenage heart leaped for joy, and the earth seemed to tilt. One of Gage's arms wrapped around my waist, and the other went to the back of my head, holding me to him. Holding us steady. The smooth slide of skin on skin ignited the coiled desire waiting inside me.

It didn't feel like any first kiss I'd ever had. It didn't feel like a second or even a hundredth one. It felt as if we'd had an infinity worth of kisses strewn behind us. And maybe we had. Maybe we'd been twined like this over centuries' worth of lifetimes.

His hand slid under my sweater, the heat of his palm burning a trail up my spine. A whimper escaped me. A damn whimper I'd never let out before. My tongue glided along the seam of his mouth, and he groaned, letting me in, and suddenly the gentle tango we'd started wasn't nearly enough. The embrace went from teenaged dream to erotic craving in mere seconds. I pressed myself into him, increasing the pace of our mouths and tongues. A deep hunger fueling us. All softness disappeared, leaving behind wild demands and brutal strokes.

Desperate to mark him as he'd long ago marked me, I let go of his shirt, twined my hands behind his neck, and dug my nails in. His hiss of pleasure only added to the blaze. He flipped us around, pushing me toward the counter. My lids fluttered open, our eyes locked, and it was then that we both caught movement in the hallway.

We jumped apart as Ivy moved toward us with one hand rubbing her eyes and the other holding her otter. She wrapped a tiny arm around Gage's knee and rested her head against his thigh. The image they made together was so sweet, I felt my ovaries flip over once again.

"Hi, Wowy," she said softly.

"Morning, Ivy," I said with my heart in my throat.

Gage's hand went to her hair, tousling the wild curls, but he was taking me in with hooded eyes. My chest was heaving, my lips stinging from the ferocity of our embrace. My reality had been altered. I'd never be able to go back to my old one now that I knew what kissing Gage felt like.

"Go get a yogurt, Ives," Gage said.

She didn't question him, just moved away into the tiny kitchen that was barely two steps away.

Gage's voice was lower and raspier than normal when he spoke. "I'm sorry."

His words had me tumbling back to earth faster than the arrival of his little sister had.

I swallowed hard. "Don't apologize."

"I'm not sure I know how to do this, Rory." He glanced in the direction Ivy had gone and then back down the hallway to where Monte must still be sleeping.

"I know."

"What I feel when I kiss you—I can't afford to get lost in that."

"I know," I repeated. The soft lick of rejection was eased by his admission of feeling something too.

Gage seemed frustrated by my easy acquiescence to his words. His voice dropped even lower. "You deserve to be someone's entire focus in a way I'll never be able to give you."

My pulse picked up another notch, my heart ramming against my rib cage as if trying to escape. I couldn't help the hope that twirled through me. He wasn't rejecting me as much as fighting with the weight of his responsibilities. I understood that maybe better than anyone.

So, I did what I could to help lighten his load. I closed the distance between us once more, and he looked at me with wariness.

"Take it easy, Gage. We shared a kiss. Not rings and I dos."

He frowned, and I pushed at the deep grooves between his brows with my fingertips.

"You keep that up, and you're going to have more wrinkles than a shar-pei."

When he didn't respond, I dropped my hands, pushed past him, and headed for the door. "I'm going to D.C., but I'll call you later and we can try to put the puzzle pieces together."

"That isn't a good idea." He looked down the hall again.

"I don't plan on shooting Dunn. I'll do everything I can to make sure Monte's vision doesn't come true, but I'm also not walking away. Now that I know my mom was involved, I can't. We can help each other. Tell Monte I want to help."

Without waiting for him to argue about it more, I pulled open the door and stepped outside. Regardless of what Gage or Monte thought or decided, I wouldn't stop.

Gage had said Monte's visions were never wrong. But *never* was a word I'd always bucked against. Especially when it came to me. Whenever someone tried to tell me I couldn't do something, it only made me more determined to prove I could.

This would be just another time I'd prove the entire universe wrong.

And in doing so, I'd get justice for my mom *and* Monte.

Where that left Gage and me when it was over, I had no

idea. I couldn't let that affect what I did or how I proceeded. There might be a possibility that Dad was wrong about tears, but he wasn't wrong about emotions messing with an investigation. I couldn't let my feelings, or a kiss, get in my way. No matter how damn earth-shattering the kiss had been.

Chapter Twenty-four

Gage

HOW MUCH LOVE
Performed by Survivor

Rory walked out the door, and I bit my cheek to stop myself from begging her to come back. She was going into D.C., which meant she was investigating, stirring up the hornet's nest. What would happen to her when she did? Look at what had happened to Monte when he'd simply talked to Dunn.

The tension in my body was wound to the top. Not just from the vision and Monte's kidnapping, but from a kiss that had splintered my soul. I would have set Rory on the counter and feasted on her if Ivy hadn't walked in on us.

Jesus. What the hell had I been thinking?

I hadn't thought at all. My body had simply reacted. A man starved for too long, I'd been unable to deny what she'd given me. I'd told her the truth when I'd said she deserved a partner who would put her at the top of their list.

And yet the thought of someone else being that person for her—the thought of someone else kissing her, twining their body with hers—was enough to make my jaw and fists clench tightly. I was torn between wanting to claim her as mine with us standing shoulder to shoulder, holding the weight of our lives above us, and needing to put my walls and boundaries back in place so I wouldn't take something I couldn't give back.

"Bubba…" Ivy's little voice called with worry in her tone. "I sorry."

I rounded the counter into the kitchen and just stared for a moment. She was covered in yogurt. Head to toe. Face, hair, clothes, and socks. How could a tiny yogurt container have covered her so completely?

"What happened?" I asked, not sure if I wanted to laugh or growl in frustration.

"I twied to open it," she said.

The burst yogurt became a metaphor for my entire morning. Messes I had to clean up right and left—at the bar, in the apartment, and with my family—all while my emotions ran so high I was swimming in them.

Throughout the day, I kept an extra close watch on Monte. His eyes were shadowed and dark, and he moved slowly, as if each motion shot pain through him. He'd taken the gauze off his hands, and the scrapes there were raw and red. But it was the mental wounds I was more worried about.

Once Ivy went down for a nap and Monte and I sat down for lunch, I finally had time to ask the question I'd been burning to ask all morning. "Do you want to talk to me about it?"

He picked at his sandwich, not really eating it. "Talk about what?"

"Any of it."

He shook his head.

"Do you want to talk to someone else? A therapist, maybe?"

He scoffed, eyes way too old for his age meeting mine. "And what? Tell them my vision drove me to D.C.? That would go over really well. They'd try to stick me in a mental hospital."

It bothered me that he was right. That he wouldn't be able to work through this with someone who knew how to help in ways I didn't, all because of the stupid abilities Demi had saddled him with.

He shoved the plate away. "I've been thinking. About Rory and Dunn. She's a private investigator, right? I mean. Maybe we hire her to find Demi. Maybe that's why she's there…"

My breath caught. "You want to find Demi?"

His eyes were tortured when he looked up. "If we don't do something, she dies, Gage. Whatever she's done… however much she's hurt us, she's still our mom."

His words echoed my thoughts from the night before. Helping her didn't mean we had to let her back into our lives—I'd be damned if I'd give her a chance to wound us more—but neither of us would be able to live with ourselves if we did nothing.

"We'll think of something," I finally said. He didn't respond, and I knew he was holding back. "What aren't you telling me?"

"Nothing."

We both knew it was a lie, so I pushed. "You don't have to protect me, Monte. It isn't your job."

He stood up abruptly, grimacing at the pain. "It wasn't your job to protect us either. But you did it. All you do is work yourself to the bone for Ives and me. We aren't your kids. We aren't your responsibility, and yet you've carried the burden of us without once complaining. You gave up every dream you ever had to be here, and I can't—I won't—be the reason you lose your freedom on top of everything else."

I stared at my brother, grief and loss running through me along with a hefty dose of frustration. I'd been careful to hide my sorrow over the loss of the future I'd seen for myself. I tried every damn day to only show the love I felt for them. To act like the tavern was where I'd always intended to end up, but he'd seen the truth.

"First, neither you nor Ivy are a burden, so get that out of your head." Monte crossed his arms over his body in a way that reminded me of myself so much I almost smiled. "I mean it, Monte. It's a privilege to be here watching the two of you become the incredible people the world is lucky to have in it. I don't know what you and Ivy will do with your abilities, but I do know, you're going to make a difference. I believe that in here." I pounded my chest. "Second, you'll see as you go through life that dreams change. Sometimes when you think you've lost something, you've actually gained. What I have here, with you and Ivy and River and Audrey, I wouldn't trade it to get back in a tank heading toward a tornado."

The truth of my words hit me hard.

If Dad hadn't died, if Demi hadn't left, I would never have had the chance to know my brother and sister the way I did now. I would have loved them, but it would have been from a distance. Instead, what I had with them—the bond we shared—was a thrill chasing a storm could never have brought me.

Monte started to speak and I cut him off. "And third, it absolutely *is* my job to protect you. That's why they gave me the title of guardian. I know you went to D.C. to prevent what happened after the train derailment from happening all over again. But it won't because we know to be careful now. You, going out on your own, all that did was stress me the hell out. It will only end up with me feeling like I failed you."

His gaze met mine, startled. "You've never failed me."

"I did. I should have taken you myself."

"Then we both would have ended up in that basement, and who would have taken care of Ivy?"

My heart couldn't take much more of those dark thoughts. Audrey and River were listed as my next of kin on any legal paperwork, and they would take my brother and sister if something happened to me. They were good people. Good humans. They'd do right by my family, but I didn't want them to have to.

I wanted to be the one there when Ivy woke up with her hair in ten different directions. I wanted to be the one Monte came to when the visions made him sick. But I also wanted to be the one he turned to after his first kiss and when he got into the college of his choice and when he eventually walked down the aisle with someone at his side if that was what he chose to do.

"Or maybe we would have been home long before they tried to come after you," I said gently. "We'll never know. But I can't live through it again, Monte. God… I thought… I thought I'd never see you again."

Monte's eyes filled with tears, and he pushed the heels of his palms into them.

"For a while there," he said softly, "I thought I'd never see you or Ivy again either. I was worried about her… about what she might feel if something happened to me. If they hurt me worse than they did… I knew she'd feel it too."

I scratched the back of my neck, chills racking my body at the thought.

"She knew you were scared."

He looked down the hall and back. "They asked me so many questions about the vision, Gage. Like how I had them and if I'd had them before. What else I saw. What other abilities I had. They asked about you too. After what I saw last night with Demi there? Maybe they're holding her like they were me."

I sat there, stunned. Even when he'd told me about Demi being in the dream, I'd never once considered the idea that she wasn't there of her own free will. After all, Demi was never anywhere she didn't want to be.

"Maybe," Monte continued, "that's why we hire Rory."

I swallowed and fought back the bitterness to say as calmly as I could, "You'd be okay with finding Demi even if Rory ends up shooting the congressman?"

"We can make her promise not to shoot him, right? Like as part of our deal to hire her?"

The truth hit me, and I said quietly, "You think you can change things this way."

Another careless shrug, but I'd landed on it. He was

desperate to have control of the situation at least one time. To see a different ending than the one he'd been shown. To change bad into good. My heart squeezed tightly as I realized Monte and Rory wanted the same thing.

But what they wanted meant keeping Rory close instead of sending her away.

It meant dancing with temptation. It wasn't just about her and Dunn. I'd kissed her this morning because I'd been helpless to stop myself. Her fierceness. Her dedication to her family… to us. It had been more of a turn-on than her tight sweater and flashing eyes. Bringing her closer would wreak havoc on the shaky boundaries I was trying to keep up for her sake as much as mine.

At the hope in Monte's eyes, my stomach fell. It was so much better than the fear and anger and trauma of the day before. When he'd first seen Rory, he'd been panicked and frightened. Now, just the idea of her being able to change what he'd seen was bringing him back to life.

Fuck.

I sighed and gave in, telling him everything Rory had told me about Dunn and her parents, and how she wasn't going to stop investigating. His eyes grew wide.

"I'll talk to her again. Make sure she knows we want her to find Demi."

Monte's eyebrows rose, and for the first time in what felt like forever, his lips tilted up. "Such a sacrifice for you."

"What's that supposed to mean?"

His face broke into a full-on grin that eased the clamp on my heart ever so slightly. "Come on, Gage. Don't pretend you don't have the hots for her."

"The hots? What are you, a seventies show throwback?" I snorted, fighting back a smile. But inside, I was wondering how I'd been so obvious. Was the electricity burning in the air when Rory and I were together actually visible to people around us?

"See. You didn't even deny it. You like her."

Like was the wrong word entirely. It wasn't anywhere near what I felt for Rory. The kiss we'd shared had been too much and not enough. My body had been addicted with the first shot. I craved her. But I wasn't sure I could afford the addiction.

"She's not entirely despicable," I said.

Monte snorted. "Looked like a lot more than not despicable when you had your tongue down her throat."

I froze, and my look only made Monte laugh more.

"Shit… that… was an accident," I stuttered out.

Which only sent him into peals of laughter, grabbing his ribs and complaining it hurt. My heart got lighter and lighter until a chuckle escaped my chest as well.

After a few moments, my smile faded again. "Seriously, though. It probably shouldn't have happened. I'm sorry if you saw it and got grossed out."

"I'm not six, Bubba. Girls don't gross me out anymore."

It was my turn to raise my brows at him. "India?"

He blanched. "No. That is gross. She's like another sibling. Besides, she's not into guys. Or girls. Not like that anyway." He gave a careless shrug and then turned serious eyes back on me.

"At first, when I saw the two of you this morning, it freaked me out. Not because you kissing anyone is weird or disgusting but because of my vision. There's her holding the gun and then there's so much blood. But that's what got me thinking about her being a PI and finding Demi. That maybe, just maybe, we can change things for once."

I wanted it so desperately I could almost taste it, not just for Demi, but for my brother.

Unfortunately, that desperation tasted a whole hell of a lot like Rory.

Honey and burned ozone. Sweetness and danger.

I wasn't sure I'd survive another sip.

Chapter Twenty-five

Rory

HOLD OUT
Performed by Aly & AJ

My time in D.C. was a flop. Lucidia had nothing to tell me about the security footage that had disappeared, and when I went to the Argento Skies office, it was locked tight with lights off. I would have snuck inside, but a counseling office down from their suite was holding a health fair, and people littered the corridor.

I retreated to my favorite coffee shop by Georgetown with every intention of heading back to Argento Skies after dark. While waiting, I pulled up what I could on the company.

According to its website and what I'd read before, it didn't have a D.C. location, and even having seen their name on the sign myself, I still couldn't find a shred of evidence that said any different. I couldn't even find a lease agreement. The office I'd seen was actually leased to a holding company that I traced to an offshore account and a shell company that screamed *hinky*.

Even the shell company was a dead end, without a list of board members to find anywhere.

Argento Skies itself was a family-owned business. My search popped up an article about its original CEO dying in a plane crash for unknown reasons a few years ago. He'd been piloting the small plane, and while there were literally hundreds of reasons it could have gone down, the fact that both his accident and my mom's had never truly been solved felt important. Another coincidence I had to follow.

My phone buzzed, and I looked down to see the text.

NAN: I didn't see you this morning.

This was really code for her being worried that we hadn't talked since I'd lost my cool with her in the car last night. I still didn't know what to say because I couldn't give her what she wanted, but I also didn't want her to worry about me.

ME: I'm working a case in D.C. I'll be by to see Mom soon. Give her a kiss for me. I love you.

NAN: Okay. I'll save you one of Harriet's pumpkin muffins. Be safe. I love you.

Her response made a lump lodge in my throat.

I stared out the window at the darkening sky filled with clouds that had threatened rain all day. I needed to know more about this cloud seeding that Argento Skies did and why it would have endangered their CEO. With a bachelor's in meteorology, Gage would likely know all about it. I could simply ask him. I could ask him and make sure he and his siblings were okay at the same time.

My heartbeat spiked at the thought of seeing him again. Of maybe kissing him again. He'd apologized for it, but he'd admitted to the attraction—the depths of it pulling at him as much as me. He'd tried to brush me off because he couldn't make me his focus any more than I could make him mine.

So, where did that leave us? With desire and no relief?

I sure as hell couldn't afford to waste more of my day thinking about it… about him.

I shoved my things into my bag and headed out of the coffee shop. As I stood next to my Rebel pulling on my helmet, my eyes fell to the bike's mirrors and the reflection of a man leaning against the brick building across the street.

Mammoth shoulders. Black jacket. Aviators. Shaved head.

It was the guy from yesterday.

I whirled around, taking a step off the curb, and a bus blared its horn at me.

My pulse raced as I jumped back.

Damn it, Rory-girl. Pay attention.

By the time the bus trundled by, the man was gone, and I had no idea which direction he'd headed. It was obvious the man had picked me up at the Argento Skies office both days. I cursed myself for not running him through my facial recognition program. If I had, I'd already know everything there was to know about him. Now I couldn't afford to go back to the building until I'd identified him and what he wanted with me.

Time I couldn't afford was literally ticking by.

I jumped onto my Rebel and flew through the streets, heading back toward Cherry Bay. I wished I could talk to Mom and not just to hear her say *I love you* again. I wished she was there to help me chase down all the different leads flying around this case. There were just too many for one person, but somehow I'd have to pull it together and fast.

I drove straight to Shady Lane, and by the time I got off my bike, I had a handful of additional texts from Nan, one from Shay, and a voicemail from Dad. My phone rang, and I would have ignored it just like I was ignoring the other calls and texts except I was surprised to see it was Gage.

"Hey, what's up?"

"I know you said you'd call later, but Monte wants to talk to you." The noise of the bar echoed around his words.

"He does?" I couldn't prevent the surprise from entering my voice.

"Yeah. He does. Do you think you could come by the apartment? I take a break around seven-thirty to make sure

Ivy goes down."

I glanced at the clock on my phone. I'd have time to say hello to Mom and start a search for the aviator glasses man before heading over. "Sure. I can be there."

In the silence that followed, I heard music and the laughter of the locals who filled the bar for Tango Tuesday. Finally, Gage responded. "After… because…" He sighed. "Just. Thanks."

It brought a tiny smile to my lips, and I wasn't sure why, but thirty minutes later, I was at their apartment knocking. Monte opened the door, and we stared at each other for a moment.

I was relieved to see there was no longer fear in his eyes when he looked at me. Instead, there was cautious curiosity. He was taller than me at thirteen, and even though he was nowhere near full grown, I could tell he'd eventually have the same broad-shouldered frame of his brother.

"Did you check before you opened the door?" I asked.

He rolled his eyes in that way teenagers perfected. "Yes. You sound like Gage."

My heart skipped a beat.

Monte stepped back to let me in.

Ivy's voice, singing the *Scooby-Doo* anthem, could be heard from down the hall.

"She's getting ready for bed. Gage will be up in a few minutes," Monte explained.

I set my bag on the counter and turned back to him. "Gage said you wanted to talk. Is it about what happened? Would you prefer to wait for him?"

Monte's stance was entirely his brother's. Arms crossed over his chest, feet wide, eyes taking me in as if they could see into my soul. "He'll want to be here for some of it. But…" Monte glanced down the hall to where the singing had stopped, and he shouted out, "What are you doing, Ivy?"

My lips twitched at the note in his voice that stated perfectly his suspicions of the quiet coming from her direction.

"Putting my pajamas on!" she yelled back as if offended he'd assume she was getting into trouble.

Monte dragged his gaze back to me. "My brother. He's given up everything he ever wanted to be here for us. Looking out for us."

I didn't know what he wanted me to say to that, so I said nothing, and he continued.

"He's not quite a martyr, but it's pushing into that territory because he doesn't do anything for himself. Ever. It's all about the bar or us."

My eye started to twitch as I got an inkling of where this conversation might be going, and I wasn't sure I could have this kind of talk. Not with Gage's younger brother. Not when Gage had insisted that pursuing whatever it was that burned between us was a mistake.

When I still didn't respond, Monte shifted on his feet, showing the first signs of being uncomfortable. "I saw you two… this morning."

A flush crept over my cheeks. There shouldn't be anything embarrassing about kissing someone. And yet, knowing his little brother had seen us and knowing how close we'd been to tossing our clothes and finding out if the counter would hold my weight, I couldn't help it.

I cleared my throat. "That was… It shouldn't have happened."

Monte grinned and a small chuckle escaped him. "That's exactly what he said."

My lips shifted up in return.

"Gage needs something—someone—who will force him to think about himself," Monte said. "To go for a motorcycle ride. To remember who he was and what he wanted before he got weighed down with a pair of siblings and a business he never intended to run."

The words were so grown up. So adult. Almost a parent's words about a child, and I realized for the first time that it wasn't just Gage who'd been forced to grow up after their dad had died and their mom had deserted them once again.

Monte may have only been ten when Demi left last, but he would have understood it. Just like I'd gotten it when my parents divorced because of me at twelve. Kids took on those burdens whether the adults in their lives wanted them to or not.

"I think…" I paused, trying to collect my thoughts. "I think Gage is very happy with his life, Monte. I think he loves being here with the two of you. He wouldn't change that."

He nodded. "I'm not saying he should go back to Kansas to chase storms. I'm saying, I want someone to remind him that he's still Gage. Not just Dad's stand-in or a bar owner or whatever. Someone who will look out for him as much as he looks out for us. He'll never let Ivy or me be that person. He never lets anyone be that for him. Not even River and Audrey. He's so worried about anyone else having to give up anything that he's determined to be the only one who sacrifices."

My breath caught for a moment as I realized the full extent of his words. Of what he was suggesting. I asked softly, "And you think I can be that person for him? What makes you think Gage will let me do that anymore than he'd let you?"

"He hasn't dated anyone since Dad died. Not once. He made me switch rooms with Ivy so I could have my own. He's twenty-seven, and he's living like a monk, sharing a bedroom with his three-and-a-half-year-old sister."

My face flushed again because Monte was talking about Gage and me having sex just as much as he was talking about me being there for Gage in some sort of relationship. As if he'd just realized what he'd implied, Monte turned red as well. He looked down, rubbing a sock-clad foot along a seam in the wood flooring.

"I'm not… I mean… Just." He inhaled deeply. "For

once I'd like for him to go somewhere, do something, and it be about what he wants, not about what Ivy or I want."

"I hear what you're saying, Monte, and I think that would be really good for Gage. I'm just not sure I can be that person for him." Monte frowned, about to say something, and I rushed forward with my words. "Not because I don't like Gage. Not because I wouldn't want to be that person, but because Gage may not be ready to let anyone be there for him in that way."

The truth of it settled between us. The reality of my words hit me as I realized just how much I would love to be the person at Gage's side, forcing him out of his shell. Forcing him to enjoy his life rather than just living to make sure his siblings had one. The irony of those thoughts and how similar they were to the words Nan had said to me wasn't lost on me.

The door opened behind Monte, and we both twisted, my arm automatically going to my back and the gun I kept there. Gage's face and body emerged from the shadowed landing. He looked from Monte to me and back, a frown appearing once again between his brows.

"You're early," he said, and then reading the tension in the air between Monte and me, added, "Everything okay here?"

Monte was the one to nod first. "Yeah. Rory just barely walked in. I'm going to go make sure Ivy really is *only* putting her pajamas on."

Gage tossed his keys into a bowl on the table by the door. An unsafe place for them. A place anyone could casually pick them up. But I had to remember I wasn't there to overhaul their security. Just like I wasn't part of the family he was coming home to even if my body was longing to run over to him and kiss him hello. To greet him like some fifties throwback that was the complete opposite of anything I'd ever want.

The truth was I'd never seen myself in a long-term relationship. Not even as a teen when I'd ogled Gage. I'd wanted him in an ambiguous way. As if I could have him without our relationship being labeled. But the person who stepped up to be in Gage's life wouldn't be able to just have him and ignore the remaining pieces of his world, because all those pieces made him the man he was.

He'd need someone who could claim his family as much as they claimed him.

And I just wasn't sure I knew how to do that.

Not when the only family I'd had was the one I'd broken.

Chapter Twenty-six

Gage

IN GOOD FAITH

Performed by Survivor

Regardless of what they'd both said, something had gone on between Monte and Rory before I'd walked through the door. There'd been a tension in the air. Not anger. Not even anything bad necessarily, but I sensed their discomfort. Monte was keeping secrets from me again. Secrets, I realized, he'd told Rory.

That hurt. And pissed me off.

Later, I'd force one—or both of them—to tell me the truth.

I read Ivy a story with Monte snuggled up on the other side of her and couldn't help but wonder what it would be like if Rory was in there with us. My heart spasmed at the idea. A reality dancing just outside my reach. When the book was done, Monte kissed Ivy goodnight and headed out of the room while I finished tucking her in.

I kissed Ivy on the cheek. "Love you to the far side of the rainbow and back, Ives."

"Love you, Bubba."

Her little eyes were already fluttering shut as I flipped off the light and partially closed the door. Ivy had never been afraid of the dark, which was nice because I hadn't had to sleep with a damn nightlight on. In fact, our sister was pretty fearless. In some ways, her attitude reminded me of Rory's.

A little in your face, not going to back down, but really, behind it, a soft wall of love and kindness.

When I walked down the hall, Rory was seated at the counter and Monte was in the kitchen grabbing a pint of ice cream from the freezer. He tossed the lid aside and started to eat directly from the container. It was only my words that halted him.

"You going to offer some to our guest?" I asked.

His eyes got wide, and he turned to Rory. "Would you like some?"

She laughed. Light and soft and enticing. A laugh that made you want to sit back and listen to it for hours. Days. Years. I'd forgotten that about her. Or maybe I'd never allowed myself to really listen to her back then. Now, her laugh was another dart that lodged itself into my soul.

"I have a feeling if I said yes, I'd be breaking your heart. So, thanks, but no."

He grinned. "I'd share. I mean, it's Cherry Garcia, and it might cost me a few more layers of skin from my hands to give it up, but I would."

She chuckled again, and it lifted more of the heaviness from the air.

"Good thing I don't like cherries then."

His smile grew wider as he dug into the ice cream. I should have yelled at him for not using a bowl, but the Cherry Garcia was all his. The three of us knew it, and he'd earned it after everything he'd been through.

I would have bought him anything today. A motorcycle he couldn't drive for another few years. The expensive Mac computer he'd been hinting about. Just having him here, after not knowing—

No. I wouldn't let myself go back to those hours of terror.

But those thoughts reminded me of why Rory was in the apartment, and my smile disappeared.

"Monte wants to hire you to find Demi," I said.

Her eyes grew wide and all the lightness that we'd finally gotten into the room disappeared, making me wish I could take it back but knowing I couldn't.

I joined my brother in the kitchen, both of us leaning against the cabinets so we faced Rory at the counter with her laptop open. It struck me how much it looked like she belonged there. As if she'd been there a thousand times before while we'd had similar conversations.

"This morning you wanted me as far away from the two of you as possible. I was the one to tell you I wasn't walking away, so what changed?" she asked. Her gaze landed on Monte instead of me, and they exchanged some unspoken words that had my eyes narrowing. What had they talked about?

"Whether I like it or not," I said, "you're involved. You're in the vision. We might as well agree to be on the same side."

"I'm not shooting Dunn," she said firmly.

"What if… what if he's like… threatening Demi or me or Gage. Would you shoot him then?" Monte asked around a mouthful of ice cream.

Rory hesitated. "If anyone was threatening another person's life, shooting them wouldn't be my first response."

"What if they had a gun to someone's forehead?"

"Wait. You never said he had a gun," I grunted out at my brother.

Monte shook his head. "I haven't seen anyone but Rory with one. I just want to know what would make her shoot him."

"If it's between me and the congressman, if he was aiming at me and I had no other options, I would shoot him like I've been trained to do. But I promise you, it will *always* be my last option."

Monte seemed calmer than I'd seen him in days, especially with visions haunting him. I was glad but also confused. He nodded. "Okay, then. You're hired."

Rory's lips twitched and a huff of a laugh escaped me. "I don't think you can actually hire her. I had to sign a contract, and you aren't old enough."

Monte shrugged. "Okay, so you hire her."

"Technically, you already have," she said. "The contract you signed said I'd work your brother's case until it was solved to your satisfaction. You have to be the one to end it."

"So the invoice you gave me this morning?"

She shrugged. "I was upset. What can I say?"

"You didn't take the money."

She shook her head. "And I won't. I'm not really charging you."

"You're not working for us for free."

She ignored me, punching away at something on her computer as she'd done almost the entire day before. Monte moved away from me to join Rory at the counter, sitting next to her on a stool.

"What do we do now?" he asked.

"You do nothing," she said. "I don't want you anywhere near Dunn. I don't want the men who took you thinking they need to do so again. I haven't heard what happened. So, if you feel up to it, could you tell me? Anything they said, anything you saw might be more important than you know. But first, do you recognize this man?"

I eased over to the counter, leaning across it to look at the image she was showing my brother. A huge man filled the screen. Military, by the looks of him. Sunglasses blocked his eyes, but his face was still grim.

Monte shook his head. "They always had their faces covered, and they were big, but this guy looks like a monster."

Rory nodded. "That's what I was thinking as well. He's as wide as a truck, and while the men who grabbed you were big, they didn't look like pro wrestlers."

"Why did you think he might be involved?" I asked.

"He followed us yesterday and then tailed me again today." Shock reverberated through me at her words. Before I could ask more about it, she waved it off, saying, "He isn't important at the moment. If it's okay, I'd like to hear Monte's story."

Monte shrugged, and then he told her everything he'd told me and Bradshaw. He repeated the story about his conversation with Dunn and West and their weird reactions, getting jumped in the alley, and the kidnappers recording him talking about the visions while asking questions about Demi and our family.

"So, your mom, she's like you? She sees things?" Rory asked.

"No. She's not like me." Monte's shoulders sagged. "She can touch people and tell you about them. Not just their past, but like what will happen to them in the future. Like that saying about your life flashing before your eyes when you think you're going to die? That sort of thing. She sees everything before, but also what can happen beyond that moment. It's not always bad like with me. Most of the time, it's not."

I could see the doubts fly over Rory's face again. We were lucky she believed us as much as she did.

"Wow. Does it happen whenever she touches anyone? Or only sometimes?"

"Not all the time, but she wears gloves just in case because if she doesn't, she can't control when the images hit her. She could hold your hand twenty times, but on the twenty-first time, *wham*, she's drowning in it."

"She sees the person's future as well as their past?"

Monte nodded, but I answered. "The future she sees is different from the past because the future has choices being made that can affect it. If she touches you today, she'll see one future, but then you might make a big decision or change your mind about something or get offered a new job, or do something little, like take a different route to work, and all of it impacts everything going forward. So what she saw today might be different from what she sees tomorrow.”

Rory had a weird look on her face. Like she’d just eaten something bad.

“What?” I demanded.

“Just think about that for a minute. Think about what kind of power it could give a politician who makes thousands of decisions every day. What if they believed in her power? And what if they had one future in mind, but every decision along the way might impact it? Wouldn’t they want someone who could tell them if they were making the right ones?”

My stomach fell, and I was sure I’d paled in the same way she had.

Monte pushed the ice cream container away. “You think… You think she’s not with the congressman by choice?”

He’d pretty much said the same thing before and I hadn’t wanted to believe it, but maybe it was true.

Rory shrugged. “Maybe she was with him for other reasons at first. Does she tell people about her abilities?”

Monte and I shook our heads. “Demi might not have been around to teach us much, but that was the one thing she drove home loud and clear. We had to be really careful who we told. It had to be people you trusted completely. People who loved you and wanted the best for you.”

And now we were telling Rory. I swallowed hard, something large swelling inside me, but it wasn’t fear I felt about Rory knowing our secrets. It was relief.

“Except on Halloween,” Monte said. “Then, she loved to dress up as a fortune teller and play it up.”

“I forgot about that,” I said softly. I rarely let myself think about Demi, and when I did, most of my thoughts weren’t good. Most of them were about her leaving. Sometimes with a goodbye kiss, but many times without. My memories of her were coated in bitterness and anger.

But we'd had some good times. She'd loved Halloween, and the Victorian we'd lived in had always been decorated to the hilt if she was around. She'd set up a purple velvet tent covered in moons and stars in the front yard, dress in a black gauzy gown, wrap her long strawberry-blond hair in a turban, and tell the parents their futures as their kids trick-or-treated.

Laughter had always rung from the tent. One year, I'd asked her why everyone was always so happy as they left when she'd obviously seen bad things too. She'd told me there was enough grief and sorrow and ugly in the world. It wasn't her job to share more of it, but she *could* spread joy and hope. That's what she focused on.

Even then, I'd wanted to ask how she could so easily spread joy to others and then walk away, leaving only pain behind for those she supposedly loved most.

"Wait." Rory's voice pulled me from my thoughts. "Your abilities." She waved a finger between Monte and me and my heart skipped a beat. Her narrowed gaze landed on me. "You told me you didn't have any abilities."

Monte shifted uncomfortably on the stool in my peripheral view, but I didn't break our stare. Instead, I lifted a shoulder as if it wasn't a big deal. As if telling her wasn't the first time I'd ever told a living soul outside of my immediate family. No one knew. Not even River and Audrey. No one.

"You asked if I had visions, and I don't."

"I also asked you what your superpower was, and you sidestepped the question," she said without any bite. Instead, she sounded resigned. As if she was used to people not being honest with her, and that stabbed at me. That I was just another person in her life who hadn't told her the truth.

"And… on that note, I'm heading to bed," Monte said with a wry grin directed toward me.

He put the remainder of the ice cream back in the freezer and started down the hall before stopping and turning to face us. "Rory?"

She shifted so she could look him in the eye. "Yeah?"

"Thanks for believing us. Thanks for helping. Whatever happens…" He shook his head and looked at me. "Whatever happens… I know you must be doing the right thing. I know that because Gage would never allow anyone next to Ivy and me who reeked of bad."

And with that, he left me to my fate.

But the truth of the words hit home. He believed in me. Even though I'd failed him a hundred times, he still believed in me. And he was right. If I sensed even one iota of ugly around Rory, I wouldn't have let her into our lives.

What I felt when I was with her was desire and a fierce determination.

But underneath her grit and strength, there was also the soft layer I'd always recognized. An innate goodness. Rory shone with it. Like the fairy godmother in those Disney movies. As if she could wave a wand and fix your life even as her own was shrouded in darkness.

I made my way around the counter and tapped her computer screen and the image of the military giant. "Where was he and how'd you know he was following us?"

"I saw him first in the building where I got the video of the kidnapping. He stood out. It was mostly just instinct until I saw him a couple more times."

"You usually follow your instincts," I said quietly. She met my gaze and nodded. "But you don't consider it a psychic ability."

She scoffed. "Not hardly. That's training and experience. And even then, I've done a shit job of listening to it lately."

I gave in to the urge to come clean. "The only abilities I have are just that. Instincts. I have an extra keen sense of people. If they're bad news, I know it. If they're good blokes, I know that too."

"Blokes?"

"Apparently today is National Use Old Words Day." I

was rewarded with a half laugh I longed to make a full one. "I can tell the nature of people. Like how I knew there was something wrong with West and Dunn. And I can tell you when a storm is coming."

Her eyes grew. "A storm?"

"It's what made me good at chasing them in college."

She sat there for a moment, not disclaiming my abilities but really letting them settle over her.

"What did you feel about West and Dunn?"

"Like they were bad news. Like they'd do anything—and I mean anything—to get what they wanted."

We stared at each other for a moment, and when she changed the subject, relief washed through me. She believed me.

"What do you know about cloud seeding?"

Just as I went to respond, my phone alarm went off.

"Sorry," I said, rising from the barstool. "I have to head back down. Tango Tuesday is wrapping up, and Audrey's off in fifteen minutes."

She nodded, shutting her laptop and gathering her things as if getting ready to leave, and I was reluctant to let her go. I tried to tell myself it was because of what she was working on for us. But I knew it had much more to do with the way I felt when she was in the room. It was how I felt in the storm tank, sitting in the eye of the storm. Both calm and full of anticipation. Knowing that what was coming could destroy me, but still craving the high of being there. Of finding out more.

Which was exactly what I wanted of Rory. More.

Not just the facts or information about the case, but more of the tantalizing feeling that coasted through me when I was with her.

With so many balls we were juggling, it was scary to add another person to the mix, but what would it be like knowing someone was there to pick one up if you accidentally dropped one? Could we do that for each other?

Would she even let me? Would she see, like I had started to, that there might be an ease in sharing our burdens even with the added weight?

It was more than I could solve in the two minutes I had left before I headed back to the bar. All I knew was I wanted her to be there when I got back so I could start to figure it out. And if, after we'd explored it, letting her walk out the door with nothing more but this case between us was the right thing, I'd do it.

But maybe I'd have the chance to taste her one more time before she did. Maybe I'd have a good memory to add to what had been a row of shitty days…

So, I reached out and grabbed the handle of her bag, our hands colliding. Her body went still, and when she looked up at me, something uncertain and yet hopeful was in her beautiful eyes.

"Don't go," I whispered. My voice was husky and low, and the words were out before I could take them back. But I didn't want to. A certainty filled my chest. Even beyond this case, our parents, and Dunn, Rory was inexplicably tied to us. To me.

I cleared my throat. "Stay. I'll be back. You can ask me about cloud seeding and tell me what else you've found out. Maybe we'll find another piece of the puzzle you're so good at putting together."

She looked away for a moment and then back. "It's probably not a good idea."

My gut fell, crushing the hope I probably shouldn't have had.

"It's probably not," I acknowledged. "But stay anyway."

I ran a finger along the top of her hand. The skin was soft and delicate but burned into me like a tattoo.

There was so much bad in the world, and Rory had seen her share of it at the ripe old age of twenty-two. Maybe what I could offer her was a chance to see something good in the darkness. A light she could hold on to when her world got really bleak as she chased bad guys down for a living. God, that thought brought terror and pride to me in equal measures.

She swallowed, looking down the hall and back to me. "Gage…"

"Not for that," I told her. "And definitely not that here with Ivy in my room and Monte across the hall. Just so neither of us has to be alone tonight carrying our burdens."

Her eyes fluttered shut and then back open. She didn't say anything, but she didn't walk out the door either, and wings of hope fluttered through my chest.

"I have a pint of mint chocolate chip I don't mind sharing."

"This morning you tried to bribe me to leave with money. Now you're trying to bribe me to stay with ice cream?" she asked, lips quirking slightly.

I leaned in, my lips barely a breath away from hers. Her eyes fell to my mouth, and I felt the caress in her look as if she'd closed the last millimeter remaining and kissed me.

"I'd bring out the big guns and offer you popcorn and Reese's Pieces, but I'm afraid I'm all out."

She huffed out a laugh, and I pulled her bag from her hand, turning to place it on the couch before walking toward the door. As I pulled it open, I turned back and said, "Thank you." Her brows rose. "For helping us even after I was an ass."

"For all of two seconds I thought about introducing you to my Vipertek, but that would be like kicking a dog for barking at an intruder. As soon as I realized Monte had seen me in his vision, I knew you were being your normal Gage protector-self. But even superheroes have weaknesses, and I'm damn good at finding them, so the next time you're an ass, be prepared to be locked in a cage with some very painful kryptonite."

I chuckled, shaking my head, but relief flew through

me. I should have known Rory would see through me. She may not have any psychic abilities that she'd admit to, but she read people. It was her own superpower.

As I jogged down the stairs to the bar, for the first time in longer than I could remember, there was a lightness to my step, and the primary reason for it was knowing Rory was waiting for me. I'd never wanted my mother's abilities, but I suddenly yearned to know what future Demi would see if she touched me. Had I grown roots deep and strong enough to find the happiness Demi had once claimed awaited me?

Would I find it with Rory and my siblings at my side?

Chapter Twenty-seven

Rory

OPEN TO SOMETHING AND THAT SOMETHING IS YOU

Performed by Aly & AJ

My heart ran wild as I watched Gage leave. Or maybe it wasn't my heart but my imagination running amuck. Waiting for him with his siblings asleep down the hall felt strange and yet right all at the same time. It felt… domesticated. It felt like a full family rather than the portions I'd been served for so long.

After the divorce, I'd guarded my heart well. Dad had been cold and reserved from the moment I'd gotten caught in the senator's home office, and then he'd started dating Sheila from the FBI before I could figure out how to fix what I'd broken. He'd spent more time with her than he had me, even canceling our weekends together to be with her.

If your own father could choose to walk away, then it was quite likely others would too. So I'd kept everyone, even those closest to me, at arm's length, hiding behind a locked door. I wasn't sure Mom or Nan had noticed. Maybe they'd just been biding their time waiting for me to let them back in.

Now it was too late. Now I might never get to tell Mom how much I *really* loved her. The casual words thrown out as we passed each other in and out of the condo didn't really count. They'd been merely alternate words for goodbye.

Ever since I'd walked into the tavern and had seen Gage, my barred door had been splintering.

Or maybe Gage was the only person who'd ever had the key.

I wasn't sure if that was sad or hopeful.

My heated body claimed it was something completely different after our almost kiss and the tender plea Gage had uttered asking me to stay.

Maybe I needed that mint chip ice cream to cool me off.

I'd just scooped two enormous mounds into a bowl when my facial recognition software pinged. I sat cross-legged on the couch with my computer in my lap, and as I opened the app, another piece of all the puzzles floating around me slid onto the board.

The guy who'd followed us was Space Force. Not only was he Space Force, but he was also an astronaut and a young one at that. Andrew Casada was barely thirty years old. Which meant he had to have double-timed his PhD before even joining the military, or maybe he'd been one of those child prodigies.

Except he certainly didn't look like the *Real Genius* nerds who'd finished school at some ungodly age of ten or twelve. He was all muscle and dashing good looks. In addition to his academic achievements, he'd accumulated a ton of flight time. He was a walking example of what determination, intelligence, and perseverance could do.

There wasn't much else to be found on him beyond that. He had to be the person from Space Force my mom had met up with. No way was this coincidence. But why hadn't he contacted me after Mom's accident? Why hadn't he just introduced himself when he'd seen me? And what did he have to do with Argento Skies?

I turned my attention from Casada back to the company itself. A town in Colorado had filed a lawsuit against them, but a superior court had dismissed it. The shell corporation that had paid for Argento's D.C. lease was a ghost that would take more time to track down.

So many dead ends. My spidey senses were going haywire trying to figure out what I was missing. It was frustrating.

My eyelids drooped, and I knew I needed to do something if I intended to be awake when Gage walked back in the door, but my body protested. The weariness I'd been feeling for over a year combined with the lack of any real sleep over the last few days was catching up to me.

I let my eyes shut. *Just for a few minutes*, I told myself.

Next thing I knew, a hand was sliding along my cheek, and I reacted instantaneously, twisting it backward and tossing my computer aside. I barely stopped myself from jamming the heel of my palm into Gage's nose as he grunted in surprise. I let go of his wrist, adrenaline crashing through me, easily pushing aside the haze of sleep.

"Crap. Don't sneak up on me like that!" I barely breathed out, trying to keep my voice down. I rubbed my chest and willed the frantic pace to slow. "You really do want to meet my stun gun."

"You get woken by bad guys often?" he asked. His voice was a mix of concern and wariness, but the truth was, he could have been one of the bad guys. He could have been one of the men who'd kidnapped Monte coming back for a second round.

"I'm a light sleeper. You must have been in stealth mode," I said, eyes narrowing in on him. I glanced at the shut door and the alarm that was now set and blinking as I sat back down.

"Habit. Ivy has always been a good sleeper, but when she was little, it took hours to get her down, and I never wanted to wake her up storming in at one in the morning."

Gage joined me, slouching down until his neck was resting on the back of the couch. His eyes closed and he rubbed his forehead. His eyes were shadowed and his face pale. He looked worn out, and I was overwhelmed with the desire to curl up next to him, massage his temples and find a way to give him a momentary respite from the burdens he carried.

As if he felt me watching him, he turned his head to the side and opened his eyes to meet mine.

"What did you find out?" he asked with a glance toward my laptop.

I righted my computer and brought up the information I'd found on Casada.

"Nothing more on Dunn. But the facial recognition identified the guy from earlier as Space Force. My mom had a meeting on her calendar with someone from Space Force the day of the accident. It's fair to say he was the one. If he's on the up and up, it's strange that he wouldn't have contacted me directly."

"Did you hack into a government system to use their facial recognition software?" There was humor in his voice, but also concern.

"I didn't hack in to run it." Which was the truth. I hadn't had to break in because I already had the software and the links to the appropriate database.

The longer I stared at the screen, the more intense his stare felt. I finally relented and looked over to see concern but also respect in his eyes. That did as much for my lonely soul as if he'd kissed me.

"Thought we agreed to no lying," he said, but it held a tease rather than rebuke.

"I'm not lying. I didn't hack in…not today," I said with a shrug and a half smile.

His gaze fell to my lips and the entire energy of the room shifted, sexual tension sifting through the air again. Magnetic. Electric. He lifted a hand, tugging at a lock of hair.

"This—your hair finally coming loose—makes me happier than you can know. I can never get Ivy's to stay up." His voice went down a notch.

"You do a good job with hers," I told him, seemingly fascinated by the way he was winding the curl around his finger. A finger I knew from experience was calloused and rough but also gentle and strong. Hands that could do such delightful things to my body.

When he'd rolled the strand to my cheek, he stroked my skin tenderly.

"Ever since you walked into The Prince Darian on Saturday, I've ached to touch you." It was a hushed admission. Not tortured. Not resigned. More… persuasive. "At first, it made me feel like a perverted creep. You were fifteen the last time I saw you."

I shook my head, and his hand on my cheek flexed.

"But the more time we've spent together, the more I've seen the fierce, beautiful woman you've become. All adult. Sexy as hell. Not a teen kid, and yet you're also not just some random woman I've met at a bar. There's no way I can lose myself in the stunning person you've become to satisfy this wild craving and then just walk away. It wouldn't be right."

My insides fluttered at his words. There'd been so many years when I'd longed for Gage to say I was beautiful. Stunning. And now, here he was saying it, and yet I still felt the "but" hanging in the air.

"Gage—"

He moved so fast it shocked me, both hands landing on my face. His thumb brushed my lips, preventing me from saying more. Our mouths were so close, it wouldn't take much more than a sharp inhale to bring them together. His eyes were dark tonight. The deepest of grays right before the lightning struck and the thunder roared.

What would it be like to get lost in Gage's storm?

He talked about craving. My entire body ached for him. Wanted what he offered. Needed it more desperately than I'd ever needed anything.

"I see you, Rory," he said, stroking my bottom lip, fanning the flames inside me until I thought he'd be able to see them through my skin. "I see the weight of the responsibilities you carry just like me. At first, the idea of adding mine to yours felt as wrong as the idea of taking you for only a night. But I think there's a way we can help each other. We're strong alone… but imagine what we would be like if we shared our burdens."

My hand circled his wrist, pulling him away from my mouth and settling our palms joined on my chest, where my heart banged as fiercely as it burned.

"Do I get to talk now? Do I get a say in any of this?" I asked.

A small smile curved over his beautiful lips—satisfaction and desire. More emotions that would spread themselves all over the case I was working, hiding the truth like the fog rolling in from the Potomac covering the cobblestone streets.

When he didn't say anything, I continued softly, "To deny I want you would be like denying *Veronica Mars* is the greatest television show ever." I watched with joy as the hunger in his eyes intensified. "But we both have more people than ourselves to consider. I don't know…"

I closed my eyes so I didn't have to see him while I turned him down. Was I really going to push him away after years of comparing every man in my life to him because of some rule my father tossed out as if it was a law of nature? Could I turn him down?

Exhaling a shaky breath, I opened my eyes and said, "Just tell me to shut up and kiss me."

His mouth pressed against mine, and my entire body convulsed with relief. But even as the sparks ignited, fanning my burning embers, I could tell he was holding back. My words had struck home. He needed someone in his life who was all in. Someone who would stick. Someone who wouldn't treat their life as if it had a revolving door the way Demi had.

If I joined the FBI, if there was any way for me to still make that dream come true, it would be just that. Me in and out. Not just because of cases I was working on, but because they'd stick me in some field office in the middle of nowhere until I proved myself. I wouldn't be here.

Unexpected tears leaked out from behind my closed lids because I knew the truth. Knew I couldn't let this moment turn into something more if I was going to disappear. I had to decide to be all in or walk away. The minute the tears landed on his hands, he pulled back.

"Why are you crying?" His voice sounded tortured.

"Because wanting you and not being able to keep you is just one more loss I'm not sure I can take."

He groaned, eyes closing, and then he was devouring me. This was not a gentle kiss that spoke of letting go, but one that demanded I give him everything. Begging me to stay instead of leave.

The darkened room seemed to fill with neon colors. Flashing signs both warning and luring me to enter as his lips sought to convince me to give him more than just my mouth—to hand over every last part of my heart and soul. To change my dreams so they were about him and his family and a very different life than the one I'd seen for myself.

His tongue swept along my seam, and I opened for him. Without any reluctance. Without regret. Only an incredible yearning unlocking secret wishes about belonging and family. He angled our mouths, joining us closer, and yet it wasn't enough.

He pulled me onto his lap, hand skimming the heated skin along my waist, sliding up under my sweater and curving along my side and to my back, palms spreading wide, pushing us together until I felt every single line of him pressed into me. Until sinew and bone merged into something new, lightning forging sand into glass.

But what if we broke?

What if we shattered?

What would remain of me after more wreckage?

I panicked, pushing us apart and shoving myself off his lap. My chest heaved. My lips stung. My heart and body demanded I go back and finish what we'd started.

His lids closed. Anguish and regret coasted over his face.

"God. Rory. I'm sorry."

"Don't!" I demanded. "Don't be sorry. I'm not." He opened his eyes, doubt swirling in them, clearly not believing me. "I'm not sorry. I just… I need to catch my breath. To think." *To make sure I don't hurt you or me or all of us.* But I couldn't say those last words aloud. They felt too raw and real and permanent.

He stared for several seconds before reaching down and righting my computer.

The tabs I'd had open had changed after being tossed aside. Instead of Casada's face, the screen now displayed the Argento Skies, Inc. website.

"You really think this has something to do with a cloud seeding company?" I could hear the doubts in his voice. I didn't blame him.

"I thought cloud seeding was just a myth? Can they really make it rain?"

"We've been doing it for decades," Gage told me. "The results are mostly inconclusive, though. It's difficult to prove whether it would have rained regardless of whether the clouds were seeded or not. Plus, it comes with its fair share of controversies."

"Like?"

"People say forcing rain to fall is stealing water from one location to give it to another. Several nations have accused China of weaponizing the weather."

"And yet we're still doing it?"

"Especially states out west because of the severity of the droughts they experience." He looked down at the information on Argento Skies. "They're on a short list for a federal contract?"

I nodded. "Their new CEO, Shawn Walden, has gone after it pretty aggressively."

"What happened to their old CEO?"

I told him about the plane crash and how the FAA ruled it an accident. "But get this," I said, opening up the article I'd found earlier. "His widow said he'd been receiving death threats from some local environmental group who insists the silver iodide in their cloud seeding is making people sick. The town tried to sue the company."

Gage shook his head. "The parts per million in the snowpack and waterways from cloud seeding are insignificant. Lower than most naturally occurring levels."

"But what if the town already had high rates of silver iodide in the water and soil from years of mining?"

Gage looked thoughtful. "I'd still have a hard time believing there was enough of it going up in the air to push into the unhealthy category."

"So the lawsuit was most likely a money grab?" I asked.

"I'd have to look at the data, but probably."

"How do *you* feel about cloud seeding?"

He raised a brow, and his lips twitched. "Feel about cloud seeding? I mean… I've never really considered it. I didn't know it was a debate that needed me to pick sides."

"Not even in the meteorological community?"

"No. At least not the circles I was in. We were about saving people's lives by increasing warning times and researching ways to prevent catastrophic events from occurring."

He'd given up those dreams of making a difference to care for his family, but watching him with Monte and Ivy, you'd never know it. All you saw was his love and devotion. Things I longed to have. Things he'd offered me. My heart squeezed. Could I change my dreams and feel the same way he did? Or would I eventually resent it?

I couldn't think about it tonight. Maybe after all this was done—once we'd stopped whatever was happening with Dunn and Demi and found the people responsible for my mom—maybe then I could really evaluate what he'd offered me.

"Can you think of any reason the Space Force would be interested in cloud seeding?" I asked.

His lips curved upward, turning into a small but stunning smile. "I mean, maybe if they were trying to make it rain on the moon. Or Mars?"

I reached out and smacked him on the shoulder. "I'm serious, Gage. You want to know why Monte was taken, where Demi is—it's all wrapped up in this somehow."

My words wiped his smile away, and I instantly regretted it.

"How did you make the leap from your mom meeting with this Space Force guy to it all being related?" he asked.

"Argento Skies is one of Dunn's donors," I told him. "Plus, Mom had the company's symbol next to notes about meeting with Casada. Her car crashed right after that meeting with him. Believe me, it's connected. I'm going back to D.C. in the morning to get into the Argento Skies office, and then I want to talk to Dunn again. See if we can rattle his cage some more."

Gage's brows drew together. "What do you plan to ask Dunn?"

"If he knows where your mom is."

Gage inhaled sharply. "You think he'll tell us the truth?"

"Not us. Me."

"If you're confronting Dunn, I'm going too," he insisted.

I shook my head, thinking about how hard it was yesterday to have Gage with me. He'd lost his cool and he'd stood out like a Hollywood A-list actor walking through the halls. He hadn't blended in at all. He was far too memorable.

"Monte and Ivy need you here," I told him.

"Monte needs this solved. For us to stop whatever is going to happen to Demi and Dunn." Gage's voice turned deep and tortured.

"You hired me to take care of this. I know what I'm doing." At least, most of the time that was true. Except this week Dad's voice had been an almost constant companion in my head, filling me with doubts.

"You absolutely know what you're doing. You're one of the smartest people I know," he said tenderly, making my heart thump happily. "But this time, you don't have to do any of it alone. I'm here. I'm going."

I tugged at the sleeve of my sweater, pulling on a thread that looked like it might unravel just like my insides were trying to do. I'd always worked by myself. Research—alone. Stakeouts—alone. Trailing a suspect—alone.

"What about the bar?" I asked softly.

"River and Audrey work Wednesdays."

"It means leaving Monte and Ivy here." That got him. I could see indecision roll through him.

"As much as I hate the idea of my brother being farther than an arm's length away after what happened, this is more important than my feelings."

He rose from the couch, went to the antique buffet where the television sat, and opened the cupboards. He pulled out some blankets and a pillow.

"What are you doing?" I asked.

"Taking the couch. You can have my bed."

I huffed out a laugh. "I can go home, Gage. I literally live ten minutes away."

"It's two in the morning and it's raining. You rode your bike, right? Just stay."

He said it casually, as if it was a simple request based on simple facts, but we both knew it was much more than that. My pulse skittered once more, bringing me right back to our heated kisses.

"I'll take the couch. I'm smaller than you," I said.

"This couch and I have lots of fond memories," he said.

I couldn't help the snort that escaped me.

"Get your head out of the gutter, Pipsqueak. I've pulled some all-nighters here but not the kind you're thinking. Quite the opposite. When Ivy was a baby, she got pretty sick a couple of times, and I had to stay awake and make sure she stayed hydrated one tablespoon at a time. And when Monte's visions get really bad, he and I stay awake watching movies."

I couldn't remember a time my dad had stayed up all night with me. Not even my mom. I'd never really been a sick kid. A cold here and there. Nothing that had been worrisome.

When I had broken ribs after the fight in high school, I hadn't been able to sleep, and Mom joined me on the couch as I rewatched *Veronica Mars*. But she'd ruined the show with all her reality versus fiction talk, and I'd told her she had to leave before I found the duct tape. She'd laughed and headed to bed.

I'd been loved. I'd been hugged and fed and taken care of. Hell, my mom had even divorced my dad for me. Or because of me? Either way, she'd chosen me over him. If that didn't say *I love you*, nothing could.

But somehow I'd still needed something neither of my parents had been able to give. This was about me and not them. Rationally, I knew that, and yet thinking about Gage sitting up with his siblings, caring for them, felt like what I'd been missing from those interactions with my parents.

But maybe what I'd really been missing was simply Gage.

Chapter Twenty-eight

Gage

YOU AIN'T BEEN IN LOVE
Performed by Nate Smith

I woke with a crick in my neck to soft whispers and a gentle clang of a pan on the stove. The sun was filtering in through the closed blinds, but it had the gentle glow of early morning.

After I'd settled Rory in my bed, I'd landed on the couch in my normal pajama bottoms and T-shirt and been unable to sleep for at least another hour. This time it was because of images of Rory tangled in my sheets.

The kiss we'd shared had been fueled with pent-up desire and emotions. I'd put myself out there in a way I'd never expected to do and yet had found myself unable to stop. She hadn't rejected it—me—but she hadn't accepted what I'd offered either. She'd pulled away, saying she needed time to think.

Maybe she was right. Maybe we both should take the time to really figure out what we wanted. Or maybe I just needed to prove to her how we didn't have to be the single column holding up a bridge all on its own.

I dragged a hand over my face and sat up, blankets falling away.

Monte and Ivy were in the kitchen. She was sitting on the counter stirring something in a large bowl, and he was at the stove dropping butter into a pan. It sizzled and snapped, and his head twisted in my direction.

"Did we wake you?" he asked with a sheepish smile.

It was good to see the grin. He'd smiled more last night than he had in a while, even with the visions haunting him. Did we have Rory to thank for it?

I rose and joined them, prepping the coffeepot and eyeing what they were doing. "Pancakes?" I asked.

Monte nodded. "You always make them for us. We thought we'd try to make them for you… and Rory."

Ah. He'd seen her then. Or Ivy had and told him.

"We were up late talking about"—I glanced at Ivy—"everything. I didn't want her driving home on her motorcycle in the rain."

Monte's lips twitched. "Sure. Makes sense."

I eased over, pulled him into a headlock, and rubbed his hair with my knuckles. "Don't get ideas, Chubby Cheeks."

He laughed, but then groaned as he grabbed his side.

I let him go instantly, a frown replacing my smile. "Shit. Sorry. How are you?"

"Shit!" Ivy repeated, waving the spoon and causing pancake batter to fly everywhere.

"Don't say that," I said, taking the spoon and putting it back in the bowl before reaching for the paper towels.

"I'm doing okay. Sore, but okay," Monte said. "Go sit down. I want to do this."

I debated. I didn't want my brother to think he had to start cooking for us. He was a kid. That wasn't his job. But I also saw the look of pride in his eyes as he pulled the bowl from Ivy and started spooning batter into the hot pan.

"You know when to turn them, right?" I asked, grabbing a coffee cup and filling it.

"When the bubbles appear."

I nodded and headed for the table crammed into the corner on the opposite side of the entryway. We didn't use it often, but it was still a piece of home I'd refused to give up. Sturdy oak with scratches and grooves from not only our life but generations of Palmers before us.

Rory appeared at the edge of the hall. She was in a pair of my sweats and an old Prince Darian Tavern tee. Her hair was down and tangled around her shoulders. She looked like the very best kind of morning. Rumpled and tired and yet with a light in her eyes. Her gaze journeyed from me at the table to Monte and Ivy in the kitchen and back.

"They wanted to make you breakfast," I said.

Her eyes widened.

"Wowy!" Ivy shouted. She squirmed on the counter, and I held my breath just as Monte caught her in time to help her down. He grimaced again, holding his side, before standing straight. My heart banged, and I almost said something, but one look at his face told me he didn't want me smothering him with my concerns.

Ivy's wild curls bounced all over the place as she ran toward Rory, colliding with her shins and holding on in a way that made Rory reach for the wall to stabilize them both.

"Morning," she said, ruffling Ivy's hair.

"Do you like pancakes?" Ivy asked.

"I do. One of my very favorite breakfast foods."

Ivy jumped and spun in a circle full of an energy I hadn't seen from her in days. Adding sugar to her already high-strung mood meant she was going to crash hard in a few hours. My eyes went back to Monte. Would he be able to handle it if I went into D.C. with Rory?

Guilt tore through me. But I was doing this for him. For us.

"Can I have some of that coffee?" Rory asked, tipping her head toward the pot.

"Please. Help yourself."

She did, watching for a moment while Monte transferred a pancake from the pan onto a plate warming in the oven.

"Those look pretty good," she said.

My brother beamed. I thought maybe he was falling in love with Rory as much as I was. My breath caught as that thought settled over me. I'd definitely wanted more than a one-night joyride with Rory. I'd wanted someone who could stick by us, but I hadn't called it love. The idea was terrifying and intoxicating all at the same time.

I desperately wanted the joy Demi had once seen for me… not just for myself but for my siblings and for Rory. Calling it love was something altogether different. More.

After Rory had joined me at the table with her coffee cup and her computer, I announced, "Rory and I are heading into D.C. in a bit."

Monte looked up from the pan, exchanging a look with me before returning to what he was doing. "Okay."

"Do I need to ask River and Audrey to come by?" I asked.

Monte's cheeks flushed. "I don't need a babysitter."

I almost snipped back something about him running off and being kidnapped proving otherwise, but I didn't. It wouldn't ease my guilt and wouldn't make him feel any better.

"I promise I'm staying here," he said in a softer tone as if reading my mind. "I'm sore as sh—heck. I think Ivy and I need a *Scooby* marathon. Right, Ives?"

"Yes!" She danced and wiggled and then stopped in her tracks. "I gotta pee."

She ran down the hall at full speed.

"Is there something I can help with?" Rory asked Monte.

He shook his head, bringing the butter and syrup over to the table. He glanced at Rory's computer as he went by and froze.

"What's that?" he asked, a hint of panic in his tone that had me setting down my cup and pulling the laptop toward me just as Rory said, "It's the logo for a company called Argento Skies. Why?"

Monte stood there staring at the screen. "I… I know it."

"From your vision?" I asked, trying to stay calm as my brother put his hands into his hair and stepped back from the table.

"I… I don't know." His eyes closed.

I was at his side in a flash.

"It's okay. Just breathe."

The smell of burned batter filled the air, and Rory jumped up, headed to the stove, and removed the pan before coming back to stand by us.

"Do you think you saw it where you were held?" she asked.

Monte closed his eyes. "I really don't know. I can sort of picture it on something. But I don't know if it's a wall… or a door… I don't know if I saw it in person or in my dreams." Frustration brewed in his voice.

He shook his head and opened his eyes. After peering down the hall, he lowered his voice. "But it reminds me. Something weird happened last night when the vision came to me again. Something I've never had happen before."

Dread filled me.

"What happened?" Rory prompted.

"The vision… It… I guess I'd say it flickered. Like one moment it was the same as I saw before with Dunn getting shot and falling. Just like the night before, Demi was in it. But one time she was falling with him… and the next, it was like she was across the room and it was just him falling. And then it was right back to them falling together."

I found it hard to breathe. What the hell did it mean? His visions never faltered. They always expanded, adding details and dimensions, but they never differed from how they started. It was Rory who expressed the inkling of hope I was feeling.

"Maybe this means we've already started to change what happens."

Monte's gaze flew from me to her and back. "Do you

think?"

I nodded, and he looked so relieved, so full of optimism, that it was almost painful. Because what if we couldn't change it? What if Demi and Dunn still fell in a pile of blood? Was a shred of hope better than being prepared for the worst? I didn't know.

Ivy came back into the room, and we let the conversation drop. Instead, we talked about Scooby and the gang while we ate.

"What show do you like?" Ivy asked Rory.

"*Veronica Mars*," she said without a single second of hesitation, and I couldn't help but smile.

"Please tell me you've watched at least a few different shows in the last decade."

She scoffed. "Yes. But you can't dislodge a cult classic from its place at the top of the pyramid. Besides, how would you even know how awesome it is or isn't? Because last I'd checked, you'd never watched more than the single movie you took Shay and me to."

"Things change," I tossed back.

"Wait." Her eyes widened. "You actually watched it?"

I shrugged. "Someone I know gave me the first three seasons on DVD."

"Gage Palmer! You watched and didn't even tell me?" The look of incredulity on her face was priceless. "I have so many things to discuss with you! Have you seen the last season too?"

I hadn't watched the series until after we'd moved into the apartment. When we'd been boxing up the basement at the Victorian, I'd found the collection among the other piles of DVDs. I'd almost tossed it into the donation pile with the rest, but something had stopped me.

Maybe it was the note stuck to it telling me I couldn't deprive myself of the greatest show on earth in Rory's tiny print, or maybe it was the memory of a girl screaming into the lightning on my bike. Either way, I'd wondered what would make someone as fierce as she'd been go head over heels for a show.

So, I'd watched it late at night when I'd been unable to wind down after closing the bar. I wouldn't go as far as Rory and say it was the best show on earth, but it was addictive. Like popcorn and Reese's Pieces. Like her.

"Yes, I even watched the last season. I almost wished I hadn't," I told her because it had been painful in ways I hadn't liked. I'd wondered what Rory thought about the final damage the writers had given her heroine. Wondered how many people were living through wreckage and loss like me and my siblings—and Rory herself.

"Can I watch it?" Ivy asked.

"No." I shook my head. "It's a grown-up show."

Ivy pouted. "I'm going to be fouwa."

"Four's a pretty cool number," Rory told her. "One of my favorites."

I looked up at her in surprise because four had always been my favorite as well. It had been my jersey number on the high school basketball team. "It is?"

She flushed in a decidedly un-Rory-like way and looked down at her plate, and I realized she'd picked that number because of me. Mixed emotions flew through me again.

I wanted to know what else of mine had left a lasting mark on her, and yet it was also a reminder of the difference in our ages. How young she'd been when she'd first looked at me with a tween crush. In our twenties, the gap seemed to have closed, but we were still five years apart. She was finishing college, and I was basically a dad with a business to run. Our lives were still miles apart.

But the thought of letting her drift out of my life felt wrong. More wrong than even the ending of her favorite show had been. Rory had always wanted to be Veronica, but it was the last thing I wanted for her because who would want someone they cared about—someone they loved—to go through life with the kind of wounds that forced you to keep a wall between you and everyone else around you? To pretend to be fine when really you were crumbling? A marshmallow melting in an open flame.

I didn't want that for anyone in my life.

And yet, it was exactly what I'd done to myself.

I'd pushed everything and everyone away to survive the loss of Dad, our home, and my dreams. I'd taken up the mantle of my life here and then used it as an excuse to keep the world away so I didn't have to feel abandoned and hurt and lost ever again.

What a lousy example that was for my siblings.

I wouldn't want this for them.

I'd insisted I was living in the present…but was this really living? I'd been drowning for a long time in the minutiae of our lives, but we needed more than that to be happy. I had to find a way to give my family that *more*. I had to find a way to give it to myself too. We deserved it, and so did Rory.

Chapter Twenty-nine

Rory

LIFE AIN'T ALWAYS BEAUTIFUL
Performed by Gary Allan

After breakfast, Gage followed me to the cottage in his SUV so I could change and drop off the bike. The sun had broken through the clouds for the moment, but they still hung in the sky, waiting to drop more rain onto the already soaked earth.

The aroma of the fallen leaves hung heavy in the air. Winter had landed fully upon us with a series of storms hitting the East Coast this week.

Which meant I'd be stuck inside a car all day when I would have preferred to be on my Rebel. Not only because it was easier to maneuver in the traffic, but because the more time I spent with Gage, the harder it was to stop myself from falling back into the teen crush of a decade ago. Especially after kissing him. Especially after kissing him and hearing him say he wanted something more than a single night with me.

It was my teenage fantasy come to life.

Except I wasn't a teenager.

I was a grown-ass woman with huge responsibilities. My mom's life literally hung on my ability to do my job and get paid.

Nan looked up from the table in the kitchen as I walked by.

"Is that Gage Palmer waiting for you?" She nodded toward where he'd parked the Pathfinder in front of the house. "You didn't say on Sunday, but I heard through the gossip line. It was his brother who was missing, wasn't it?"

I nodded.

"That family has been through so much already," she said softly. "What happened?"

"We think it's tied to something with Demi," I said, wondering if I should tell her that it might be tied up with Mom too, and then deciding until I had proof, it would seem like I was trying to connect dots that were on completely different pages. Even Gage, knowing everything, had hesitated last night.

"So you're still on the case, then?" Nan asked.

I nodded, placing my bag down on a chair. "I'm going to shower and change real quick. I probably won't be by Shady Lane until late."

Guilt twined through me, and Nan read it.

"She isn't there, Rory. She won't even know."

Sadness. Regret. Anger. They burned inside me.

"I can't believe you've given up on her." I started down the hall, tossing over my shoulder, "I don't have time for this today. She's in there. We just have to reach her."

"How long, Rory? How long are you going to keep her in that state and you along with her? You're both in limbo, withering away."

I whirled around to see her standing at the table, face red with frustration and anger and hurt. I strode back to her. "I'm not withering away."

"You are, damn it! And Hallie would hate it. As much as I despise siding with that man who fathered you, this may be the one and only time he actually knows what's best for you. I'm glad he didn't give you the loan."

My mouth dropped. "You knew? How?"

"I have my own nose for lies and secrets, Rory."

"He told you."

"He texted me."

"You've been talking behind my back this whole time?" God, did it hurt.

She shook her head. "No. Just since you went to see him on Friday."

Tears pricked my eyes but I fought them back. "I really don't have time for this, Nan. But trusting Dad and believing he knows what's best is the last thing either of us should *ever* do."

When I could see she didn't entirely believe me anymore, when I realized Dad had somehow used those Bishop charms on her, I broke and told her the one thing I knew would push her back into my lane. "Did you know her car's computer was messed with? That it wasn't an accident?"

Nan's face paled, and she grabbed hold of the back of the kitchen chair to stabilize herself. "What?"

"Dad knew! He knew! And didn't tell me! He had Detective Muloney withhold that information from us. Someone tried to kill her…" My throat closed, and I had to fight to breathe. "So do not *ever* tell me Sutton Bishop knows what's best for me or this family."

I wheeled around and headed for my bedroom.

After a quick shower, I pulled my hair up in a ponytail and made my way toward the front door. Nan met me, wrapping her arms around me before I could protest. I held myself stiff for all of two seconds, but then I hugged her back.

Life was too short. I'd had my walls up too high for too long. Mom had been there and then gone in a flash. I couldn't leave Nan without letting her know I loved her as much as she loved me. I let the warmth of her affection bleed into me.

She stepped back and put a wrinkled hand on my cheek. "I just want you to be happy. That's what she'd want too."

I swallowed hard. "I know, Nan."

I wanted to tell her that sometimes happy wasn't in the cards for everyone.

Except last night and this morning, I had felt happy. Being with Gage and his siblings had felt… right. The love floating between them had been contagious. A virus you wanted to catch rather than push away.

I loved Nan. I loved being with her, but both times I'd moved in with her, it had been because of traumatic things happening in my life. The cottage was tainted with those reminders. Reminders of how I'd failed both Dad and now Mom.

Looking back at those few months before Mom's crash, I could see she'd been worried. Harried even in a way my cool and collected Mom had never been. Even when she and Dad were fighting as they had been for months before I'd messed up at the senator's house, they'd always fought with an impressive control. Raised voices happened, but rarely. The words they used were more powerful than the volume.

But now, I wondered if the calm they'd exhibited even in the middle of arguments was because they'd never loved each other enough to truly fight. After mere hours with Gage, I was struggling to imagine leaving. If we spent weeks, or hell, years together, and he tried to walk out, I didn't think I'd be anywhere near calm. I didn't think I could let him pack up in silence without fighting for him to stay the way my dad had let my mom.

I squeezed Nan's hand and forced every single bit of meaning into the words as I said, "I love you."

"I love you too," she said, glancing toward the window and Gage. "Please stay safe out there."

I nodded, a lump in my throat preventing me from saying anything more. But by the time I'd closed the passenger door of the Pathfinder, I'd pulled myself together. Letting my emotions out with Nan was fine, but they needed to stay carefully locked away while I worked this case.

"Dunn will be at Margetto's for lunch at eleven

o'clock," I told Gage. "If we get there ahead of him, we might be able to talk to him before he goes inside."

"A hangry congressman, great," he said. "How did you get his schedule?"

"I told you, my dad works for him. In addition to internet security, Dad's team does physical security for Dunn whenever he's outside the Capitol."

"You hacked your dad's system?"

I glanced over at him, and I could tell he was fighting a smile. I shrugged.

After Dad had caught me looking into Dunn's files, I'd closed the backdoor again so he couldn't have Chanel backtrack it. And this time, I'd been sure I hadn't left any windows open. I'd locked everything down tight with a set of trip alarms I'd designed that hadn't gone off. Not yet anyway.

"You're Mac *and* Veronica rolled into one," Gage said, losing the battle and allowing a grin to spread across his face. I didn't know if it was his stunning smile or the fact that he knew about Mac as well as Veronica that had my heart flipping over. Whatever the reason, it shot pure pleasure through my veins and straight to my core.

"Don't try to butter me up with your Veronica knowledge."

"Not buttering you up, Pipsqueak. Facts are facts. You're like your hero in more than just the investigator and broken home ways. What does Wallace say to her? Something about Veronica's angry shell hiding her desire to bake him something? And her being decidedly marshmallow-like?"

I couldn't help the laugh that escaped me. "Trust me, you don't want me baking you anything. You might end up in the hospital with food poisoning. I'm lucky I can make a grilled cheese or heat up a frozen burrito."

"I notice you didn't deny being a marshmallow."

"Mars-mallow. It's what they call fans of the show. I'll

admit to being that and nothing more." An unfamiliar feeling of happiness settled in my veins at our teasing. More locks deep inside me seemed to open. More walls tumbling down for the one man I'd always wanted and never thought I'd have.

I turned my head to watch the trees flying by outside the window, forcing myself back to the case and the facts I needed to move around until they slid into place.

Gage slammed on his brakes, the ugly commute traffic slowing us down.

"We should have ridden our motorcycles," I told him. He didn't disagree. I looked at the car seat in the back and thought about what Monte had said about Gage and his motorcycle and the sacrifices he was making. "Do you ever get to ride your bike at all?"

"It's hard to find the time."

"What happened to your Charger?" I asked.

"Traded it and Dad's truck in for this," he said.

"Why?"

"You ever try to get a car seat in and out of the back of a Charger? Gives lessons in geometry a whole new name. Plus, this has side airbags in addition to the front ones."

I didn't say anything, and his lips twitched again. "This is way sexier, right? Come on. Talk of airbags and car seat safety… You never knew it could be such a turn-on."

I knew he meant it as the opposite, but the fact Gage had given up so much to take care of his siblings was exactly that. One oversized, endorphin-driven turn-on.

"You have no idea what turns me on," I teased back.

"You're right, I don't. So tell me. What does?" His voice was low. Sexy. My breath caught as he gave me another quick glance in the stop-and-go traffic, eyes thundering more than the clouds outside the car.

I fought to find my voice, and it sounded uncharacteristically sultry when I finally answered, "Sacrifice. Honesty. Honor. People who keep their word.

People who stick when the going gets tough."

"At least I'm in the game then," he said. "I may not be in the right shape to stick any three-pointers, but I'm on the court rather than sitting on the bench."

My smile grew. "I think you have some three-pointers left in you. You aren't some ancient wash-up looking back on his time in the pros with longing. You still have plenty of game."

"Yeah?" he said, eyes drifting to my mouth and then back to the road.

I pulled the sleeves of my sweater over my fingertips, swallowed, and then said, "Trust me. You got it in the net last night."

I didn't think it was possible for Gage's smile to be more beautiful than it already was, but he lit up at my words. A wild joy rushed over his face so beautiful it made me quiver.

"But I hit the rim. I need nothing but net next time."

"If you keep going with the corny basketball analogies," I teased, "I might have to take back everything I said."

His soft chuckle rolled through me. I wanted to freeze the moment. Capture it. Hold on tight so that neither of us remembered anything but the hint of desire and the overwhelming sense of belonging that filled the air. What would I give up to keep this? To be unlike my television heroine and actually hold on to the one person her heart had always wanted?

Chapter Thirty

Rory

BIG MAN, LITTLE DIGNITY
Performed by Paramore

Margetto's was one of the restaurants in D.C. that politicians went to when they wanted everyone to see who they were having lunch with. Dunn was meeting with the senator from Colorado who was due to retire next year. Which meant he was trying to maneuver his way into the upper house with the old guard's backing. This was good for us because he wouldn't want to make a scene at the restaurant. He'd want to appear strong and confident and squeaky clean.

Gage parked the car in a lot not far from the restaurant, and we hoofed it down the sidewalk, stopping just beyond the valet stand. The building wasn't old, but it liked to act like it was. Glazed windows were set in carved black wooden fronts, and ivy climbed the sides of the red brick with wrought iron trellises. The entire thing looked like it belonged in New Orleans rather than the heart of D.C.

We didn't have to wait long before two dark-windowed SUVs pulled up. I recognized two of the guys from the first car as men who worked for my dad, but the rest of the entourage was unknown to me. I greeted the two I knew, and they gave me a chin nod in return before scanning the sidewalks for danger.

As soon as the congressman's perfectly shined dress

shoes hit the ground, I raised my voice, "Congressman Dunn! We'd like to have another word with you about the missing boy we mentioned."

It drew not only the security team's eyes, but also those of the other politicians and voters coming and going. Dunn and West stepped toward me. West's face showed a flicker of anger before he locked it away. Dunn's remained decidedly congenial.

"Did he show up, Ms. Bishop?" Dunn asked. "I've been worried."

My breath caught at my name pouring from his lips, knowing for a fact I hadn't given it to him on Monday.

"He was kidnapped, but let go," I said.

I watched as a film-perfect expression crossed Dunn's face—as if he'd practiced it in the mirror as I'd once practiced a lifted brow. It was full of concern and empathy. "Is he okay?"

Gage shifted beside me, and I could feel his impatience and frustration as if they were my own as he growled out, "Okay is a relative term."

I shot him a look that said, *Let me handle this.*

"I'm glad he was returned to his family," Dunn responded, a little frown creasing his brow. "Although I fail to see how this has anything to do with me."

"His mother is Demi Palmer. I believe you two know each other."

His look fully centered on me for a beat. For the first time, I felt a dark and dangerous intensity in his gaze before it vanished. His affable smile returned and he said, "Demi. Beautiful woman. Kind soul."

"Did you know Monte was her son when he showed up on Friday?" I asked.

"Ms. Bishop. Now is hardly the time or place for this discussion. Representative Dunn has a very busy day, and you're making him late for an important meeting." West stepped forward as if to put himself between the congressman and me.

"With Senator Ackley," I responded. "I know. Sounds like Congressman Dunn is planning a senate run. Big step. I wonder what would happen if he was suddenly caught in the middle of a scandal with missing kids, missing women, and corrupt sponsors?"

West's eyes narrowed, but Dunn's glimmered with humor as if I was an adorable little kid to pat on the head. "Aren't all politicians surrounded with conspiracies their opponents stir up? I'm not worried. I have it on good account that I can weather any storm that's coming."

Gage's entire body stiffened at the precise words Dunn had used. The representative looked Gage in the eye and asked, "Is it your mother who's the missing woman? Seems like the problem runs in the family."

I stepped in front of Gage as rage rolled through him. It put me close enough to West that I could smell the man's cologne. Aggressive and over-the-top just like him.

"Tell me the last time you saw her," Gage demanded.

"Demi was a great comfort to me when I was going through my divorce. Promised me it wouldn't impact my political career. And look." He waved his hand around. "She was right. Here I am, doing exactly what I was destined to do."

"Demi is only as right as your last decision," Gage retorted, and the congressman's face faltered again.

"Can you tell us the last time you saw her?" I repeated Gage's question.

"It's been a while. I miss her. She was a bright light, but you know Demi." Dunn would have said more, but West spoke over him.

"She always found it hard to stay in one place for long, didn't she? Unfortunately, that's what the congressman needed in his life. Stability and loyalty. I'm not sure she really knew the meaning of either word."

Gage pressed forward so that his chest was to my back,

and I reached a hand out to grab his arm in case he tried to move around me and hit West.

A silent standoff bubbled between all of us for a moment before Dunn smiled once again and West's grim face turned even darker.

"Let me know if you find her," Dunn said and then started toward the restaurant.

I called out after him. "What really happened to the Argento Skies's CEO?" He and West kept going, and I had to raise my voice to be sure I was heard. "The new CEO has become a big fan of yours, hasn't he? Lucky you. I forget, how much money did he contribute to your last election? How much is he giving you for your senate run?"

Dunn never turned around, but West looked at me in the window's reflection. His face was pinched and angry. Furious, even. The two men disappeared inside right as the clouds above us broke. Rain poured down outside the green-and-white awning we were standing beneath.

One of Dad's guys looked at me, shaking his head. "Mr. Bishop is not going to be happy about this, Rory."

I shrugged. "Nothing I do makes dear old Dad happy these days. Maybe you can give him a message. Tell him if he knew anything about what Dunn did to Monte Palmer—what is happening to Demi Palmer—I won't go easy on him just because I have his DNA running through me."

The man's jaw tightened, but he whirled around and headed into the restaurant.

The wind was cold as it blew over us, and yet the air felt heavy. The street was oddly silent, making the steady drip from the awning all the more prevalent.

"Stay here. I'll run and get the car," Gage said.

"It's just water," I told him. But then, through the restaurant's windows, I caught sight of West, on the phone, weaving through the tables toward the patio on the side of the restaurant that was shut down due to the winter weather. "Fine. I'll wait here."

Gage's eyes narrowed as if he knew I was up to something, but he took off at a jog, lifting the collar of his jacket, boots splashing in the puddles. I watched to make sure he didn't turn around and then headed around the side of the building. The rain instantly drenched me, leaking down the back of my leather jacket.

I slipped over the waist-high wrought iron railing and quietly pushed aside the clear plastic cordoning off the patio for the season. After a quick glance to make sure I wasn't being watched, I made my way over to the corner where several closed sun umbrellas were stacked. I pulled my phone from my pocket, hit Record, and hoped the rain pattering on the copper roof wouldn't make West's conversation incomprehensible later.

"First, he made that ridiculous decision on Monday, and now he can't see how she's become a liability. He won't free himself from this addiction because he believes the bullshit she spouts about the senate seat. We need to cut the cord for him," West ranted. He paused to listen briefly before saying, "I don't care how it's done." Another beat. "Fine. I'll have Shawn make the drop when you have a location."

He punched the phone off and then dialed another number.

"We have another meeting for you." Silence as he listened. "It's too late. You're tangled up in this even more than we are. Just remember, it was my calls that got the FAA off your back and the judge ruling in your favor for that ridiculous lawsuit. You owe me."

His eyes narrowed at the response I couldn't hear. "No. You haven't even come close to paying your debts. Just take the goddamn call when it comes in and do your part."

He hung up and stared out into the rain beyond the plastic, deep in thought.

My pulse raced. God. Was he talking about Demi being the problem? And was Shawn the Shawn Walden who'd inherited Argento Skies after his brother died? Were they talking about his brother's plane crash the FAA had determined was an accident? And was the lawsuit the one filed by the Colorado town against the company?

West ran a hand over his goatee, shoved his phone inside his suit pocket, and turned to go back inside, glancing my way. I held my breath, hoping the darkened corner of the patio and the umbrellas were enough to hide me.

"Who's there?" he demanded, taking several steps in my direction. There was no way I could slip out of the plastic now without him seeing me, so I did the opposite.

I moved out into the open and asked, "Problems, West?"

"I don't know what you think you heard, but—"

"Shawn Walden isn't a fixer. He's a nerdy little scientist and a semisolid businessman." I wasn't sure if he was more pissed at me for cutting him off or the fact that I had a good idea who he'd been talking to.

"Your father isn't going to like it when we cancel his contract because his little girl is playing spy games and messing around where she doesn't belong," West said, his voice oily and threatening.

But all it did was make me chuckle. "If you knew me at all, you'd realize just how little of a threat that is."

He'd expected me to be upset, so my laughter only fueled his anger. He darted a look toward the restaurant where the blinds were pulled so no one could see us, and then he closed the distance until there was only a table left between us. My hand slipped into my pocket where my fingers curled around my stun gun. I hadn't brought my Glock, which was stupid in hindsight, but I'd been worried about Monte's vision. About actually pulling the trigger and killing someone.

"Daddy issues? How trite. Do you have mommy issues, too?" His face turned snide. "Oh wait, she's practically dead, isn't she? I bet she was nosing around in other people's business too."

My heart stopped for so long I thought it wouldn't start again. Knowing he expected me to run with my tail between my legs, I forced myself to inhale and surprised him by lunging forward and placing my stun gun to his neck. "What. Did. You. Say?"

His look shifted to my weapon and back, but he didn't look afraid. Maybe it was because it looked like a flashlight instead of a hundred-thousand-volt stun gun.

"What do you think happens if you push that button, little girl? I can have your pitiful little contracts with the DoD stopped just like that." He snapped his fingers. "I think those background checks are the only things keeping you afloat these days, aren't they? How ever will you pay for dear Mommy's care facility if you lose them?"

I hated that he knew so much about me. Hated even more that it might have been my father who'd given him the information. My finger lingered on the button, wanting to see this arrogant asshole's eyes roll back in his head as electricity ran through his body.

"Rory?" Gage's voice called out beyond the darkened patio, worry bleeding through it.

"Run along, now," West said. "We wouldn't want Mr. Palmer to lose yet another person tied to him. The police might find that just a little too coincidental, don't you think? First his brother, then his mother, and finally his girlfriend?"

I didn't bother wasting time saying we weren't dating, mostly because my throat was clogged with fury and disgust. I pushed West away from me, stepping back toward the translucent plastic and the rail I'd entered the patio by.

His face twisted into an evil grin, and he wiggled his fingers at me. "Go on now."

"It's always the smug ones who have the thinnest shells. I'm going to enjoy cracking yours."

"I've been in this game since before you took your first breath. Keep digging and see what happens to those just learning how to dip their toes into the water. You can drown in the shallows just as easily as the depths."

"Rory!" Gage's voice held an edge of panic to it now.

I swirled around, pulled back the tarp, and eased over the rail without looking back.

"I'm here!" I called out, jogging around the corner of the restaurant and running smack into Gage.

"Thank God," he said on an exhale, wrapping me into his embrace as the rain poured over us. "Where the hell did you go?"

As the warmth of him mixed with the cold rain, I realized I was shivering, or maybe quivering with fury. Regardless, my body was trembling. Gage seemed to feel it too, because he pulled back to look into my face, worry cresting his brow.

"What's wrong? What happened?" he asked.

The pancakes I'd eaten felt like a twenty-pound weight in my stomach.

I looked back the way I'd come, but no one was coming after me. It meant West hadn't told Dad's team… not yet anyway.

"Let's go. I'll tell you in the car," I said, pushing away from Gage and heading toward the valet stand where the Pathfinder waited with a black F-150 pulled up behind it.

As I slid into the running vehicle, dark emotions welled. Even with the recording, nothing West had said was enough to prove he and Dunn were involved in something underhanded. It was all vague talk that could be interpreted in multiple ways, easily explained away, and even if the authorities believed us, none of it would be admissible in court. They wouldn't even be able to use it to get a search warrant.

It might get some airtime with a journalist, but it would be easy for West to spin.

I'd played my hand too soon.

I'd fucked up. Now West knew we were coming after them, and it might have cost Demi her life.

Chapter Thirty-one

Gage

I CAN'T HOLD BACK
Performed by Survivor

Whatever had happened in the few minutes I'd been gone to get the car had Rory shaking. But her face was blank, so I didn't know if the trembling was in fear or anger or just because the rain was cold as hell.

I shifted the SUV into drive, merging into the traffic and heading toward the Capitol and the building with Argento Skies's offices.

"Tell me what happened," I said quietly.

As she played back the encounter for me on her phone, my fingers tightened on the steering wheel until I was almost crushing it. God. What the fuck had Demi gotten us all involved in now? What had she gotten herself into?

"The asshole basically admitted to everything!" I growled out.

"Everything and nothing all at the same time," Rory added. "We need more proof, Gage. No one is going to listen to us. No one is going to bring him or Dunn or Shawn Walden to justice without more than what we have. And we need to do it before someone else gets hurt."

I'd thought I'd stopped caring about our mother years ago, but ever since Monte had first told me she was in his vision, I'd been plagued with a multitude of feelings for her. As much as I didn't want to see her again, I also didn't want to bury another parent. Monte's talk about Halloween last night had reminded me that we'd had good times.

After Dad was gone and we'd moved out of the apartment, I'd come home to find the entire living and dining area covered in a sea of sheets and blankets.

"We made a fort," Monte said with a smile, peeking out at me. "And we're having a picnic. Come join us."

Seeing it brought back bittersweet memories of Demi making the same kind of fort for me. After a moment's hesitation, I joined them, and we spent the rest of the afternoon and evening inside the homemade tent, playing board games and eating junk food.

As night started to fall and it neared bedtime, I told Monte we had to clean up. He moaned, and Demi smiled at me softly before she slammed a pillow into my face saying, "Lighten up, Gage."

It stunned me. The attack as well as her laughter that followed it—light and whimsical. My frozen state allowed Monte to crawl on top of me and pound his pillow into my face a few times before I rolled out from beneath him. I returned their attacks with vengeance until we all lay exhausted and smiling on the floor beneath a flowered sheet, the world hazy and dreamlike.

"I can't believe you did that," I said, but I was grinning.

Demi shrugged at me. "You only get one life. Don't let your responsibilities leak all the joy out of it."

Her hand was resting on my bare skin, and I saw the moment she got the vision. Saw the way it changed her eyes and made her face blank out. When she came back to me, there was sadness in her eyes. Grief I'd never seen in Demi before when she'd looked at me. As if she'd lost me rather than the other way around.

"Trust me," she said. "It's important to savor every happy moment because you never know when it'll be ripped

away."

She got up and crawled out of the fort. I almost called out after her, asking what she'd seen that made her so sad. Almost asked if she was okay. But then Monte hit me again with his pillow and I turned to my brother and tickled him until he howled.

My mind and heart whirled with those memories as I turned into the same garage I'd parked in on Monday. I didn't want to remember the good times with my mother because those moments were the ones that made her abandonment so much harder to bear. She'd left us again mere days after the fort-making incident, taking the joy and draining it away.

As Rory went to get out of the SUV, I stopped her with a hand on her arm. She turned back to me with furrowed brows.

The vague threat we could interpret as being aimed at Demi was nothing to the direct one West had lobbed at Rory. I inhaled and exhaled several times, trying to get ahold of my emotions as she watched. The air between us was charged as always, but the desire was now blanketed by fear for the people I loved. "I don't want anything to happen to Demi, but if trying to stop it means putting you or my family at risk… If I have to choose…"

God, could I even say it? My thoughts were torturous, drawing deeper crevices down all the breaks inside my soul that had bloomed into existence since the first time my mother had walked out the door.

Rory leaned over the center console, cupping my cheek. "I won't let anything happen to any of you. I promise."

I could hear the surety in her tone as much as I could read the determination in her eyes.

"But what about you? Do you promise nothing will happen to you?"

Her hand dropped away, and I felt the loss of it as she shifted in her seat, avoiding my gaze. I grabbed her wrist, twining our fingers together, setting the joined hands over my heart, and forcing her to focus on me.

"What happens if he sends someone after you? What if *you* end up shooting a U.S. congressman, even in defense? We don't know what happens after Dunn falls in Monte's vision. What if one of the men guarding him returns fire? What if you…"

It made me want to throw up. Rory was tied into my soul as much as my family. She was part of me. I wasn't sure when it had happened. It was ridiculous, as I hadn't seen her in years before Friday night, but I couldn't deny it. Maybe she'd *always* been part of me. Maybe everything between us had been part of some big cosmic plan Demi had been the only one able to see.

You'll have to fight for the joy, she'd told me.

This felt bigger than a fight. It felt like a war. Battles I didn't know how to wage and were likely to end in someone getting hurt. Killed.

I slid my thumb over the top of her hand, and she watched the movement before looking up at me with pain in her eyes.

"I won't let anyone get away with hurting my mom," she said quietly. "I'm not going to let them get away with hurting yours either. If they're involved, I'm taking them down."

"You're one person without any—"

"Don't say it, Gage. Please. I'm not just a little girl playing games. I don't know what I'll do if you don't believe in me either. I need someone." Her voice cracked. "I've made mistakes. But I'm not making any more. I promise you can trust me."

I felt the wounds she carried around in her words. They layered over my own cracks and scars, digging in deeper.

"This isn't about not believing in you," I told her. "This

isn't about you being female or twenty-two or five foot whatever. This is about you being one person on her own without a team to help her. Even an FBI agent has backup. Someone looking over their shoulder when they can't."

Her eyes turned even more tortured, and I couldn't stand it. My palm went to the back of her head, pushing her toward me until our mouths met. Until the softness of her lips was pressed against the hardness of mine. I wasn't sure who I was trying to soothe—her or me or both of us. But this, my lips on hers, was the only way I knew how to show her exactly what I meant.

And just like both times we'd kissed, the soft press of lips became not nearly enough in a nanosecond as shockwaves rolled through my body. I invaded her mouth with my tongue, and she responded with a little moan that made me instantly hard.

The embrace became a hungry feast where we took turns devouring each other. Lapping and licking and tasting as the world came to a blurry halt around us. Until there was nothing but us, the sounds of our heavy breathing, the pounding of our hearts, and the ache of souls that had gone far too long without connecting to another human in just this way. The absence of love that had existed for too many years being filled with touch.

That thought, along with the console biting into me, had me slowing the kiss. I knew nothing about Rory's love life. It had been years since I'd held someone, but she could have been with someone last week.

Except, somehow, I knew it wasn't true. Maybe because this was another way in which Rory and I were alike. We'd given up our own pleasure to focus on caring for the ones we loved.

When we finally broke apart, her lids fluttered open, and I was caught in eyes that were heated and sad and yet somehow hopeful. She retreated to the passenger seat, and I dragged my hand over my face, unsure if I should apologize or drag her back across the console and keep going.

"A complete swish. Every time, you sink it in without ever touching the rim." A smile broke over her face, and the brilliance of it along with the tease lightened the heaviness in my chest and drew a half smile from me in return.

"Now who's caught up in cheesy basketball analogies?"

She laughed softly but opened the car door and slipped out. "Come on. You can be my backup as long as you do exactly what I say without an argument."

I joined her, meeting her gaze and saying in a gruff voice, "I'll do my best, but I don't know if you noticed, I kind of like being in control."

Her eyes dropped to my lips and back up. "It takes a lot of trust for me to let someone else drive."

I arched a brow, tossed my keys up in the air, and caught them. "And yet you've let me all week."

She snorted but didn't respond as we made our way out of the garage.

I raised my umbrella over our heads and did my best to keep up with her fast stride. We were almost to the entrance of the Argento Skies building by the time the sexy flirting disappeared and my skin started to crawl. I darted a look out from under the umbrella, taking in the street, but couldn't see anything out of the ordinary. Just the normal hustle of people darting from doorway to doorway in the downpour.

Inside, I shook off the umbrella, leaving it in a stand at the entrance, and followed Rory's confident stride toward the bank of elevators. She never paused. Never looked at the guy at the reception desk, just acted like she'd been there a million times doing exactly this.

In the elevator, she glanced up at the corner briefly, and I realized she was looking for cameras. Or maybe she already knew where they were from all the hacking she'd done. The door dinged open on the fourth floor, and she strode out, hanging a left and going around the corner to where the hallway branched off. She stopped at a corner suite with glass doors that read Argento Skies, Inc. with the logo Monte had recognized. Behind the doors, the suite was dark in the middle of the day on a Wednesday, but maybe they were closed for Thanksgiving.

Rory took a wallet-like item from her inside jacket pocket, flipped it open, and pulled out two small metal tools. She stuck them into the lock and jiggled.

My breath caught. I looked both ways down the hall and leaned in to whisper, "What are you doing?"

She winked at me. "Nothing like a little B and E before lunch to brighten your day."

Before I could even think of an adequate response, she'd pushed open the door and slipped inside. I followed, full of that same mix of pride and worry I felt every time I'd seen her in action.

She directed a penlight at an alarm box on the wall, and when she turned around, confusion was written on her face, weirdly shadowed by the glare of the light.

"They don't have the system connected to a service." She moved past me, heading to the large empty desk where a receptionist would normally sit. She lifted the phone's handset. "No dial tone."

She moved farther into the suite with me trailing her, but she stopped me with a hand. "No. Stay here. Keep an eye out. If anyone shows up, just text me. I'll feel the buzz in my pocket."

"Rory…"

She put her hand up. "No arguing, remember. Just stay here."

I watched, doubts swirling through me as she marched off. She peeked over low, cloth-walled cubicles, ducked her head into offices, and finally disappeared inside a doorway at the end of the hall. My gut turned nastily.

Something was wrong. Goose bumps broke out over my skin.

Outside the plate glass windows, lightning flickered. I counted to three and the thunder cracked through the air loud enough to cause the glass to vibrate.

From the direction she'd gone, a printer was barely audible over the sound of the storm.

Laughter drew my eyes to the hall. I tucked myself up against a wall, looking around the corner as a man and a woman meandered past without even glancing into the Argento Skies office. It was lunchtime. Maybe that was why the Argento Skies offices were closed. Maybe everyone was just at lunch, but the silence and smell of disuse belied that thought.

A touch on my back had me jumping and whirling around. Rory's face shifted from surprise to laughter. "Nervous much?"

"You may be used to this cloak-and-dagger stuff, but I'm not. What did you find?" I nodded to the paper in her hand.

"There's only one office with anything in it," she said, tilting her head toward the room she'd disappeared into. "Everything else is completely empty. Either they were here and left, or they never intended to be here at all."

"What does that mean?"

"I don't know yet."

Rory moved toward the doors, and I followed. She used her kit to lock back up, and then made her way toward the elevators with the same calm, smooth stride she'd used on the way there. She acted like we'd just been out for a little stroll in the park, whereas my palms were clammy and the back of my neck was damp from more than just the rain.

We didn't say anything until we'd made it all the way back to the Pathfinder.

"All the file cabinets were empty, and there was no computer, but there was a printer. Someone has been there recently because the dust on the desk and side table had been disturbed. I managed to reprint the last document."

She flipped through the pages. Her hand stalled for a moment before she glanced up at me. "It's a list of warehouses for sale or rent in D.C."

My mouth went dry. When Monte had described where he'd been held, it had sounded industrial. Roll-up doors and concrete floors. Plus, it had been near the river. Dunn was shot in a warehouse—was it one of these? Was Demi there? Had Demi been in the same place as Monte? Had she known they'd kidnapped him?

"How many?" I asked.

"Twenty," she said. "Too many to canvass them all today. But we can hit a few, and then I'll research them tonight and narrow it down further."

I programmed the first warehouse into the GPS with my heart thudding.

"Is this what it's like for you all the time? Sneaking into places, breaking into computers, living in the shadows?" I asked as the GPS's voice navigated me onto the streets of D.C. once again.

Rory shook her head. "Honestly, most of the time I'm behind my computer doing standard background checks or staking out a motel waiting for the money shot."

"But you do this too?"

"Mom usually took the cases that required more stealth," she said, and then immediately went on the defensive. "That wasn't because she didn't think I could do it, but because I was in school and didn't always have the time. I could study in the car waiting for some asswipe to show up. That wouldn't be possible if I was sneaking in somewhere."

She acted like all of this was normal. Like what she and her mother did for a living was just another job like mine, serving drinks and taking out the trash.

But it wasn't the same at all. The biggest risk I took in my job was from a broken bottle and tossing an ornery drunk out. I had mixed feelings about everything she did, but I knew she'd hate it if I told her the truth.

If she joined the FBI, she'd be in much worse

situations.

I couldn't stand the idea of her getting hurt.

Of something happening.

How did law enforcement and military families live with it? She'd always be at risk, and that meant my family might lose, yet again, someone we loved. That made my stomach fall.

But I also didn't want Ivy and Monte to see me never letting anyone in. Never loving again. And God help me, I didn't have the strength to walk away from her. I craved more time with her, not less.

When I was with her, I felt as if I'd walked through the doors of the Victorian all over again. As if I'd come home after months away. As if her arms were the one place I truly belonged.

Chapter Thirty-two

Rory

CAN'T AFFORD A HERO
Performed by Night Ranger

As Gage drove out of the parking garage, my gaze landed on a black truck with its extended cab and long bed. It looked out of place on the streets of D.C. Was it the same one I'd seen outside Margetto's? I watched the side mirror, but the truck didn't follow us. Maybe I was just being paranoid.

I flipped through the list of warehouses, pulled out my laptop, and loaded them into a database used for property searches.

"When was the last time you went on a date?"

My head whipped up in surprise at Gage's question. "What?"

He grinned. A delightfully flirtatious smile just like the one that had accompanied his tease about control before we'd broken into Argento Skies. It was so much like the Gage of my teen years that it seemed like we'd opened a wormhole and slipped back in time. My heart hammered harder than it had while picking the office lock.

I ducked the question, saying, "You first."

"Three years." He said it instantaneously and without the least bit of embarrassment. "After Demi left, I had my hands full learning to take care of a baby. Later, I convinced myself I didn't want to let more people in our lives who would leave again.”

The openness of his words was both a balm and a cruel jab I was sure he hadn't intended. My thoughts returned to the ones I'd had the night before—all reasons why I should walk away before I hurt them. But the thought of leaving, of not seeing Gage and Monte and Ivy again, caused as much pain as the idea of turning off Mom's life support.

My throat bobbed, and any response I might have given dried up. I looked away with my pulse hammering, taking in the industrial area we'd driven into. My eyes fell to the side mirror and landed on a large black vehicle several cars behind us. In D.C., black SUVs were the norm with the number of security teams trolling the city. But this looked decidedly like the grille of a F-150.

“Your turn,” he prompted, not letting me off the hook.

I wanted to say something light. Something funny that would keep the smile on his face, but all I could come up with was the truth. So, instead of watching my words rip the grin away, I watched the traffic behind us as I said, “Shay and Nan keep telling me I need to go out more, but the idea of trying to enjoy myself while Mom is lying in a bed unable to move… It just feels wrong.”

“It's been almost a year, right? What are her chances?” he asked.

My chest squeezed tight. “The doctors have already given up. Dad gave up months ago. It was just Nan and me, but now…”

I still couldn't look at him because if I did and I saw any kind of pity or caring, it would wreck me. I swallowed hard and breathed out the worst of it. “Now, Nan wants to take her off life support too.”

He inhaled softly as if feeling the blow as much as I did.

“I'm truly sorry you're having to make that kind of decision, Rory.”

I finally turned away from the window to find he wasn't

looking at me but at the road ahead. I watched his profile as he drove. He looked so damn sturdy and stable. A rock radiating strength. What had he said to me last night? *We're strong alone… but imagine what we would be like if we shared our burdens.* What would it be like? To have Gage at my side if the wind knocked me down?

I couldn't think of it right now. All that mattered at the moment was getting the proof we needed to stop Dunn and West.

We pulled up in front of the first warehouse on the list to find it was a hive of activity. Vans with a cleaning company logo on the side zipped in and out of the parking lot. Not exactly a place you could bring a kidnapped teen—or hold a woman—without anyone noticing.

"I don't think this is the place. I'll check their financials and run any ties they might have to Dunn and Argento Skies, but this looks like a regular business."

He nodded. "What's the next address?"

I read it off, and he punched it into the GPS before flipping a U-turn and heading back in the opposite direction. My gaze caught on the black truck parked down the street. The man inside was a shadow, but he was wide enough to fill the space behind the driver's wheel. He wore a baseball cap that he tugged as we drove by, blocking his face.

I snapped out a command over the GPS voice. "Take the next right."

"What?"

"Gage, now, turn right."

He did as I asked, tires screeching a bit.

"There! Pull over," I said, pointing to an open slot among a row of cars parked along the curb. "Stay here!"

I jumped out. My hand immediately settled on the stun gun at my waistband as I ducked behind a sedan, grateful the rain had stopped for the moment. The street was quiet. Nowhere near the bustle of people there'd been outside the Argento Skies building. I'd barely inched forward to the edge of the sedan's bumper when the black truck turned onto the street. The F-150 drove past Gage's SUV and pulled in a few cars ahead of us.

I stayed low to the ground, glad in a way I rarely was for my small size. It allowed me to stay out of his rearview mirror while closing in on the truck. I'd just reached the tailgate when the cab door opened. I moved quickly and quietly, approaching the driver just as he slammed the door shut. I placed my stun gun on the back of his neck.

"Freeze, asshole."

Both his hands went out.

"I can explain," he said in a deep voice. He turned his head slightly toward me, and I caught sight of his aviators and the square face I recognized from the Space Force website.

"Why are you following us?" I demanded of Casada.

Behind me, I heard a door slam and Gage's feet pounded as he ran up behind me.

"What's going on?" Gage demanded.

"I need your help," Casada said.

"And following us around D.C. is your way of asking?" I scoffed.

"I know you don't have any reason to trust me, Rory."

I bristled at my name falling from his lips. I pushed the gun into his neck a little harder and had to give him credit for not reacting.

"But your mom did," he added. "She was working my case before she crashed."

My chest nearly exploded at the mention of my mom. A month ago, I would have believed I'd known every file she was working on, but the last few days had crumbled that belief like a sandcastle being washed out to sea.

"Tell me why a Space Force astronaut needed a private investigator, Casada." I used his name on purpose. So he knew I was aware of who he was just like he'd known me.

He glanced down at my weapon, and I pulled it away, returning it to its spot underneath my jacket. I took a step back, running into Gage. He put a hand on my waist as if to steady me, and the warmth of him drifted through me as I warily assessed the mammoth man in front of us.

Casada wasn't taller than Gage, but he was twice as wide, and it was all carefully crafted muscle. He pushed his sunglasses up, resting them over the brim of a NASA cap, and I was hit with the same pair of green eyes that had looked out at me from his bio page.

"She really didn't tell you anything about what we were investigating?"

The *we* stung almost as much as the disappointment in his eyes. Why had she trusted him and not me?

"I know she was worried enough to encode her notes."

He lifted a large hand, scratching the back of his neck, and then glanced around. "Can we go somewhere to talk? This isn't exactly—"

"No," I said. Behind me, Gage stiffened. "But you can sit in the back seat of our car, and I'll hear you out."

I whirled around and headed for the SUV. After a beat, I heard two sets of footsteps following me. Gage and I got in up front, and Casada stuffed himself into the back next to Ivy's car seat. He glanced at it and then up to me as if surprised by it.

"Talk," I said.

"Hallie was helping me investigate Argento Skies."

Because I'd already suspected it, I simply met his stare with a steady one of my own.

"My family lives in Parkerville, Colorado. Ever heard of it?" he asked.

I'd read about it last night, but he continued without waiting for my answer.

"Its claim to fame now is being one of the highest elevations in the United States, but it once was known for its silver and turquoise mines. The silver mining left contamination in the soil and water. Kids, pregnant women, and people with weak immune systems are tested regularly to make sure they don't end up with silver iodide toxicity."

"This is about the cloud seeding lawsuit."

His eyes flickered with a surprise that came and went. "My mom died. Kidney failure caused by silver toxicity. Except my mom had never had symptoms until a year before her death. She'd lived there her entire life and had never been sick."

"Cloud seeding doesn't put enough silver iodide into the air or the water to be harmful," Gage said with a frown as he repeated what he'd told me the night before.

"Normally, that's the case. Except, Argento Skies is running five times the ground-based generators they're reporting. And there was a major spill from a tanker hauling the chemical in 2020 that no one did anything to clean up. They cited some bullshit about it not being more than what was naturally occurring. A year later, my mom was dead and large portions of our community had their skin changing color and were having breathing issues along with constant nausea. Toxicity that had been all but dormant for several decades came roaring back to life."

"If the number of ill people is that large, there has to be an investigation going on," I said.

Casada's face grew tight. "You'd think, right? But their CEO, Shawn Walden, has ties here in Washington."

West's words from the phone call came back to me. He and Dunn had to be the ones who'd helped Shawn bury this.

"I tried to convince Argento Skies to stop what they were doing. After they stopped taking my calls and emails, I cornered their former CEO, Tim Walden, in the bathroom of his favorite restaurant. I shoved a printout of the numbers at him, and when he read it, he acted like he was completely surprised. Even looked sick about it. He said he hadn't received any of the information I'd sent, but that he'd get to the bottom of it. A month later, his plane crashed and his brother took over. Shawn made it very clear if I pursued my so-called attack on his company, he had people who could end my career as an astronaut."

"You think he killed his brother?" Gage asked, surprise in every syllable.

"I think it's an awfully big coincidence otherwise," Casada said, an echo of what I'd been thinking, and my mom must have thought it too. Every word only continued to confirm that West had been talking to Shawn Walden on the phone earlier.

"Argento Skies is one of the largest sponsors of Representative Dunn's campaigns," I said. "He's making a senate run next year. They wouldn't want to be tied to a scandal like this. Murdered CEOs and a sick town aren't exactly the stuff political dreams are made from."

"Plus, West is a silent partner in Walden's company," Casada said.

I shook my head. "He isn't listed on any of the legal documents."

Casada shrugged. "That's what your mom told me before…"

My back went rigid. It never got easier to hear people talk about the wreck. I'd wondered if the person she'd met with had planted a device to hack into her car's computer. I watched Casada, waiting for his reaction as I said, "It wasn't an accident. Mom didn't crash. She was driven off the road."

His face fell. It could have been an act. He still could have been involved, but it seemed highly unlikely given that she was working with him. Casada's voice was full of regret as he said, "I'd hoped that wasn't the case. The last day I met with her, she said she was followed and that she'd found a bug in her office."

I tugged at my sleeves as pain welled through me all over again. Why hadn't she told me?

"Do you have any leads? Does it tie back to Argento Skies?" he asked.

"I didn't even know about it until this week. The

detective involved hid it from me." I barely kept the bitterness from my voice. "It's going to take me a while to trace the hacker who wormed into her car's computers. They've had almost a year to cover their tracks."

As I said the words aloud and pictured Dad's new little friend and her computer skills, my stomach fell. With his connection to Dunn and West, my father was in the perfect position to cover it all up. But even with all his failings, I couldn't imagine him hurting Mom. I couldn't imagine him running on the wrong side of the law like this.

"With your mom gone, I've been trying to follow Walden on my own. I keep hoping I'll catch him doing something, anything, that I can use to go to the authorities. But he's rarely in Colorado anymore, and I'm not always able to follow him to his house in the Hamptons or his place in Aruba."

The money Argento Skies brought in wasn't lucrative enough for Walden to be able to afford homes in those high-end locations, and his family hadn't come from money. They were essentially crop dusters who'd stumbled into cloud seeding.

When I said as much, Casada nodded. "Your mom was following the money trail. Argento Skies has become the number one cloud seeding company in the United States, but Hallie said there was no way the dollars added up."

Following the money wasn't just a television show ploy. It was almost always the way to find out who was in bed with whom and what was really happening behind the scenes. I instantly thought about the shell corporation that had paid the lease on Argento's D.C. office. I'd been running checks on the people involved with both Gage's case and my mom's, but I hadn't had the time to fully dig into their financials. I'd been spread too thin all week, but my focus tonight had to be on the warehouses and the money.

"Do you know where Walden is now?"

"In a suite at the Willard Hotel," Casada responded.

"He's in D.C." It wasn't a question because it wasn't really a surprise. Casada was here, and there'd been someone in the downtown office. The printout on the warehouses proved it if nothing else. I just hadn't been sure whether it had been Walden himself or an employee.

"Dunn and his sidekick had just come from a meeting with Walden when I saw you at the restaurant today. I haven't wanted to bring anyone else into this after what happened to Hallie, but if I don't leave for Colorado Springs tonight, I'll be AWOL. I'm pushing it now if I drive straight through, and I've already extended my leave as much as possible," Casada said. He scrubbed his face and then glanced at Gage and back. "I know it's a lot to ask you when you're only—"

"The best at what she does," Gage cut him off. "Rory will get to the bottom of this."

Casada shifted in his seat, taking me in, and I knew what he saw. It was what everyone saw. A girl who looked like she was barely eighteen. Some teen wannabe trying to play girl detective. For some reason, his doubts didn't ruffle my feathers as much as they normally did. Maybe because Gage's confidence in me was filling the holes that people's disbelief had caused.

"Your mom was proud of you," Casada said, tugging at the brim of his hat.

"What?" I asked over the lump that formed in my throat.

"She told me if she let you loose on this, you'd find answers quicker than she could. Said you'd never stop digging until every bone was unburied, but she was also worried. She didn't want to drag you in… But after I saw you at the Argento Skies office and then again with West, it didn't feel right to *not* contact you."

My chest felt tight and my eyes burned, but I couldn't afford to really think about what he'd said. Maybe later. Maybe when I was alone in the dark I could relive his words and hold on to them and let them sink in.

"Do you know what room he's in at the hotel?"

Casada rattled off the number and reached for the door handle. "I liked Hallie." I cringed at his use of the past tense. "She was smart and savvy, and she gave a damn. There aren't many people out there who would've put themselves at risk for the truth. Especially for a woman who was already dead and buried in a town thousands of miles away. But my family—my town—they deserve answers, and they deserve to have the cloud seeding stopped if it's killing us."

After he stepped out of the Pathfinder, he reached into his jacket pocket and pulled out a business card. He handed it to me through the open door.

"I'd appreciate it if you kept in touch. Your mom wouldn't take my money. But I've been setting aside some anyway. It's yours if you can pick up where she left off."

He got out and drove away leaving behind him almost as many questions as answers.

Chapter Thirty-three

Rory

ANGEL WITH A SHOTGUN
Performed by The Cab

Silence settled between Gage and me after Casada left. We still had no real proof of anything. No matter what Casada said, my mom hadn't trusted me. Not enough to bring me in. If she had, maybe I could have found out the truth before she'd ended up crashing into the Potomac. Maybe she'd be here.

Maybe would do nothing but leave holes in a sinking boat I couldn't plug.

"What now?" Gage asked.

"The Willard. But I need to make a stop first."

I gave him the address, and he punched it into his GPS.

As we drove, I made a list of the supplies I needed. I felt Gage's eyes drifting back and forth from the road to me. Concern but also something else—the trust I'd thought I'd lost when he'd shut me out on Monday.

"Thank you," I said quietly.

"For what?"

"Defending me. Believing in me."

"I don't know how anyone can see you do the things you do and not. You're really good at this sleuthing stuff."

He said it with a raised brow and a grin as if he was trying to lighten the heavy mood. I was sure he had no idea just how much those words both healed and broke me.

Casada's words had done the same. I hadn't wanted to think about them yet, not with a case to focus on, but they still lingered. Still burned their way through me with the same force as Gage's look.

"No matter how proud anyone thinks she was of me, she never would have seen me as a true partner. She would have always looked at me through a parental lens, protecting instead of trusting."

He was quiet for a moment. "For what it's worth, I don't think it's because she didn't believe in you. If anything, it was because she loved you so much."

My jaw ticked, teeth grinding as I attempted to pull myself away from emotions that wouldn't help us.

"I know you don't see it as a good thing," Gage said. "But her wanting to keep you safe, wanting what's best for you—it's what a parent should do."

I glanced over and saw his body was tense. He had to be thinking about Demi. The way she'd never stayed. The way she'd abandoned all her children. The way her actions were actually putting them in danger now. My heart skipped a beat as I realized we were doing the same, putting our loved ones in the crosshairs. West had basically threatened all of us if I kept poking, and here I was doing exactly that and planning to do more of it.

Over the huge lump that had formed in my throat, I said, "I need to stay in town. I can get a CarShare back to Cherry Bay when I'm done, but I think you need to go back to your family."

His eyes narrowed as if trying to figure out why I was sending him packing. "You think they're going to come after us? After Monte or Ivy?"

I wanted to say no. I wanted to say they were safe, but I just wasn't sure. Instead, I told him the truth. "I think it's better if you're with them. Is there anywhere else you can stay for a few days?"

He was quiet, a range of emotions flooding his face before he asked quietly, "And who's going to be with you, covering your back? And what about your grandmother?"

I was already texting Nan. Harriet had wanted us to come over for Thanksgiving. There'd be no issue with Nan spending the night with her.

Gage hit a button on his steering wheel. "Call River."

The phone rang a couple of times before the man picked up. "Hey, Gage. Audrey and I were just about to leave for the bar. How's everyone doing?"

"Monte's doing better than I expected. I'm worried he'll break down at some point, but he's showing me his brave face. I'm sorry to do this, but I need another favor," Gage's voice held guilt and worry that I was familiar with.

"You know better than to be sorry, Gage. We're family. Whatever you need, we're here."

"I'm in D.C. with Rory. We're trying to find Demi."

Silence for several beats on the other end. "Why the hell are you looking for her?"

"Monte's vision, what happens, she's there. And what happened to him is related. We have some leads, but I'm not going to make it back for a while. I don't want Monte and Ivy there alone. There's just too much going on."

River was quiet again before he said, "You think whoever this is will come looking for all of you?"

Worry coasted over Gage's brow, and disappointment filled my mouth. Bitter and harsh. Disappointment at myself. I'd promised him earlier I wasn't going to let anything happen to him or his family, and here we were stirring up bees who might do exactly that—zip out to Cherry Bay and sting from the darkness. And I wouldn't be there to stand in their way.

"I think it's better if they aren't at the apartment. Can you take them to your place tonight?" Gage asked.

"I'll have Audrey pack them up and bring them over before we open the bar."

"Monte's going to freak. I'll text him, but he's going to worry."

"You were coming to our house for Thanksgiving anyway. Just tell him we decided to make a night of it so we had more hands to help in the morning."

Gage breathed out a sigh. "Thanks, man."

"I'm going to get seriously pissed, Gage, if you don't stop with this shit. We're in this together. No guilt. No favors. Just family doing for family. You understand me?"

I'd felt so much loneliness in Gage since I'd walked into the bar on Friday, and I'd thought it echoed mine. But he'd never really been alone. He'd had Audrey and River just like I'd had Shay and Nan. So, why had we both put up so many walls it ended up feeling like we were in solitary confinement? Why had we kept the people who cared about us from showering us with their love and support?

Gage and River said their goodbyes, and I swallowed over the lump in my throat to say, "I'm sorry, Gage…"

He swiped a hand through his hair and then looked over at me. "I'd say I'm the one who should be sorry for dragging you into this with Monte's vision, but just like you said yesterday, it seems like we're in it together. Whatever happened to your mom and is now happening with my family, it's related. River's right, we need to stop feeling guilty for it and just figure it the hell out before anyone else gets hurt."

The words were exactly what I needed to hear. Regret, wishing for something different to have happened in our pasts, wouldn't help either of us. It wouldn't help us find Demi or change Monte's vision or bring down Dunn and West.

I tucked all my emotions, doubts, and what-ifs aside as Gage pulled to the curb.

His eyes widened. "What are we doing at a pawnshop?"

My lips twitched. "It's not just a pawn shop. Gary has equipment I need." I opened the door. "Give me ten minutes."

I slipped out of the car, headed into the store, and exactly ten minutes later I walked out with my credit card screaming. I couldn't really afford to spend what I had, but money wasn't going to stop me from keeping the people I cared about safe.

I walked up to the SUV, pulling a beat-up, hard-sided silver suitcase. Gage gave me a puzzled look but popped the hatchback. I tossed the case inside and then climbed into the passenger seat.

"I'm checking in to a hotel. I'll need luggage," I explained. "And I needed equipment I left in Cherry Bay."

"*We're* checking in, Rory. Us. Not you. I'm not letting you do this alone." Before I had a chance to argue, he added on words that almost killed me. "Besides, isn't it Veronica who says you can't declare a victory if you walk out of the ring in the middle of the fight? I'm not leaving."

The hero is the person who stays… I wanted to whisper back but caught my words.

In the show, Veronica lost the love of her life in a fiery bomb. She'd thought everything was finally behind them, the good ahead, and she'd lost him anyway. What would happen if I lost Gage?

Determination welled through me.

I wasn't going to let these arrogant assholes get away with any of this. I was going to put a stop to it. And I guessed, in that way I was exactly like my hero.

West and Dunn might not think I was worth even batting an eye at, but holy crap were they going to care when I got my revenge on. They were going to be wishing it was Veronica Mars and not Rory Marlowe Bishop coming for them, because Veronica was fictional and I was the real deal. I was going to take their crappy little world down.

♫ ♫ ♫

The iconic lobby of the Willard Hotel greeted us as we

walked in. The gold-flecked marble pillars, antique glass, and carved ceilings shimmered in stately elegance. It was a hotel fitting its nickname as the Presidents' Residence with every president since Franklin Pierce having stayed there.

I didn't have any connections here, not yet. But as close as it was to the White House, and with as many foreign dignitaries who walked through its doors, it would be smart for me to cultivate some. As it was, we were lucky that Casada already knew Walden's suite number. I'd taken a quick look at the floor plan using the hotel's online map and chosen a room across from his to set up shop.

When the front desk clerk informed us the room was already booked, I pouted. "It's our anniversary. That was our very first room together." I fluttered my lashes. "Has the person checked in yet? Isn't there any way you can move them to another room? We'll pay extra. Or we could pay to upgrade their room for them."

As I said it, I put three twenty-dollar bills on the counter with my palm covering most of them. It was more money I couldn't afford, but I still slid it toward him. The guy was around my age, and he looked at the money with a flicker of hope in his eyes. He turned back to his computer, banged around a bit, and then said, "There is an upgraded room I can move them into."

Five minutes later, Gage and I were on our way upstairs. We made our way down the lushly carpeted burgundy hall to the room across from Walden's. I tilted my head in the direction of his door, listening for sounds coming from the suite, but heard nothing.

Gage slid the key card over the reader, and we ducked inside.

I hardly noticed the lavishly furnished blue-and-white interior as Gage rolled the suitcase inside. The single king-sized bed made my heartbeat pick up and my stomach twirl. But if I did my job right, we weren't going to be here at night. We weren't going to be here long enough to even pull back the covers.

I went to the house phone sitting on the nightstand and punched in the hotel code for Walden's room. It rang and rang, the hotel's automated voicemail finally picking up.

He could be in the shower. I'd give it another ten minutes and then try again.

I pulled the suitcase up on the bed and unzipped it.

Gage stood across from me, eyeing the packages inside. "What's all this?"

I ripped open the first plastic container, palming a device the size of a dime. "Wi-Fi enabled camera with audio."

"That tiny thing?"

I nodded. Turning it on, I connected it to my phone in practiced moves before stepping out our door. I flipped the lock so the door didn't shut all the way and took a slow breath as I eyed the hall, grateful to find it empty.

My gaze scoured the wallpaper and wainscoting, wishing I'd gotten a white device instead of black before finally placing it as inconspicuously as possible along the door frame.

Back inside our room, I brought up the app and checked the view to ensure it captured the door across the hall.

It would do.

I went to work on the rest of the equipment, tearing open two more camera packages. The first was like the one I'd just stuck outside, but the second looked like a USB charger I could plug into any electrical outlet. I pocketed them both before opening another square box and pulling my computer out of my messenger bag. I set the devices on the desk in the room.

"What are you doing now?" Gage asked, leaning over my shoulder.

The scent of him surrounded me and his breath coasted over my neck. My body reacted as it always did, jumping to attention, begging me to turn my head and join our lips once more. To find some relief from the insatiable yearning I'd had for him for a decade. The bed was right there. How long would it take to lose ourselves in each other?

I cleared my throat, forcing myself to focus on my computer.

"This is a key card machine," I said. I logged into the hotel's Wi-Fi, opened the internal code, and found my way into the employee-only access. From there it was an easy jog into their admin systems, including the key card software. I hooked the machine I'd bought to my computer and pulled the second key card the clerk had given us from the envelope. I placed it into the machine and reprogrammed it for Walden's room.

"Won't that make his card not work?" he asked.

I shook my head. "No. If he'd declared it lost, they would have generated a new code, but this is just creating another version of the one he already had."

"And you're going in there? To his room?"

I rose, the movement forcing him to move back slightly, but our chests were still practically touching. Energy zipped between us. We stood there for a few beats before I eased around him to pick up the hotel landline, once again calling Walden's room. It rang unanswered.

"Give me your phone," I said. He handed it over without question. I installed the camera app on his phone, logged in, and brought up the camera I'd installed outside our door. "Watch this and text me if you see Walden."

"It'll be too late if he's already at the door. I'll wait in the hall. There was a bench by the elevator. If he comes, I can text you with enough time for you to get out."

"Won't matter. If he's already in the hall, he'll still see me come out of his room."

"Rory."

"You said you believed in me," I told him, and my eyes locked on his. He was worried. But for the first time in a few days, I finally felt in control. Cameras, technology, and surveillance were the things I excelled at.

"I do."

"Then watch the camera and text me."

I didn't wait for him to argue again, just checked the camera feed myself, pulled on a pair of disposable gloves, and slipped into the hall. Not even thirty seconds later, I was inside Walden's room. I went immediately to the desk and plugged in the charger with its hidden camera. Normally, if I needed a money shot, I would place the camera so it had a view of the bed, but I didn't need information on Walden's sexual proclivities. This time, I really needed to hear who he was talking to and what they were saying. Still, out of habit, I stuck the smaller camera at the base of a lamp on the bedside table.

With those items in place, I moved over to the closet. His luggage was tucked inside. Expensive. Just like the handmade suits hanging there, and the silk ties draped over the rod. Several pairs of high-end shoes, perfectly shined, were lined up on the floor.

I punched in the standard master code on the safe, but it didn't open.

In the bathroom, the counter was littered with a shaving kit and more creams and lotions than even Nan had. A cologne bottle that had to have cost him a pretty penny sat next to them. Everything about Walden screamed of a wealth he shouldn't have.

Out in the room, I eyed the desk and the computer cord sitting there, wishing he'd left his computer. My phone buzzed, and I looked down at it, worry coasting through me, but it wasn't Gage, it was Shay.

> *SHAY: Where are you? Your Nan said you asked her to stay the night at Harriet's. What's wrong?*

I ignored the text, looking around the room one more time before bringing up both cameras on my phone. "Testing. Testing." My voice echoed through, clear and strong.

I went to the door, looked back, and noticed the edge of a silver box barely sticking out from under the bed. I jogged back, pulling out a hard-sided gun case. What the hell was Walden doing with a gun when there were none registered to his name?

I pulled a pocketknife from the inside zipper compartment of my jacket, flipped it open, and stuck it into the lock. I did my best to not leave a visible mark, but if someone stuck the lock under a microscope, they'd know it had been broken into.

When the case opened, my breath caught in surprise.

Money. Bundles of hundreds. At least two hundred thousand dollars stared up at me.

I swallowed hard. He'd left the money casually lying around under the bed. In a locked case, sure, but easily broken into. It had taken me under thirty seconds to get inside it. What the hell was in the safe if he had this much money just sitting here?

I lifted several of the bundles, thinking about how long this money would keep Mom at Shady Lane. Thinking about how easy it would be to take it, and knowing I never would. Mom would hate it. She wouldn't want to live off bad money. Never in a million years.

Below the bundles was a Smith & Wesson SW1911. All black, with extra bullets.

A good gun. Not my favorite. I preferred my Glock 19 with its 9mm cartridge allowing room for more ammo and less recoil. Plus, owning and shooting it gave me experience with the gun of choice of the FBI. Looking at this one, I regretted again not bringing mine today.

I debated taking the Smith & Wesson as nothing good could come from Walden having it.

But then I remembered Monte's voice and the promise I'd made. I didn't plan on shooting anyone. I wouldn't have to if I did my job right. I fought with the instinct urging me to take it, and instead, took a picture of the serial number so I could run it and see what came up.

My phone buzzed once more as I was putting everything back inside the case. Gage. My heart skipped a beat, and I eyeballed the closet, which was pretty much the only place to hide if Walden walked in.

GAGE: Are you okay?

I didn't waste time replying. I'd already been in the room longer than I'd planned.

After putting the gun case back exactly where it had been, slightly sticking out from the bed skirt, I headed for the door. I'd checked the camera app on my phone, rechecked the hall from the peephole, and started to open the door when voices halted me.

I closed the door most of the way, heart hammering as I watched through the crack while a couple walked by arm in arm. They were laughing and smiling as if they didn't have a care in the world, and my chest squeezed at the image they made. I had no idea what that was like… feeling light and free and in love.

I'd never loved anyone but my family and a boy I'd never really known. Shay had once accused me of holding on to a mirage I'd created as a teen. But after having spent several days in Gage's presence, I knew the truth.

It wasn't a mirage. I hadn't made up anything about him. He was exactly the noble, kind hero I'd thought he was even back then. Wounded and tormented for sure, but life hadn't broken him. It hadn't turned him into something ugly or dark. Broody maybe, but not dark.

He'd laughed today. Laughed and winked and shown me a glimpse into that boy I'd first fallen for. What would it be like to see him that way all the time? To be the reason he got some of his joy back?

The couple's voices drifted away, a door down the hall clicked shut, and I made my way out of the room and over to ours. As I stepped inside, Gage froze, caught in what I presumed was pacing along the edge of the bed.

"Thank God," he said quietly.

Why did the simple relief in his voice make my entire being light up?

Why did every word and look he directed at me seem more poignant and real than anything anyone else had ever sent my way?

How could I possibly experience this with him and then leave it behind?

Why the hell would I want to?

Chapter Thirty-four

Gage

WRECKAGE
Performed by Nate Smith

I paced the length of the suite, tugging at my hair as each second felt like a lifetime while I waited for Rory to return. I debated leaping into the hall, pounding on the door, and demanding she get out of there.

But none of that would win me any points with her.

I'd told Rory and Casada that I trusted her. Believed in her. And I did. I trusted she knew what she was doing. But that didn't mean I wouldn't worry about her getting caught. Because what would Walden do if he found her? If he'd killed his own brother, or hired someone to do it for him, killing some meddling PI wasn't above him.

What if I lost her just as she'd swept back into our lives?

Texting her would make her think Walden had arrived, but I couldn't stand not knowing if she was okay a moment longer. I typed out the words and then waited for the dots to show up saying she was responding. They didn't come.

I swallowed hard.

The camera app she'd installed flickered with a notification just as I heard laughter outside the door. When I opened the app, a couple, twined together, sauntered down the hall, and I realized I didn't even know what Shawn Walden looked like. I held my breath as they continued past our door.

In the silence that followed, our door lock beeped and then Rory was there.

Dressed in black from head to toe, she looked exactly like what she was—a PI. A real-life Veronica Mars. Her hair was in a ponytail, and even though we'd both gotten drenched in the rain earlier, it was still smooth and straight, pulled back from her face.

Her eyes glimmered with emotions across the room. Ones I couldn't read.

The innate goodness that spread from her aura was layered with grief, but the strength that rebounded off her like some sort of shield seemed to pull all the air from my lungs.

She was beautiful. And brave. A stunning soul.

The kisses we'd shared had done nothing but increase the desire that had flickered to life since she'd walked into the bar last weekend. I craved more. I wanted to be burned from the inside out by it. Consumed by it until there was nothing left but her.

I'd never wanted to be lost in that way. The tease I'd dropped earlier had been true. I'd always needed to be in control, and the women I'd been with had been happy to hand it over to me in the bedroom. Been happy to let me lead while I brought us both the satisfaction we sought.

But with Rory… I didn't think I'd be able to hold back.

"Thank God," I uttered, dropping my phone onto the bed and taking two long strides to reach her. One hand went to her waist, jerking her to me, the other tangled in her ponytail, drawing her head back so I could see every inch of her face glowing in the soft lamplight.

I didn't hesitate. I kissed her. It wasn't gentle. It wasn't regretful or wondering. It was me demanding she let go and be devoured by the same emotions I was feeling. My tongue invaded her mouth, seeking the inner softness. The honeyed taste of her. The sweetness that existed beyond her tough outer shell that so few got to see.

I moved so she had her back pressed up against the wall while my hands tugged off her leather jacket, all while my lips plundered hers. Days of worry. Days of grief. Days of desire all seemed to slam together requiring release.

She let the jacket slip from her fingers before she wrapped her hands around my neck. Her short, neatly filed nails dug into my skin, and the spike of pain and lust it brought had me driving my body into hers. I pressed my hard length into the softness of her stomach.

My palms skimmed under her shirt where her skin was cool from rain-dampened clothes, and yet somehow it still felt like putting my hand on a flame. Burning with electricity that was all chemistry-driven hormones but might as well be the lightning that had flashed all week long in the skies.

The storm had finally settled over us.

My lips slid down her cheek, finding the soft hollow below her ear, and she gasped. A little throaty noise that made me impossibly harder. One of her legs wrapped along my thigh, drawing me closer, and I lifted her until our cores were aligned.

My lips journeyed down the long slope of her neck until I was shoving aside her clothes and leaving open-mouthed kisses along her collarbone and shoulder. I braced her against the wall and lifted my head to pull her shirt off.

Our eyes met. Reciprocal flames burned in the depths of hers.

My eyes slid down to her purple lace bra and the peaked tips pushing against the material. I slid a finger over one before rubbing it between my thumb and forefinger. Her head slammed into the wall as a moan escaped her. I drew the material aside, baring the rosy perfection, and bent to pull it into my mouth. My tongue twisted it, nipping at it, and her thighs pulsed around me.

I'd taken off my jacket while she was across the hall, and now she fisted my T-shirt, drawing it over my head and breaking our contact. She slid her hands over my chest, and

I was glad that lifting crates and kegs and cases at the bar had kept me in decent shape.

I snapped open her bra's front clasp, flinging it aside, and then feasted on the other breast while my hand worked the first. Her fingers dug into my scalp. I grunted at the pleasure of it just as she made another little whimper that had my lips returning to hers, claiming them.

Our hands were as desperate as our mouths and tongues. Touching, digging in, and then soothing. But it wasn't enough. I needed more. I needed to have all of her.

I lifted her up and carried her to the bed, and as her back hit the mattress, I bent to slide down the zippers on her boots and pull them off. When I risked looking at her again, the green in her eyes seemed to have taken over the brown. Green flames. Want and need and trust…

I tugged off her jeans, toed off my shoes, and let my pants fall to the floor. Then, I knelt on the mattress, drawing a hand down the middle of her bare breasts, over her taut stomach, and down to the thin lilac fabric of her underwear. I cupped her and she writhed beneath me from just the simple touch.

My mouth found the soft skin of her inner thigh, and she embedded her hands in my hair as I found new pieces of her to worship. To taunt. To taste and lick.

Her breathing came in sweet little gasps as her hips bucked, and a shudder rocked through me, my control slipping further away. Something wild in me needed to absorb every sound, every emotion, every whimper that escaped her. As if by doing so I could absorb her heart and soul along with them. As if I could embed her into me one kiss at a time.

Thunder boomed, rattling the glass.

Inside, we made our own lightning. Shedding boundaries between our worlds as we shed the last vestiges of our clothes until there was nothing keeping us apart where we crossed an unknown barrier into a netherworld where pleasure and joy were all that existed.

I'd almost slid inside her, almost found my way into the delightful heat, when my conscience finally broke free enough for me to pull back. I rested my forehead on her chest, my shoulders heaving as my lungs tried to find oxygen.

"Fuck."

"Don't you dare stop, Gage Palmer. Do. Not. Fucking. Stop." Her voice was all command and control I wanted to give in to. I wanted to heed her demands and let her lead the way.

My fingers slid down, curling into her, and she gasped, pushing into my palm. I circled her with my thumb, and she moaned, eyes fluttering closed.

We found a rhythm together, her hips shifting, my hand seeking, and I watched with glorious wonder as pleasure coasted over her face. The fierce beauty that was Rory became the joy of angels as her release burst through her body. She quivered against me, body shaking.

I kissed her, slower this time. In awe of what I'd seen. In awe of her.

Her hands slid down my back, squeezing my ass before one hand slipped around to surround the length of me. I growled in pleasure and twisted pain, my hips shoving into her palm.

"I need you inside me, Gage. I want to see those gray eyes of yours become a thunderstorm when you break apart. I need that. I need to know it's because of me."

My eyes searched hers. I ached to give her what she asked and cursed my stupidity for not planning this. "I don't have a condom."

Her brows went up. "I have a birth control implant. I haven't done this with anyone without a condom. I'm clean."

My breath hitched. The idea of her being with anyone like this made me want to lose my damn mind. A ridiculous and unwarranted jealousy raged through me, slicing through bone and marrow. But I finally caught up to what she'd said. What she wanted. She wanted me bare inside her. Feeling every slide of skin. Every pulse and flicker.

"I haven't been with anyone in over three years. And I was tested after."

The glimmer in her eyes grew. She leaned up slightly, taking my mouth with hers, dipping her tongue inside, as she shifted her hand, leading me to her center and the wet heat I yearned to sink into.

"You're sure?" I asked her.

In answer, she spread her legs wider, digging her heels into the backs of my thighs, and I responded by sliding in. As I bottomed out, pleasure rippled through my body and the world grew hazy, until there was nothing but the fire burning between us and the honeyed sweet taste and smell that was Rory.

That overwhelming sense of having found home coursed through me all over again.

I belonged with Rory.

At first, our pace was steady and measured as we learned each other's shape and angles, but it quickly grew frantic. Wild. As if we were consumed by nature and the storm that grew to a torrent both inside us and out.

The bed rocked. Another round of thunder boomed, and I hit the top, the crest of the wave, the eye of the storm. As I came, her body shook around me and a cry escaped her that was the most beautiful sound I'd ever heard. Pleasure and love and goddamn hope.

Our bodies slowed, the trembling of our limbs coming to a stop. I had no desire to remove myself from her, but I rolled slightly, bringing her with me, so that we were on our sides, joined in the closest possible way. Not just body parts. It was deeper than that. Holes in our souls had been filled as well.

It felt like peace.

For a moment, there was a quiet where only the beat of

our hearts could be heard.

"A complete swoosh," she said, and I laughed softly.

I caressed her arm as her fingers slid along my chest and down my biceps. Her fingers settled on the words wrapped ivy-like around the sword inked onto my skin.

"What's this quote from?" she asked, her voice low and sultry in a way that made me pulse inside her again. Her eyes found mine, a slow curl of her lips letting me know she'd felt it.

"Nothing," I said.

Her eyes found mine. "You made it up?"

"It may have been inspired by a couple of things."

"Such as?"

"The fairy tale the tavern is named after, for one."

"I've never heard of a fairy tale with a Prince Darian."

"It's called the Light Princess. She's born with this glow emitting from her." I slid my hand over her collarbone, cupping her cheek. "Kind of like someone else I know."

Rory rolled her eyes, and I continued. "The glow frightened her parents and the people of her land, so she was sent to live with a giantess in the mountains. When her parents finally called her back, it was because they were at war. They'd tried to invade the kingdom next door and had failed, and now their enemy was in their land, wreaking the same horrors on their people that they'd done to his. So, they offered her up as a trophy in an attempt to appease the enemy's prince.

"At first, the princess refused to be handed over, but then the prince offered her a way out. Give him one kiss, and he'd forgive her parents their sins and leave her people in peace. She chose to protect those who'd never shown her any kindness, and that kiss cleansed the world. Her flame— her light—joined with his and burned the evil from both their kingdoms. She chose to be the hero in a world full of villains."

Her hands stilled on my chest, and she swallowed.

"That's a pretty powerful story."

I nodded. It was. A story that had been handed down in my family for generations, but no one was really sure of its origin.

"What else?" she asked.

"What else what?"

"What else inspired the tattoo?"

My gaze held hers. In that moment, the power of the universe overwhelmed me—the power of fate or magic or God—whatever you wanted to call it. Because somehow Rory and I had always been meant to end this way.

Souls joined.

Epic love filling us.

Did she feel it too?

Chapter Thirty-five

Rory

Tangled up with Gage in a way I'd always dreamed about but never thought would happen made my entire being rejoice. Tingles of pleasure coated every vein and synapse. What I'd felt when we'd been joined together… it had been… otherworldly. Like we'd stepped beyond the veil to some other existence.

Landing back in reality should have been painful, but instead, I was surrounded by his warmth, his scent, and his touch. It felt like… belonging. Like here and only here would I ever be truly safe and whole.

As he told me the story of the Light Princess, my heart seemed to grow. A girl who was forever on the outside choosing to stand up for those who'd banished her. It was Veronica. It was me.

And maybe that was the fourth time I truly fell for Gage Palmer.

I stared up into his eyes. They'd thundered when we'd made love, flashing with passion and desire instead of lightning, but the heat had been just as intense. Now they'd softened into the gray of a fading storm. As if the sun would break through at any second and shimmer white beams onto the earth. Maybe he wasn't the prince in the story but the princess. Maybe he was burning the evil away.

He watched me, and I wondered if he was ever going to tell me what else had inspired the tattoo. When he finally spoke, his words sliced through me in the most beautiful way possible. "The hero is the person who chooses to stay."

They weren't quite Veronica's words, but I knew that was what he'd intended them to be. And the reality of it thundered through me.

"How many times have you actually watched *my* show?" I asked quietly.

"More than any twenty-seven-year-old guy should probably admit," he said, lips curving upward.

"Why?"

"Escape. And hope."

"Hope?"

"That after all the wreckage, after all the damage, there's still a chance for a happily ever after."

My breath caught again, tears flooding my eyes, and I squeezed my lids shut to hold them back. I turned so my cheek was on his chest. My voice was choked as I said, "She doesn't get her happy ending."

"We all know Logan wasn't in the car, Pipsqueak," he said, hand running over my hair. "No way they could survive the tragedies they'd both experienced only for her to end up without him."

"I don't think Rob Thomas agrees with you."

"What does he know? He may have created the characters, but they became something bigger than him the moment they landed in our hearts. And that little bit of hope the fans feel, the little bit of wonder that exists no matter what he says, that's worth keeping."

The tears I'd been holding back escaped, running down my cheek, and I moved my hand but wasn't fast enough to catch the first one before it landed on his chest. He shifted, and the movement broke us apart. He lifted my chin with his finger.

"Why are you crying?"

It was the second time I'd done this with him. Tears that I hated. Weakness. Distraction. I couldn't respond, so I simply shrugged.

"Rory…" Worry coated that single syllable.

I cleared my throat enough to say, "I've felt like Veronica in that final episode for almost a year. Panicked and sort of broken. Out of hope."

"You think she was broken?"

I nodded.

"If anything, that ending shows how fucking resilient she is. How *not* broken. And I don't believe she was out of hope either. There was more waiting for her. Even if it wasn't Logan. There were decades left of epic stories in her future."

My eyes fluttered closed. I pulled away from his grip on my chin and rested my cheek against his chest once more.

Gage's arms banded around me, drawing me impossibly tighter to him, and he kissed the top of my head. "Besides, you're not her. You've never been her. You're stronger and even more badass. You know what I think?"

I didn't answer, and he kept going.

"The only mistake Veronica ever made was in thinking she had to do the big stuff on her own. You won't make that mistake. Because I think you know the truth. I think you know that the only way to be epic is if we do it together."

My heart literally spasmed inside my chest.

Before either of us could really register I'd moved, I was kissing him. It had the same fierceness as before—the same passion—but the edge of desperation we'd felt had been curbed. This was something bigger. Better. More. This kiss held the beauty of his words and the hope that he was trying to give me. It offered a future filled with times like this that I hadn't quite believed in but somehow he could see.

Sitting up, I pushed him onto his back and straddled him. His eyes roved over my body and the small curves I'd never hated nor adored. They were just me. But the love in Gage's eyes made me appreciate them in a way I hadn't before.

I kissed him again, nipping at his lower lip, and we got lost once more in mouths and fingers and limbs. Retreating into the bubble of passion and lust we'd just left where we didn't have to think of anything more than the way our bodies fit. Where we moved together as if we'd been doing this for an eternity.

When I finally lifted myself up to sheathe him inside me, it was Gage who cried out this time. As if the joy and pleasure were too much to be contained. I savored his cry, swallowing it with another kiss. Making it mine.

Making him mine in the way I'd always been his. Since I'd climbed the stairs to the apartment above the bar and heard The Guess Who drifting from the open doorway.

I thought I'd be able to keep control as I set the pace. I thought I'd be able to slowly lead us to the summit, but the more we moved, the harder the thrusts became and the more the world around me blurred until it completely disappeared. Until all I could do was race with him toward the finish line.

Gage flipped us over, and I grabbed the headboard as he moved faster and harder, and it still didn't feel like it would ever be enough. He dragged his hand down between us, swiping a single finger along my core, and I exploded, crying out, trembling as my entire body seemed to leave the earth. He thrust inside me one last time, going over the edge himself with a deep groan that would forever enchant my dreams.

He collapsed on top of me. If it had been another guy, I would have felt suffocated. Instead, he comforted me like a weighted blanket and my entire body relaxed. My eyelids closed, and I found it impossible to lift them. For the first time in months, I felt nothing but peace.

♫ ♫ ♫

The notification sound I'd set up for the cameras in

Walden's room jerked me awake. I was tucked up against Gage, his arms wrapped around my waist.

I'd slept with Gage.

The thought didn't fill me with the panic it should have.

Instead, it felt right. Like we were home and not in a hotel room in D.C. on what was essentially a stakeout.

The notification pinged again, and I pulled away from him with reluctance, searching for my phone in the pile of clothes we'd shed from the door to the bed.

Picking up my jacket, I looked back and found him watching me with a somber look on his face. The smile and heat were gone.

Did he regret it? Was he going to give me a line about our ages, our lives, or the impossible situation we were in and why we shouldn't have done what we had? No… he couldn't. Not after talking about this being epic.

My heart pounded fiercely.

I hated looking away in order to swipe the camera app open.

We'd missed Walden going into his room, but he was there now. I rewound the video. He'd shed his suit jacket the moment he'd entered the room and headed for the bathroom where the shower was now running.

The perfect time to go in.

I started pulling on my clothes, and Gage moved to do the same.

"What's the plan?" he asked.

"Surprise him when he comes out of the bathroom, demand answers."

His lips quirked. "Just like that."

"Just like that."

I made sure I had my stun gun, backup pen stun gun, pocketknife, and pepper spray on my body before pulling a set of zip ties from my bag and sliding them into a pocket as well. I handed him a pair of gloves while I slipped into my own. He eyed them like they were going to sting him, but reluctantly put them on.

The two key cards were on the floor where they'd fallen after Gage had swept me off my feet. My veins hummed at the thought of how he'd dragged my clothes from my body and branded me with his touch. His smell lingered on me.

For the first time, maybe in my entire life, I didn't want to do the job or be Veronica interrogating a villain or a witness. I just wanted to pull the covers back and drag Gage underneath, losing ourselves in each other's skin for at least a month.

I swallowed back those thoughts and headed for the door with Gage on my heels. I checked the cameras one more time. Walden was still in the bathroom. We stepped across the hall, I swiped the key card across the reader, and the lock clicked open. I pushed the handle down as quietly as possible, slipping into the room.

The door had barely shut as the shower turned off.

I motioned for Gage to stand on the other side of the open bathroom door. It meant Walden would see me first. Gage didn't seem to like that, but I was the one with the stun gun. I pulled it from my waistband, waiting for Walden to appear.

Walden was naked, towel wrapped around his waist, and he barely registered my being there before I'd pressed the nodes of the gun to his neck.

"Don't move. Don't scream. Don't twitch a damn muscle," I warned.

His eyes narrowed briefly, anger and a hint of fear washing over his face. "Who the hell do you think you are?"

"Nemesis, here for retribution," I replied.

He looked down at the object pressed to his neck and snorted, starting to pull away. "Is that a fucking flashlight?"

"Stun gun, asshole." I pushed it harder into his skin. "Feel the nodes pressed against you. They'll shoot a hundred thousand volts into your body. Enough to completely immobilize you. It's a lot more painful than the television actors make it look. Hurts like a son of a bitch for days."

He raised his left arm, fisting his hand as if to take a swing, and in a flash, Gage had twisted it behind Walden's back. He grunted out in surprise and pain. He'd been so focused on me that he hadn't seen the other, much more intimidating, body in the room.

I stepped forward to push the gun into him again. "Looks can be deceiving, don't you agree? Take you for example. You look like a respectable CEO saving the world one rain cloud at a time, but instead, you're just a murderer in a thousand-dollar suit.

"Me? I look like a sweet co-ed instead of La Femme Nikita, and this"—I pushed the barrel farther into his neck—"looks like a hapless flashlight, when it can almost stop your heart."

Walden kicked out at me while trying to take a swing at Gage with his free arm. In response, Gage yanked the arm he held up until Walden's shoulder was fully strained and his face contorted in pain. Even then, Walden didn't stop fighting.

The two men stumbled backward into the room. The asshole got a jab into Gage's side that made him grunt. But Walden had completely forgotten about me, and I moved with rapid succession, sweeping his legs out from under him and landing an elbow to his spine.

He crashed down, head bouncing into the dresser, and falling face-first on the blue-and-gold carpet. He'd barely groaned and reached for his temple by the time I was straddling his back, pulling his already strained arm backward and pushing the stun gun into his neck again.

"Grab the ties from my pocket," I told Gage. When I risked looking at him, concern mingled with awe on his face.

He did as I asked, reaching in and grabbing the zip ties. Between the two of us, we moved the dazed and befuddled CEO to a straight-backed chair at the table in the corner. We tied his arms behind it and his ankles to the legs.

When I stepped away to look at him, I expected to see anger or even fear on his face, but instead, it held a strange calm that made the hair on the back of my neck stand up.

"I didn't recognize you at first, Rory," Walden said. The fact he knew who I was carved a little thread of worry through me, but not enough to stop what we were doing. "You've made a huge mistake."

"I don't think so. You're the one who made a mistake."

"West isn't just going to let you walk away from this. He told you to back off."

"As you weren't at the conversation I had with him, I'm pretty sure you don't know what he said. Maybe he's where I got the information about how you murdered your own brother." Walden didn't react. "You have one chance to come clean before we turn you over to the cops."

He scoffed. "For what? What exactly do you think you have on me?"

"Why don't we play a round of twenty questions and you can tell me?" He just stared at me, and I stepped forward, pulling my pen-like stun gun from my pocket. I leaned into his face. "Did you know my mother was investigating Argento Skies?"

He didn't respond, so I shoved the pen into his neck and hit the button.

His entire body convulsed as a grunt of pain escaped him.

"Jesus," Gage said, looking at me with wide eyes.

"That little beauty was my backup, Shawn. She hurts, don't you think? But not nearly as much as my friend here," I waved my Vipertek at him. "So, I'll ask you again. Did you know my mother was investigating you?"

"Yes," he said, struggling against the ties and the tremors the zap of electricity had sent through him.

"Did you send her car off the road?"

He just glared, but when I went to push the button again, he caved. "I didn't, but they did."

"You can say their names. We all know who you're talking about."

"Look. None of this was what I wanted. I didn't have a choice."

"What are you saying? You were blackmailed into killing your brother? Nearly killing my mom?"

"Do you even know who West is? You're playing with fire, little girl."

Gage stepped forward before I could push the button and said, "She's not a little girl. She's a fucking brilliant woman who just immobilized you in less than a minute. So stop tossing around half-assed, ignorant insults and explain yourself."

Walden scowled at Gage, eyes dropping back to the gun in my hand before giving a shuddery breath and saying, "When the people of Parkerville filed their suit against us for the silver iodide poisoning, I didn't believe them. I thought it was just another money grab since the town has a history of toxicity from centuries of mining, but Tim wanted to do our own testing. We fought over it, and I told him it was stupid to open a door we couldn't close.

"I happened to be meeting with Dunn that day and poured my worries out over several martinis with him and West. They told me they had a friend who could help us take care of it if that's what I wanted. I told them I'd think about it. When I told Tim, he freaked out.

"The next thing I know, his plane has crashed, and West shows up telling me they have evidence that ties me to the wreck as if I'd paid someone to do it. Everything that's happened since then has been out of my hands. I'm just following orders so I don't end up dead. So my brother's wife and son don't end up dead too."

"You want me to believe you had nothing to do with this? That you're being blackmailed by Dunn?" I asked, scorn ripping through my words.

Walden's laugh filled the air. Sarcastic and cruel. Filled with bitter venom. "Fuck. You really have no clue who you're screwing with if you think it's Dunn. He's just the happy puppet whose strings are being pulled. An idiot who thinks some cheap fortune teller and his smile are going to get him into the White House someday, when really it's his powerful friends who will make it happen."

My stomach fell as I realized he was telling the truth. He believed there was someone, or multiple someones, much more powerful behind Dunn and West.

What had I missed?

Chapter Thirty-six

Gage

ANGELS (CAN'T HELP YOU NOW)
Performed by Def Leppard

My heart pounded furiously as I watched Rory in action. She was so damn cool and collected. Strong and calm, whereas I was rattled to my core, so when Walden dropped the line about the fortune teller, all I could see was red. He knew where Demi was.

I stepped up behind him and yanked his zip-tied arms up until he grunted in pain. "Where the hell is my mom?"

"I don't know!" he cried out.

"Did you have my brother kidnapped?" I growled.

"I told you. I don't know shit. I'm just following orders."

"Whose?" Rory demanded. "West and who?"

"If I tell you, they'll kill me, my sister-in-law, and my nephew. Hell, I may already be as good as dead." He scanned the room furtively, and Rory's gaze followed his.

"That's my camera," she told him, chin nodding to the dime-sized object she'd hid earlier on the base of a lamp.

"There'll be more. There's always more."

My eyes found Rory's, and her jaw clenched tight. She immediately started searching the room, and I stepped in to help even though I didn't know exactly what I was looking for. We touched every piece of furniture, turning it over.

Bedding was tossed aside, and every single plug, appliance, and device was inspected. When the room looked like a hurricane had flown through it, she stopped, returning to stand in front of Walden.

"The only cameras here are mine," she said. "You were just wasting our time. Why?"

He shook his head as if not believing her.

Rory bent and pulled a briefcase out from under the bed. "What's the gun and the cash for?"

"A drop I was supposed to make."

"A murder for hire, just like you murdered your brother. Like you paid someone to run my mom off the road! Was this drop for me?"

He didn't respond.

"Was it for Demi Palmer?" Rory demanded.

My heart had already been pulsing at a weird, off-kilter beat, and now it halted completely before thundering back to life as if she'd hit *me* with the stun gun. Rory had said they might come after us—her. But fuck, she really thought they'd hired someone to kill her. And Demi. It hadn't just been a precaution when she'd told me to send my family away.

"I never ask. I never want to know what it's for," Walden said, and for the first time since we'd tied him, he struggled again before dread seemed to scroll over his face.

"Who's in charge, Shawn? Who's giving the orders?" Walden just stared at the carpet until Rory shoved the stun gun back at him. "Who?!"

"The Lovatos."

Rory went perfectly still, and something crossed her face I wasn't sure I'd ever seen before—fear. Shit… if Rory was afraid…

"You mean the Lovato Cartel?" she asked, the tone breathy from shock.

Walden barely nodded.

"Why would the Lovatos care about your cloud seeding company?" Her brows scrunched in concentration before realization made her eyes widen. "That's where you're getting the money. You're laundering money through your company for the Lovatos. That's why West is a silent partner."

Walden didn't say anything.

"Are you talking about a drug cartel?" I asked Rory.

"They started as a drug cartel, but they've got their hands in everything. Guns. Identity schemes. Price gouging. Investment fraud. You name it, they've done it."

"And they're trying to put their puppet into the White House?" I asked.

Rory shrugged. "I'm sure they have more politicians than Dunn in their pocket along with moles in every law enforcement agency in the country. It's how they've been a step ahead of anyone trying to bring them down."

Rory paced the room, coming to a stop again in front of Walden. "Which warehouse is yours? The list you printed off. Which one were you going to buy?"

"I didn't. They decided at the last minute they were going to do it through another avenue."

"Is that where Demi Palmer is being held?"

His eyes genuinely looked surprised. "Held? You act as if she's been kidnapped. She's Dunn's mistress."

My stomach rolled.

"Dunn doesn't need a mistress. He's single," Rory said.

"You think he wants to be associated with a woman who can't stay put and abandons her family?" Walden shook his head. "He keeps everything about her quiet so he doesn't get dragged over the coals when he talks about how family values are the cornerstone of our society."

"Where is she?" Rory demanded.

Walden shook his head again. "You keep acting like I'm someone in the know, and I keep telling you I'm just a pawn on their chessboard. Dunn, he's just a pawn too, but he likes to pretend he's their king. The carefully guarded piece that will win the game for them. And hell, maybe he is, but the real power is with the Lovatos."

"I'm calling someone I know at the FBI. They'll come and get you. You tell them what you told me, and they'll probably get you a deal with witness protection."

Rory whipped out her phone, and Walden said, "You make that call, and I'm dead."

"You cooperate and tell the truth, and they'll make sure you're safe."

Walden shook his head. "You truly have no clue. You really are just a little girl playing in a league you can't possibly understand."

"I'm trying to save your life, asshole, and Demi's and mine along with it."

"You want vengeance for your mom, and that's blinding you to the truth. You're over your head so deep you're going to get yourself and anyone around you killed."

As he said the words, he glanced at me, and I could tell by the flicker of worry that crossed her face that he'd hit home. She wouldn't want to put me and my siblings in danger, but the way I saw it, Demi had already put us on the Lovatos' radar.

"If Demi is with Dunn and Dunn is with this cartel, they already know everything about us, Rory. They already know they can get to Demi through us. What happened with Monte…" I shook my head.

This was so much more than just Dunn trying to get himself into a senate seat by using Demi's and Monte's psychic abilities. Maybe Demi had threatened to walk and they'd decided Monte was good leverage. Maybe she'd just decided to flit away again on her light feet, but they needed her so they'd kept her.

I headed for the door, suddenly desperate to get back to my family. To be a physical shield to whatever might come after them. Rory was on my heels. "Gage?"

"I need to get home. I need…" God, my breath was uneven. The room spun. I was going to pass out like some fucking wuss.

"We'll go. I'll call the FBI from the car," she said.

Rory whipped back around to Walden, searching his pockets. She came up with his cell phone and wallet. She left the wallet on the dresser, pushed the phone in front of his face to unlock it, and swiped through a bunch of screens.

"Code?" she demanded, and when he didn't answer, she shrugged. "It doesn't matter. I can work around it."

She returned to where I was waiting for her at the door.

Walden called out to us, terror in every syllable. Not a shred of the calm he'd had when we'd shoved him into the chair remained. "You leave me here, and I'm dead."

"The FBI will be here in just a few minutes, Shawn. Sit tight."

I was heading toward the elevator already, but Rory halted me. When I turned, she was going back into the room we'd rented. I desperately needed to get back to Cherry Bay. To my family. God, what had Demi led to our door? What had Rory and I done poking at the sleeping bear?

I waited for a beat, and then she came out of the room pulling the silver suitcase she'd gotten from the pawnshop. She had her phone on her chin, waiting for someone to pick up. I took the handle from her as we got into the elevator.

"Do you actually know someone at the FBI?" I asked.

She nodded. "Yes, but I may have oversold my relationship to Walden. Sheila was Dad's first girlfriend after the divorce. They haven't been together in years, but they're still friends. I haven't spoken to her myself in years. I guess I was always afraid if I reached out to her for anything, she'd tell Dad."

"You don't think she'll tell him now?"

Rory took a deep breath. "She probably will, but we don't have a better option."

"What about Detective Bradshaw or Muloney?" I

asked.

"No way they'd have the resources for this." A muffled voice registered on her phone, and Rory said, "My name is Rory Bishop. I'm a private investigator in D.C. I need to speak with FBI Agent Sheila Gates urgently. I have a witness with critical information about the Lovato Cartel who needs to be protected."

She was put on hold, and we made our way out of the hotel to my car, which we'd parked in the Willard's lot. I'd just backed out of the spot when the other phone in her lap buzzed. Walden's phone. She looked at the screen and hit the button.

"You were warned to stay out of this," a deep, accented voice said on the other end.

Rory didn't say anything. Instead, it was Walden's voice that came across the line, panicked. Desperate. "No. Please. I've done everything you've asked."

Rory turned wide eyes to me, and I braked sharply.

A muffled sound, like a soda can being popped open beneath a pillow whooshed over the call, and Rory gasped.

"That's one," the dark voice returned. "I wonder who will be number two?"

The call dropped.

"What the hell just happened?" I asked as Rory swiped through screens on her phone, pulling up the cameras she put in Walden's room with shaking hands. When she got them up, the screen was black.

She looked at me with wide eyes and shouted. "Go, Gage. Go! We need to get to Cherry Bay."

She didn't have to ask me twice. I put my foot on the gas pedal and sped out of the garage with tires squealing. I couldn't afford to get pulled over, but I also couldn't afford to slow down. I needed to get to my family before anything happened to them.

Rory put her phone on the console, elevator music filled the air as she whipped out her laptop and started typing furiously. When I glanced over, I noticed her hands were still shaking. Calm and collected Rory was gone.

"What just happened, Rory?"

"They killed him."

"What? How do you know? The screen was black, maybe—"

"That was suppressor fire, Gage."

I weaved through the streets of D.C., anxious to get to the freeway so I could really put my foot down. When I glanced back at her computer, it showed us interrogating Walden.

"What are you doing?"

"Getting ready to send this to Sheila. I was going to edit us out and just leave his confession, but this proves we left the room. That we weren't the ones to shoot him."

My heart fell to my stomach.

I was going to jail, and Monte and Ivy were going to grow up thinking I was a murderer and their mother had abandoned them. They'd hate all of us.

"Won't they just think we went back into the room?"

"We're on cameras leaving the hotel and in the parking garage. I'm going to grab those videos as well just in case they get deleted before the FBI asks for them. I wish I'd had time to clone his phone before they called so I could have recorded it."

Her hands trembled, but she was still thinking. So damn smart. My brain was frozen on the simple act of getting to my siblings.

"Rory? This is Sheila? What's going on?" A woman's voice asked through the phone.

Rory explained what had happened. The conversation with Walden as well as what she thought had happened to him. The agent swore, told Rory to send her the videos, and said she would get a team over to the Willard. She told us not to go anywhere because agents would be coming to talk to us as well.

My mind flashed to memories of the FBI tearing our apartment apart after the train bomb fiasco. My heart fell. I didn't want to put Monte through that again. To put Ivy through it when she might actually remember it.

Even though the traffic was no more of a bear than it normally was leaving D.C., my skin crawled. I wanted to scream and ram cars out of my way so I could hurry home. I called River and told him to close the bar and go back to his house because people might be coming for my family. He swore under his breath using worse, more violent words than the FBI agent had.

"God, Gage… I'm so sorry…" Rory's voice cracked, and she turned her eyes away from me.

"I don't see how this is your fault."

"I should have done more research before I confronted Walden. Fuck, fuck, fuck!" She banged her hand on the seat. "I knew there was something funny about the amount of money Walden had. Knew there was something off about West being the silent partner Casada had suggested. If I'd slowed down, I could have put it together that they were tied to the Lovatos. I'm sure my mom did."

Rory pulled a day planner out of her bag. Old school. She flipped through it, reading what looked like a bunch of doodles. Things you made when you were bored in class.

Her phone rang, and she picked it up. "Hey, Nan. Are you at Harriet's?"

Her voice was an attempt at calm, but I heard the edge beneath it.

"Nan… Slow down… I can't understand you…"

Rory's face went pale and a guttural cry ripped from the depths of her. She folded over on herself.

"No! No! I didn't! God, no!"

I swerved to the side of the road, horns honking, people flipping me off. But I needed to help her. Hold her. Do something other than just fucking drive.

Chapter Thirty-seven

Rory

KEEP YOUR EYES ON ME
Performed by Tim McGraw and Faith Hill

Pain took over as the aftershock of Nan's words rolled through me. She was sobbing, crying on the other end. I'd barely understood her, and even when the words finally hit home, I still didn't want to believe them. I squeezed the phone so tightly I thought I might break a finger.

"I'm coming, Nan. I'm on my way. Tell them I didn't sign it. Tell them…" God. My words were as choked as Nan's. I could barely understand myself.

Tears welled and poured down my face.

Mom.

I wasn't sure if I'd hung up or Nan had as the phone slipped from my grasp. My arms pulled tight around my waist as sharp barbs landed inside my chest and stomach. I barely registered Gage whipping the car to the side of the road as horns blared. He slammed the SUV into Park and reached for me. I recoiled. If he touched me, I'd never be able to hold myself together. I'd crumble.

"D-don't stop, Gage! I n-need to get to Sh-shady Lane."

It was already too late. I was already too late! I wouldn't be able to say goodbye. A raw and feral sound broke free of my chest. Some weird combination of a scream and a sob.

"Rory. What happened?"

I couldn't look at him, but I could hear his concern, and it spiraled me more. This was my fault. It was all my fault. Dad had been right all along.

Dad!

Maybe this wasn't all on me.

My hands fumbled to find my phone. He picked up after two rings. "What did you do?" I hollered into it.

"Rory? What's wrong?" His voice was calm but concerned.

"Did you do this? Just tell me…" Another tortured sob broke free.

Before I knew it, Gage had lifted me over the console and onto his lap. He cradled me in his arms. His warmth bled into me, and all I could do was sob.

"Rory, honey, where are you? What's wrong?" Dad's voice held more emotion than I'd ever heard from him.

"Someone signed the order to shut off M-mom's life s-support!" My voice was garbled with tears and emotions.

I could barely breathe. My lungs were squeezed tight, unable to perform their simple function. The world swam in front of my eyes.

Gage grunted out a shocked huff, and his arms tightened. His forehead settled in the crook of my neck as he whispered, "Rory." That single word was full of compassion and sadness and loss. And it made the tears flow faster and harder.

Dad had gone silent. I didn't know if it was shock or guilt.

I pushed away from Gage, climbing back into my seat. "Please, Gage. Please. Get me to my mom."

Gage's face was contorted with grief and pain, but he put the car into gear, looked over his shoulder, and whipped back into the lane.

"Rory… Jesus… I can't believe you think I'd do that." Dad's voice finally came over the line. "You're the only one who can."

"S-someone forged my signature, Dad. S-someone…" I couldn't even say it. But I could think it. Someone had signed Mom's death warrant.

That's one. I wonder who will be number two?

Hatred filled me. Hatred and anguish and regret because it wasn't Dad who was responsible. This was all on me. All of it.

"I fucked up, Dad… I fucked up… and they k-killed her…"

Sobs escaped me. Loud and angry.

"Are you at Shady Lane? I'm on my way, honey. I'm on my way."

I hung up. I wasn't there. I'd be there before him, but it wouldn't be in time.

An entire lifetime went by as Gage weaved through traffic and changed lanes, pushing safety to the limits as he raced toward Cherry Bay. We squealed into the Shady Lane parking lot, and I bolted from the car, leaving everything behind me.

My boots were loud, pounding the same ferocious beat of my heart as I sped through the doors and down the sterile hallway. Someone at the front desk yelled at me because I hadn't stopped to sign in, but I just kept running until I was skidding through the doorway of Mom's room.

Nan had her face buried in the blankets on top of Mom, holding her hands. The machines that had been beeping out a rhythm for almost a year were silent, and it felt wrong. It felt wrong and awful and terrifying.

Chills ran over my skin as I crossed to the other side of the bed. Normally, I had to be careful of the tubes and the wires. Now there was nothing. Nothing but my mom's body that had withered slowly away and a heart that had come to a complete stop. I climbed in with her. Climbed in, even though I knew there was nothing there. Her chest wasn't moving. No breath escaped her pale lips.

She was gone.

She was gone, and I hadn't gotten to say goodbye. Not before she'd crashed into the Potomac almost a year ago. Not before some asshole had forged my signature on the order to turn off her life support.

"I'm so sorry, Mom. I'm so sorry. I'm so sorry. I'm so sorry," I cried, holding an empty shell.

Nan raised a tear-stained face, letting my mother's hands drop as she reached for mine. "I tried, Rory. I tried to get them to stop." The pain in her voice sent another sharp crack through my chest and more sobs escaped.

"B-betty at the front called me… She didn't understand why we weren't here… She kn-knew we'd never let her go alone. They'd already removed everything… They showed me the order with your signature. I told them there was some m-mistake."

She shook her head, and I could see she was trembling as hard as I was. I squeezed her hand as we both cried. Horrified awful tears. Even knowing that Nan had thought we should do exactly this, we never would have done it this way. Never.

Movement in the doorway behind Nan revealed Gage. He had my bag and my phone in his hands. He stepped inside the room, dropping the items on the love seat where I'd often done my work while keeping Mom company.

When he turned back to me, his eyes were full of grief and sorrow. A huge knot formed in my throat. I couldn't breathe again. I gasped, trying to get air.

Gage rushed over to me, brushing my hair away from my face as his hand fell to my back. "God… Pipsqueak… I'm so sorry."

His voice held the same guilt I was feeling. Guilt that wasn't his. He wasn't the professional. He wasn't the one who'd fucked up. He wasn't the one who'd led a cartel to our doors.

I struggled to gain control of the sobs so I could speak. "Go, Gage! Go to Monte and Ivy. Call Muloney. Get an officer at your door."

His eyes rounded, large and frightened. I could feel the debate within him. The need to stay with me battling with the need to protect his siblings. And the bittersweetness of it bled through the agony inside me.

It mattered more than I'd ever be able to express that he was debating—that he cared enough to actually want to stay. But I'd already lost my mother. There was nothing we could do here, whereas he could still protect his family.

"Go!" I all but yelled.

It shocked him. I hadn't meant that I didn't want him with me. I ached to let myself get lost in his comfort. To lose myself in the warmth of his embrace, but that would just be another mistake. He needed to be with his brother and sister. That's where he belonged first and foremost.

He stepped back, wavering still, looking from me to Nan and back. Sadness and indecision poured from his eyes.

I swallowed hard, trying to soften my tone so he knew I wasn't angry with him. So he knew I needed him to do this. "Please. I'm okay. But you need to get to them. I… I won't be able to live with myself if something else happens tonight… if they get hurt."

That was all it took. He whirled around and was gone.

I turned back to Nan. Her tears were slow and steady while mine ravaged my body and poured down my face.

I'd lost Mom.

I'd lost her because I'd thought I was smarter than them. Because the damn chip on my shoulder had me trying to prove that I could outwit them.

Nan and I lay there, tucked against my mom until my tears turned into a silent stream rather than a torrential wave. My face felt swollen and pained. My entire body ached as if I'd run a marathon.

I'd fought for so long to help her survive, and now she would never have the chance to prove to the world she hadn't given up. That she was a Marlowe through and through, fighting for every inch of life she could gather.

I wasn't sure how long we'd lain there tangled together before Dad showed up. He wasn't in his typical suit but a pair of jeans and a button-down with loafers on his feet. It was the most casual I'd seen my father in maybe a decade. A frown twisted his face as he moved into the room, glance darting between the three of us.

He rubbed a large hand over his chin, tears welling in his eyes, and I wasn't sure who they were for—him or me or Mom. He approached us slowly, squeezed my shoulder, and asked, "Do you know what happened?"

I did. I did but couldn't bring myself to say it. To see the disappointment in his eyes… and in Nan's. So I closed mine.

I turned back to my mother. I kissed her cheek. It was already cold.

It was always cold in this room, but this felt different. As if there was now ice instead of blood in her veins. As if she was gradually becoming stone instead of flesh and bone.

Dad moved back so I could climb out of the bed. My legs wobbled, and I would have fallen if he hadn't caught me. He pulled me against his chest with both hands, holding on tight.

This wasn't the loose, one-handed hug I'd become used to over the last decade. This was strong and sure and full of love. A hug that whispered all-but-forgotten memories of my childhood and feelings of safety I'd long ago pushed to the recesses of my mind.

More tears came. These were slow. A drip, drip, drip that echoed the pounding of my heart.

"I'm so sorry, Kora," Dad said to my grandmother. His voice vibrated through his chest and into my body.

Nan sniffled, and when I opened my eyes, I saw her reach for the tissues on the side table. She blew her nose and wiped at her tears.

A doctor appeared at the door, and Dad took over. "Explain to me what the hell happened here today."

The doctor tugged at the collar of his white coat. "When I came in today, the order to remove life support was in my box. I assumed Ms. Bishop and Mrs. Marlowe had already come and said their goodbyes." He cleared his throat. "I don't understand. The order had Ms. Bishop's signature. It was witnessed and stamped by a notary."

"I'll need to see it," Dad told the man. "I'll need copies of it and all camera footage for the day."

The doctor nodded, spinning around and leaving.

Dad took me by the shoulders, pushing me away enough to scour my face.

"Now, tell me why you think this has anything to do with you."

I swallowed hard. I still didn't want to tell him. Still didn't trust him because his client was tied up in this. Was Dad with the Lovatos as well? Was he being blackmailed into helping them?

"I didn't heed a warning to back off."

His eyes narrowed. "And you think they did this"—he looked over at my mom's lifeless body—"as retaliation?"

I didn't answer.

"Who?" he demanded, voice turning stony.

"The Lovatos."

His jaw ticked and his throat bobbed. Was it a sign of guilt? Regret? "Damn it, Rory. I told you not to fuck around in your mother's case."

The fact that he already knew the connection caused fury to blaze through me. I was almost grateful because it pushed aside some of the guilt and overwhelming sadness. Pushed it aside enough to give me a purpose and a person to direct all my emotions toward. And I did.

"You knew! You knew the cartel was involved and didn't tell me? I can't believe you!"

I sidestepped him, going toward my gear that Gage had left on the love seat, but not quite getting there before his words halted me.

"I suspected. I didn't have proof. I told you to stay the hell away from this."

"Well." I whirled back around. "If you'd trusted me enough to tell me what was really going on, maybe I wouldn't have stumbled into the middle of the hornet's nest unaware. Besides, I was working on a different case. It just happens to tie together with Mom's."

Disbelief appeared in his eyes, but I didn't give him a chance to say anything.

"I don't care if you believe it or not. It's true." I waved a finger at him. "And you and your cushy little political friend are involved too. I just haven't decided how much of a villain you really are in this story."

I expected him to be angry, to maybe even raise his voice when it was something he rarely did. Instead, sadness greeted me. "You think I'd do this? You think I'd endanger you and the woman I loved?"

I scoffed. "Loved. You didn't love Mom. I'm not sure you know how to love anyone. Not even your own daughter. I was a tool for you to wield, and when I disappointed you and Mom wouldn't let you use me anymore, I became even less important. Something to forget rather than keep close."

He rubbed his hand over his eyes. "I've made mistakes with you Rory, but I've never once given you a reason to doubt I loved you." I didn't respond, and he moved on. "If you don't believe that, then at least believe I would never risk everything I've built working with the Lovatos. And I sure as hell wouldn't let them put Hallie into the Potomac."

I didn't know what I believed. My emotions were too wound up. My thoughts were too convoluted. I had to step back. Step back and look at everything from a clearer angle. I had to do it before more people got hurt. Nan or Gage or his siblings. Demi might already be dead.

Bile rolled up the back of my throat. The bitter taste was an apt reminder of what I'd done. Of the failures hanging on me tonight. But the voice on the phone hadn't threatened three people. Only two.

Did that mean they were done? That as long as I stopped, they'd walk away? Or would they keep cleaning house, sweeping aside any debris that could land back on them? I needed to finish this. I needed to stop them before they hurt more people I loved.

Time was slipping away. Time I couldn't afford.

Then my look landed on my mom's cold and unmoving body and Nan standing by her side looking so lost and alone, and I knew I couldn't leave. Not yet.

I needed to be here. I needed to be here for Nan in a way I hadn't been for Mom.

Chapter Thirty-eight

Gage

YOU BETTER BELIEVE
Performed by Train

Every muscle in my body hurt from being held tight for what felt like a week straight. Fear and anguish and now incredible sadness leaked through me. The brief respite I'd had while lost inside Rory back at the hotel seemed like a dream that had vanished into the night. A mirage that had disappeared with a blink.

I lay on one side of the pullout couch in River and Audrey's living room, listening to Monte's breathing as he slept on the other sofa. I was grateful he was asleep, but I wondered if it would be broken with nightmares. We had to be getting closer to the day his vision came true. Too many strings had been pulled for it not to be happening soon. Rory and I had stepped into a field full of landmines we'd never expected.

My heart ached for Rory. I couldn't shake her tortured cries from my head.

Monte had sounded like that at Dad's funeral.

I'd cried a thousand tears on my way from Kansas to Virginia after I'd gotten the call about Dad. I hadn't been able to say goodbye to him, but on the drive, thousands of memories had flooded me.

I'd cried for Dad, for the father I'd admired and loved more than words. I'd cried for myself. For the lost dreams

and my lost future because even then I'd known the truth—
I wouldn't be going back to Kansas.

What worried me most now about Rory was the guilt
I'd seen written all over her in that hospital room. She
believed this was because of her. That somehow she could
have stopped it from happening. Her voice screaming at me
to leave Shady Lane and get to my siblings had filled me
with terror not just for my family but for her.

Would she ever recover from this? Would it become a
new wound that would fester and grow until it absorbed her
entire being, taking all her light and dousing it?

I rose from the bed, stepping quietly to the window and
shifting the blinds to look outside. Mist curled up from the
ground, shrouding the world in more than just darkness. A
thick heaviness hung in the air.

More thunderstorms were coming.

Through the dim spotlight the streetlight cast in the
gloom, I barely made out the shape of a patrol car parked at
the curb. I'd been surprised Muloney had sent someone,
especially when I hadn't given him all the information. Just
enough to know I'd witnessed a murder and that what had
happened with my brother was tied up with the Lovatos. I'd
told him the FBI was getting involved, and maybe that had
spurred him into helping.

I pulled my phone from the side table where it had been
charging, dashing off a note to Rory.

ME: Are you awake? Are you home?

I wanted to ask how she was. I wanted to ask if I could
call or if I could come over or how the hell I could help. But
all of it seemed pointless. Useless. I knew from hard
experience that no one could help. No one could take the
pain away.

There was only one way to travel the road of grief—
alone. All your friends and loved ones could do was walk
beside you and try to catch you if you fell. So, I'd do that for

Rory. When she collapsed, when she needed someone to carry her for a few feet, I'd be there for her.

When she didn't respond, I didn't know if I was relieved or worried. Was she actually sleeping or was she ignoring me on purpose? Was she off doing some sort of Rory supersleuth work? Or was she grieving in silence?

Noise from down the hall had my entire body going still and my ears straining. I eased quietly on my sock-clad feet down the dark planks. At the door to the garage turned art studio, I paused. A desk lamp cast a beam on River standing at his workbench shoved up against a side wall.

His large hands worked tweezers as he moved pieces so small he had to use a magnifying glass to maneuver them. Behind him, a large statue took up the rest of the garage. Audrey's new piece was made of large chunks of granite wrapped in swirling, thick metal.

River looked up from his work as I moved closer, giving me a nod. I took a seat at an old barstool that had been perched near his bench for decades.

"I'm sorry if you couldn't sleep because of us," I said gruffly.

"The truth is, I'm up at this hour a lot of times anyway. When I'm working on something new, I often can't sleep until it's done," he said. He carefully put down the items he'd been holding.

"Everything's spiraled out of control," I told him. "People are dying… Hallie Marlowe… That Walden guy I told you about."

In my mind, I heard the whoosh Rory had identified as a suppressor fire all over again. I heard Walden's fear as he begged for his life, and my stomach coiled tightly, threatening to lose the sandwich I'd picked at earlier.

"And Demi. She might be dead too." I swallowed hard, those same unexpected emotions from all week overwhelming me—loss I never thought I'd feel over our mother.

River leaned up against his workbench with his heavily tattooed and muscled arms crossed over his chest. Normally, his face was hard to read. A blank sketch. He was calm and cool-headed ninety-nine percent of the time, but if you did enough to actually rile the man, he was hard to bring back down. Now there was only sadness in his eyes.

"You're not responsible for that woman, Gage. Never have been. She was the adult. The parent. She was supposed to look out for all of you, not the other way around. If she got tangled up into something ugly, it's her fault for pulling you into it."

I knew that. At least, logically, I did. But every instinct told me it wasn't that simple. Worse, I'd dragged Rory into it too. Her mom was dead as a result of our actions over the last few days. My chest grew tighter and tighter until I thought it might implode like an atom bomb, causing even more wreckage to strew across our lives.

I tried to give myself an out. Rory's mom had already been involved. Her car accident was proof she'd been working this case long before Monte's vision and kidnapping, but what would have happened if I hadn't asked Rory to find Demi? Would everyone still be breathing?

Rory wouldn't stop now. Not until she got justice for her mom. Not because she envisioned herself as some Veronica Mars clone, but because exacting justice was in her DNA. It was at the core of who she was. And what would happen then?

What would happen after?

I'd told her I wanted her at my side. Wanted her in my life. And I'd meant it. Hell, I'd basically told her I loved her. But what if keeping her meant bringing this kind of evil closer to my siblings over and over again? What if the worst happened and I lost one of them? And yet…

I still didn't know if I could let her go. Just the idea of walking away made me feel like my arms were being ripped from my body. As if I wouldn't ever be able to move again until she was at my side.

"What else is going on in that brain of yours?" River asked.

"I slept with Rory." It slipped out before I could even debate saying it.

His eyebrows lifted, and his lips twitched. "Well. Good for you, man. It's been too damn long."

I rubbed the scruff on my chin. "It should have been weird. Hell, she was twelve when I first met her." I shook my head. She was an adult now. A stunning force that drew me like gravity. "Instead, it just felt…"

"Right," he finished for me.

I nodded.

"Once when I was a teenager, I asked my mom how she knew my dad was the one for her," River said. "Her response was, 'I just knew.' When I told her, 'That was fucking useful,' she slapped me for swearing. But it was the truth, because as soon as Audrey turned her smile on me in Art 101, that's how I felt. It was like my entire life slid into focus. As if I'd been stumbling around in the dark until she showed up."

His words settled inside me. That was how I'd felt next to Rory. Like everything else was out of focus except her. As if she was the only place where I'd find peace again. Except now, everything was in chaos.

"Regardless of how this ends with Demi and Dunn and the Lovatos, Rory is going to be out there putting herself at risk. If not as a PI, then as an agent. It's who she is. It's what she's wanted from the moment I met her. How do I invite that uncertainty into Ivy and Monte's world?"

"Plenty of law enforcement types have families, Gage."

"But my family has lost so much already," I said, my doubts showing in every syllable.

He stared at me for a moment. "Who are you really trying to protect? Your brother and sister or yourself?"

River picked up a roll of wire from his bench. "You're afraid to unwrap the metal cage you've locked your heart inside. For four years I've watched you going through the motions, keeping everyone at bay. This isn't the life you're supposed to live, man. You gotta put it all on the line. So what if it gets stabbed once or ten more times? At least you will have actually lived."

I bristled. "I don't have my heart locked up. I give it every day to Monte and Ivy."

River's eyes narrowed, and he shrugged. "Yeah. You love them. You keep them safe. But you don't show them how to live. How to put yourself out there. How to accept love as much as you give it. You've taught them how to shield themselves, which isn't a bad skill to learn, but learning to open yourself up is also important."

Before I could respond, Monte's scream ripped through the air, and I bounded out of the room with River on my tail. Monte's cry died away into a choked sob as I skidded into the living room. He was sitting up on the pullout bed, eyes wild, hair standing up.

I landed on the bed, dragging him into my arms. "It's okay, Monte. I'm here."

He was trembling so hard that it made my body quiver too.

"They're all there, Gage. Demi and Dunn and Rory."

I nodded, my chin grazing the top of his head as I squeezed him tight.

"No... What I mean is"—he pulled away from me, terrified and tortured eyes meeting mine—"they all die."

Chapter Thirty-nine

Rory

EYE OF THE TIGER
Performed by Survivor

I felt like I was moving through a fog as Nan, Dad, and I watched the coroner arrive and take Mom's body from the room. The staff at Shady Lane were nervous and jumpy, as if they were afraid we were going to sue them. But this wasn't their fault. This was mine.

While we'd waited, anxiety had crept in, growing stronger and stronger until I thought it might choke me. An invisible countdown sat above my head, approaching zero and fast.

When the room was finally empty except for the three of us again, the silence made me want to scream. No machines. No Mom. Nothing but agony and regrets dripping from all of us, pouring on the floor like acid ready to tear apart the frayed edges of our relationships.

Dad broke the quiet with words that surprised me. "Let me take care of the arrangements with the funeral home tomorrow. Neither of you should have to deal with it."

"She didn't want to be buried. She wanted to be cremated," Nan said. Her voice was so hoarse from crying that it made me wince.

Dad nodded. "I know. When we were married, we had it all written down in our will."

Nan looked at me to see if I was okay with this, and I

shrugged. It didn't really matter what happened, did it? She wasn't here. She was gone. What we did now was for us and not her, and all I wanted to do was catch the assholes who'd killed her. That was what I wanted to do for my mother.

"Do you need a ride home?" he asked.

"I've got my car," Nan said. "Rory?"

"I'll go with Nan." There was no way I was getting into the car with Dad. My feelings were too much of a jumbled mess, and I was afraid he'd see through me. That he'd see what I was going to do.

I grabbed my things from the couch, and we walked out of the room. As we exited the building, tears filled my eyes once more. It wasn't that I would miss Shady Lane, but the finality of what had happened hit me all over again. I ground my teeth together, fighting to hold myself together.

"I'll call tomorrow," Dad said, taking in my splotchy and swollen face. "Take a moment to breathe, Rory. Don't do anything until I call you."

I shrugged, and his eyes narrowed. But I wouldn't make promises to him I didn't intend to keep. I couldn't.

"I don't want you to get hurt too. Don't go looking for revenge without me," he insisted. "If you've learned anything from watching that damn show of yours, remember the mistakes she made in not telling her dad the truth. In not waiting for backup."

My stubborn defiance must have shown on my face because he growled, "Keith Mars isn't the only man who loves his daughter."

And it hit me in the chest like a brick. The words about love. The fact that he knew so much about my favorite characters. That he must have watched the show.

But I couldn't do this with him right now. Love or forgiveness… or whatever he was hoping for. I didn't know if I'd ever be able to work with him on Mom's case or any other, and especially not when I wasn't a hundred percent sure I could trust him.

So instead of responding, I spun around and followed Nan to her car. The mist whirled around us in thick spirals, making her Beetle almost impossible to see even when we were right on top of it.

Everything about tonight felt wrong. Like watching the ending of a movie but knowing it wasn't the way it was supposed to be. Like watching Logan's car blow up in the series finale.

Wrong. Wrong. Wrong.

The quiet in the car was as painful as it had been in the room. I finally broke it, saying softly, "This is my fault."

She reached over and squeezed my hand. "I hate that it happened this way, Rory. I hate it. But this was *not* your fault. You didn't cause the accident. You didn't sign those papers."

I squeezed my eyes shut, tugging at the cuffs of my jacket. Throat bobbing.

"I hate that it happened this way," she repeated, and then inhaled and let go of an unsteady breath. "But it did need to happen."

I turned away from her. It was pointless to have the argument anymore. The choice had been taken away from us. My mother was gone. The thought was accompanied by splintering pain.

When we pulled up to Nan's house, a dark sedan screaming government was parked out front with two people inside.

As we got out of our car, they did as well. Two women. One I knew—Sheila. A decade ago, she'd been a new agent, fresh-faced with her brown eyes shimmering in equally brown skin. Now there was a layer of confidence about her that had nothing to do with the suit she was wearing even though it was nearing midnight.

The person with her was in an outfit not far off from mine—black jeans and a black leather jacket—but a pair of royal blue cowboy boots were on her feet instead of my heavily buckled motorcycle ones.

Nan looked startled at first, but then her back went stiff as they approached. "This is not the time. I just lost my daughter. Rory just lost her mother. Whatever you have to ask or say can wait a day or two."

Sheila's lips twisted in regret. "Unfortunately, Mrs. Marlowe, it can't."

I put a hand on Nan's arm. I needed to talk to them. If I was going to bring the men behind this to justice, I needed these two women and their resources.

"It's okay, Nan," I said.

We let them inside, I punched the long-ass code into the alarm, and we headed back toward the kitchen. I poured two shots of bourbon for Nan and me and looked at the two agents. "Want a glass?"

Sheila shook her head, but the other woman said, "Sure."

I handed the woman her drink, taking in her long dark hair, hazel eyes, and thick brows. Her cheekbones were high and sharp. "And you are?"

"This is—" Sheila started only to have the woman interrupt her.

"G. Just call me G."

"And you work for the FBI?"

Neither woman responded, and I wasn't sure whether to be pissed or impressed. Undercover then.

"You're familiar with the Lovatos, I take it?" I asked.

"Painfully," G responded.

"We have some questions about what happened today. What you know. How Gage Palmer is involved," Sheila said.

The other woman looked over at Nan. "I'm sorry, but I'd really prefer it if you weren't here for this."

Nan bristled again. "This is my home, my granddaughter—"

"It's probably for the best, Nan," I said. "The less you know, the better."

I would have taken them into my makeshift office, but I wasn't sure I wanted to hand over my corkboard to these women, and I could guarantee they'd want it. They'd want it all. Here I could control what I gave them.

Nan glared at us. I put my drink down and pulled her to me, hugging her tightly. "I love you," I whispered. "Please. I need to do this."

She squeezed me back, tight and full of love that had me swallowing back more tears. Then, she let me go, downed her drink, and left the kitchen without another word.

I was exhausted. My body ached. My soul ached. But if I sat down, I might never get up again, and I couldn't afford to rest. Not yet. So I stood at the counter and told them what I could about my mom's accident, Casada, Argento Skies, Dunn, and West.

When it came to Gage and Monte, I held back the psychic piece. It wasn't my place to tell, and I doubted they'd believe it. Instead, I told them Monte had known Demi was seeing Dunn, and he'd gone to try to find her. I ended with the first of my failures, telling them I didn't know my mom's case was related to Monte's until the trail twirled around Argento Skies and Walden.

The women asked a few questions as I went along, but mostly they just listened.

"How much trouble are Gage and I in?" I asked after silence had settled uneasily in the room.

Sheila shot a glance at G. "At the moment, none. We can't afford to have any of this come out. It puts a longtime operation at risk."

"You're undercover," I said to G.

She didn't respond.

"Just tell me you know the asshole they hired to pull these jobs. My mom…" I swallowed back the emotions. "And Walden."

"We have a good lead on Walden's shooter. But he wasn't the person who messed with your mom's car or pulled the stunt at Shady Lane tonight," Sheila said.

I barely bit back my angry retort at her poor word choice. That *stunt* had ended my mom's life.

G watched me closely, the action grating on my already shredded nerves. As an undercover agent, it was her job to be good at reading people. Her life depended on it, but I couldn't afford for her to see through me. I didn't want her to see my anger or to figure out my next steps, so I fought harder than I'd ever had to keep a straight face.

"The person who was responsible for my mom is a hacker. A really good one. That's a short list."

G nodded. "Yes."

"You going to share?" I asked.

The two women exchanged a look before G responded. "All we can tell you right now is that the signature on the order at your mom's facility was pulled from one of your canceled checks. This person gets in and out of banking systems, car navigation systems, and more without leaving a trace.

"We've been trying to find them for several years. Every time we think we've narrowed down their location, they move. We've trailed them to Colombia, Venezuela, Nicaragua, and the Caymans. What we know for sure is they have a role in almost every aspect of the Lovato business. We find them, we get to take them down."

I wanted to offer to help track them. I knew my way around every backdoor and code out there, but I also knew the FBI had plenty of experienced technophiles at their disposal. I doubted I could find anything they hadn't already uncovered. I hadn't even known the Lovatos were involved whereas my mom had.

I could try to give myself some grace for the limited amount of time I'd had since Friday. Finding Monte had been the priority, and ever since, I'd been chasing down different leads.

But deep in my soul, I felt like it was my inability to do the job on time and in the right way that had cost two people their lives. I'd never forgive myself for Mom… Tears welled, and I barely held them back by focusing on the bourbon in my glass. I swirled it around, unsure if I could even swallow liquid with the tightness in my throat.

"Are you going to put Walden's sister-in-law and nephew in protective custody?" I asked.

"We've got agents going to talk to her now."

It really wasn't what I'd asked, but I moved on. "What about Gage and Monte?"

"The Palmers weren't at their apartment when we went by. But my understanding from talking to the local police is that they sent a car over to River Kane's home. Is that where they're staying?"

How would Gage's family react to more agents showing up to question him?

My stomach turned. "Gage was my client. He didn't have any say in what went down today. He shouldn't even have been with me. I take responsibility for anything you want to charge me with but leave him out of it."

The women stared, and I tried not to give them an inch. Tried not to show the way my heart pattered and ached. How the love I felt for Gage made me want to shield him from any backlash. I couldn't have him hurt. I couldn't have him taken from his family.

"He was there. We'll still need to debrief him," Sheila said.

I didn't respond.

Instead, I started toward the door, signaling we were done. It took a minute, but they followed me.

"I wish you'd called me sooner, Rory," Sheila said.

"Tell that to Dad. He's the one who knew about Mom all along. He even knew the Lovatos were involved."

Her cheek tightened, but she didn't respond. Maybe she'd get more out of him than he'd been willing to share with me, but I doubted it.

I closed the door behind them, set the alarm, grabbed my things, and headed down the hall. Nan's lights were out. I doubted she was sleeping, just like I doubted I'd ever close my eyes tonight.

I went directly to the office and stared at the corkboard for a long time. Then, I added the new information we'd gathered today using handwritten sticky notes and printed images. Last, I put pushpins up for the locations of all the warehouses on the printout from the Argento Skies office.

One of them near the water could be where Monte had been held, but I couldn't necessarily be sure his impressions had been right. The sounds and smell he'd experienced could have been a fountain or a pond.

But he'd said he'd only been in the trunk for about fifteen minutes before they'd pulled him out. And about the same amount of time when they'd dropped him off at the police station. I drew circles for the distance they could have gone based on what I knew about D.C. traffic.

I plugged in my computer, set it up, and started my research on the locations in the overlapping area. Of the five in the circles, Gage and I had checked out one, and only two others had transferred hands within the last month. One of the purchasers was a corporation and one was a privately held company.

I pulled bank statements for all the board members and owners. Then, I logged into our private investigators' database and ran background checks on everyone involved.

Nothing jumped out.

I pulled up the two warehouses on the internet, switching over to a satellite view.

Nothing.

But one of these two buildings had to be the location.

I closed my eyes and weariness immediately assaulted me.

I didn't have time to be tired. I needed to get to them

before they disappeared from the warehouse altogether.

Before they left Demi behind as collateral damage.

I pulled myself up from the chair and reassembled my bag with my computer and equipment before reaching for my stun guns. I only found my pen-like one. My Vipertek was missing. Had I left it in Walden's room? I was almost certain it had been with me when I'd gotten back into Gage's Pathfinder. Which meant it was likely in his car. I opened the gun safe and stared at my Glock. I'd wished for it more than once today—or rather yesterday—but having it with me upped the probability of Monte's vision coming true.

Did I care?

If Dunn was involved with those who killed my mom and turned around and threatened Demi, would it matter if I shot him?

I knew the answer was yes and despised myself for it.

But I also needed protection. They'd killed Walden, partly because I'd left him tied up and defenseless. If he'd been able to reach for the gun that had been in the case, would he have had a chance? Or would he have ended up dead sooner? That was assuming he even knew how to use the damn thing.

Knowing how to handle a gun wasn't an issue for me. I not only knew how to use mine, but I was a damn good shot. I could control my emotions, couldn't I? I wouldn't shoot someone unless another person was at risk. I put the gun in my bag and headed for the bathroom.

I took a cold shower, hands lingering over the red marks from Gage's scruff on my neck and thighs. I was sore and tender from using parts of my body I hadn't used in a long time. Those moments in the hotel room seemed like another lifetime already. More like a movie I'd watched or maybe an alternate version of my life where I'd been able to keep the man who'd brought me peace...

I shook my head and finished washing off the scent of our lovemaking along with the sweat and tears of the day before stepping out. I braided my hair so it would stay out of my way and didn't even bother with makeup. There was no point.

There was no escaping the anguish and grief that marked my face. Instead, I purposefully avoided my eyes in the mirror as I tugged a knit beanie over my hair. Then, I slipped into more black clothes. I traded my leather jacket for a padded vest that hugged my body and wasn't as likely to get hooked on anything if I had to slip in and out of a building through a window.

The sky was still dark and thunder-filled. The weather app predicted another onslaught throughout the day, so I grabbed the keys to Pop's old Jeep. It would be safer traveling in the rusty classic, but it would also be more conspicuous. If the color didn't make it stand out, the noise would. A beefy growl that was louder than a pack of dogs burst through the air as I turned the engine over.

Nan would know I'd left. She'd worry. More guilt rolled through me. Could you die of guilt? Maybe not the guilt itself but the physical response to it?

As I pulled onto Main Street, a pair of headlights fell in behind me, following at a distance. If it wasn't three o'clock in the morning, I wouldn't have thought anything about it. But Cherry Bay was quiet at this hour. Especially on a holiday.

It was hard to believe it was actually Thanksgiving. I didn't feel very thankful at the moment. I felt tattered and torn and angry. At myself and the assholes behind all of this.

In the dark, with the clouds and mist, there was no way I could make out the make and model. It was fairly low to the ground. A sedan most likely. Maybe Sheila. I flipped off my lights, made several right turns, and by the time I ended up on a dark country road, I'd lost them. Or maybe I'd just overreacted, and they hadn't been following me at all. But right now, it paid to be paranoid.

I turned my lights back on and headed down the pitch-black back road. As I made my way north, lightning lit up the sky, striking a tree close to the edge of the road, and my heart skipped a beat. It was followed by a clap of thunder so loud it rattled the soft top of the Jeep, air rushing in and causing a shiver to creep down my spine as the sides flapped.

Once upon a time, I'd ridden down this road on the back of Gage's motorcycle in a similar storm. I'd thrown my head back and laughed at the lightning. I wondered if the fates had heard me that day and decided I needed to be taught a lesson.

If everything that had happened was because I'd dared the universe.

Then, I thought of what Gage and Monte had told me about Demi's psychic abilities. How one little decision you made today could change everything about your future. One decision. And I'd made thousands of them since being on the back of Gage's bike.

I gritted my teeth, determined that the decisions I made today would bring only justice for my mom and Gage's family. I was going after my enemies like Veronica Mars had, but not just for revenge. Not just to get even or take an eye for an eye. This was so the people I loved would never again be hurt by those who'd come after us.

I vowed that no matter what happened—whether I shot Dunn and ended up behind bars, or I changed Monte's vision and *they* all ended up behind bars—my loved ones would be safe. I wasn't sure how, in just a handful of days, my loved ones had come to include Gage and his siblings.

But maybe I'd never stopped loving Gage. Maybe he'd never left my heart from the time he'd entered it when I'd been too young to really understand the meaning of it. I did now. I understood it just like I understood that there was a huge chasm that resided between us.

I couldn't think about it at the moment. I couldn't think about anything but catching the bastards who'd put these wheels into motion.

Chapter Forty

Gage

WITH OR WITHOUT YOU
Performed by U2

River and I had calmed Monte the best we could, but his eyes were as red-rimmed as Rory's had been earlier. My stomach was full of knots that would be impossible to work out. I called her phone several times, and she didn't pick up. Just like earlier, I didn't know if that meant she was actually sleeping, if the FBI was questioning her, or if she was ignoring me to take matters into her own hands.

I paced River's living room while three sets of eyes watched.

The need to get in my car, drive over to her nan's cottage, and pound on the door competed with my need to stay right where I was. To remain here and be another line of defense between the murdering assholes and the people I loved most.

Except, I loved Rory too.

And out of all the people in my life, she was the one putting herself in direct danger. She wasn't just going to sit on her hands after what they'd done to her mom. She wasn't going to just let the police and some FBI agent try to take these people down without doing everything in her power to help them.

I understood. When they'd taken Monte, when I'd seen

the bruises on his body, I'd wanted to strangle them with my own hands.

If they'd killed him… I couldn't even fathom it. I couldn't even begin to understand the depths of Rory's feelings at the moment.

"You need to stop her, Gage," Monte said, drawing my eyes back to him. "She's there because of us…" His voice cracked. "Rory got involved because of us."

I pulled him up from the couch and into my arms. "She's also involved because of her mom, Monte. This isn't all on us."

Even though I knew it was the truth, it didn't feel like it. Our lives had been woven together because of decisions we'd all made.

"Look," River said. "We've got the police outside our door. I've got plenty of instruments in the studio that I can use as weapons. I promise you, they aren't getting to Ivy and Monte. If you need to go with Rory and stop this, then go."

Audrey stood, sliding her arm around River's waist and meeting my gaze with serious eyes. "I've got a blowtorch and a nail gun that will do some serious damage if anyone tries to get in here."

Monte pushed away from me, locking me with his blue eyes. "It's not us in my vision, Gage. You and I both know if something was going to happen to Ivy or me or you, I'd see it. What's happening right now, it's Rory and Demi." He rubbed his chest. "In here, I feel like… We have to be there."

"There's no we, Monte. You're not going anywhere near this." Monte's jaw tightened, unhappy at my words, and I tried to soften them by adding, "If you want me to go with Rory and try to find a way to keep them both safe, I'll do that. But if you're with me, I'm going to be worried about you first and foremost."

We argued with our eyes for a long moment, and then finally, Monte caved with a reluctant nod. "Fine."

I hugged him tightly to me. I wanted to go kiss Ivy and

hug her as well, but she was the only one of us actually sleeping. There was no way I'd wake her just to satisfy some panicked need to hold her. Like Monte said, I wasn't the one with a death threat hanging over me. Neither were my siblings.

I grabbed my jacket, phone, and keys, and headed for the door.

"Call me if you see anything else."

River followed, reaching out to grab my arm before I was fully outside. "Just because Monte doesn't see something doesn't mean you have some damned protective bubble around you. You can still get hurt. You can still get dead."

I swallowed hard and met my friend's eyes. Emotions welled through me. "I know. I promise to be careful. I promise to not get dead."

His lips twitched, and we shared a look full of unspoken words. I was so grateful to have him and Audrey in my life.

"Thank you—"

He slammed a fist into my shoulder powerful enough that it made me collide with the doorframe.

"Knock that shit off."

I smiled, rubbing my arm. "Just because we're family doesn't mean I'm not supposed to say thanks for all you do for me. For us."

"Yeah, well, I hate it, so stop."

Without another word, I turned and sped down the path through the mist and the rain to the Pathfinder. The Cherry Bay patrol car was parked behind it. I stopped at the officer's door, and he rolled down the window. He was the young kid from the day I'd reported Monte missing. He looked barely old enough to drive. Did I trust him with my family?

But then I thought of Rory. Every single person she met underestimated her. I wouldn't do the same with this man.

"My family is staying here. They need protection. I'm going over to Rory Bishop's. Do you know if someone is protecting her as well?"

He frowned and shook his head. "No, our orders are for you and your family."

"Well, my family is here. This is where you're needed. I think the FBI has Rory covered," I told him. I wasn't sure it was true, but I didn't want this guy following me instead of staying here.

I turned and jogged over to my SUV with the rain beating down on me.

Driving to Rory's place from River's required me to go past the Victorian I'd grown up in. Regret always ripped through me when I did.

I missed our home. Wished that Ivy had been able to experience growing up there, playing on the swing set tucked between the hedges and roses. Wished that, somehow, we'd been able to keep it.

The retired couple who'd bought it had moved out of D.C., saying they were ready for a slower pace of life. It had felt wrong for it to be just the two of them in the house. I'd wanted it to be full of family—kids laughing and pounding their feet down the wide, Scarlett O'Hara-worthy staircase. Playing hide-and-go-seek in the multitude of rooms. Hosting holiday dinners in the large dining room. But beggars couldn't be choosers, and at the height of the pandemic, I'd needed the most money I could get and they'd made the best offer.

As I passed the house, my heart flipped as it always did, but this time it was because of the For Sale sign sticking out of the sculpted grass of the front lawn.

Maybe this time it would be a family who bought her after all.

I kept driving, but my eyes found the sign in the rearview mirror. If the recovery from the pandemic hadn't taken so long and Demi hadn't taken the meager savings we'd had, maybe I'd have been able to swing buying it back.

But then I rolled my eyes at myself. There was no way

I could afford it now. Not likely ever again with the way the real estate market was off the charts these days.

I tried to leave all thoughts of our family home behind us as I turned down Rory's street and parked in the driveway behind her Nan's Beetle. The lights were off in the cottage. It was three in the morning, and I wasn't sure what I expected. I texted Rory again.

> *ME: I'm outside. Can you let me in? We need to talk.*

I waited five minutes for a response that never came. I knew there was a possibility that she was sleeping, but every instinct told me she wasn't. After everything that had happened, Rory would be champing at the bit to avenge Hallie's death.

I made my way to the front door, rang the bell, and then followed it with an immediate loud knock. After several minutes, when nothing happened, I repeated it.

Eventually, the porch light came on, and I felt eyes on me through the peephole. The door opened a crack, the chain lock stopping it. Kora Marlowe peeked out at me through the few inches. Her face was puffy and tear-stained. She wore a terry cloth robe and her short hair was pushed up at weird angles as if she'd been tossing and turning in bed.

"Gage?" she said, bemused.

"I need to talk to Rory."

She hesitated, removed the chain from the door, and opened it all the way.

As I stepped inside, rain rolled off me onto her wood floors. "Sorry," I said, grimacing.

"It's fine. Just a little water." She headed toward the back and the hallway that led to the bedrooms. "Her light's out in her bedroom, but the office light was on. She must have fallen asleep in there."

She knocked on the door and then opened it. The space was small, but a large desk, file cabinets, and bookshelves had been shoved inside it. Rory wasn't there.

Kora pushed past me, going down the hall and knocking on another closed door. She opened this one and flipped on the light, revealing a room done in vibrant teals and aquas. But the bed was perfectly made, and there wasn't anything out of place to indicate Rory had been there recently.

Kora turned to me with a worried expression. She rushed down the hall and opened a bathroom door. "Rory?" she called.

My heart lunged at the panic in her voice. It echoed my fear.

But I wasn't afraid of what had come for Rory. I was afraid of what she was going to do.

In the kitchen, Kora went straight to a set of hooks by the back door.

"She took the Jeep," she said, waving a hand at an empty hook. Her eyes were huge as she said, "She went after them, didn't she?"

We stared at each other because there was nothing to say. She had. We both knew it. A wave of panic flooded my veins. Where had she gone? My brain flashed with the list of warehouses she'd printed out. I wished I had my own copy.

Maybe I'd get lucky and she'd have left the list here. I went back to the office, headed straight to the desk, moved papers around, and eyed the empty computer cord. Kora emerged in the doorway, and as I glanced up, my gaze froze on the wall next to her. A huge corkboard was covered in paper and pins and even strings. It looked a bit like something you might find in a serial killer's house… or maybe the conference room of a police station.

I made my way over to the board, staring at all the information she'd gathered. Jesus. There was so much. It looked like chaos to me, but Rory would have seen exactly how it overlapped.

Kora came to stand by me, inhaling sharply. "She… she had to have just put this together. It wasn't in here last week."

I was more impressed than I'd ever been. Rory had gathered all this intel in a matter of days. Hours, even. I had no doubt that, given time, she would have solved her mother's case one way or another and found Demi in the process. Or vice versa. She knew exactly what she was doing. She'd been made for taking down criminals.

My hand landed on a couple of pushpins with addresses near the river. They were in the center of pink highlighter marks drawn in circles like a Venn diagram. The circles overlapped with the Argento Skies building where Monte had been taken and the Metropolitan PD headquarters. The warehouses. She had to have narrowed them down to these two.

I snapped a picture of their locations with my phone and turned back to Kora. She had her face in her hands, and her shoulders were moving. Silent tears. Fuck. My throat closed, and I squeezed her arm gently. "It's going to be okay."

She looked up at me with a bone-weary expression. "I can't lose her too."

"I'm going after her, but she's smart, Kora. And she knows how to take care of herself. You should have seen her today…"My throat grew thick with emotions as I thought of Rory all week. The confidence with which she'd walked into the Rayburn Building. The way her fingers had sped over the keyboards. The lack of fear she'd shown as she'd stuck a stun gun to Casada's neck when the man was three times her size. The way she'd taken Walden down with a sweep of a foot and an elbow to his back.

She was strong and intelligent and so much more than her television heroine had ever been. Pride and love welled through my chest.

Any man would be lucky to have Rory at his side. A partner. A lover. A friend.

I ached to be that person. I ached to be the one she came home to at night and lost herself in so she could forget the horrors of her day or the burdens of the case she was working. I wanted to be the one to kiss her and touch her until the only thing she experienced was love that washed away the ugly she'd seen.

I'd been worried that Ivy and Monte would see someone always leaving. Someone we might lose in a brutally painful way. But I hadn't thought about what they'd see and learn and feel while she was with us.

The strength of Rory's character. The goodness that vibrated from her like a light. The determination and ferocity with which she protected the people she loved. Having my siblings see that… feel that… have it as a role model… It could only be a good thing.

I'd shielded us for way too long. I'd tucked our love for each other into a cave and sealed the door, letting only Audrey and River sneak in the back entrance. River was right. My family deserved more than that. A full life, including the heartache that came with fully loving others.

"You love her." Kora's voice brought me back to the cottage and the corkboard and the danger Rory had just driven into.

"I do."

She smiled. It was a weak smile but real.

"She adored you from the moment she met you. We all saw the teenage crush and were grateful you were always kind to her when you could have been cruel."

My heart tightened and loosened at the same time. A strange dichotomy.

"She was a force of nature that even a dumb teen like me could appreciate."

Before I knew it, Kora had wrapped me in a hug. She squeezed tight. "Go get her. Tell her. Give her something to feel other than the guilt she's drowning in. When life throws our girl a curveball, she thinks she was supposed to see it coming. She thinks this is her fault."

I hugged her back. "I promise I'll find her."

Kora stepped away, and we shared one more look. This one was full of things neither one of us wanted to speak about. Fear and sadness and worry.

I made my way down the hall, but at the door, I looked back. "It's going to be okay, Kora."

And I felt it. In my bones. This woman was getting her granddaughter back.

I didn't know if it was Demi's abilities she'd passed to me or just my love for Rory that made me feel that way. But it was like being in the eye of a twister. Calm and quiet. I could feel the storm whirling viciously around the hollow core, danger in any direction, but I also knew it was going to lift. It would evaporate into nothing but wind and rain.

I'd always been saddened by the debris left behind after a tornado—the wreckage strewn about as nature took homes and businesses and lives. But this time, after the storm, there would be something new waiting for me.

Love. Hope.

Rory.

I just had to find her and make sure she saw it too. That she didn't dive off the cliff thinking there was no other way. To show her the only way we would survive the catastrophic events that had ripped apart our lives was if we did it together.

Chapter Forty-one

Rory

BURNING HEART
Performed by Survivor

The first warehouse was a bust. The lot had been empty, and the building had appeared to be vacant. It hadn't taken much effort to evade the smattering of cameras, sneak in a back door, and search the joint. There was no basement and there was nothing in the building. It was emptier than the Argento Skies offices downtown.

I spent a few minutes longer than I wanted making sure there wasn't a hidden hatch in the ground or some other sign that people had been there recently. The entire building reeked of oil and gas. The owner had run an auto repair shop out of it before closing down. If the Lovatos had been there or if Dunn and West had brought Monte there, no signs of them remained.

My gut twisted as I made my way through the shadows back to Pop's Jeep.

Maybe I was too late again.

Back in the car, I checked my phone and saw I'd gotten another message from Gage. He was at Nan's—outside. Shit. I didn't want him to worry. Worse, I didn't want him to wake Nan up and make her worry too, but if I responded, I'd either have to lie to him or risk him coming here. I couldn't do either.

I couldn't afford for him to show up and distract me

simply with the energy that zapped between us. My heart twisted as I put my phone down and drove through the darkened streets to the second address.

I parked in the lot of a building across the road and picked up my nightscope.

This warehouse had been bought by a company selling gourmet tea and coffee blends. Many of their products were shipped from South America. It would be a stereotypical way of smuggling drugs into the country and would likely have had customs and DEA all over it, if it were true. But if the Lovatos were involved, they could have paid off individuals in those organizations.

This early in the morning, the building was quiet, but a couple of box trucks were parked in front of a loading dock. The roll-up doors were shut. Floodlights illuminated the entire frontage of the building and a sign that read Bishop Security.

Whether I wanted to believe it or not, Dad was involved.

It would make it easier for me to get inside. I just had to reopen the back door of Dad's system. But I couldn't afford to trip the hidden code that had notified Dad last time.

I scanned the roof of the building. It was futile to think I could enter that way. Dad would have those entry points locked down as if they were a bank safe. Maybe tighter. My eyes slipped to the side of the warehouse where a couple of dark Escalades were parked in the shadows. Dunn and West had arrived in similar ones at the restaurant yesterday.

But then again, three-quarters of the politicians and military leaders in and around D.C. rode around in similar models. Hell, even the lobbyists scurrying around the Hill and CEOs of companies vying for federal contracts showed up in them. I wished I'd taken snapshots of their license plates.

I opened a secure link on my computer and started to type in the IP address for my hack into Bishop Investigations. Then, I hesitated. What if I went in the front door instead of the back? What if I used Dad's access?

And then my mind settled on Dad's words from earlier at Shady Lane about working this together, and my throat closed. What if I used my own access? One he'd never given me before… one I'd never asked to have.

I opened the Bishop Investigations employee portal. I typed in my name for the user I.D., and then my fingers hovered for a moment over the password field. What would he have chosen if he thought I'd come knocking? I thought back to his words at Shady Lane once more, and my heart squeezed another notch tighter.

With shaking fingers, I typed Keith-Mars-Isn't-The-Only-Man-Who-Loves-His-Daughter and then held my breath. A fresh wave of unexpected tears hit my eyes when it was accepted. Did this mean he now believed in me? Trusted me? Or had he simply known I'd never stop?

I shook my head and concentrated on what I was there for.

When I found a file waiting with my name, surprise rolled through me.

I hovered over it, wary. So many things could go wrong when you opened a file. I'd planted many of the rotten eggs myself over the years. But there was only one way to find out, so I clicked on it.

The file loaded an image of Mom's accident scene— the tire marks that had given Dad his first clue that something wonky had happened with her braking system. There were more, and I swiped through each of them before something funky caught my eye. I went back two photos. The license plate was wrong in just this single image. It wasn't Mom's. It was a random string of numbers. Code.

Dad had left me a message.

I opened a new screen and typed in the code.

What the hell was this? It looked like some of Chanel's files from the front desk. Innocuous drivel. Things Dad had asked her to handle. Why the hell had Dad encrypted any of it?

Headlights burst through the darkness of the storm, and I scooted down in my seat. Another box truck headed straight into the lot opposite me, backing in next to the other two already there.

The driver got out as one of the doors rolled up. A couple of men stepped out of the warehouse, and the three men talked briefly before starting to unload crates from the back. With the doors wide open, this was my chance to get inside. I just had to shut the cameras off and back on quickly enough.

I logged into Dad's site on my phone, grateful I'd spent enough time snooping around to know exactly where to look for his on-site security cameras. My pulse increased. Even knowing the layout of his system, it took longer than I wanted to drill down to this specific address and the correct cameras.

Finally, I had the right ones at the ready. I pocketed some of my tools and slipped my Glock into my waistband at the back. Leaving the Jeep and keeping to the shadows beyond the streetlights, I slipped past the chain-link fence. Then, I carefully stepped in time with the cameras as I flipped them off and on again.

Just as I reached the box truck, the men emerged from the building, and I rolled underneath the truck. They were talking in Spanish. Laughter filled the air as they stepped into the back. The truck moved above me as they grabbed more cargo. As their voices faded away, I spun out, pulled myself up onto the dock, and flattened my body against the side of the warehouse next to the entrance.

I used the cameras on my phone to identify where the men were, and when their backs were turned, I swiped off the video feed, eased around the doorway, and edged back into the darkness behind crates piled up on the warehouse floor. I'd barely ducked down before they were heading back into the mist and rain to grab more boxes.

Above the main floor of the warehouse, a metal grate

walkway led around what looked like a set of offices. The blinds and doors were shut, but light peeked through them. At the back of the building, another set of stairs led underground. Everything about it fit with the description of where Monte had been held.

Was Demi here?

Was this where Monte's vision came to life?

The Glock at my back suddenly felt hot and heavy.

The door to the offices opened, and West stepped out onto the landing, removing any doubt that I was in the right place.

He spoke to the men in Spanish, and once again, I was grateful I'd stuck with it through college in order to give me a leg up on my FBI application.

"Everyone clear out," West told them.

The men looked up at him, brows furrowing. One of the men tilted his head and said, "We were told to stand guard."

"And now I'm telling you to leave. We won't need anyone here after today."

The men looked uncertain, but then did as they were told, heading out onto the loading dock. The noise as the metal door hit the concrete sent shivers along my spine. Was one of the men who'd left the one who'd killed Walden? Or the one who'd ordered my mom's death?

They were the right size to have been the men in masks who'd kidnapped Monte. They might even have pulled the trigger that killed the CEO, but I wasn't sure any of them were the type to hack into a bunch of computers.

Then again, maybe I was doing exactly what everyone did to me, judging a person by their appearance. But in this case, I just didn't see the Lovatos' golden computer genius hauling boxes around.

Behind West, Dunn appeared in the office doorway, carefully shutting the door behind him. The two men started arguing, but their voices were too low for me to hear what they were saying. I had to get closer. I eased my way through the boxes, keeping low and to the shadows and taking a wide route so I'd stay hidden.

As I neared, Dunn pushed his hands through his hair, ruining his perfectly coifed locks, clearly upset. He raised his voice, and it carried over the warehouse, bouncing around the cavernous space. "We need her! She's gotten us this far!"

"I can't trust your decisions anymore, Roland. I told you not to let the kid go, and you went behind my back and did it anyway."

"She was freaking out. She knew her son was here. I had to calm her down."

West's response to Dunn's claim was too quiet for me to hear even though I'd finally made it to the far wall. To get beneath them, I'd have to cross a small area with nothing to hide behind. I'd be exposed for a moment, and once I reached the stairs, it wouldn't be much better. The landing they were on was made of metal grates. I'd be clearly visible if they looked down, but I didn't have much of a choice.

I waited until Dunn started to turn back toward the office before I moved. I sped along the space as West caught the congressman's arm, halting him. I'd just ducked under the stairs and pressed my back against the wall when West said, "You don't have a choice, Roland. It isn't just the little girl who's suspicious now. Sutton is as well. We need to make sure nothing ties us to this."

"Then get rid of *them*. But I *need* her."

Above me, the office door swung open for the third time, and another person joined them. A pair of purple Prada heels stopped next to their polished black loafers. I recognized those shoes. My mind scrabbled to place them, twisting to try to make out the woman's face around the tablet she was holding. But all I could see were tailored slacks and a silk white button-down.

"We have a problem," she said. And at the sound of her voice, everything clicked.

My palms turned sweaty and my body shook. How

much had Dad known? How much had he been involved? West said he was now suspicious. Did that mean he wasn't on the wrong side? God… I wanted that to be true more than I'd ever thought possible.

"What's he doing here?" West demanded, looking at the computer screen she was showing him.

"Does it matter why? If he's here, Rory is too."

My name on her lips caused me to squeeze back against the wall. Was it my dad? Had it been his headlights that had followed me out of Cherry Bay in his Jaguar? Low to the ground, it made sense.

"Get Demi. We'll take this down by the river and toss all three bodies in," West said.

He turned and headed down the stairs with Chanel on his heels.

"We can't do it here. Not yet. I haven't cleaned out all the ties to Lovato."

"You have five minutes. As soon as we walk outside with Demi, the son will follow us easily enough. And Rory will follow them," West told her.

My entire body froze… the son… God. Gage was here.

I wanted to scream. I wanted to send a scathing text telling him to get the hell out of here, but there was no time. They were already on the move.

Above me, Dunn reappeared, and this time he had his arm around another woman. It took me way too long to recognize Demi. She looked nothing like the vibrant, fairy-like woman I'd once met.

She looked so frail I wasn't sure she'd make it down the stairs. Her strawberry-blond hair was stringy and thin, clinging to her face. She wore a tank top that allowed every bone in her neck, chest, and arms to stick out in the worst kind of way while a pair of sweats hung from her nonexistent hips.

I pulled my gun from my back, trying to quell the shaking, as the truth of Monte's vision hit me. I was here.

Demi and Dunn were here.

Someone was going to die.

I sent a prayer out into the universe, hoping it wouldn't be Demi.

Hoping I wouldn't be the reason another mother died tonight.

Chapter Forty-two

Gage

SEND ME AN ANGEL
Performed by Scorpions

As I climbed back into the Pathfinder, I shook off the rain that had settled over me while I'd explored the first empty warehouse and tossed my phone in the cup holder. A dark object on the passenger seat caught my eye. Rory's stun gun. The one that looked like a flashlight rather than an actual weapon.

I reached over and picked it up. The light on one end actually worked, and when I pushed the side button, electricity zipped through the nodes. Had I just wasted the charge? I hoped not. I could use a weapon. Something that wasn't an actual gun.

My jaw tensed. I set the stun gun with my phone and drove through the quiet streets of D.C. to the second warehouse. A wave of relief flew through me upon seeing Rory's grandfather's old Jeep in the lot opposite. I pulled up next to it, cutting my engine.

The sun was fighting for purchase against both the night and the storm clouds, but in the dim shadows, I could see the Jeep was empty. I peered across the street to the building she'd been staking out. My chest seized as I realized she was already inside… Inside a warehouse where Monte had seen my mom, Rory, and a crooked politician all die at different times.

Every instinct was screaming to sprint across the street, throw open the front door, and demand the assholes hand back my family. I grabbed the stun gun, pocketed my phone, and headed across to the building.

As I slipped through the chain-link fence, I noticed the first camera. There were likely more I couldn't see, which meant whoever was inside was probably already aware I was there. I could only hope that in dealing with me, I could be the distraction Rory needed to get Demi and whatever other information she needed. Because even though they'd seen me coming, I knew for a fact they hadn't seen her.

I walked straight up to the main door and pulled it open with a shaking hand. I stepped inside, dread filling me because I didn't know what I was walking into. But I believed in Monte, and he'd know if something was going to happen to me. Whenever I died, it wasn't going to be here. Not tonight. But it might be Rory. The woman I loved.

The wind caught the door, whisking it out of my hand and banging it against the wall. The sound echoed into the warehouse, any last chance of surprise being wiped away.

I strode deeper into the building, feet halting as I caught sight of Dunn coming down the stairs with a woman who I hardly recognized as my mother. She was nothing more than a skeleton of the free spirit who'd had Ivy and then left us. Her skin was pallid, with dark circles under her eyes making her look ghost-like—as if she'd already died and they were hauling a corpse around.

Unexpected fury raged through me. "Let go of my mother!"

From my peripheral, I caught movement. West and another woman I didn't recognize stepped around a stack of boxes bearing a coffee company's logo. They joined Dunn and Demi, their tailored pants and suits hiding the sleaze that radiated around them as if a vat of oil covered their auras. The darkness around West had grown stronger, shimmering into an evilness that I could almost smell.

West pulled a gun from inside his jacket and pointed it

in my direction.

I took three steps toward him. My lack of fear seemed to confuse him, and he turned the gun in my mother's direction. That did stop me.

"I don't care what you're doing here," I growled, waving to the crates. "I don't care about who you're working for or what bribes you've taken. I just want Demi and me to walk out these doors alive."

It took great effort to keep my gaze on the men and my mother when I really wanted to search the shadows for the five-foot-five supersleuth I knew was here somewhere. I could feel her. I could sense her almost as if she was right at my side.

"We're well past that now," West said. "I'd say neither of you are leaving."

A sudden pounding on the metal roof of the warehouse almost drowned out his words. Hail drummed loudly as the tail end of the storm drifted overhead. Lightning flashed outside the upper windows, and I'd barely taken a breath before thunder shook the entire building. It rattled the metal doors and echoed around the concrete floors.

Some people were terrified of storms, and they had reason to be. Hurricanes and tornadoes ripped through water and land, leaving devastation in their wake, but I knew with every fiber in my being, that this storm would help us. It would hide any noise Rory made.

"I get why Dunn took my mother. I understand him believing in her ability to predict his future. I even get how Hallie Marlowe investigating Argento Skies made you nervous. I mean, if she looked too close, there was a chance she'd find your money laundering and the ties to the Lovatos, right? But she didn't have any proof, and I know better than anyone how hard it is to get law enforcement to act without proof, so why did you really run her off the road?"

"We don't have time for some evil villain monologue," the woman next to West said. "Take them all outside."

"Have you studied storms?" I asked, looking the woman straight in the eye. She was probably the same age as Rory. Maybe a hair older or younger. But she had the same confidence as the woman I loved. "Because I have. I've spent years chasing them, and I can guarantee heading outside with the lightning striking near a metal building with you holding a metal object in your hand is just asking to be struck yourself."

"Gage?" My mother's confused voice drew my eyes to her face as she tried to step away from the congressman. Physically, she was a distorted version of the person I'd last seen, but when my eyes locked with hers, a new torture wound through me because her stare was as hazy as the rest of her. Had she been drugged or just held for too damn long and lost her mind? She shook her head, her once-beautiful curls thin and greasy, clinging to her, as she said in a slurred tone, "You're not supposed to be here."

She stumbled trying to take the last step off the stairs, and Dunn held her up, concern flitting over his face. God. Did he actually have feelings for her? Some warped kind of affection?

"Just do it here," the woman said, dropping the tablet she'd been working on, and it hit the ground with a loud crack. "I've wiped out any connection to our boss and left a trail back to Sutton instead."

West cocked the gun still pointed at Demi.

"You shoot her, and you're dead," Rory said as she stepped out from beneath the metal staircase to the right of Dunn and Demi. My heart skipped a beat as my gaze landed on the gun she had pointed at West. "Hello, Chanel."

"You don't seem all that surprised to see me, Rory."

"I'm not. And my father would be even less so. You aren't as good at hiding your trail as you think."

The woman, Chanel, narrowed her eyes. "What's that supposed to mean?"

Rory shrugged. "Every hacker leaves a fingerprint somewhere."

Chanel looked at West. "What are you waiting for? Kill them all."

Rory's voice was firm and calm as she said, "You pull that trigger, and I guarantee you'll be dead before you even finish."

"You assume he's the only one with a gun. You assume a lot of things. It's almost laughable. You hated being judged for your size and your age, and yet you do the same damn thing." Chanel reached behind her, and Rory aimed her gun at the woman instead of West.

"Don't move."

"How do you think this will play out?" Chanel asked. "West shoots Demi, you retaliate, but I shoot you and then your boyfriend. I'll be the only one left standing with a gun."

She hadn't even finished talking when West swung his aim toward Demi again. As he pulled the trigger, Dunn screamed, "No!" and leaped, blocking my mom. A hole bloomed in the center of his forehead, blood spraying from the back as he tumbled sideways, taking the skeleton that was my mother with him.

West's gun now pointed at Rory, and Chanel having alluded to having her own, I had to even the odds. With my finger on the stun gun's button, I lunged toward Chanel, who was closest to me. Rory dove to the side as both she and West shot their weapons, and the sound reverberated through the room.

West's body jerked backward as a bullet hit him in the shoulder. He tripped on the stairs behind him, landing near Dunn and Demi with a furious scream.

"Rory!" I screamed, watching as she skidded along the concrete toward my mother.

Chanel pulled a gun from her back, her aim following Rory's movements as the woman I loved rolled to her knees. My breath left my body, and I took another gigantic leap, diving forward.

I was too late. Chanel's gun went off, but it was

matched by another loud report from behind me. The air next to my ear whizzed, and red bloomed along the white silk covering Chanel's chest. A stunned expression filled her face just before she joined West and Dunn on the floor at the base of the stairs.

My feet propelled me forward until I landed on my knees beside Rory, calling her name again. I reached for her just as she reached up and our hands collided as thunder shook the building.

"I'm okay!" she said. "Chanel may have been a good hacker, but she was a really crappy shot."

I pulled her to me. Heart thudding. Body trembling.

"Gage. I'm okay." Her voice was muffled, buried against my chest.

A fierce grip on my leg had me shoving Rory behind me and pressing the stun gun I was still grasping into the person's arm. West's entire body spasmed, and the pistol in his hand clattered to the concrete. Rory kicked it away from him as we both scrambled to our feet.

Her eyes focused on a movement behind me, and I shifted, attempting once again to put myself between her and whoever this new threat was when her words stopped me. "Thank you for taking the shot, Dad."

My gaze found Sutton Bishop's before drifting back to Chanel's body. Rory's dad had saved her. Chills flooded me.

How he'd known, how he'd gotten there, I wasn't sure, but he'd saved her.

He joined us, looking down at the bodies on the ground with a grimace. My heart thudded loudly as I took in the awful reality of the vision my brother had been seeing for days in his head. Bile rose in my throat.

Demi... Fuck.

I took two unsteady steps toward the heap, unsure of what I'd find. Unsure of which of Monte's visions had finally forged itself into reality when the warehouse doors rolled up. Rory and her dad shifted their weapons in that direction as men and women with FBI emblazoned on their vests came streaming in with more guns drawn.

"FBI, freeze!"

For several tense seconds, everything in the room went still.

"At ease, everyone. These three are with me," a tall woman in an FBI windbreaker said, striding toward us.

I turned back to the pile of bodies. Dunn was clearly dead. I couldn't even be sorry for it, but God, there was so much blood covering Demi's ragged clothes I was almost sure she hadn't made it either. I knelt beside her and a soft, whispered groan left her lips. A tsunami-sized wave of relief flooded me.

"Mom?!"

I pulled Demi up and away from the chaos, sweeping her into my arms.

She felt like nothing. Like a piece of paper easily crushed. For so long I'd thought I'd hated her, but I barely held back tears at the thought of her almost dying. At the shape she was in.

"H-how are you here?" she whispered.

"That's a long story, but Monte is part of the answer," I told her. She met my eyes with a glassy look.

"We have an ambulance on its way," the agent said. "But I'd suggest having her sit down."

I eased Mom onto the bottom step and squatted in front of her.

"How long have they been holding you? How did you even get involved with Dunn?"

She seemed confused. "I… don't know."

Rory slid a hand over my shoulder, squeezing gently. I settled my palm over hers and squeezed back. I wanted to wrap the woman I loved in my arms and get her away from here—get both women away from this ugliness. But with FBI agents swarming the place, I doubted we'd be able to leave without answering their questions.

I didn't know what I'd say or how I'd keep the truth of my brother's abilities from them.

Monte. I needed to call him. I needed him to know that while his vision had partially come true, Rory and her father had prevented the worst from happening.

My finger hovered over the call button as I really took in the scene that my brother had seen over and over again. Bodies strewn. Blood. The stench of death. Sadness filled me for the things Monte had lived through in his dreams.

Next to me, Demi's eyes closed, and she seemed to slip away. I couldn't help but feel sad for her too. Because she might be able to see the good in people's futures—she might have told me that she only shared the positive because there was enough ugly in the world—but it hadn't prevented her from seeing the worst.

My throat bobbed.

"Where are the men who took Monte?" I asked Rory, but it was the FBI agent who responded.

"We detained three men in a box truck down the street."

It wasn't quite relief that hit me, but something along those lines.

Rory rubbed a hand on my cheek, drawing my attention back to her. "Call Monte, Gage."

I swallowed hard at how she'd read my mind.

Tears hit my eyes as relief overwhelmed me again. She'd made it. I'd been so certain when I'd left Cherry Bay that I'd be okay, but I hadn't been so sure about her. I pulled her to me for a moment, resting my face in the curve of her neck, breathing her in. Allowing myself to acknowledge that she was still there.

I wanted to yell at her for coming on her own.

But even more, I wanted to tell her I loved her.

And I would. Just not now in the middle of a crime scene with blood surrounding us.

Instead, I lifted my head, pushed the button, and called my brother.

Chapter Forty-three

Rory

As Gage helped his mom into the back of an ambulance parked at the warehouse loading dock, my emotions bounced around erratically. Relief should have filled me at knowing the people who'd done this to Mom would answer for it, but instead my chest burned with anger, and my mind swam with unanswered questions.

While I was damn glad Gage had Demi back, it was also a brutal reminder that I was never going to hold my mom again. She was gone. They'd taken her away in a body bag just hours ago, and the guilt of that still hung heavy on me. I fought another influx of tears.

I felt eyes on me and turned to find Dad and Sheila shooting looks in my direction as they talked. A bitter taste coated my tongue. If they'd trusted me, maybe tonight would have ended differently. I made my way over to them and handed my gun to Sheila, and she accepted it with a gloved hand.

Then I turned to my dad and demanded, "How long did you know Chanel was behind Mom's accident?"

"Only for a couple of months," my dad said.

"Only!" Frustration welled.

"Your mom called me the day of the crash. She knew Dunn was my client and wanted to give me a heads-up about her suspicions that he and West were tied to the Lovatos. So, when I saw the police photos and the tire marks, I knew what had happened wasn't an accident."

"Your dad called me, and I hooked us up with a multi-agency task force that's been working on taking down the Lovatos. That's where G came in. We've been following West and Dunn for a while now," Sheila said.

"Why did you put Chanel's file where I'd see it once I signed into your system?" I asked.

Dad's lips twitched upward. "You logged in?"

I nodded. This seemed to make him happy in a way I would never have suspected.

"Two months ago, one of the task force members took a picture of Chanel talking to West at a coffee shop. They were just waiting in line to order, and it might simply have been a coincidence—"

"But there are no such things as coincidences when working a case," I finished with Mom's words burning through me and pricking at the back of my eyes.

G sauntered up to us with the tablet Chanel had dropped in her hands. "We'll get this over to the task force and see if we can unwind the last things she did. But we really needed her alive."

G glared at my dad.

"She had a gun aimed at my daughter," he said as if that was the end of the discussion.

"You didn't have to kill her!"

There was something beneath the words, and I realized G had her suspicions about my dad. Dunn was his client, which meant he'd been a breath away from working with the Lovatos himself. Maybe she thought he was working both sides.

"Chanel said she removed any trail to her boss and instead was pointing everything at my dad," I told them, not knowing if that would make things better or worse but unable to just sit back and let Dad get blamed for this.

"She knew I was on to her," he said. "That's why I left you those photos with the encoded number. In case something happened to me too, I knew you'd find them."

The idea of losing him in addition to Mom made my stomach twist. I'd spent so much of my life hating him, hating what had happened… My voice was choked as I asked, "Why didn't you tell me, Dad?"

He ran a hand over his chin, and then suddenly reached out and pulled me to his chest like he had at Shady Lane. For the second time in less than a day, love radiated between us. Maybe my feelings for Gage had opened me up so I was more receptive to it, or maybe Dad was just showing it again for the first time in years. I wasn't sure which was true. Maybe they both were.

"I knew if I told you my suspicions you wouldn't stop until you found answers, and I couldn't stand the idea of losing you on top of losing Hallie." His voice was choked.

The feelings he seemed to have for Mom threw me for a loop. I stepped back, needing to put some space between us. I shot a glance in Sheila's direction as I said, "You act like you still loved her."

Sheila snorted. "Which is exactly why your father and I never worked."

Was that why none of Dad's relationships had lasted? He'd still been in love with Mom?

Mom had never really dated. She'd seen a few people, but she'd always used her job as an excuse to keep from getting serious. What if the truth was that they'd both still been madly in love? God. That felt terribly sad. To have loved each other and not been together all these years.

What if I'd been the reason they'd stayed apart?

Pain washed through me, sharp and fierce.

Sheila and G were called away by one of the other agents, and it left me alone with my dad.

He put his hand to my chin, tipping my eyes up to meet his. "What happened with your mom and me wasn't your fault."

I wasn't sure I could ever fully believe that, just like I'd never let go of the guilt over how Mom's life had ended, but it still eased the knot in my chest ever so slightly.

"I'd done a whole list of stupid things that cost me your mother's trust. Not just what I'd done to you…" He stopped, clearing his throat before continuing. "I was willing to do anything to get the job done, even if that meant—"

"Sleeping with other women?"

"I was never unfaithful," he said forcefully, shaking his head. "But I pushed the boundaries enough she could never be quite certain. Plus, I was always trying to protect her, and it made her feel like I didn't see her as an equal when really I was just trying to keep her safe. I guess that made it even harder for her to understand why I had sent you into some of the situations I had."

"I was never in danger."

"The senator could have become violent with you. He had a history of it."

I hadn't known any of that of course, and I wasn't sure knowing it then would have changed how I felt responsible for the demise of my parents' marriage.

"Even if I was just the final straw… I was still the straw," I told him. "I screwed up." I looked around at the dead bodies and the agents scouring the scene. I thought of Walden and Mom. And suddenly I couldn't stop the tears that leaked. "Just like now. I screwed up so many times. And people lost their lives. I think you're right. I'm not cut out for this work."

He shook his head. "I'm so proud of you. You uncovered in a matter of days what it took Sheila and me months to find out."

His words felt like a balm, but they were coming too little, too late. Too little for the lives I had on my conscience now.

Gage jogged over to us, and when he saw the tears on

my cheeks, his face took on a dark glower as he turned to my father. "Don't you dare—"

"Stop, Gage. It's okay. Really."

He looked from me to Dad and back again. Dad actually smiled. "I kind of like knowing there's someone watching your back, Rory-girl. Let him bluster a bit. I can take it."

A soft laugh escaped me, and Gage's face relaxed. "They're taking Demi to the hospital. I'm going to follow the ambulance."

I grabbed his hand. "I'm sorry… that we didn't stop…" I glanced over to where crime scene photographers were shooting the bodies.

His hand slid to my cheek, and if my dad hadn't been standing there, I knew he would have kissed me. Instead, I wrapped my hand around his wrist and leaned into it.

"Demi's alive. That's because of you." His voice was deep and emotional just like Dad's had been. Too many feelings that were never good for an investigation were floating in the air.

Except there was nothing left to investigate. Not for me. Demi was safe. Mom's murderers were gone. Two cases closed.

But like Veronica at the end of most seasons, I didn't feel like celebrating. The loss had been too great to be seen as a win.

The ambulance doors slammed behind us, and Gage stepped away. Our eyes clung to each other for a long moment before he said, "I'll call you as soon as I know anything about her condition."

And then he spun around and hurried out the cargo bay doors.

"You should go with him," Dad said. "I can have someone take the Jeep back to Cherry Bay for you."

"I haven't been debriefed."

Dad shrugged. "It's not like they don't know where to

find you. They'll want to talk to Gage too."

A week ago, I would have wanted to stay. I would have soaked up everything about the crime scene, watching and learning and filing it away for the future I'd seen for myself. But the thought of Gage having to go to the hospital alone, worrying about his mom, and not having someone there when he needed it, suddenly felt more important than anything else. Just being with him felt more important. I needed the comfort of him as much as I needed to offer it.

Maybe that was where Dad and Mom had gone wrong. They'd put the job above their marriage. Above the love they'd felt for each other—and me. Did I want to repeat their mistakes? Especially when I wasn't even sure I could continue with the career I'd laid out for myself?

I leaned up and kissed Dad's cheek and then ran for the doors.

Outside, the sun had eased its way over the horizon, the soft glow peeking through the clouds as the storm broke. A soft mist still fell, and in that rare moment of sun and moisture, a rainbow appeared. It arched over the buildings across the way, and Gage was caught in a glow at the midpoint

My feet stopped, my heart thudding loudly at the breathtaking picture he made painted in the vibrant colors. With a sudden clarity, I knew there had never been a first or second or last time I'd fallen for Gage Palmer. The number of times would be unending. He'd always been and always would be the person I loved.

I took off at a sprint, calling his name, and when he looked up, a soft smile took over his face. I ran straight into his arms and kissed him. With love and passion and hope. I handed over my heart and soul to him and he took them, mouth angling over mine and offering the same pieces of himself right back. We'd hold on to them for each other. Hold on with all we had.

"I love you," I said, breaking away. "I've always loved you. Since the minute you played The Guess Who and smiled at me. I can't go another day without acknowledging it. Without you knowing it. I may not fit into your life, and I may not be what you need—"

He cut me off with another kiss. Wet and hungry and passionate. But also fierce and almost angry. "You're exactly what I need, Rory. I want to have the brave, smart, beautiful woman you've become, showing me how to live past all the damage that's come before."

"My teenage self would have exploded at those words." I swallowed hard, rubbing a thumb over his bottom lip. "But adult me would really like to hear three very different words."

The glint of humor in his eyes matched the wide grin he gave me. "Yeah? Three words? Like… let's get breakfast?"

I shoved him in the shoulder and went to pull away, but his arms wrapped around me, tugging me closer as his smile disappeared. "I love you. Is that what you needed to hear, Pipsqueak?"

"It's not completely despicable," I said softly.

He kissed me again. Long and hard, until our breath came out in small pants and our bodies were aching to be joined.

"As much as I'd like to continue where this is going, I really need to get to the hospital," he said.

I nodded, stepping out of his embrace and heading for the passenger side. "I'm coming with you."

His smile returned, and as he glanced over at me with a look that was everything I'd ever wanted from him—desire and love and belonging—my heart finally did explode.

Inside the Pathfinder, his hand found mine, lifting it to his lips. "What's the Logan line?"

"Which one?"

"The one about their relationship being epic?"

I swallowed hard. In my opinion, those lines were the most romantic in the entirety of the show, even if Logan did screw everything up after he'd said them. "He said he thought their story was epic. That it would span years and continents. That it would last past all the lives ruined and all the bloodshed. That they'd be epic together."

Gage nodded, but his face turned somber once again as he looked back across the street at the warehouse. "I like the epic part. Not sure I want to experience the bloodshed and lives ruined anymore. Let's try to limit that, shall we?"

I choked out a laugh, and he grinned, turning on the car and backing out of the lot.

The love between us didn't promise to be any easier than Veronica and Logan's had been. Too many things were still up in the air and unknown about us and me and our future, but I wanted the epic. I wanted it so badly I was willing to set aside a few of the things I'd once thought would be mine. The sacrifice would be worth it to keep Gage and his siblings. To have this feeling with me every single day. I'd do just about anything to hold on to them.

Chapter Forty-four

Gage

EVER SINCE THE WORLD BEGAN
Performed by Survivor

Rory and I spent hours in the emergency waiting room as the doctors assessed Demi. We paced to keep ourselves awake, swallowed a whole lot of coffee, and when that got to be too much, we simply sat with arms twined.

My burdens should have felt heavier after seeing my mother in the shape she'd been, seeing the shoot-out and the reality of Monte's visions, but instead, they lightened. Maybe it was because Rory and I had admitted we loved each other. Maybe it was just knowing we were standing there holding our responsibilities together instead of alone.

When a doctor came out asking for Demi's relatives, Rory and I stood up and joined him in the hall.

"She's severely malnourished and dehydrated," the doctor said. "It's my understanding she was being held against her will. Is that correct?"

"It's what we believe. We won't know more until she can tell us herself what happened," I said.

"There is a significant amount of opioids in her system. Did she use drugs before this?"

I shook my head. As flighty as Demi had been, I'd never seen her on drugs. She didn't even drink much. She was just high on life most of the time.

"Well, they may have been used as a way of keeping

her subdued. It's going to take some time for that to work through her system, and the withdrawals are likely to be painful. We'll start the process here, but I highly recommend she be removed to a rehabilitation center afterward. They'll be able to support her with counseling in addition to the physical aspects of the withdrawal."

I swallowed hard and nodded. I wasn't sure I could talk even if I wanted to. My fingers tightened on Rory's, and she squeezed them back, taking over the conversation for me.

"Were there other signs of abuse?" Rory asked, and my lungs constricted because I hadn't even thought about what Dunn and West and whoever was guarding her might have done. The doctor shook her head.

"None that the team noticed at this time. The only physical injuries were the marks on her wrists from where they'd restrained her."

"Can we see her?" Rory asked.

"I've given her a sedative because she was a bit hysterical and not making much sense. I'm not sure if it was from what she experienced or the drugs wearing off. I'm hopeful that with some sleep, she'll be more coherent and be able to tell us what she needs."

"Do you know how long that will be?"

"Several hours at least."

I cleared my throat, and when I finally spoke, my voice was raw and raspy. "Thank you for taking care of her."

"They're moving her to a room now. The front desk can tell you the number in a few minutes. She'll be here a few days, but I'll have the nurses give you a list of the centers I recommend. With time and rest, she'll be okay. Try not to push her too hard."

The doctor walked away, and Rory wrapped me in her arms. I rested my cheek on the top of her head and just held on. I was still a knot of conflicted emotions over my mother. Pissed that she'd gotten mixed up with Dunn to begin with. Pissed that she put Monte and the rest of us at risk. But I was also still terribly sad for what she'd gone through.

"Maybe we should head back to Cherry Bay. Shower and change—"

Just as the words escaped me, my family walked through the door. Monte was holding Ivy, with River and Audrey trailing them. As they shifted, another person became visible—Rory's grandmother.

It wasn't just my family. It was ours. Together.

My throat closed.

I moved toward them, wrapping my siblings in my arms, holding them tight as Rory did the same with Kora. Then, Audrey and River were there, surrounding me and my siblings until we were nothing more than a mound of arms and legs. Ivy giggled, and that was enough to break us apart.

Ivy stuck her hands out, and I took her from Monte. "I missed you," she said.

"I missed you too, Ives."

"We bwought Tanksgiving to you," she said, and my heart squeezed tight.

With everything that had happened, I'd forgotten the holiday. I looked over at Audrey and River, who were grinning. At their feet were several warming bags and a cooler.

Rory's grandmother gave me a one-sided hug and a kiss on the cheek, but the real surprise was Monte dragging Rory into an embrace. Rory patted his back as she shot me an uncertain look.

"Thank you," Monte said.

Tears welled in Rory's eyes, and I gently punched my brother in the shoulder. "Don't make her cry."

He stepped back, a gentle smile on his face as he looked from me to her and back. "Does this mean you two are a thing now?"

"A thing?" I joked, just as Rory said, "Yes."

It was almost comical the way both Kora's and Monte's

faces lit up. If I'd had any reservations left about Rory coming into our lives—which I didn't—that would have removed them. Rory belonged with us. We belonged to her.

Life together might be rocky at times. Seeing her leave and come back while she went to FLETC and shipped off to some unknown location might be the hardest thing I'd ever do, but I'd do it because we were meant to be together. I knew it with the same confidence I knew that the storms ravaging D.C. were gone.

♫ ♫ ♫

Afternoon had drifted into evening by the time one of the nurses came and told us Demi was awake and had asked to see me. Monte's face flashed with hurt, but it was better if I talked to Demi alone first. I didn't know what she had to say, and it might not be anything I wanted my brother to hear. He was only thirteen even though it was hard to remember that sometimes.

I made my way to Demi's room only to be shocked all over again at the sight of her. Frail was almost too kind of a word. Her eyes flooded with tears at seeing me. She reached up a shaky hand to pull a tissue from the box on a bedside tray. She wiped at her eyes as I made my way to the chair next to her.

"How did you find me?" she asked.

"Monte had a vision, but it was actually Rory who found you." I told her everything about Monte being kidnapped and how Dunn and West were tied up with the Lovatos and how they'd had Hallie Marlowe killed. Demi closed her eyes several times, slow tears leaking from the corners.

When I was finished, she somehow looked even worse than when I'd walked into the room. I wasn't sure if I felt guilty about it or not. Maybe she wasn't in the right condition to hear the full truth of what she'd tangled herself in, but years of anger and hurt made it almost impossible to shield her from it either.

"I knew Monte was there, Gage... I sensed him. Saw him... I begged Roland to let him go..." Her voice cracked. "At first, he said he couldn't. But I told him I'd kill myself before giving him any more answers if he didn't release him."

Her words piled more emotions onto the heap I was already feeling. Gratitude I'd never felt for her mixed in with frustration because she was the reason my brother had been in danger in the first place. I leaned in, elbows on my knees. "How did you get mixed up with Dunn? How did he even learn the truth about your abilities?"

"I met him at a party." Her focus was far away, as if looking backward through time and memories. "He was so... jovial... charming. Happy. I needed that. I needed that because I was feeling the pull to go home again, and I knew I couldn't."

My chest ached, and my voice was deep as I growled, "Couldn't or wouldn't?"

Her hand, which was all skin and bone, shook as she ripped at the tissue. The action was so like Monte's when he was tearing the sandwich wrapper in the police station interrogation room that it was almost painful. Of all of us, Monte was the most like Demi.

"Everything I did was to protect you. It was the only way for you to become who you were supposed to be. To find joy."

"Joy!" I growled, and then took a deep breath, trying to control my anger. "Don't start that bullshit again about how leaving was good for me. Like you were just feeding me broccoli. Every time you left, it cut deep grooves in Dad. In me. In Monte.

"Ivy doesn't even know you! How on earth was that for the best? Do you know she has abilities too? She can feel when we're hurting. She's linked to us. And I don't know how to help her with that any more than I know how to help Monte with his visions. And you—the one person who could help them, who'd lived through your own experiences with these fucked-up abilities—you left. Over and over again."

For the first time since seeing her in the warehouse, I saw a bit of spirit come back into her face. She dropped the tissue pieces and reached a hand toward me. I pushed back, not wanting her to touch me. If she did, I'd be dragged right in again to whatever bullshit she wanted to spout.

I wouldn't become Dad. I wouldn't put Ivy through what Monte and I had been through. A repeated cycle of love and loss.

I was glad Demi hadn't died. I was sad she'd gone through this horrific experience, but I was damn sure I didn't want her destroying my siblings like she had me.

"How did you feel when Monte was missing, Gage?" she asked softly.

"How do you think I felt? Terrified! Out of my mind. But then again, maybe you wouldn't know because you've never cared about anyone but yourself."

"Would you have done *anything* to make sure he lived?"

My stomach turned as I relived the moment I realized Monte was actually not with India. And then, the god-awful pain I'd felt watching him on the video being shoved into a trunk by masked men. I'd been filled with agony and desperation.

"Yes. I would have done whatever it took."

"Even walk away?"

I didn't want to think about the scenario she'd laid out. If the kidnappers had said they'd hand Monte back, send him home if I'd walked out of their life forever, would I have done it? Nausea rolled through me.

"What are you saying?" I asked, my voice low and guttural.

"I had to choose between staying and watching you die or leaving and you getting everything you wanted."

I shook my head. "Fuck that." But a chill coasted over my skin, and I could tell she was telling the truth. She thought I would have died if she'd stayed. Her gift… she'd seen it. My mind reeled as I remembered the times her smile had vanished after she'd touched me.

The fort incident. The happiness that had dissolved into grief.

My heart felt like it was imploding as the terrible realization hit me.

She'd done everything. The years of leaving. The grief she'd caused my dad. Monte. It had all been for me?

Barbs of guilt and remorse landed in my chest, tearing me open.

Just another way for her to have struck at me.

When I didn't say anything, she continued. "Whenever I looked into your future, that's what I saw—you dying in my arms. I didn't know why, but I could sense it was because of me. So, I chose to leave. Whenever I came back, I hoped that the choices we'd both made in my absence would have changed the vision. I hoped what I saw would be different. Hoped I'd be able to stay."

My throat felt like it was closing. I gasped for air, inhaling sharply, and the intake of oxygen caused almost as much pain as the emotions she'd set sailing through me.

"After Holland died… after I had Ivy. It was gone for a while. And then, that day you'd come back to find Monte and me in the sheet fort we'd made, I touched you, and I saw you fighting with one of Roland's men as they tried to take Ivy. I saw you…" Her voice cracked and faded away.

"I don't understand. Why would Dunn…" Then the realization hit me. "Dunn was her father."

She swallowed, not meeting my eyes, but nodded. "He was already threatening to come into my life and ruin it— ruin everyone I loved—if I didn't come back to him. And that vision… I lost you both. You died, and he took Ivy and kept her hidden from me."

I didn't know how to reconcile everything she was telling me. Guilt flooded me, knowing she'd stayed away because of me for so many years. Anger because she'd brought Dunn into our lives. Frustration that my family had been torn apart repeatedly by the paranormal abilities she'd passed down to us.

"Did Dad know why you kept leaving?" I asked.

"Not at first," she said. "But later…"

It suddenly made sense why he'd kept allowing her back into his life. Why he'd never even dated someone else. Never filed for a divorce. He'd loved her, and he'd taken her back even when she'd been pregnant with another man's child.

I stood up. I needed out. I needed to get away. I needed to… I didn't know what.

Squeezing my eyes shut, I pushed my palms against them.

Fuck.

"Let me touch you, Gage." It was a desperate beg. A plea to see something different from what she'd seen in the past. But God, what if she saw something worse? What if she saw Rory dying? Or Monte or Ivy? What if it was me who had to leave?

I shook my head.

"No."

That one word made her crumble, and I almost took it back.

"I can't let you do that," I said. "I can't live my life for a future that may or may not happen. I don't want to. I want to live in the present, holding on to the people I love and care about, experiencing as much joy as I can right now.

"You were the one to tell me we aren't guaranteed anything. Not even the future you see. We both know that what happens tomorrow isn't just dependent on the decisions *we* make. It could be some jerk who gets into a car after one too many beers and crashes into us. It could be some person walking into the mall with a gun. It could be a million other things that change what happens next.

"Dunn was so obsessed with the idea of what you could predict that he held you hostage for years. He was addicted to what you saw. I can't do that. I won't live that way. I have to follow my heart and my gut and hope it brings goodness into our lives and not darkness."

She sobbed, and her bony shoulders shook.

I set my hand on her leg over the top of the blanket, avoiding the skin-to-skin contact she required for her to get a vision of me and my future. I squeezed gently.

"If you want to come home, Demi…" I stopped. Was I really going to invite her back in? To allow her the power to hurt Ivy? Monte? Me?

"If you want to come home, I need you to promise that you won't try to see our futures on purpose. And if you accidentally see something, you still have to stay no matter what it is you see. If you can't make those promises to me, then I can't let you into their lives again. It's my job to protect them now, so you'll do it my way or no way."

She started to say something, and I shook my head. "No. Don't answer me right now. You're going to be here for a few days at least and then in a rehabilitation clinic for a while. Just think about it. Really and truly consider what I'm saying, and then we'll talk."

A knock on the doorframe brought my eyes to Rory. I wondered how much she'd heard. Her eyes were large and sad, but they'd been that way for what felt like days now. The only time I'd seen her light up was when we were teasing each other or kissing or making love. "I'm sorry to interrupt, but the FBI is here. They want to debrief us."

I nodded.

"Can I see them?" Demi asked. I knew she was talking about my siblings, but there was no way I was letting them in here without me.

"Yes. If I'm here too. So, it'll have to wait until after I've talked with the FBI."

Demi accepted my decision, eyes shutting.

I headed for the door, and as we stepped outside, Rory wrapped me in her arms, squeezing me tight.

"Are you okay?" she asked.

I rested my cheek on her head. "No. But I will be. All of us will."

I didn't mean just my family. I meant her too, and she must have understood it because she moved, rising on her toes to kiss me softly. It was a brief, barely there kiss, but it was full of caring and comfort. A peace I'd only found in Rory.

And for the first time in days—maybe years—I felt the truth of my words. We really were going to be okay. I'd been focusing on the present because I'd been full of pain from my past and uncertainty over my future, but I hadn't really been living either.

I promised myself to be better at it. To live in the now because it was all we were guaranteed. To live in the now so I could fully experience the love and joy that were offered to me. To give that love freely in return, with no reservations. I didn't need tomorrow or yesterday. I just needed the beautiful moments I'd make with Rory and my family today.

Chapter Forty-five

Rory

OPEN ARMS

Performed by Journey

The days after the shoot-out at the warehouse were a blur that included multiple debriefings with the FBI and the Lovato task force for Gage, Dad, Demi, and me. Good to his word, Dad made the arrangements for Mom's funeral, and Gage offered the bar for a celebration of life ceremony on a Sunday.

The normally closed bar was packed to the brim with people who'd loved my mom. The 5-H club, clients, and people she'd cultivated as contacts in D.C., many of whom were also mine and Dad's.

I'd been surprised when Casada had shown up. I'd called him after everything had happened at the warehouse, and he said he'd come to pay his respects to my mom. He thanked me again for uncovering Argento Skies' ties to the Lovatos as it meant the end to the company's cloud seeding around his town.

But the damage to his community would take decades to heal. He'd offered me the money he'd been saving for my mom's investigation, and I'd declined, telling him to use it to help the people in his town who needed it more.

When classes resumed after the break, my head was barely there, but I finished the semester without screwing up my grades too much. I'd finally earned my bachelor's degree but didn't know what I would do with it.

Guilt still tore through me on a regular basis as Nan and I grieved. Our lives had a gaping hole in it. Not just because Mom was truly gone, but because so much of our time over the last year had been spent taking care of her. I had hours at my disposal that I hadn't had before. Not only because I wasn't spending all my free time at Shady Lane, but because I wasn't taking on any new cases.

I kept up with the background checks for the DoD, but that was it. No cheaters. No deadbeat parents. No missing kids. Instead, I divided my time between Nan's cottage and the Palmers' apartment. I even helped out in the bar a few times as Gage went back and forth to D.C. to visit Demi in the hospital and then the rehabilitation clinic.

To my surprise, Dad began showing up several times a week in Cherry Bay, bringing takeout to Nan and me or just to visit for a few hours. It was the start of repairing a relationship we'd spent ten years forcing behind a glass wall. I was surprised by how much I truly wanted to fix it. To keep close the one parent I had left.

By some unspoken agreement, we didn't talk about his work or my work, and it allowed us to mostly get along. In fact, the only time we fought was when he found out I had no intention of attending the winter term graduation ceremony.

"Hallie would have wanted to see you in a cap and gown getting your diploma."

"You know it's not a real diploma, right? They mail it to you later."

He huffed. "That's not the point."

"I've never been a normal college student, Dad. Trying to force me into that box now would be stupid even if I wasn't grieving. I don't feel like celebrating. Not yet."

"That's exactly why you should do it. Exactly why we need you to. It's something good, Rory-girl. Everyone in your life could use a bit of good right now."

Later that night, when I sat across the bar from Gage and told him what my dad had said, he looked at me for a long time and then said, "He's right."

I scowled, and he smiled at me. He leaned across the bar and kissed me. Long and slow. My entire body ignited from that single kiss, and I almost gave in.

When Nan added her vote to Dad's and Gage's, I did give up.

Which was how I ended up walking on stage to accept a fake diploma the Friday before Christmas with the people I loved sitting in the bleachers, screaming my name. Unexpectedly, it brought me to tears. When had I gone from being completely okay on my own to needing this large group of people like I needed air?

Afterward, we celebrated at the bar once again. This time, there wasn't a crowd of Mom's friends. There was just Shay and her dad and my family—Gage's family. I wasn't sure whose smile was larger, my dad's or Gage's… or mine.

As I watched everyone laughing at a huge table set up where the dance floor normally was, I knew my family had been right. We'd needed this. I'd needed this. It was a moment of joy after months of barely living. Maybe it would allow me to turn a corner. Maybe we'd all turn it together, finding our way out of the rain into the sunshine.

By the time Dad decided to leave, most of my friends and family had taken off, leaving the crowd in the bar the normal Saturday mix of college students and locals.

Dad hugged me and then stepped back to hand me an envelope.

"What's this?" I asked. When he didn't respond, I opened it and gasped at the amount on the check inside. "What the hell is this?"

"Hallie had a life insurance policy. She must never have gotten around to taking my name off it as the beneficiary, but it doesn't belong to me. She would have wanted you to have it."

"Dad…" It was a serious amount of money.

He looked over to where Gage was talking with River and Audrey. They were staffing the bar so Gage could celebrate with me.

"From what I've been hearing… and what I've seen over the last couple of weeks"—his lips twitched as he glanced at Gage and then at me—"I'm guessing you need somewhere bigger to live."

It took several seconds before I realized what he was suggesting. That Gage and I move in together. I'd be lying if I hadn't been thinking about what it would be like to make a home with Gage—to truly be a family.

I wanted all of it. I wanted to wake up next to him every morning and tuck Ivy into bed with him at night. I wanted pancake mornings and lazy Sundays sprawled together on a couch. For nearly a decade, if not longer, I'd never seen anything in my future but a job. The FBI.

Now I wanted a complete life. Not just a one-sided one.

I wanted his family to be mine, and I wasn't sure what that meant for my old FBI dreams. But keeping Marlowe & Co. running had also lost some of its appeal. That had been Mom's dream way more than it had been mine.

ZeoTech, one of the companies I'd applied for when I'd thought I needed money for Shady Lane, had called me back and offered me an interview. I had one set up for the first week in January. But the thought of working for them in a cubicle every day also made me feel like I couldn't breathe.

I was a mess of indecision. Something I was unaccustomed to and didn't like.

Dad pulled me into a hug, kissed me on the top of my head, and then stepped back. "I'm really proud of you, Rory-girl. I'd offer you a place at Bishop Investigations, but I don't see that future for you."

"No?" I said, my throat clogging.

"No, I really don't." He glanced behind me, and I was surprised to see G sitting at a table in the corner. I hadn't seen her since the last debriefing in D.C. days ago. He started to walk away and shot back, "Tell me what your plans are for Christmas. I'd like to be around at some point."

"Okay," I croaked out, watching as he and Gage shook hands, and then he left the bar.

I made my way over to G. She was spinning the glass in front of her, making the amber liquid twirl.

"Hey," I said.

"Congratulations," she said, head tilting toward the banner with my name and grad year that Monte had hung on the back wall.

"Thanks."

"What are your plans now?" she asked.

The hundred-dollar question. "I'm not exactly sure yet."

"Don't take the job at ZeoTech."

I raised my brows at her, and she smirked. She tossed back the contents of the glass, leaned in toward me, and said quietly, "I don't work for the FBI."

Somewhere along the way, I'd figured that out. It wasn't just because she never dressed like the other agents—it was something in the way she held herself. Her training had been different.

When I didn't respond, she asked, "Have you ever considered working for the NSA?"

That surprised me. It wasn't what I'd expected her to say. I'd been expecting DEA or CIA or some other group known for its clandestine activities. "You don't look like a computer analyst."

She laughed. "And you don't look like a private investigator." When I didn't say anything, she went on. "Truth is, I'm in the field a lot. Publicly, the National Security Agency does not conduct human-sourced intelligence gathering. We do, however, assist in the installation of required software and tools. We're the tech buddy our partner agencies can't live without, especially in foreign locations."

I looked at Gage as he threw his head back and laughed at something Audrey had said. He'd been happier in the last few days than I'd ever seen him.

Even as a teenager, there'd always been this layer of sadness to him. Pain. Regret. All caused by the repeated cycle of his mother being in and out. I'd tangled my life with Gage's, and I wanted it. I wanted all of it—the burden and the joy of each relationship. But it also meant I couldn't leave them.

"Truth is," I told her with a shaky breath, "I think my goals have changed."

She looked toward Gage and then back and smiled. "I can understand that. My brother was Secret Service until recently. He resigned so he could be with his fiancée. Family is important. But just because you have a family you want to stay close to doesn't mean you can't work for the NSA.

"We need smart analysts, Rory. We have plenty of people who can code and hack and install the right technology, but people who understand the data coming in and who can put the pieces all together? That's rare. You have an innate talent for it. My boss has told me to ask you what it would take for you to join. Not quite a carte blanche—we are the federal government after all—but you'd be able to set some terms. Push the salary a bit. Maybe get a signing bonus."

The check from Dad was burning a hole in my pocket.

I was pretty sure I knew what I wanted to do with it. But it would eat up the check. I'd have to find a way to support myself. To help support a family.

She rose, sliding a business card over to me. All it had on it was a phone number.

"Give me a call after you've had a chance to think about it."

She started to walk away, and I called out after her. "Hey G."

When she looked back, I swallowed hard, guilt flooding me so hard I almost passed out. "I made a lot of mistakes recently."

"Don't we all. In this job, this way of life, you'll make more. We'll never have all the facts. We'll never be able to fully trust the people or the systems we get our intel from. But from where I'm sitting, you've done a hell of a job with the cards you were dealt. Don't underestimate yourself, Rory. I'm sure you've already realized there are plenty of people who will do it for you."

She walked away, blending into the crowd of college kids before disappearing completely.

Gage's eyes met mine across the room, and as if he could see and feel my uncertainty, he frowned. He started toward me, and I met him halfway. I rubbed at the frown line between his dark brows. The touch of him, as always, filled me with energy that coiled and grew, desperately needing a release.

"You're going to be wrinkled and gray if you keep this up. Then people will really believe you've robbed the cradle because I don't plan on having any wrinkles before I'm fifty."

He smiled. That slow stunning smile that had first stopped my heart at twelve. Now, it curved through my chest and stomach and lower. Filling me with heat.

When he looked down, gray eyes turning stormy, I finally saw all the pieces of my life coming together. My past. My future. My present. And I knew what I wanted to do with the check in my pocket and with the offer G had made.

But even more, I wanted to surprise Gage with all of it.

♫ ♫ ♫

The surprise had taken some finagling. More than I'd thought it would, but all the parts of my plan came together on New Year's Eve. It was a big night for the bar, and Gage was supposed to be working, but I'd enlisted his family and mine into helping me execute the plan by freeing him up.

When he came downstairs from the apartment to start prepping the bar for opening, he found all of us waiting for him, including Dad and Nan.

"What's all this?" Gage asked hesitantly.

"I have a surprise for you, but it means leaving with me now."

He swallowed hard, looking around at everyone waiting there. "It's New Year's Eve, Pipsqueak… It's a busy night. I can't afford—"

"I'm filling in for you," Dad said. "I don't know how to mix drinks, but I can pour from the tap. River and Audrey can do the hard stuff."

"And I'm helping Audrey with the tables," Nan said.

"And India and I are watching Ivy," Monte added.

I could feel the debate within Gage. He wanted to come with me, but the years of responsibility that had weighed on him made it nearly impossible for him to just toss it all aside to run away. Not that we were running far, but he didn't know that.

I pulled Gage's hand into mine. "Trust me. Trust them. We've got you."

His throat bobbed.

"Go," River said. "You have your phone. If disaster strikes, we'll call, but it won't."

Gage looked down at me. My anticipation and excitement were all but pouring from me. I couldn't wait to show him. Couldn't wait to have a night alone with him again.

But I was also nervous. I'd made some huge assumptions in the last two weeks. I thought I knew what he'd say. I believed I knew him well enough to know he'd want this too. A tiny part of me, that teenage girl who'd been lovestruck by a boy so far older than her and so far out of reach that he might have been the moon, was afraid she'd tried to grab hold of something that was never meant to be hers.

He cupped my cheek, a thumb sliding along my lower lip, causing my breath to all but evaporate. "Okay. I'm all yours."

Our family cheered, and happiness flew through me.

"Must be some surprise?" he said, his brow rising and eyes heating.

We'd get to that tonight too. But first, I had to show him how I'd made our past and our futures into our present, just like he was determined to live.

Outside, I made my way over to my Rebel. It was cold, but there was no rain or snow predicted tonight, and I wanted Gage to take a ride. I wanted him to remember the exhilaration of being on a motorcycle again. I handed him a helmet, and his eyes widened.

"You're driving?"

I laughed. "Yes."

His lips twitched, but he didn't hesitate. He simply trusted me, giving me control as he buckled on his helmet and I tugged on mine. I swung my leg over the bike, stabilized it, and then patted the seat behind me. He climbed on the back, arms wrapping around my waist, and I started the engine.

Driving with him nestled behind me, cocooned between the heat of his thighs, made it really hard to concentrate. But I did my best, taking us out of town and along the route Gage had taken me when I was fifteen and riding behind him. The wind whipped by, bitterly cold, but the sky was clear and the damp smell of earth and fallen leaves filled the air as we rode alongside the Potomac.

Gage's arms loosened around me, and he let out a huge whoop of joy. It was full of life and happiness and freedom. It was a repeat of the sound I'd made all those years ago.

And I fell for Gage all over again.

I knew enough by now that there hadn't ever really

been a first time I'd fallen, and there would never be a last. My life would simply be a constant barrage of times where I fell for him. And every time I did, the love would be fiercer and stronger and all the more beautiful.

I pulled off at a vista point along the river. We removed our helmets, left them on the seat, and stood watching the scenery as the sun set behind us. The wildlife was quiet with winter having fully set in, but the slosh of the water on the shore was relaxing. Peaceful. Everything about my life felt that way now that I'd made these enormous decisions. I just hoped he'd feel the same.

Gage pulled me into his chest, nose nuzzling the curve of my neck, breath coasting over my skin, and I broke out in goose bumps that had nothing to do with the frigid air. His mouth trailed over my jaw, and I turned slightly, our hungry mouths finding each other. The lick of those flames that had been tamped down for too many days burst free.

In no time, we were all but consuming each other. I turned into his embrace and let our bodies take over, lips seeking, tongues twining, and hands exploring.

The cold seemed to disappear with the pace of our caresses.

A car drove by, honking, and we lifted our heads, grinning.

"I hope these plans you have end with a bed. Hell, I'd settle for a couch or a floor as long as there's privacy," he said, raising a single brow.

I stepped back, grabbed his hand, and drew him to the bike. From my pocket, I pulled out a blindfold. "Do you trust me?"

Once again, he didn't even hesitate. He took the material and wrapped it around his head, securing it tightly, and my heart skittered. I handed him his helmet, and he pulled it back on, while I did the same.

We got back on the bike and drove through the winding back roads until we got near the town limit. I made a couple of turns I didn't have to make because I didn't want him to suspect where we were going. When I finally pulled into the driveway of the Victorian that had once belonged to his family, a wave of panic hit me, making my palms sweaty.

The porch light was on as I'd left it. A light was on in the kitchen and another was on in the main bedroom. That was the only room with furnishings at the moment. I wanted the bedroom to be full of furniture that was new to us. That would be ours and ours alone. A haven of our present while the rest of the house would be filled with the items from generations of his family and my life with Mom.

I guided him, still blindfolded, down the path and up the front porch. I unlocked the enormous maple door with its oval stained glass and wrought iron trim and pushed it open. Would he know where we were simply from the smell of the place—the antique wood and hint of generations that had lived there? Another family had been here, adding their aura to the house, but their stay was just a blip in the time it had belonged to the Palmers.

I led him down the hall to the kitchen. My gaze landed on a picnic basket on the marble counter. A champagne bottle rested in a silver ice bucket with two crystal flutes standing next to it. A charcuterie tray sat beside a little sign I'd made with shaky hands this morning.

"Okay," I said, my voice breathy and shaky. "You can take the blindfold off."

He didn't right away. Instead, I was surprised when he pulled me to him and kissed me again. Full of love and heat and trust. My heart banged furiously from both the passion and the sweetness of it. From knowing that no matter what else happened, Gage Palmer loved me just as much as I loved him.

Chapter Forty-six

Gage

THE SEARCH IS OVER
Performed by Survivor

Something about the steps we'd taken into the building tickled at the back of my brain. My mind was trying to assemble the pieces when Rory was really the one who was best at puzzles.

For whatever reason, bringing me here had made her nervous, which she rarely was. Whatever this surprise was, she'd given it lots of thought and put her heart into it, and yet she was still unsure of whether I'd like it. I didn't want her to feel that way.

I knew, without a single shred of doubt, that whatever she'd put together for us tonight would be something I loved. Just like I loved her. Bringing in the New Year with her tonight—twined together as I hoped we would be—was going to be perfect.

To show her how I felt, I kept the blindfold on even after she'd told me I could remove it, and I pulled her toward me until our fronts collided. I placed my palms on either side of her face and leaned in to kiss her.

Just like on the shore minutes ago, the simple act of joining our mouths seemed to unlock a storm inside me. Waves of lightning that I wanted to turn into the thunder of our bodies pounding together. A rhythm I'd been almost desperate to find again since the time in the hotel room in

D.C., and yet our daily lives had kept it from us.

Now, there was nothing to stop us.

At least, I hoped not. Maybe there was a room full of people watching us fondle each other. That brought a smile to my lips, and I lifted my head.

"What's so funny?" she asked.

"We don't have an audience, do we?"

She laughed softly. "No. But take off the blindfold because I'm not sure I can handle the suspense any longer."

I chuckled and lifted my hands to undo the knot.

"Wait!" she said, capturing the material before it fell from my eyes. Then, she turned me slightly. "Okay."

She pulled the blindfold away, and it took me several seconds longer than it should have to realize where we were. The familiar dark cherry cabinets. The granite counters Dad had added to the kitchen. The recessed lighting and beautifully stained floors. My throat squeezed tight.

"What are we doing here?" I asked, the words barely getting out as my chest and lungs felt like they'd stopped working.

She waved at the counter where a picnic basket sat open next to a silver bucket. A note written with Rory's tightly formed letters read "Welcome home to the Palmer-Bishop residence."

I pushed the heels of my hands to my eyes. Fuck.

Then, I swung around, examining the kitchen that had once belonged to my family. The place where our dining table belonged stood empty. The walls were bare. There was nothing inside the glass-fronted cabinets. The house felt abandoned.

I looked down to see worry lines pulling her brows together.

"Say something," she said with panic in her voice.

"I'm not sure I understand…" I said slowly, trying not to get my hopes up too high. Maybe she'd just rented the place for the night. Maybe the realtor had given her the keys so I could have a last moment in the home I'd loved.

Because there was no way Rory had the money to even put the down payment on this house. It was so far out of both our price ranges, it was ridiculous. We'd be lucky to own a house the size of her Nan's cottage someday.

"It's… ours," she said softly. "Is that okay?"

I swallowed hard, damn hope crawling through me again. "I love this house, Rory. I love the idea of building a family with you in it—my siblings, our own kids if that's what you decide you want. All of it. I might lose my fricking mind if we got to do that here, in my family's home, but I don't see how it's possible. I can't… There's not enough—"

She cut me off with a kiss that was passionate and fierce just like her. But it was also telling me to shut the hell up. When she pulled back, a huge smile was on her face. "It's ours, Gage. I already bought it."

I stared at her, attempting to pull her words into some semblance of meaning.

She laughed. "I should have been filming this. The look on your face." She shook her head. "My mom had a life insurance policy. There's still a mortgage, but it's small and I think I can handle it… or we can… together… if you want…"

As the realization settled in, my heart almost exploded.

The house was ours.

I yanked her to me, kissed the hell out of her, and then looked down into her face. "I want it all. I want the house. I want our families to eat holiday meals here. But what I want most is you."

My tongue slipped inside the soft, heated recesses of her mouth, curling and tasting and caressing. She let out a breathy sigh. A sweet and tantalizing moan that made my dick hard and my chest ache. I tugged at her jacket, forcing it to fall to the ground, and she did the same with mine. My hands slid under her shirt and ripped it up over her head, and mine went the same way.

She was wearing a black lace bra, taut tips visible through the thin fabric. I dipped my head and sucked on one through the material. Her fingers found my hair, tugging, digging in as more sensual sounds escaped those pretty lips.

She pulled away, and I reached for her.

"Come on." She grabbed my hand, linking our fingers and leading the way to the staircase. The only lights on in the first floor were the ones in the kitchen, but as we moved toward the stairs, I could see the rest of the house was empty. The couple who'd lived here was gone.

My free hand trailed over the smooth, glossy banister, and I was overjoyed to realize the previous owners hadn't changed much. The wainscoting was still a beautifully stained cherrywood. The stairs were still smooth and dark. They'd painted the walls in the entry a soft green, but it wasn't totally despicable.

At the top of the stairs, Rory led me in the direction of the main bedroom, which had once been my parents' room.

"I know this might seem weird," she said, pushing open the carved wooden door.

The bedroom was alight with hundreds of candles. The fake kind, but they still danced along walls someone had painted a pale blue—the color of the sky on the clearest of days. The antique chandelier wasn't on, but its hundreds of crystals still sparkled in the flickering candlelight. A pair of dark wooden side tables sat on either side of an enormous sleigh bed piled with linens and fabrics in shades of blue and white and yellow. Across from the bed, above the marble-pillared fireplace, was a large television. On the screen, a show had been paused.

Episode one of *Veronica Mars*.

My lips curled upward.

I looked down into Rory's face and saw excitement all but bleeding from her. "It's all new furniture. I figured, if we wanted to make the Victorian ours, we'd have to make sure this was the one place—"

I kissed her, lifting her up, and taking the handful of steps to the bed before tossing her on it. I yanked at her boots, stepped out of mine, and we both hurried out of our jeans. Then I joined her on the silky comforter, both of us in nothing but our underwear and smiles. She'd worn her hair down today, so it was a tangled mess from the motorcycle ride, but it looked perfectly Rory. I gently tucked a few strands behind her ear as I stared into eyes that gleamed in the twinkling lights.

"I love you," I said, my voice deep and raw with lust and longing.

She ran her fingers over my brows and down my cheeks. "I love you too. In epic proportions."

We got lost in each other's eyes, and then she tugged me toward her. I kissed her briefly before sliding my mouth down her jaw, her neck, and her collarbone. Her tantalizing scent was a heady, pheromone-induced aphrodisiac. She gasped when my lips found her breasts, fingers curling into my hair, nails biting into my scalp.

God, I loved it. The sound, the smell, and the feel of her under me.

Last time we'd taken this too fast. Tonight, I wanted to take my time.

I worshipped and plundered and claimed until she was finally convulsing around my fingers and tongue. No one was ever going to see Rory this way. Completely unguarded, completely relaxed.

This moment was mine, and I was damned sure not going to be foolish enough to let it go. To let her go. Not ever again. I was the only one who would ever see the way her bright light turned into a fiery inferno as she came. The only one to see the pulse of green flame surrounding her pupils burst into existence.

"You're so damn beautiful," I growled as I moved up her body again to kiss her slowly, sensually.

Her nails dug into the skin at my waist, pulling so that our hips slammed together.

"Gage, I'm seriously going to lose my fricking mind if you're not inside me in the next ten seconds."

I huffed out a breath and was rewarded with goose bumps covering her skin.

"Don't rush me. I need to take my time with you."

"Later. Take your time later. Right now, I need you!"

I smothered her perfect lips in a fierce kiss. I'd give her what she needed. What we both needed, but I had to do it my way tonight. I had to make love to her. I had to embed every single ounce of emotion I felt into each and every movement. So, even when she gripped me harder, nails digging into my skin, I didn't go where she wanted.

Instead, I slowly took my time until she was panting and writhing all over again.

When I'd taken her almost to the edge once more, when I felt like I might explode myself, I eased back and asked, "Bare? Or I have a condom in my wallet."

She shook her head. "We've already established I'm on birth control, and I got tested last week. I need you. Right now."

I dropped my forehead to her shoulder, attempting to regain an ounce of control before I slid home. Otherwise I'd go off like a teen with a wet dream.

We'd done this once before, but it felt like it had been in another lifetime. Like it had been so long since we'd been joined that we were completely different people. And in some ways, we were.

That night in the hotel, there'd been fear and anger and loss surrounding us. And now, there was joy and love and healing. We were finding a path. One neither of us had to travel alone.

I lifted my head and met her gaze as I slid inside her. A deep groan escaped my chest that was echoed in her breathy exhale. It felt like heaven. Like leaving this earth to dance among the clouds while simultaneously landing home. A dichotomy I'd never understand.

Part of me was demanding I move—pound in and out of her so fast and furiously that we'd reach the summit in a flash—but part of me wanted nothing more than to stay put. To stay buried inside her where we were joined as close as we could ever be. Where the connection was more than just physical. Where it was souls tying knots around each other, whispering promises of forever.

Rory let me set the pace, even as her hips shifted and her nails continued to bite into my skin. I'd never felt anything like this. Not even in the epicenter of a storm. Here the lightning was inside us rather than around us, but I found deep pleasure in chasing it. I sought every bolt, every charge, and every roar until it was shaking through us like our own little thunderstorm.

Her body tightened, trembling, before she sang my name and let go. I joined her, leaving pieces of me inside her that I'd never get back. That I didn't want back. They belonged to her.

We lay, still joined, our breathing uneven. Eventually, I moved to place a gentle kiss on her lips, and when my eyes found hers, my entire body froze. Her eyes were cloudy with emotions, tears filling them.

"What. God. What's wrong?"

She shook her head.

"Pipsqueak…" Worry and love merged together.

"It was just… perfect. So damn perfect."

And I couldn't deny it. It was. It had been.

Nothing in my life could have prepared me for this. For her. For us. For the amount of love that I felt pouring through me. Not even the love I had for my family. What I felt for them wasn't necessarily less, but it was light-years different.

What I felt for Rory was unnamable. Uncatchable.

The magic of a rainbow that I got to hold and the peace that came with it.

Epilogue

Rory

BEAUTIFUL AS YOU ARE
Performed by Journey

TWENTY-SIX MONTHS LATER

The commute home to Cherry Bay had left me more exhausted than anything that had happened at work. I used to think driving into D.C. was ugly, but going around D.C. and up to Fort Meade for my job at the NSA was downright grueling. Even though I'd requested an early shift, most of the time my days depended on how and when our intel came in and how we were repackaging it. If an op was in play, sometimes I was there for twenty-four hours or more.

But I loved it.

I loved pulling together all the pieces of the puzzles that were sent to us, seeing things that others didn't. I'd been there for two years now and had the opportunity to work on some incredibly rewarding cases, including G's final takedown of the Lovatos.

The information we'd gathered from Chanel's computers hadn't been enough to get an arrest, but it had sent us whirling in a surprising direction. G had uncovered the leader of the Lovatos in a place no one had expected. She should have been awarded a medal for it. But no one outside the intelligence community knew what she'd done except the man attached to her hip ever since.

As I pulled into the driveway of our house in Cherry Bay, I was surprised to see Demi, Monte, and Ivy making their way over to Nan's Beetle with the kids' overnight bags. Ivy ran straight for me as I climbed out of the Pathfinder I'd driven that morning because of the rain. February had been a cold and wet month so far.

I swung Ivy up into my arms, squeezing her tight. "Hey, Ives. Where are you all heading? And why wasn't I invited?"

I tried not to let myself be disappointed. Sunday was my birthday, and I'd been hoping to spend the weekend with all of them. One big messy family including both my dad and Sheila, who'd started dating after everything that had gone down. But instead, my family was leaving.

Ivy giggled. "We're going to dinner and a movie." Weeks away from turning six, she'd outgrown her Rs sounding like Ws and I missed it. "And then we're spending the night with Nan-Nan and Mom."

I raised my brows in the direction of the adults, but it was the way Monte wouldn't meet my eyes that had me immediately suspicious.

"We'll have them home late tomorrow," Demi said, a glimmer in her eye that only added to the feeling of something being up.

Some days, Gage still had his doubts about his mother—years of pain and abandonment hadn't simply disappeared. It was going to be a long time before he could fully trust her again, if ever.

But the pain Demi had caused him was also twisted with the guilt he felt knowing she'd left to save his life. He was slowly trying to reconcile these conflicting realities and his relationship with her just like I was trying to reconcile my relationship with my dad and my guilt over Mom.

For more than two years, Demi had respected Gage's wishes to live in the present and not try to see their future. She'd also given us our space, moving in with Nan instead of staying with us at the Victorian. We'd been taking it a day at a time, rebuilding from the ground up, as the months ticked by.

"We have to go, Ivy, or we'll miss our dinner reservation," Nan said, coming over and prying Ivy from me before hugging me tightly. "Demi and I thought it would be nice for you and Gage to have a date night before the wildness of your birthday party."

I smiled. "You know I hadn't confirmed there was a party happening, right?"

She laughed and said, "Don't spoil the secret."

He'd been acting a bit off over the last week or so, and I'd thought something was up because every time I'd mentioned my birthday, he'd clammed up. Knowing Gage, he had a list of tasks he'd doled out to everyone in the family.

She winked and headed back to the car with Ivy.

I smirked to myself as Monte practically doubled over to try to squeeze his six-foot-two frame into the back of Nan's Beetle. He still wasn't done growing. He was going to surpass Gage before he was done, I was sure.

"Hi, Monte. Bye, Monte," I called.

He stuck his head back out and said, "Love you. See you tomorrow." Then he disappeared with what I was sure was a blush.

Something was up. More than just the not-so-surprise party.

I waved as they backed out of the driveway before making my way up the front steps.

The house felt oddly quiet with no one inside it. Friday. Gage was already at the bar. I'd have a few hours of alone time before he returned at around ten o'clock. He rarely closed anymore. Instead, he'd hired additional help once we'd moved in together. It made our finances tight some months, but Gage said it was worth it because he could spend more time with me. With our family.

The table in the entryway had once been in the Palmers' apartment and had the same bowl on it that Gage always dropped his keys into. I hadn't been able to break him of the habit. He'd laughed and said, "You've installed an alarm with a code that would require another secret code in order to break. I don't think anyone is going to be able to get inside and take my keys."

The bowl was empty now with Gage at work. I hung my jacket on the coat tree, tossed my boots into the basket full of all our shoes by the door, and hauled my bag down to the study that once had been Gage's dad's. I locked my gun and laptop away in the safe, left the rest of my things slung over the cozy armchair sitting in front of the fireplace, and headed for the stairs, determined to take a long, soaking bath and let my brain noodle on the latest round of intelligence we'd received.

When I opened the bedroom door, my feet came to an abrupt halt. The fake candles that I'd used when I'd first bought the Victorian were spread all around the room. The chandelier was off, the fireplace was lit, and the atmosphere was decidedly romantic. At the foot of the bed, on a long, tufted bench, sat a tray of snacks and the same silver bucket I'd used when I'd first surprised Gage with the house. A bottle of champagne was tucked into the ice.

The familiarity of it squeezed my heart almost as much as the romance of it.

I turned around, and instead of the first episode of *Veronica Mars* on the screen, I saw the final episode. The heart-shattering, you-almost-never-want-to-watch-it-ever-again episode. The one I'd been able to watch only twice before. Gage knew I couldn't stomach watching the ending, and yet he had it cued up and ready to go.

As I started to make my way toward the bathroom, Gage appeared in the doorway. He wore nothing but a gray towel wrapped around his narrow hips. His muscled torso was on display, still defined and shaped in a way that made my mouth water just looking at it. All my suspicions from the moment I saw everyone getting into Nan's car came rushing back. But they weren't accompanied by fear. Instead, a sweet expectation started to hum through me.

A smile spread as I said, "Do we have big plans tonight?"

"You're early."

"I'm actually late. Traffic was hell."

He looked down at the clock on the bedside table. "Shit."

My grin grew. As I started across the room toward him, I began losing clothes. Sweater, jeans, socks. By the time I reached him, I was in just a bright blue bra and panty set. Gage's gaze wandered over my body, taking in every ounce of me. My workout routines had suffered some from spending so much time with my family and being on the road a lot, but it was worth it. I was still strong and lean, but my curves were a little fuller. Gage didn't seem to mind.

"Nan mentioned something about date night. I take it we're not going out?"

Gage's throat bobbed and his eyes turned cloudy as his hand caressed my collarbone, down over one breast, lightly rubbing the tip through the silky material. My eyes fluttered closed for a moment before opening again.

He leaned in and kissed me, but it wasn't with the intensity that meant we'd be lying tangled in the sheets in two seconds flat. Instead, it was with a tenderness that almost overwhelmed me. A sweetness that took all those suspicions and amplified them.

He backed up. "Stop distracting me."

I laughed. "You're the one who was practically naked when I walked in, and who, I might add, kissed me."

He took my hand and led me into the bathroom we'd remodeled last year, making it another little haven that was all ours in the family's Victorian. We'd converted a bedroom next door into a walk-in closet and bathroom with a giant claw-foot tub and a walk-in shower made decadently for two.

The bathroom was as full of fake candles as the bedroom. Here they led up to the bathtub already full of bubbles. Gage quickly divested me of my last two layers of clothing and then held his hand out to help me in. He dropped the towel, and my eyes fell to his hard-on. As I reached for it, he lifted an eyebrow, waved a finger at me, and then stepped into the tub behind me.

He pulled me back against his chest, arms banding me, fingers working into the tight muscles along my neck and shoulders. The tension of the commute and the intelligence work that had consumed me on the way home disappeared. Instead, I was utterly in my present. Body alert in a very different way with Gage's thighs encasing mine. With the heat and scent of him blending in with the soft citrus of the bubbles and the warmth of the water.

He lightly brushed my taut tips, lowering his mouth to my ear and nibbling on it. "You're so beautiful, Rory. Beautiful and strong and brave and I rejoice every day that you're mine."

I turned my face to find his lips, and the temperature in the tub tripled. As our slick bodies slid along one another, pleasure coursed through me, and I was already seconds away from going over the edge. I moved swiftly, rising and turning around so I came down on top of him, taking him inside me all in one smooth motion. His eyes widened in surprise, a delicious moan escaping him that I swallowed with my mouth.

Gentle sounds filled the air. Our panting, the slosh of the water against the sides of the tub, and the slap of our skin. It was intoxicating. Sensual.

Every moment that Gage and I had come together over the last two years had been like this. Overwhelming. Emotional. Beautiful. Every time we made love, I felt our souls stitch together another notch tighter. Someday, there would no longer be two of us, but some merged being. We'd finish each other's sentences and hand each other things before the other asked. We'd be a perfect organism that had been joined by love and time.

It didn't take long for each of us to find release. To go over the top and tremble back to reality…

I laid my cheek on his shoulder as our breathing evened out. His hands slid over my hips and up my sides to my back. A slow, comforting caress.

"That was supposed to be last," he said, a smile in his voice.

I sat up to look at him, locking him with a stare that my coworkers called Scary Rory. "What was supposed to be first, Gage Palmer?"

He grinned in response, not at all scared.

Gage wrapped his arm around my waist and stood, bringing me with him. He hauled us both onto the soft mat beside the tub, reaching for towels. When I tried to grab mine from him, he swatted my hand away and proceeded to gently dry me from top to bottom, kissing me along the way.

My entire body was trembling again by the time he was done.

He pulled my silk robe from the back of the bathroom door and helped me into it. He tied the belt around my middle and then stood back, eyeing me. "That isn't much help. I'm going to want to take it off again."

I huffed out a little laugh. He stepped into a pair of pajama bottoms. Once upon a time I might have thought pajama bottoms were for old men and little boys, but Gage made them look sexy. Especially because I knew he'd started wearing them back when he was sharing a room with his sister. It hadn't been a natural state for him. He'd learned to live with it in order to take care of his family. Like the million other things he'd done to care for them.

In the bedroom, he had me climb into bed and brought me a glass of champagne and the tray full of snacks. He joined me, hitting the remote, and allowing my least favorite Veronica Mars episode to fill the screen.

It felt like the exact opposite of what this evening should have been about. Not sexy at all.

"You're ruining our date night," I said, waving the champagne flute toward the television.

"Wait. I need to record that. Rory Marlowe Bishop saying *Veronica Mars* was ruining something. Can you please repeat it?" he teased as he reached for his phone.

I punched his shoulder softly.

We watched the episode in near silence. Just eating and drinking. I wondered if I was wrong. If my thoughts about what was happening tonight were way off base. As we got toward the end, my chest started to ache and my eyes started to water because I knew what was coming. I knew the pain and loss and sadness.

I couldn't help the slow tear that drifted from the corner of my eyes as Veronica drove away and the credits rolled. Gage took my champagne glass from my hand and put it and the tray to the side. He pulled me onto his bare chest, reaching out to wipe at my tears.

"I keep telling you, Pipsqueak, he's not dead."

I huffed out a half laugh, half sniffle. "Even if that's true, *she* still thinks he is."

Gage brushed a finger slowly over my lower lip, and my body forgot Veronica and Logan and the episode. Instead, I was right in the moment. Right with Gage and our time together. Our present that would always be more important than anything else in our lives.

"Logan is wrong, you know," Gage said.

"Yeah, about what?"

"He says he wants to marry Veronica because he respects her, and he wants to have children with her that will inherit her qualities. Because she's the toughest human he's ever met, picking herself up after blows that would destroy most people."

My eyes narrowed at Gage as I dragged out my single-word response. "Yeeesss."

"That's a way to admire and respect someone. But it isn't a reason to marry them." He waited for another beat before continuing. "You marry them because, as cliché as it might be, you love them so much you can't imagine a world that doesn't have them in it. You marry them because they're the piece of your soul that was always missing until you miraculously collided together. You marry them because there is no other choice. Because the loss of each other would be a blow neither of you could ever recover from."

Those sweet words didn't help my tears. Instead, they were suddenly coming faster. It was exactly how I felt. As if there was no way I could ever survive the loss of him. And yet I knew it wasn't true.

Gage and I had survived wreckage after wreckage in our lives, and if one of us lost the other, we'd be Veronica, holding ourselves together once again. But God, did I hope that never was the case. I hoped we'd live until we were both too old to move and then died together in our sleep.

Gage reached under his pillow and brought out a dark blue velvet box.

"Will you marry me, Rory Marlowe Bishop? I couldn't survive this world without you, and I think you feel the same."

He opened the box to reveal a ring shining with stones that glimmered in the candlelight. The middle stone was an emerald, a beautiful shade of green, surrounded by a band of chocolate diamonds. None of it was large or ostentatious. It was quiet and understated. A simple statement. I looked up from the ring to his gray eyes, and I thought, I've fallen for Gage all over again. For the millionth time, and I'll still be falling for him every day for the rest of our lives.

His throat bobbed because I hadn't answered him. I was still trying to find my voice.

"Or… maybe you don't like the idea?" he asked a bit breathlessly.

"It isn't entirely despicable," I said. His face broke into a huge smile. He snapped the box shut and tossed it aside before tackling me to the bed, the heavy weight of his body trapping me.

"Say yes," he said, trailing kisses along my jaw and down my neck, moving the robe and continuing downward until his tongue circled my tip.

I gasped. "Yes."

He looked up, a huge grin taking over his face. "Yes, what?"

I ran my fingers through his hair. "Yes, I'll marry you."

He eased up, lips finding mine again. Kissing me slow and steady as another new feeling bloomed inside me. Something I couldn't name but that felt like forever. That felt like not just our present but our future and our pasts all merging into one huge timeless entity that would forever be us.

♫ ♫ ♫

Thank you so much for reading Rory and Gage's heartfelt romantic suspense. I hope they'll stay with you for a really long time and that if you aren't already a Marsmallow, you've found a new show to watch. 😊

If you're not quite ready to let Rory, Gage, and their families go, check out this **swoony bonus scene where Rory has to reassure Gage after all the things for her not-so-surprise party go wrong**.

https://bookhip.com/LWJXLQN

♫ ♫ ♫

If you were **intrigued by G** and want to find out how she takes down the Lovatos, you can catch her *standalone, HEA*, romantic suspense later this year from LJ Evans. G's hunt takes her to the small town of Willow Creek, bringing along a surprise for a broody rancher who's vowed to never love again. Catch *The Last Promise You Made* in May, 2024. https://geni.us/TLPYM

And in the meantime, if you want a look at **more single-dad romantic suspense**, keep reading the first few chapters of the growly rancher's brother's story in ***The Last One You Loved***. It has a small-town sheriff and the woman he could never forget who comes back into town threatening the careful balance in the life he's built without her.

The Last One You Loved - Sample

Prologue

Maddox

AIN'T ALWAYS THE COWBOY
Performed by Jon Pardi

The lake shimmered in the moonlight. The warm breeze stirred up tiny waves, sending white sprinkles shifting across the surface as it drifted toward the shore where we were parked.

We were on the tailgate of my beat-up Bronco with our hands and limbs joined. McKenna's jean-clad legs were flung over my lap, and her head rested on my shoulder. Her cowboy boots were off, lost somewhere behind me in the chaos of blankets and food wrappers. I ran the fingers of my free hand over the gentle arch of her foot, and she jerked it away, laughing.

"Don't you dare tickle me unless you want to end up with a busted nose," she teased, her soft voice washing over me.

It wasn't like I hadn't known she'd pull away. Ten years of knowing her meant I knew just how ticklish her feet were, but I'd done it anyway in an attempt to lighten the mood. But the sound and scent and feel of her made it almost impossible to feel anything but sorrow. It might be the last time I would hold her like this, and my heart screamed as if it could change what was happening by merely twisting inside my chest.

"Wanna go for a swim?" I asked.

It was still humid outside, even though the sun had set hours ago. Long enough that the twilight sounds of the bugs and wild animals had almost disappeared. Instead, a quiet had taken over the space, a preview of what would happen once she drove down the road tomorrow and my life was forever changed.

In answer to my question, she slid off of me and started discarding clothes. She was wearing a string bikini under her jeans and floaty blouse, as if she'd known I'd ask for this—us in the water. I swallowed hard at the gentle curves I'd spent years getting to know as well as my own. I glanced down at my sinewy body toughened from years of working on the ranch. She'd always said my muscles were the very best kind—built from hard work. Would anyone else ever care about them the way she had?

I hadn't been as prepared as she'd been for a swim, so my boxer briefs were going to have to do. Once I'd stripped down, I recaptured her hand, determined to touch her for as long as possible, and led us toward the water, picking our way through the twigs and rocks as we went.

As soon as we hit the cool water, I shivered. It was a soothing relief to the heat and heaviness of the day. If only it could lift the weight inside me as easily as it chilled my skin.

We swam toward the makeshift dock someone had fastened to the middle of the lake decades ago. We didn't pull ourselves up on top. Instead, we hid in the shadows. She wrapped her long limbs around my waist, and I looped an arm through one of the ropes hanging off the wooden slats to hold us steady while my hands continued to touch her.

She kissed me. Wet and wild. Slow and torturous. Love and goodbyes blended into the movements as we rejoined our bodies in the way we'd been doing over the last couple of months. Like a flame on the wick of a firecracker, burning, burning, burning until it finally ignited into a shower of light and sound.

Until it became nothing but us.

She moaned into my mouth when my fingers slid under her bikini, touching pieces of her that were aching for me. I wanted to cry out as well, but with a different ache. I wanted to let my tears wash into the lake.

But it would be selfish because I wouldn't be crying for her. I'd only be crying for me, and that didn't seem fair. McKenna deserved the future she was heading toward—her dream of becoming a doctor finally starting. But her desire to escape this town and her mother hurt because it meant she was escaping me and my family as well—the people who'd loved and sheltered her.

Knowing it was coming hadn't eased the pain of its arrival. As much as I wanted to follow her, I couldn't. My life was here with my family, and the ranch, and my own dreams of serving my community. Even if everything at home had been perfectly fine, I wasn't sure I'd want to leave our small town for a place where you couldn't see the stars. Here, they were so bright it seemed like you could grab them, put them in your pocket, and take them with you. If I was forced to live in a city, I'd burn out just like those faraway suns. If you forced her to stay, she'd wither like the roses I'd given her last week. Dust into dust.

We loved each other more than I'd ever thought was possible, especially considering we were just two kids, barely legal. I knew her smiles and looks and moods better than she knew them herself, and vice versa. But this was where the road we were on finally divided after a decade of running side by side. A bitter taste rose inside me because I wasn't sure our roads would ever cross again.

"I'll come visit," I told her, breaking my mouth from hers. "Thanksgiving or spring break. Whichever works."

Could I get through to spring without seeing her? Touching her? Loving her? How would I even come up with the money for the trip?

She rested her forehead on my shoulder, placed a gentle kiss there, and then looked up at me with sad, tormented eyes.

"Maddox…between college, medical school, and a residency, it'll be at least eleven years before I'm done. I'll always be your friend. I'll always love you…but…I just…" A choked sob broke free from her, and my throat bobbed, eyes watering.

"You want to break up. You don't even want to try?" I asked, that bitterness coating my tongue and my mouth growing. She had choices. She could have applied to Tennessee State. She could have kept us closer, but even as I said it, I knew she couldn't. McKenna needed to put her childhood behind her…even if that meant giving me up along with it.

She put her hands on my cheeks, cupping them and kissing my lips sweetly.

"You're my favorite thing. My favorite memory. My favorite gift. My favorite person," she said quietly.

I could no longer hold the tears back. I didn't know how to let her go. But I'd have to because it wasn't always the cowboy who ran away.

Sometimes, it was the golden-haloed woman with a future so bright the gods had to be jealous.

That was my McKenna.

And tomorrow, she'd be gone. No longer mine, but the

world's instead.

Chapter One
McKenna

YOU ALL OVER ME
Performed by Taylor Swift with Maren Morris

TEN YEARS LATER

Bouncing on my bed woke me. I forced my eyes open and then slammed them shut upon seeing Sally's glowing face. It was too early for this kind of over-the-top happiness.

"Happy birthday, McKenna!" she practically screamed, forcing me to look at her again.

I groaned and tried to bury my head under the covers, but my roommate wouldn't let me. Instead, she ripped the blankets back with surprisingly strong hands and shoved a heavy present at me. Her large, mahogany eyes twinkled in her light-brown face as her pink-tipped waves swung around her sharply defined cheeks and chin.

I hated birthdays, while Sally was from a family who celebrated them like they were a bigger deal than Christmas. In the three years I'd been living with her, she'd made sure I had cake, presents, and whatever I wanted for dinner. Last year, she'd even thrown a surprise party for me at the nurses' station. I'd wanted to run as soon as I'd turned the corner, and I'd made her promise never to do it again.

Growing up, my birthdays had been a painful reminder of what had gone wrong in Mama's life, and she'd done everything to make sure her worst day would also be mine. Only one person besides Sally had ever tried to make this day something different.

I pushed aside the memories that threatened to weigh me down and groused without any real heat, "It's too early for presents and celebrations, Sal."

"Shut up and open it!" she said, ignoring my grumpiness and shoving the box at me with her wide smile fixed permanently in place.

I sat up, and my naturally blonde hair tumbled around me in knots. I'd regret going to bed with it wet, but I'd been exhausted after my twelve-hour shift at the hospital had turned into a sixteen-hour one. I'd barely been able to shower, let alone worry about my hair.

I pulled the bulky gift onto my lap and shot Sally a frown. "I hope you didn't do something stupid, like spend some of your car money on me. I don't want to be the reason you can't get it in January!"

She flicked my shoulder. "Just open it and stop being ridiculous."

I slowly undid the ribbon and pulled off the lid. Inside was a DVD collection of *Buffy the Vampire Slayer*. Every season. I swallowed hard. The DVDs weren't new, but they still had to have cost her a pretty penny to get the entire set. With both of us barely scraping by due to the enormous college debt resting on our shoulders, this wasn't a little gift.

Tears hit my eyes for real, but I refused to let them out, like I'd learned to do early in life by biting my cheek and clenching my nails into my palms. But my voice was still clogged with emotions when I choked out, "Dang it, Sal."

She hugged me to her, and I did my best not to stiffen, letting my head land briefly on her shoulder.

"Now, you'll always have Buffy when you need her," she said softly.

"I need her less these days because I have you," I responded. She was the best female friend I'd ever had. I'd say she was my best friend ever, but there was a teeny-tiny place inside my heart that knew it would be a lie. But I wouldn't hear from him today. I'd shoved him out of my life for a dream—a mirage—that had disappeared in the shimmer of the hot sun.

My gut twisted.

I couldn't think of that today. Of him. Of my mistakes.

I had to get my head on straight, put on my white jacket, and head to the ER—to the real dream I was mere months away from finalizing.

Once my residency was over, I'd be one-hundred-percent official. I'd not only be a doctor, but I'd also be able to call the shots. Goosebumps covered my arms. Ten-year-old me would hardly be able to believe it. That I'd actually escaped and made it happen.

"Get dressed. Your birthday breakfast awaits," Sally said and basically pushed me out of the bed. I stumbled, barely catching myself on the dresser.

"Geez, if this is how you treat a friend on her birthday, I don't want to see how you treat your enemies," I teased.

She headed for the door. "If you're not out in five minutes, I'm going to shove your pancakes—whipped cream and all—in your face. Dickwad Gregory is in charge today, so neither of us can afford to be late."

My stomach knotted thinking of the head of the ER department. He was obnoxious, and egotistical, and thought everyone should swoon over his fifty-year-old, married self. Worse, some people did. Made me pukey even thinking about it.

"McK, I'm not kidding. Five minutes," Sally said, bringing me out of my thoughts.

"Okay, okay."

I slipped into the bathroom, washed up, and pulled on my scrubs. As I fought to drag my messy hair into a high ponytail, the shadows under my hazel eyes caught my attention. They'd pretty much become a permanent feature since starting my residency and were almost as black as my heavy brows. My hand stalled as it hit me suddenly—I looked like Mama.

That scared me. My tired expression wasn't from drugs and alcohol, but it was from running fast and furious for too many years.

"McK!" Sally hollered.

I shoved my phone, water bottle, and keys into a small backpack and hurried out of the room before coming to a complete stop, mouth dropping open.

The entire apartment was full of balloons and streamers.

I bit my cheek hard, tasting blood, and blinked rapidly to hold back the waterworks. Sally was all but dancing around me, excitement on her face from the pure joy of doing this for me.

I didn't care about my birthday. But I thanked the universe for the day Sally had found me on the bench outside the hospital, in a rare fit of tears, and befriended me. It was almost as important as the day Maddox Hatley had found me cowering in a shed behind his uncle's bar when I was eight.

Too bad I didn't have Maddox anymore.

It made this, what I had with Sally, that much more important. So, I'd celebrate today because she wanted me to. Because she was literally the only soul left on this planet who would care if I disappeared tomorrow.

Chapter Two

Maddox

SLOW BURN
Performed by Zac Brown Band

I pulled back just in time, letting the fist barely graze

my chin. The movement was enough to send my Stetson flying, landing amongst the straw where it was going to get trampled. It was the sight of my hat on the ground that pissed me off more than the fist or Willy Tate's drunken, angry snarl as he lunged for me again.

I ducked the second shot and shoved my shoulder into his gut, taking him down to the ground with me. The music had stopped, the customers in the bar quiet as they watched two burly men wrestle. Several chairs were tipped over, tables were bumped, and drinks were spilled as we rolled around. It took me one too many moves before I finally had him pinned facedown with his hands behind his back and my knee holding him in place.

"Damn it, Willy, you owe me a new hat!" I growled.

Clapping filled the air along with hoots and hollers that made my eyes roll.

"Thanks for the show!" someone in the back yelled as someone else shouted out, "Brings me back to my sheep-tying days!"

"Thanks for the help, y'all," I said sarcastically, eyeing my brother sitting calmly on a stool at the bar with a crooked grin.

"Why, Sheriff Maddox, no one would ever presume to think you needed help." Ryder's grin grew, and then he had the audacity to wink at me as he raised a beer in my direction. I barely resisted flipping him the bird as laughter erupted from him, causing his blue eyes that matched mine to crinkle at the corners. He brushed a hand over his perfectly tousled dark-brown hair that should have been smashed flat after wearing a hat all day but instead looked like he'd stepped off the page of a damn magazine.

I was not anywhere near picture-perfect. My dark-blond hair was standing up in places, and the stubble on my chin—a day past trendy—was dripping and sticky from the whiskey Willy had thrown at me. The alcohol had stained my tan shirt, and our scuffle had snagged the ends of my olive-green tie, almost ripping it from my neck.

"She left me, Maddox. For a goddamn suit from Knoxville." Willy was crying now, and it almost looked ridiculous on the six-foot-three mechanic with the hair and beard of someone who'd been lost in the wild for one too many years.

"Taking it out on everyone here isn't going to make the pain go away, shithead," I grumbled. "You gonna start swinging again if I get up?"

Willy shook his head. I stood and then helped the man to his feet. His sad, puppy-dog eyes were full of tears that tumbled down his cheeks.

"You going to arrest him for hitting a lawman?" Gemma asked, trying not to giggle. My sister was sitting next to Ryder at the bar. Her long hair was the same color as mine, but her hazel eyes were full of our brother's laughter. Ryder tapped her elbow with his in appreciation of the taunt she'd thrown my way.

Willy hunched his enormous shoulders. "Fuck. I forgot you're the sheriff now."

"I've been an officer of the law for damn near six years, Willy. Hitting me before or after I'd been elected wouldn't change a damn thing." I leaned down and picked up my hat, brushing it against my thigh and shoving him toward the door of McFlannigan's. It was the only bar in town and normally looked as Irish as my uncle who owned the place, but on Thursdays, they had two-dollar beers, line dancing, and a live band. Uncle Phil brought hay in from the ranch to make it more *Tennessee barnyard* than *Dublin dive*.

I'd told him more than once the hay was a hazard, but as he was friends with the county health inspector, who just happened to be in one of the booths tonight with his wife, my uncle clearly didn't have to worry about being fined. That was the way everything in this town worked, and while I'd been able to turn a blind eye to some of it as a deputy, since I'd been elected, it had been harder to do.

The people of Winter County had put their trust in me. Maybe it was because Sheriff Haskett had thrown his hat in my direction when he'd stepped down, or maybe it was because the Hatley family had been in Willow Creek since its inception. Regardless, they'd taken a chance on a green twenty-seven-year-old last year, and I'd spent twelve months proving to them it had been the right choice.

Willy and I were at the door when Ryder called out, "Going to come back and have a beer with us after you get him home?"

I shook my head.

"Come on, Maddox, one drink!" Gemma called.

I had no desire to sit at the bar, shooting the shit with my siblings, after the long day I'd had. If the bar hadn't been mere blocks from my house when the call had come in as I walked out the station door, I would've let one of my deputies handle the call. Now that I'd done my civic duty for the night, I had only one goal, and that was getting home to my girl.

I directed Willy into the passenger seat of my ancient green and rust-covered Bronco, wishing I'd driven my sheriff truck instead. But the Bronco had called to me this morning—the date dragging at me as it did every year.

The date I tried to ignore and failed miserably to do.

I got Willy tucked into the small apartment above the garage his family had owned almost as long as mine had owned the ranch and then headed to my 1950s-style bungalow two streets over. After three years of hard work, the house was pretty much how I wanted it. The wood siding had a fresh coat of pale-yellow paint, new black shutters edged the multi-paned windows, and a burnt-orange custom door invited you in, just like the swing tucked in the corner of the front porch.

An antique lamp on the hall table cast a gentle light onto the dark plank floors as I let myself in, and the murmur of the television in the open-space living area greeted me. Rianne looked up from the cushy, leather couch I'd spent a small fortune on as I hung my destroyed hat on the rack by the door.

Her bright-red lips curved upward in greeting, and her dark-brown face was just starting to show signs of wrinkles even though she was as old as my grandparents. Her black-and-white corkscrew hair was tucked beneath a vivid-blue scarf littered with pictures of baby ducks. She had so many head wraps I thought she could wear a different one every day of the year and still have more.

"How is she?" I asked.

"Like always. Pretending to sleep but really waiting for you," she said, turning off the TV and rising. She was wearing soft jeans and a long tunic top, looking far more casual than she ever had as my third-grade teacher. When I'd been a rowdy eight-year-old, I'd adored her, and now that she'd turned in her teacher badge and taken on helping me, I loved her almost as much as I loved my mama.

"You smell like a liquor cabinet." Rianne's nose squished up, but there was a smile on her lips.

I sighed, ran my hand over my half-assed, alcohol-soaked beard, and grimaced.

"Had to pull Willy out of McFlannigan's before he tore it apart."

Rianne's face fell. "Aw, he's taking the loss of his woman pretty hard."

I nodded. It was why I'd tucked him at home instead of locking him up in a cell at the station. I knew what it felt like to watch your woman drive away. The agony I'd felt didn't make me want to bleed out on the floor anymore, but the reminder on this day, more than any other, made the hurt tumble through me as if it had happened yesterday instead of a decade ago.

Rianne gathered her things, and I walked her to the door.

"Try to get some rest tomorrow, and I'll see you on Sunday," she said before leaving.

I was technically off the clock for a whole day, but that never meant much when you were one of only twelve people holding down the only law enforcement agency in the county. We didn't have a lot of crime in Willow Creek, but we did have a lot of work. On any given day, I might be helping round up stray chickens one moment and taking beer from underage kids at the lake the next. The biggest pain in my ass was the motorcycle club, The West Gears, who used their headquarters up in the mountains right at the county line to deal drugs and store stolen merchandise. The Gears were the reason I was dead on my feet tonight after a day of hunting them down.

I headed down the hall, feet stalling as I passed Mila's door. She'd expect me to crawl into bed with her, and I didn't want to do that smelling like whiskey, so I continued on to the one room I hadn't let Mama or my sisters help decorate. Instead, the main bedroom reflected me like almost no other part of the house. It was full of dark woods, navy linens, and black-and-white photographs of the lake and the ranch.

I locked my weapon away in the gun safe, showered in the bathroom filled with teak woods and blue linens, and then changed into sweats and a long-sleeve T-shirt before padding on bare feet back to Mila's room. I turned the knob as quietly as possible in a vain hope that she might actually be asleep but chuckled to myself when I saw her dart her head under the covers.

Her room looked like a rainbow had thrown up in it. She was obsessed with them. She'd even convinced me to paint her white headboard in rainbow stripes. Between that, her four pastel-colored nightlights, and the pile of stuffed unicorns that filled an armchair in the corner, it felt like walking into a cartoon world. I crossed the faux-fur white rug and stood looking down at the rainbow comforter that shed glitter like it was a cat changing seasons.

"Oh good, Mila is asleep. I don't have to read *The Day the Unicorns Saved the World* for the one-thousandth time," I said softly.

The covers were thrown back, and beautiful wheat-colored eyes stared at me under thick brows that were almost black and contrasted with the honey-blonde hair spiraling in waves around her round face. "I'm not sleeping, Daddy! You *have* to read it, or I'll be up all night."

There was a little whine to her sweet voice and a pout to her lips that made my mouth twitch. I sighed dramatically, looked up at the ceiling, and pretended to contemplate the fate of my life before pulling the book from her nightstand.

"Scootch over," I said as if this wasn't our nightly routine.

She pulled back her covers and moved to the side as I slid in with her. Her tiny, five-year-old body curled up against me, and I put one arm around her, holding her tight. She smelled like the berry shampoo Mama had bought for her birthday, and she had on a pair of fuzzy, pink-striped pajamas that had been from my sister. Her body was warm and her tiny hand soft as she placed it on my arm. My heart filled to near bursting just by having her there.

"How was your day?" I asked.

"I learned that the letter L says *lllll* like in lion, and that five and two more is seven. Seven is my birthday number, so Mrs. Randall let me use the butterfly pointer and lead the class in the alphabet song."

Kindergarten. My baby had started kindergarten at the end of August. I hadn't expected it to be as hard as it had been to drop her off at school and walk away. I mean, I'd been leaving her every day for the four years of her life that she'd been mine. But there was something different about leaving her with Rianne versus taking her into a classroom full of kids who I couldn't guarantee would be nice and adults who were strangers. I'd run the name of the principal and every teacher at the school to make sure there weren't any scumbags hiding in the system, even when I knew the state wouldn't have given certificates to criminals. I'd sort of gone off my rocker for a day or two. The only thing that made it easier was knowing Mila liked being there.

"That sounds like a really good day," I told her.

"Yeah. But Missy wouldn't give me a turn with the hula

hoop." She pouted, and every vein in my body tightened. The need to protect her, even from other five-year-olds, was a strange sensation. There was a time in my life when I hadn't wanted to be a dad, when I'd promised another blonde-haired girl that we wouldn't have kids because she was adamantly opposed to having them.

"I'll buy you your own damn hula hoop tomorrow," I told her, voice gruff with emotions. She giggled.

"You cussed again, Daddy. You owe me another dollar for the cuss jar."

I smiled with my lips against her hair. She'd have enough money in that jar to go to college if I wasn't careful. The thought of her being grown up and going away to college threatened to rip some more at the scars that had already cracked open today.

I pushed the pain away, opened the book, and started reading as my girl snuggled deeper into my chest. My heart expanded until it was quadruple the size it should have been. This was perfect. I didn't need anything else in my life but this.

Keep reading *THE LAST ONE YOU LOVED* now!
Free in Kindle Unlimited

Thank you for taking the time to read *After All the Wreckage*! This book started with my love of all the underestimated young female sleuths like Veronica Mars, Wednesday Addams in the new *Wednesday* show, and of course, Nancy Drew. I had an overwhelming urge to write my own tough, sassy female PI and the man who not only fell in love with her believing she was strong and brave but who could show her just exactly how courageous she was at the moment when she doubted herself most. I hope you enjoyed every moment of Rory and Gage's heart-stopping story.

All my books are inspired by music, and there's usually one song that becomes the novel's anthem. For this story, it was "Wreckage" by Nate Smith, but a close second was "I Can See You" by Taylor Swift. I hope the way Rory and Gage's story with its mix of resilience and music leaves marks on your soul that you'll feel every time you hear one of the songs on the playlist from now on.

If you like talking about music, books, and just what it takes to get us through this wild ride called life as much as I do, you should join my Facebook readers' group, LJ's Music & Stories, and the conversations happening there. Hopefully, the group can help *you* through your life in some small way.

Regardless whether you join or not, I'd love for you to tell me what you thought of the book by reaching out to me personally. I'd also be honored if you took the time to leave a review on BookBub, Amazon, or Goodreads, but even more than that, I hope you enjoyed it enough to tell a friend about it.

If you still can't get enough, you could also sign up for my newsletter, where you'll receive music-inspired scenes weekly and be entered into a giveaway for an autographed paperback by yours truly each month. Plus, you'll be able to keep tabs on what's coming next in my bookish world.

Finally, I just wanted to say that my wish for you is a healthy and happy journey. May you live life resiliently, with hope and love leading the way!

Acknowledgments

I'm so very grateful for every single person who has helped me on this book journey. If you're reading these words, you *are* one of those people. I wouldn't be an author if people like you didn't decide to read the stories I crafted, so THANK YOU!

In addition to my lovely readers, I must also acknowledge these people:

My husband, who never ever lets me give up on myself, even when he's struggling himself. You've had a really hard few months, my love, and I am in awe of your resilience, your strength, and the way you sacrifice for those you love most. Thanks for being my Gage. For pushing me forward whenever I needed it.

Our child, Evyn, owner of Evans Editing, who remains my harshest and kindest critic. Thank you for helping me create my stories and believing in me when my critics didn't. Thanks for being your own kind of snarky Veronica. Love you, kiddo.

The folks at That's What She Said Publishing. Thank you for not giving up when it would have been easy to do so.

My sister, Kelly, who made sure I hit the publish button the very first time and reads my crappy first drafts, still loves my stories anyway, and is never afraid to say, "You can do better."

My mom, who tells me the truth, even when it hurts her to do so, as she beta reads my stories and then loves them enough to buy them repeatedly and reread them over and over.

My dad and my father-in-law, who are my biggest fans and take my books to the strangest places, telling everyone they know (and don't know) about my stories.

Michelle Fewer, who patiently reads, uplifts, and plots without judgment and so much grace. Thank you for giving me your time, energy, and love.

Jenn at Jenn Lockwood Editing Services and Karen Hrdlicka, who have been on this journey and continue to have faith in me no matter how far apart we get pulled.

The folks at HEA Author Services, who helped polish the story into perfection.

The entire group of beautiful humans in LJ's Music & Stories who love and support me. I can't say enough how deeply grateful I am for each and every one of you.

The host of bloggers who have shared my stories, become dear friends, and continue to make me feel like a rock star every day. Thank you, thank you, thank you!

A host of authors, including Stephanie Rose, Erika Kelly, Kathryn Nolan, Lucy Score, Hannah Blake, Maria Luis, Annie Dyer, and AM Johnson, who have shown me that dear friends are more important than any paralyzing moment in this wild publishing world. MWAH!

All my ARC readers, who have become sweet friends and true supporters. Thank you for knowing just what to say to scare away my writer insecurities.

Leisa C., Rachel R., Lindsey R., and Stephanie F. Thank you beyond words for being the biggest cheerleaders, partners, and friends I could ever hope to have on this wild ride called life.

I love you all!

About the Author

Award winning author, LJ Evans, lives in Northern California with her husband, child, and the three terrors called cats. She's been writing, almost as a compulsion, since she was a little girl and will often pull the car over to write when a song lyric strikes her. A former first-grade teacher, she now spends her free time reading and writing, as well as binge-watching original shows like *Wednesday, Ted Lasso, Veronica Mars,* and *Stranger Things*.

If you ask her the one thing she won't do, it's pretty much anything that involves dirt—sports, gardening, or otherwise. But she loves to write about all of those things, and her first published heroine was pretty much involved with dirt on a daily basis, which is exactly why LJ loves fiction novels—the characters can be everything you're not and still make their way into your heart.

Her novel, **CHARMING AND THE CHERRY BLOSSOM**, was *Writer's Digest* Self-Published E-book Romance of the Year in 2021. For more information about LJ, check out any of these sites:

www.ljevansbooks.com

FaceBook Group: LJ's Music & Stories

LJ Evans on Amazon, Bookbub, and Goodreads

@ljevansbooks on Facebook, Instagram, TikTok, and Pinterest

Books by L J

Standalone

After All the Wreckage

A single-dad, small-town romantic suspense

He's a broody bar owner raising his siblings. She's a scrappy PI who's loved him since she was a teenager. When his brother disappears, she forces aside years of pining and family secrets to help him.

Charming and the Cherry Blossom

A contemporary romance with hints of magical realism

Today was a fairy tale…I inherited a fortune from a dad I never knew, and a thoroughly charming guy asked me out. But like all fairy tales, mine has a dark side...and my happily ever after may disappear with the truth.

The Hatley Family Standalones

The Last One You Loved

A single-dad, small-town romance

He's a small-town sheriff with a secret that can unravel their worlds. She's an ER resident running from a costly mistake. Coming home will only mean heartache…unless they let forgiveness heal them both.

The Last Promise You Made

A single-dad, small-town romantic suspense

He's a grumpy rancher who swore off all relationships. She's a spitfire undercover agent who brings danger to his life. Not even a common enemy can force them to trust each other. Desire is an inconvenience. Falling in love is absolutely out of the question…

Perfectly Fine

A fish-out-of-water, celebrity romance

He's a charming, A-list actor at the top of his game. She's a determined, small-town screenwriter hoping for a deal. They form an unexpected connection until heartbreak ruins their future. Available on Amazon and also **FREE** with newsletter subscription.

My Life as an Album Series

My Life as a Country Album — Cam's Story

A boy-next-door, small-town romance

Cam's diary-style, coming-of-age story about growing up loving the football hero next door. She vowed to love him forever. But when fate comes calling, will she ever find a heart to call home? Warning: Tears may fall.

My Life as a Pop Album — Mia & Derek

A rock star, road-trip romance

Bookworm Mia is attempting to put years of guilt behind her when soulful musician Derek Waters strolls into her life and turns it upside down. Once he's seen her, Derek can't walk away unless Mia comes with him. But what will happen when their short time together ends?

My Life as a Rock Album — Seth & PJ

A second-chance, antihero romance

Recovering addict Seth Carmen is a trash artist who knows he's better off alone. But when he finds and loses the love of his life, he can't help sending her a host of love letters to try to win her back. Can Seth prove to PJ they can make broken beautiful?

My Life as a Mixtape — Lonnie & Wynn

A single-dad, rock star romance

Lonnie's always seen relationships as a burden instead of a gift, and picking up the pieces his sister leaves behind is just one of the reasons. When Wynn enters his life just as her world is disintegrating, their mixed-up pasts give way to new beginnings neither of them saw coming.

My Life as a Holiday Album – 2nd Generation

A small-town romance

Come home for the holidays with this heartwarming, full-length standalone full of hidden secrets, true love, and the real meaning of family. Perfect for lovers of *Love Actually* and Hallmark movies, this sexy story intertwines the lives of six couples as they find their way to their happily ever afters with the help of.

My Life as an Album Series Box Set

1st four Album books plus an exclusive novella

In the exclusive novella, *This Life with Cam*, Blake Abbott writes to Cam about just what it was like to grow up in the shadow of her relationship with Jake and just when he first fell for the little girl with the popsicle-stained lips. Can he show Cam that she isn't broken?

The Anchor Novels

Guarded Dreams — Eli & Ava

A grumpy-sunshine, military romance

He's a grumpy Coast Guard focused on a life of service. She's a feisty musician searching for stardom. Nothing about them fits, and yet their attraction burns wild when fate lands them in the same house for the summer.

Forged by Sacrifice — Mac & Georgie

A roommates-to-lovers, military romance

He's a driven military man zeroed in on a new goal. She's a struggling law student running from her family's mistakes. They're entirely wrong for each other…except their bodies disagree. When they end up as roommates, how long will it take before intense attraction shatters their resistance?

Avenged by Love — Truck & Jersey

A fake-marriage, military romance

When a broody military man and a quiet bookstore clerk end up in the same house, it isn't only attraction that erupts. Now, the only way to ensure she gets the care she needs is to marry her.

Damaged Desires — Dani & Nash

A frenemy, military romance

A grumpy Navy SEAL reeling from losing his team fights an intense attraction for his best friend's fiery sister. Until a stalker put her in his sights, and then he'll do anything to protect her, even if it means exposing all his secrets.

Branded by a Song — Brady & Tristan

A single-mom, rock star romance

He's a country-rock legend searching for inspiration. She's a Navy SEAL's widow determined to honor his memory while raising their daughter. Neither believes the intense attraction tugging at them can lead to more until their futures are twined by her grandmother's will.

Tripped by Love – Cassidy & Marco

A broody-bodyguard, single-mom romance

He's her brother's broody bodyguard with secrets he can't share. She's a busy single mom with a restaurant to run. They're just friends until a little white lie changes everything.

The Anchor Novels: The Military Bros Box Set

The 1st 3 books + an exclusive novella

The Anchor Suspense Novels

Unmasked Dreams — Violet & Dawson

A second-chance, age-gap romance

Violet and Dawson had a heart-stopping attraction they were compelled to deny. When they're tossed together again, it proves nothing has changed—except the lab she's built in the garage and the secrets he's keeping. When she stumbles into his dark world, Dawson breaks old promises to keep her safe.

Crossed by the Stars — Jada & Dax

A second-chance, forced-proximity romance

Family secrets meant Dax and Jada's teenaged romance was an impossibility. A decade later, the scars still remain, so neither is willing to give in to their tantalizing chemistry. But when a shadow creeps out of Jada's past, seeking retribution, it's Dax who shows up to protect her. And suddenly, it's hard to see a way out without permanent damage to their bodies and souls.

Disguised as Love — Cruz & Raisa

A chemistry-filled, enemies-to-lovers romance

Surly FBI agent, Cruz Malone, is determined to bring down the Leskov clan. If that means he has to arrest or bed the sexy blond scientist of the family, so be it. Too bad Raisa has other ideas. There's no way she's just going to sit back and let the infuriating agent dismantle her world… or her heart.

The Painted Daisies

Interconnected series with an all-female rock band and the alpha heroes who steal their hearts. Each story has a HEA.

Sweet Memory — Paisley & Jonas

An opposite-attract, second-chance romance

The world's sweetest rock star falls for a troubled music producer whose past comes back to haunt them.

Green Jewel — Fiadh & Asher

An enemies-to-lovers, single-dad romance

He did it. She'll prove it. Her body's reaction to him be damned.

Cherry Brandy — Leya & Holden

An opposites-attract, forbidden, bodyguard romance

Being on the run with only one bed is no excuse to touch her…
until touching is the only choice.

Blue Marguerite — Adria & Ronan

A celebrity, second-chance, frenemy romance.

She vowed to never forgive him... Not even when he offers answers her
family desperately seeks.

Royal Haze — Nikki & D'Angelo

Nikki and D'Angelo's bodyguard, on-the-run romance.

He was ready to torture, steal, and kill to defend the world he believed
in. What he wasn't prepared for… was her.

Free Stories

FREE with newsletter signup

https://www.ljevansbooks.com/freeljbooks

Perfectly Fine – A Hollywood, second-chance romance

He's a charming, A-list actor at the top of his game. She's a determined,
small-town screenwriter hoping for a deal. They form an unexpected
connection until secrets ruin their future.

Rumor – A small-town, rock-star romance

There's only one thing rock star Chase Legend needs to ring in the new
year, and that's to know what Reyna Rossi tastes like. After ten years,
there's no way he's letting her escape the night without their souls
touching. Reyna has other plans. After all, she doesn't need the entire
town wagging their tongues about her any more than they already do.

Love Ain't – A friends-to-lovers, cowboy romance

Reese knows her best friend and rodeo king, Dalton Abbott, is never
going to fall in love, get married, and have kids. He's left so many
broken hearts behind that there's gotta be a museum full of them
somewhere. So when he gives her a look from under the brim of his hat,
promising both jagged relief and pain, she knows better than to give in.

The Long Con – A sexy, antihero romance

Adler is after his next big payday. Then, Brielle sways in with her own
game in play, and those aquamarine-colored eyes almost make him
forget his number-one rule. But she'll learn… love isn't a con he's
interested in.

The Light Princess – An old-fashioned fairy tale

A princess who glows with a magical light, a kingdom at war, and a kiss that changes the world. This is an extended version of the fairy tale twined through the pages of *Charming and the Cherry Blossom.*